HOLIDAY HEIST AT DUNHAVEN CASTLE

ALSO BY NELLIE H. STEELE

Cate Kensie Mysteries:

The Secret of Dunhaven Castle

Murder at Dunhaven Castle

Holiday Heist at Dunhaven Castle

Danger at Dunhaven Castle

Jack's Journal Versions:

The Secret Keepers

Murder in the Tower

Lily & Cassie by the Sea Mysteries:

Ghosts, Lore & a House by the Shore

Duchess of Blackmoore Mysteries:

Letter to a Duchess

Shadow Slayers Stories:

Shadows of the Past

Stolen Portrait Stolen Soul

Gone

Trouble

Clif & Ri on the Sea Adventures:

Rise of a Pirate

Maggie Edwards Adventures:

Cleopatra's Tomb

Secret of the Ankhs

HOLIDAY HEIST AT DUNHAVEN CASTLE

A CATE KENSIE MYSTERY

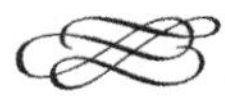

NELLIE H. STEELE

A Novel Idea Publishing

Cover design by Stephanie A. Sovak.

❀ Created with Vellum

For Jacob, Arabella and Jillian
Never stop trying.
We only fail when we fail to try.

ACKNOWLEDGMENTS

A HUGE thank you to everyone who helped get this book published! Special shout outs to: Stephanie Sovak, Paul Sovak, Michelle Cheplic, Mark D'Angelo and Lori D'Angelo.

Finally, a HUGE thank you to you, the reader!

MacKenzie Family Tree

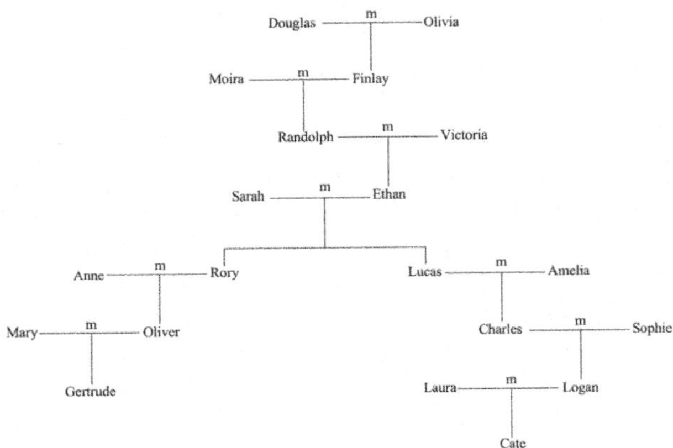

CHAPTER 1

Lady Catherine Kensie strolled up the path from the loch toward Dunhaven Castle. Her two best friends, her dogs, Riley and Bailey, trotted at her side. As the two dogs stopped to sniff at a set of bushes edging the path, Cate glanced up at the castle. Her abode for the last seven months, she was still settling in, yet already felt at home.

Her life had been a whirlwind since finding out she inherited the castle. With her stalled career and living in a small apartment, she jumped at the chance to move to the beautiful castle nestled in the Scottish countryside. Riley, her black and white dog, made the trek with her from her former home in the midwestern United States. Shortly after arriving here, Riley found Bailey hiding in a folly on the property. The two had been instant friends and Cate readily adopted Bailey when given the chance.

Soon, another old friend of Cate's would arrive from the States. Molly Williams, her former department secretary from her days as a college professor, suffered a turn of bad fortune just as Cate experienced an upturn in her own luck.

After a visit to the castle for Cate's first major party, a Halloween ball, Cate offered Molly the opportunity to rebuild her life in Scotland as housekeeper-in-training. Cate's current housekeeper, Mrs. Fraser, planned to retire in the coming years. Mrs. Fraser approved of the idea, welcoming Molly with open arms. Molly was due to arrive in less than one week. Cate smiled as she contemplated Molly's arrival.

A shiver passed through Cate as the wind blew past her. She shrugged her coat higher on her neck. "Yikes, come on, boys! It's getting too cold out here!" Cate encouraged the two pups to follow her back to the castle.

She entered through the kitchen, greeting Mrs. Fraser who was busy preparing dinner for the evening. Cate ushered the two dogs up to the library, where she planned to complete work on her book before dinner.

A historian by training, Cate's project when she arrived at the castle centered on writing a book on the castle's history and its inhabitants. Her most recent work on the book centered on Randolph and Victoria MacKenzie. Randolph was the owner of the castle from the 1850s until the 1880s. Cate smiled as she perused her notes about these two.

She was lucky enough to have met and interacted with them. While it seemed astounding and often felt like a dream, Cate possessed the ability to time travel due to an anomaly within the castle walls and a specially designed timepiece created by her ancestor. The timepiece, when activated in specific spots within the castle, allowed the user to slip backwards or forwards in time. The anomaly, termed "rips in time" by her ancestor who discovered it, allowed her to visit other time periods.

Though Cate enjoyed their time traveling experiences, Jack, her estate manager and friend, hated time travel. Part of Jack's role as estate manager was to protect the castle's secret and its proprietor, a duty handed down through the generations of Reids who had worked on the estate. Though when they used the anomaly to assist Randolph and solve a murder, he found the experience gratifying. Cate spent the rest of the afternoon summarizing her notes about these family members. She wrote a few paragraphs in her first draft before Mrs. Fraser brought her dinner to the library.

Cate thanked her, closing her laptop for the day and digging into her supper. As she ate, she opened a new folder. Mrs. Isla Campbell, the town's librarian and president of the historical society, provided it for Cate's research. The last set of articles Mrs. Campbell provided her alerted Cate to the murder at the castle and to Randolph's predicament following it.

Cate flipped opened the folder. The article she read soon after solving the centuries-old murder sat on top. The headline read THEFT AT DUNHAVEN CASTLE. Cate re-read the article. It fascinated her. The article detailed a theft occurring on New Year's Day in 1925. The theft robbed the family of two expensive jewelry pieces passed through generations.

Cate flipped through the other articles supplied by Mrs. Campbell, all of them connected to the theft and the subsequent investigation. Neither the jewels nor the culprit were ever found. Cate studied the information. The description of the pieces sounded familiar to her.

As Mrs. Fraser returned to collect her tray, Cate closed the folder. "Oh, thank you, Mrs. Fraser. I wish you'd let me return these myself," Cate chided.

"Nay, I wouldn't hear of it, Lady Cate. Besides, in a matter of days, I can have that whippersnapper, Molly, running up for it." Mrs. Fraser chuckled, winking at Cate.

"Good plan." Cate laughed.

"Aye, no rest for her when she comes," Mrs. Fraser joked. "Now, is there anything else I can fetch for you, Lady Cate?"

"No, Mrs. Fraser, nothing at all. Please enjoy the rest of your evening."

"You do the same, Lady Cate. I plan to pack a few things this evening for our upcoming stay," Mrs. Fraser informed her, referring to when she and Mr. Fraser would stay in the castle. After a discussion, Cate and Mrs. Fraser agreed having the couple stay for three weeks, beginning just prior to Molly's arrival and through the new year was advantageous. Molly would arrive to begin her training to take on the housekeeper's role for the estate, a holiday party would be held at the castle days before Christmas and Cate would entertain houseguests until after the new year. While the decorating had already begun for the Christmas holiday, much work remained. This made it easier for both Cate and her staff during the hectic holiday season.

After Mrs. Fraser departed, Cate glanced at her schedule for the rest of the week. With the Christmas party ten days away, meetings filled her calendar. The next meeting with Isla Campbell, the town's librarian and historical society president, was set for this Friday. With a week to go after that meeting, Mrs. Campbell would be in full-blown party mode. The mere idea exhausted Cate. Mrs. Campbell, however, thrived on it. In less than two months, she had thrown together not one but two holiday parties on the estate. The first, entitled the Snow Ball, occurred days before Christmas and was open to anyone who purchased a ticket. Tickets to the event sold out within hours of going on sale. The second, entitled a New Year with our New Countess, was an exclusive VIP event. By invitation only, it was the area's most exclusive party of the season.

Cate shook her head, trying to recall how Mrs. Campbell persuaded her to host two events in the matter of one week.

An introvert, Cate cherished her quiet alone time. She had never excelled at social events, finding herself awkward in most social situations. Yet her inheritance thrust her into a public role, particularly within her local area. She was still adjusting to her new circumstances, but she was growing into the role. While she was uncertain she'd ever be a pro at it, she already was transitioning from "just Cate" to "Lady Cate."

Cate turned her attention back to the folder containing the articles about the theft. She flipped open the file, perusing them again. She planned to share them with Jack tomorrow. She would spend the rest of the night preparing for the inevitable argument that would ensue. Jack would maintain the past should be left alone. "What's done is done," he would say, "and we've no right to mess around with it."

Cate would remind him how satisfying it had been to help Randolph. While Jack would agree, he'd still oppose another trip to another era to solve another crime. Forever curious, Cate couldn't help but want to unravel the truth and, being a historian, to experience life as it was lived in another era.

She flicked the folder closed. It would be an uphill battle to convince Jack to investigate, but she felt prepared to make and win her case. It also helped that she was his boss.

She gathered both pups, carrying them to her room and settling in near the cozy fire for a night of reading. She spent the rest of her evening in her sitting room with a good book and her two best friends, Riley and Bailey.

The following morning Cate was up early, bounding out of bed, ready to discuss her latest project with Jack. The chill in the mid-December morning air chased her back into the castle after a brief time outside with the dogs. She enjoyed her breakfast, warmed by the fire in the library.

After breakfast, she gathered her materials about the theft

and wandered the castle in search of Jack. She came upon him near the ballroom, adjusting a few artificial Christmas trees near the doors leading inside the room.

"Good morning," she said as he crawled from under one of the trees.

"Good morning, Lady Cate. Would you mind doing me a great favor, lassie?"

"Not at all," Cate answered. "What do you need?"

"Tell me, does this tree grouping look acceptable? I don't want any mistakes before the party czar shows up tomorrow."

Cate giggled at his new name for Mrs. Campbell. She stepped back to inspect the tree placement from all angles. "It looks acceptable to me," she answered.

Jack climbed from the floor. "No doubt, she'll still find something wrong about it," he lamented.

Cate chuckled. "Now that you've got your tree placement worked out, could I have a moment of your time?"

"Sure, lassie, what is it?" Jack questioned.

Cate held up a folder. Before she could speak, Jack said, "Oh, no. No, no. If this is about that bloody snow machine the party czar wants, the answer is no. I will not have a snow machine dragged onto these grounds…" he began.

Cate shook her head, waving her hands in the air to stop him. "No, no, it's not. Although you may prefer it was," she admitted.

"Oh, no. Worse than the snow machine?"

Cate crinkled her nose. "Not to me but…"

"The only thing worse than dragging a snow machine through the gardens of Dunhaven Castle is time travel."

"You're such a stick in the mud," Cate complained. "Just take a peek at these articles."

He waved his hands at her, dismissing her comment, but accepted the folder. He flipped it open, glancing through the articles. He snapped it shut, handing it back to her. She raised an eyebrow at him. "Well?" she asked.

"Well, it appears due to a very unfortunate turn of events, some of your inheritance was stolen, Lady Cate. I dare say you'll do all right without it. I've seen the estate's financials. You should be able to get by." He winked at her.

She rolled her eyes at him, sighing. "You know very well my interest in this has little to do with recovering my lost inheritance."

"Yes, yes," Jack replied. "Righting wrongs and experiencing the past by living in it and all that, I know."

"Oh, come on, you had to have noticed the interesting bit about the missing items at least."

Jack raised his eyebrows at her. "Interesting bit?"

"Yes, they describe the missing pieces of jewelry in the first article. And the third article has a picture of the items. Notice anything?" Cate asked, calling his attention to both articles.

"They're very pretty, Lady Cate."

"No, not that. Look closer!" Cate shoved the picture to his face.

"I'm still not getting it," Jack said, staring at it.

Cate frowned at him. "Jack, that's the necklace I wore to the Halloween Ball Randolph and Victoria held when we investigated the murder!"

"Ohhhhh," Jack responded. "Oh, yes, I remember it. It was quite a necklace."

Cate nodded. "Yes, it was. I recognized it right away when I saw it. It was Victoria's. It appears the other stolen piece was also hers. It's the necklace she wore that night."

"Whoever stole those made off with a fortune," Jack admitted.

"Yes, and it would have broken Victoria's heart to realize someone stole her jewelry," Cate answered.

"Yes, it would have," Jack agreed. "It's a terrible shame."

"You know this year is one of the ones we can travel to. Well, the year when they discovered the jewelry was missing. It appears to have been stolen on New Year's Day. While everyone was sleeping after ringing in the New Year, someone else was busy helping themselves to the family jewels. I wonder…"

"Nay, Lady Cate," Jack interrupted her. "I don't like when you wonder. Your wondering gets us in trouble most times."

Cate shook her head at him. "That's not true."

"It is! The last time you wondered, we went back to 1856, we became embroiled in a murder investigation, we were almost killed and…"

"And solved a murder and saved my ancestor's life and reputation. Along with the life of a young woman!" Cate finished.

Jack scowled at her. "That's not exactly where I was going with that."

"But it's true," Cate added. "Wouldn't it be wonderful to solve another mystery? Stop a theft, help the family again?"

"Oh, Cate," Jack replied, shaking his head at her.

"Consider this: whatever progress we make on finding the lost jewels of Dunhaven Castle distracts me from finding a link to Douglas MacKenzie. If I can't find a link to Douglas MacKenzie, I can't determine how he's harnessed the castle's powers. And if I can't determine how he's harnessed the castle's powers, we're stuck only traveling to times with locations we know of!"

"You've still not got that comment from Randolph out of your head, huh?" Jack questioned, wincing.

"I have not," Cate admitted. "Randolph was Douglas' grandson. In two generations, they lost the secret of how Douglas harnessed time travel? Did he never tell them? Was it kept secret? If so, why?" Cate rambled. "Oh! To have a conversation with Douglas..."

Jack shook his head at her. "I'll never understand your mind, Lady Cate."

"Oh, come on," Cate replied. "You can't tell me these questions don't cross your mind."

"I can and I will, lassie," he countered. "These questions have never crossed my mind. I've no desire to play with a power we don't fully understand and can cause tremendous damage."

"I'm not planning to damage the past irreparably," Cate promised.

"Whether you plan to or not, it could happen. We have no idea what might damage the past irreparably. And it's not just that, Lady Cate. If anyone ever discovers this secret, do you realize the danger the entire world may be in? Not to mention us! I don't like time traveling to begin with, but we may be damn lucky that we've only got a limited ability. Let's not push too far and chance more things going wrong."

"So, we'll just focus on the jewelry heist then?" Cate queried.

"Bah, Lady Cate, how do you always manage to turn my adamant arguments against all your plans into support for at least one of them?"

"It's a talent, I suppose," Cate answered, grinning.

"I'd call it something different," Jack mumbled.

"Anyway," Cate answered, ignoring his comment, "there's nothing we can do now. With this party fast approaching, there's no time to travel to the past..."

"Thank heavens," Jack interjected.

Cate grimaced at him. "And I should research more. So, you are off the hook. At least until I've done that."

"Oh boy," Jack exclaimed. "I hope you're busy with no time to research!"

"I do have the meeting with Isla tomorrow," Cate answered, frowning. "That meeting will eat up most of my morning. And I've got to finish a few things before Molly arrives on Sunday."

"I never imagined I'd appreciate Isla Campbell so much as I have today," Jack joked, laughing loudly.

"Very funny," Cate quipped. "While I have her here, I'll ask her about the theft and get some research done, anyway." Cate made her best "so there" face at him, to which he grimaced.

Jack rolled his eyes at her. "As long as I live, I don't imagine I'll ever understand you, Lady Cate."

Cate shrugged. "What's hard to understand? It's fun visiting other time periods!"

"I don't consider it fun to chance radically changing history."

"Oh," Cate voiced, shaking her head and waving her hand at him, "you worry too much."

"Somebody's got to do the worrying! And I've got to worry double, once for me and once for you!"

Cate shook her head again, but laughed. "Okay, deal," she agreed. "I'll do the researching and you do the worrying. And now I'll leave you to your trees."

"They're only MY trees until they are set up, then they become YOUR trees, Lady Cate."

"I haven't forgotten! I'm excited to decorate the trees over the coming week for the party. I hope we have enough lights, garland and ornaments!"

"We've got boxes and boxes, don't worry about that," Jack answered.

"Good! I've never had a Christmas tree this big! Riley and I always had small trees in my apartment. Even when I was a kid, our trees were never this large!"

"Nothing like days of decorating to put you in the holiday spirit," Jack replied.

"And hot chocolate and cookies, courtesy of Mrs. Fraser," Cate added. "She's got quite a lot planned for our upcoming decorating parties!"

"I'll bet," Jack answered. "Mrs. Fraser's cookies. Mmm. Now, that I can get excited about."

"Noted," Cate responded. "Perhaps I can pack a tin of her cookies for our trips to the past. Maybe then you'll be excited!"

"Doubt it," Jack responded, ruining her ploy.

"Oh, well." Cate sighed. "I tried! Well, I should get back to work. I've a million details to go over before my meeting tomorrow. Have fun with the trees!"

"Will do, Lady Cate." Jack gave her a quick salute before returning to setting up another grouping of Christmas trees on the opposite side of the doorway.

Cate wandered to the library, her mind in the clouds. Her brain whirled as she imagined outfits for their visits to the Roaring Twenties. Plenty of clothes were stored in the castle by generations past for the purposes of time travel. She practiced conversations complete with customs and jargon from the time. Despite Jack's reluctance, Cate's mind surged with excitement at the idea of time travel. As a historian, she felt fully prepared for the endeavor. And despite her brush with death during their last trip, she experienced no hesitancy about jumping in headfirst with this mystery.

The last mystery they solved proved satisfying, resulting in them helping a young woman to live a full life and saving her ancestor from death row. She hoped her latest venture proved as rewarding.

Exhilarated, Cate stepped into the library, finding her two dog friends playing with a ball. She smiled at them as she set up shop on the desk overlooking the side garden. With immense reluctance, Cate shoved her research on the jewelry theft under a stack of papers at the back of the desk. Instead of pursuing her desire to dive straight into that mystery, she opened her party planning dossier. The file had grown from a small manila folder to an accordion file organizer containing several color-coded folders.

With a heavy sigh, Cate withdrew several of the folders to verify detail after endless detail concerning the upcoming event. After this, she mused, she'd have to move on to the other accordion folder, filled with details for the fast-approaching VIP event.

As she ticked off tasks on her party-planning to-do list, Cate marveled at how Mrs. Campbell kept all these details straight. During their meetings, she rarely referenced her notes, able to recall even minute details with ease off the top of her head.

Cate giggled as she read a memo from Mrs. Campbell asking Jack and Mr. Fraser to reconsider the use of a snow-making machine to "add a magical ambiance" to the castle grounds. The memo, written in red ink and underlined three times, highlighted the persistence of the so-called party czar. She had requested the machine four times and four times been denied her request. It didn't seem to matter. She was like a squeaky wheel with her repeated requests.

Cate's chuckle drew the attention of the two small pups who raced over, certain her utterance signaled a sign of distress. "Hello, Riley and Bailey," Cate greeted them as they danced on their hind legs. "Do you have any input concerning the battle of the snow machine?"

Riley cocked his head to the side, staring at Cate. Bailey stood on his hind legs, waving his paws up and down, issuing a high-pitched note that Cate nicknamed "singing." "Hmm," Cate murmured, "I'm not sure Jack would agree." At the sound of Jack's name, Riley danced on his hind legs. Cate chuckled at him and his love for his newfound friend.

Cate glanced to the mound of paperwork still awaiting her attention, then back to the two small dogs. "This can wait until this afternoon," she told them. "How about a nice walk?" Both dogs danced at the "w-word," earning another chuckle from Cate. Despite the chilly winter air, Cate still enjoyed their walks.

She bundled herself and both dogs in warm coats and proceeded outside, ball in hand, for a sojourn around the property to fill the rest of the morning hours. As they walked, Cate took in her surroundings. She shook her head in firm disagreement with Mrs. Campbell. These grounds didn't need a snow machine to achieve a magical ambiance.

After lunch, both dogs, tired from their walk, lounged near the roaring fire in the library, allowing Cate to finish her party-related tasks. Despite the lack of physical activity, she was spent by the time her dinner arrived.

Cate stuffed the folders for the VIP event into her accordion organizer just as Mrs. Fraser arrived with her tray. "Still working on those parties, Lady Cate?" Mrs. Fraser asked as Cate cleared a spot on the desk.

"Just finishing," Cate admitted. "Wow! There are so many tiny details!"

"With that woman at the helm, there'll be no shortage of those, without a doubt!" Mrs. Fraser, never a fan of Isla Campbell, was still gleefully anticipating the parties despite their organizer.

"Do you have your gowns ready for both events?" Cate queried.

"Aye, Lady Cate. I've a beautiful black ball gown with a plaid sash tied in a bow for the Snow Ball. And, well..." Mrs. Fraser paused, her features reddening, "Mr. Fraser talked me into a black gown with silver sparkles for the New Year's Eve party. Oh, I'm not sure why I allowed myself to be talked into it. At my age, marching about dressed as a disco ball." She shook her head.

"I'm sure it's just beautiful. The sparkles are perfect for that party!"

"Oh, thank you, Lady Cate. I just hope no one considers me dressing too young for my age."

"I've no doubt your gown is appropriate for you! Mr. Fraser has great taste!"

"Aye, aye, he does," Mrs. Fraser answered, nodding. "I've never been to such a party before, Lady Cate. I'm at sixes and sevens about it. I cannae believe at my age I'm attending my first VIP party with the lords and ladies of the country!"

Cate grinned at Mrs. Fraser's excitement. This made her endless cycle of party work worth it. Molly's excitement was also building for the two parties. Cate invited her staff as guests to both parties to allow them to enjoy the castle as she did. While Molly was excited about her new journey, her gushing about the two parties made it obvious how thrilled she was to be included. Molly's latest emails babbled about her gowns, being sent straight to Dunhaven, shoes, hairstyles and more. With only days to go before her arrival, Molly's nervous energy was at an all-time high.

As she ate, Cate checked her email, finding an update from Molly. She stated she had checked into a hotel for her last night in Aberdeen. The following morning, she had an early morning flight to London. With no love lost between Molly and her current home, she was counting the hours until her flight.

Cate snickered as she blew on her soup to cool it before eating. Cate imagined Molly staying up all night to count the minutes down until she could kiss Aberdeen goodbye. Cate didn't blame her. Molly's divorce left her in a bad financial position. Her ex-husband, who still lived in town but now with her former student assistant with whom he'd had an affair, made the situation even more uncomfortable. Cate smiled as she reflected that in a matter of days her friend would join her and settle in to her new life.

Her excitement for Molly's arrival might temper her enthusiasm for travel to the past. She planned to spend the next two days preparing Molly's new room. Cate finished her dinner and curled up afterward with a good book to relax for the evening. Her mind fought to concentrate on her book, but it wandered to Molly's arrival and daydreamed of travel to the past.

CHAPTER 2

Friday arrived before Cate was ready. Despite the full night of sleep she enjoyed, she felt nothing prepared her for Isla Campbell's party-planning meetings. After breakfast, Cate took her usual walk with Riley and Bailey before settling them in the library with a couple of bones. She planned to meet with Mrs. Campbell in the sitting room. Mrs. Campbell, not a fan of animals, would find the addition of two pups unwelcomed, so Cate made other arrangements.

Cate stood waiting at the front door twenty minutes prior to their scheduled meeting time. Mrs. Campbell had a habit of arriving at least fifteen minutes early. Often, to Mrs. Fraser's dismay, if no one was available at the front door, she'd wander through the halls until she came upon someone. By now, Cate caught on to the woman's antics and was always prepared for her early.

Like clockwork, Mrs. Campbell's car glided down the drive fifteen minutes early. The woman bounded out of the car, dozens of folders, swatches and other party paraphernalia in hand. Cate greeted her, stepping from the door to relieve her of some materials.

"Wow!" Cate exclaimed, eyeing the materials. "You've been hard at work!"

"With only a week to go, Lady Cate," Mrs. Campbell's Scottish brogue answered her, "we cannot be too careful. We must make sure everything matches perfectly. Are the trees set up?"

Cate led the way into the sitting room off the main foyer. "Yes, Jack set them up yesterday. We can take a look after we've finished these details," Cate answered, waving her hand over the multitude of items now sprawled on the loveseat.

Mrs. Campbell nodded her head in agreement. "Yes, there are many details to check and double-check. I will NOT risk another debacle like the one at the Halloween party." Mrs. Campbell gave her a knowing glance coupled with a grimace. Cate held back laughter, recalling the so-called debacle Mrs. Campbell referred to: linens in the incorrect color. Mrs. Campbell's reaction had been typical of the woman's personality. She had turned the entire situation into a Greek tragedy and the solution, keeping the red tablecloths despite having burgundy napkins, left Mrs. Campbell less than satisfied. After the mix-up, Mrs. Campbell was determined to avoid another "costly mistake." Cate, too, was determined to avoid one after the tizzy it sent Mrs. Campbell into for Halloween.

Cate retrieved her folders from the nearby table, settling into a small space she carved out on the loveseat across from Mrs. Campbell. "I wanted to begin with the linens. As I mentioned earlier, I do NOT want another issue. I have checked, rechecked and triple checked with the linen company. Ugh," she groaned, dropping her head between her shoulders and rolling her eyes. "Can you imagine the issue if they bungled the linens this time? Oh!" she exclaimed, squeezing her eyes shut. "I've had nightmares of clashing plaids all week! I will feel so much better once they are delivered tomorrow."

Cate offered her a smile. "I'm sure we all will. And I hope they get the selections correct," Cate added, picking up the fabric swatch. "These patterns are so beautiful. They will be lovely for Christmas."

"There is no room for error!" Mrs. Campbell said, nodding her head in agreement. "Particularly with the tight turn around between the two parties!"

Cate nodded, selecting another swatch. "And with such different looks!" she commented.

Mrs. Campbell nodded as Mrs. Fraser entered the room carrying a tray. "Can I offer you some tea, Mrs. Campbell?" Cate asked as Mrs. Fraser settled the tray on the coffee table between them.

"Oh, yes, thank you! Hello, Emily," Mrs. Campbell nodded to the woman. "How are you? Almost out the door, eh?" she queried, needling about the older woman's retirement.

"Oh," Mrs. Fraser responded, "I wouldn't put it that way. I've got a good deal of training to provide the new lassie."

"Oh?" Mrs. Campbell replied, playing dumb. "Lady Cate, you won't let her retire until she's properly trained the staff, is it?"

Cate opened her mouth to answer, but Mrs. Fraser beat her to it. "Nay, you've got it backwards, Isla. I won't retire until I'm good and ready, and the new whippersnapper has a complete handle on every aspect of the estate and Lady Cate's care!"

Cate smiled at Mrs. Fraser's response. "And I will be happy to have you here every minute, Mrs. Fraser. And once you've retired, I expect you to be here often as my guest!"

"Well," Mrs. Campbell responded. "You'll have good practice playing guest at the two parties." Mrs. Campbell, despite her agreement, had obviously been miffed to have the estate's staff invited to the VIP event. She less-than-tactfully pointed out the guest list may not mix well with Cate's staff. Cate disagreed, stating the Frasers, Jack and Molly were VIPs to her. Unable to argue with the countess, Mrs. Campbell yielded.

"Aye," Mrs. Fraser agreed. "I'm looking forward to them both. Now, is there anything else, Lady Cate?" she asked, turning to Cate.

"No, thank you, Mrs. Fraser," Cate answered. Mrs. Fraser nodded to her, exiting the room. Cate poured Mrs. Campbell a cup of tea, handing it to her along with the tongs for sugar. She offered the cookie plate to her next. "Cookie? Mrs. Fraser bakes them and I've never tasted anything better."

Mrs. Campbell offered a slight smile, pulling one from the plate with her fingertips as though it may poison her. She nibbled a corner, searching for some flaw she could point out.

Cate bit off a chunk of cookie as she stirred her tea. "I swear these taste better with every batch!"

"Mmm, yes, no doubt Emily learned her baking skills from our many excellent neighborhood bakers! Oh, that reminds me, the cookie selection!" Mrs. Campbell dropped the rest of her cookie onto her saucer next to her teacup and placed the saucer on the coffee table. She searched through her folders, pulling a legal-sized paper from a red folder. After sliding it to Cate across the tabletop, she pointed out several starred items.

The women spent the next two hours checking final details, making final arrangements and wrapping up loose ends. Cate enjoyed several of Mrs. Fraser's cookies as a reward for the tedious work. As they finished these tasks, Mrs. Campbell finished her second cup of tea before asking if she could view the progress on the ballroom preparations.

"Yes!" Cate answered, standing and placing the teacups and saucers onto the tray. "Follow me." Cate led Mrs. Campbell to the ballroom.

As they approached, Jack emerged from the room. "Ah, Lady Cate, good day!" he greeted her, bowing. "And Isla, hello."

Mrs. Campbell smiled at him for a moment, offering him the briefest of glances. She turned her eyes to the groupings of trees on either side of the doorway. "As you can see," Cate said motioning to the trees, "Jack has done a great job getting these ready to be decorated!"

"Hmm," Mrs. Campbell mumbled, still eyeing the trees. She pursed her lips, squinting at them. "Does this appear... off to you?"

"Ah..." Cate began.

"Lady Cate assured me they were spot on," Jack answered, giving two thumbs up.

"Perhaps a fourth tree..." Mrs. Campbell suggested, waving a hand in the air.

Jack's jaw dropped as he searched for an answer. "I'm not certain that's necessary," Cate answered. "Three is a nice number! Four would look too... square."

"How enlightening your analyses always are," Mrs. Campbell responded, a sarcastic tone creeping into her voice. "Oh, Mr. Reid, with the trees settled, I wondered if I might bend your ear for a moment."

"Of course," Jack answered, offering a polite smile to the woman while casting a sidelong glance at Cate.

"I'd like to make one final plea for the snowmaking machine. We've no assurances of snow next week..."

Jack interrupted her, holding up his hand. "I'll stop you there, Mrs. Campbell. After a lengthy consultation with

Lady Cate, we have all agreed a snow machine is inappropriate for the grounds. I realize and appreciate the effect you intend to achieve, however, to pull it off may cause damage to the grounds and we aren't willing to take that risk."

"Jack is correct," Cate added, backing Jack's response. "We gave it extensive consideration. We both realize how important it is to you. I can assure you we did not dismiss it out-of-hand, but in the end, we were not comfortable with the idea."

Mrs. Campbell frowned for a moment before responding. "Well," she began, again eyeing the Christmas tree setup, "I suppose if you're decided, there is nothing more to say!" She lowered her voice, mumbling, "Except what good is a Snow Ball with no snow."

After overhearing her mumbled comment, Cate responded, "The forecast seems favorable for some snow the evening of the event. Maybe we'll get lucky. Shall we take a peek inside the ballroom?"

"Oh, you Americans, always with the optimistic point of view," Mrs. Campbell replied. "Yes, I'd like to see the tree placement inside."

Jack followed the women into the ballroom to ensure everything was in order. After a few minor adjustments, Mrs. Campbell declared everything acceptable. "We will decorate over the next week. The next time you see these trees, they will be transformed!" Cate promised.

"And you've got my schematic? Showing how you should place the decorations and colors on the trees?" Mrs. Campbell asked.

Cate patted her folder. "I've got it right here and have already made copies for everyone who will assist with the decorating. We will have everything just as you proposed!"

"Excellent, excellent!" Mrs. Campbell pronounced. "With everything in order, I will see you on Thursday! Jack, keep up the good work. And if you change your mind about the snow machine, call me at once!"

Jack simulated an amused chuckle, finding the comment anything but amusing. "Oh, I will," he assured her.

"Well, I guess that's everything then. We'll see you again on Thursday," Cate agreed, nodding. "I'll walk you out." Cate showed Mrs. Campbell to the front door, saying her good-byes and watching the car pull down the drive. She breathed a long sigh of relief before returning to the sitting room, intending to return the tea tray to the kitchen. To her surprise, Mrs. Fraser had already retrieved it.

Cate glanced at her timepiece. It was almost lunchtime. She decided to take the dogs for a short walk before returning to the library for lunch. Cate made her way to the library. As she entered, she found both Riley and Bailey staring at a bookcase near the door. Cate's brow furrowed, wondering what held their attention.

"What has you two so interested in that bookcase?" she inquired of the two pups. Riley glanced to her, then directed his gaze back to the bookcase. Cate wandered over, giving both dogs a scratch on the head. Riley leapt to his feet, approaching the bookcase, then staring at Cate.

"What is it, buddy?" Cate questioned. "Did you lose a toy or bone?" Cate approached the bookcase, sweeping her hand around the bottom and glancing at the bottom shelves. The small dogs couldn't reach much further up the bookcase, so she doubted any of their belongings could have landed higher. "I don't see anything here," she stated, standing and shrugging her shoulders.

Riley glanced to her again, then returned his gaze to the bookcase, issuing a small whine. Cate screwed up her face, confused as to the dog's interest in the bookcase. "What are you trying to tell me, Riley?" she queried. The small pup remained silent on the issue beyond his interested gaze. Cate shrugged again, glancing to Bailey. "I don't suppose you want to fill me in on the details, do you, Bailey?" The other dog met her gaze with bright eyes but offered no explanation. "Well, since we're at a standstill on this subject, how about a walk?"

Riley whipped his head around to stare at Cate. Bailey jumped to his feet. "I'll take that as a yes." Cate laughed. "Come on, you two."

Cate started toward the door with the two dogs in tow. She almost collided into Jack, who approached the library. "Whoa!" she exclaimed. "Sorry!"

"Oops!" Jack replied. "A near collision, sorry, Lady Cate! But I'm glad I ran into you, pun intended!" Jack answered with a jovial laugh.

"Very funny," Cate responded. "What did you need?"

"Do you have a moment? I wanted to vent about the party czar," Jack confessed.

"I'm about to take the dogs for a quick pit stop. Care to walk with me?" Cate questioned.

"Sure, perhaps the fresh air will soothe my frayed nerves," Jack answered.

They proceeded to the front door, letting the dogs out and heading toward the side garden. "I just wanted to ensure," Jack began, "that we are on the same page with that bloody snow machine."

"We are," Cate assured him. "I trust your judgement."

"I cannot believe that woman brought that infernal machine up again. This has to be the fourth time we've told her no. I'm sorry for jumping into the conversation, Lady Cate. Perhaps it wasn't my place, but I couldn't take anymore."

Cate snickered. "It's okay," she assured him. "I'm not sure how many more ways we can say it before she's convinced we mean it."

Jack rolled his eyes, recalling the conversation. "Ah, that damned woman," he replied, shaking his head.

Cate kept an eye on the dogs frolicking through the bushes. She held in a laugh at Jack's last statement. "Careful," she warned, "you're starting to sound like Mrs. Fraser."

"Aye, Emily and I have the same view of her, I'll admit it," Jack answered.

"You can swap horror stories over lunch," Cate added then called the dogs back to her.

"Oh?" Jack questioned as they turned back to the castle.

"Yes," Cate replied. "Mrs. Fraser brought tea to us for the first part of our meeting and had a small conversation about her retirement with Isla. I'll bet she was boiling when she left the room."

"If the conversation went beyond a standard 'hello,' I'm sure she was!" Jack responded.

They entered the castle through the main doors. The dogs raced off to the library as soon as they opened the door. "What's with them?" Jack inquired.

Cate shrugged. "No idea," she replied. "I found them both staring at one of the bookcases in the library. I'm not sure what is so intriguing about it, but it seems to have captivated their attention."

"Perhaps they'd like to take up reading," Jack joked.

"Yes, I'm sure that's it," Cate answered. "Sir Riley is really fitting into his role as lord of the manor. He only needs a pipe and a monocle, and he'll be all set."

Jack chuckled at Cate's joke as Mrs. Fraser approached them with Cate's lunch in hand. "Oh, I can take that from here, Mrs. Fraser," Cate stated, reaching for the tray.

"Enjoy your lunch, Lady Cate," Mrs. Fraser expressed. "I'm sure you'd like a quiet moment now that the ninny left."

Cate chuckled at Mrs. Fraser's nickname for Mrs. Campbell. "Oh, she could use it," Jack answered. "The ninny was even more of a ninny than usual!"

Cate grinned at them. "I'll leave Jack fill you in on the details. I've already told him I was sure your conversation about retirement with Mrs. Campbell exasperated you."

"Oh, you've no idea," Mrs. Fraser admitted. "Come along, young Jack, wait until you hear what that woman said this time!"

Another giggle escaped Cate's lips as she watched them disappear down the hall together. Cate carried her tray to the library, where she found the two dogs on either side of the bookcase. Two sentinels guarding some unknown treasure. Cate shook her head at them as she set the tray on the desk.

After opening her laptop, she browsed her emails as she ate. An email from Molly with the subject *On my way!* appeared in her inbox. Cate smiled as she opened and read it. The brief email said Molly's plane was about to take off and she'd be in London by afternoon. She promised to text once she was settled at her hotel. It wouldn't be long before Molly was a permanent resident of Dunhaven Castle.

Cate glanced at her watch. In just over forty-eight hours, Molly would call Dunhaven Castle home. Cate monitored the second hand as it ticked off the seconds, drawing Molly's arrival ever closer. As Cate reflected on her friend's arrival, her mind swung from the future to the past. The case of the stolen jewelry pushed itself to the front of Cate's brain. Who had stolen the jewelry, and why? Why was it never recovered? Where did the case go cold? Cate's mind turned the limited details from the newspaper articles over and over, searching for a clue.

She found none. With a sigh, she opted to begin her weekend early, curled up with a good book by the room's massive fireplace. After receiving an email stating Molly was settled in her hotel room, Cate relaxed into her evening.

CHAPTER 3

Cate spent the early morning hours of Saturday pacing her bedroom floor. She watched the sun rise over the moors while Riley and Bailey lounged in their beds, too lazy in the cold weather to crawl out. The warm yellow sun painted the sky a rainbow of colors, brightening the frosty morning.

Cate's mind swam with a variety of topics. A true over-thinking introvert, Cate bounced from topic to topic, planning, pondering, organizing, reminding, listing tasks and reaffirming her schedule. She cataloged the final details to be completed before Molly's arrival. Some decorating would begin today. It would take several days to complete all the decorating of Christmas trees, hang wreaths and set up holiday displays.

True to form, Mr. Fraser developed a magical plan for the gardens outside. Even with the cold weather predicted for the party, many partygoers would likely still escape the heat of the interior to enjoy the gardens. The plan promised to provide an ethereal effect, snow or not. Cate found the design charming, like an enchanting walkthrough light show.

She appreciated the fact that Mr. Fraser had captured a nostalgic American holiday display to remind Cate of home for her first Christmas in the castle.

Cate's mind turned to another Christmas, one that occurred in 1924. In 1924, the MacKenzie family gathered to celebrate their Christmas and New Year. As they rang in 1925, however, someone robbed them. Cate plodded into her sitting room, retrieving the folder containing the articles of the theft. Cate glanced through the articles again. Pencil in hand, she noted a few items in the margin to follow up on. Cate's overcrowded mind longed to spend a quiet day researching this mystery, but she had many duties to attend to. She glanced at the timepiece. "Soon," she promised. "I'll visit soon."

Cate dressed for the day and took the dogs for a quick walk before breakfast. Monday was her usual day to breakfast with her staff, but she also joined them today to discuss the decorations. Everyone planned to pitch in, each decorating a tree or more inside and outside the ballroom. Within minutes of arriving in the kitchen, Cate found herself able to push her longing for research aside, filled with giddy excitement to decorate a Christmas tree.

Mrs. Fraser, who stayed with Mr. Fraser in the castle the night before, arose early and was already baking cookies. Mr. Fraser sat at the kitchen table studying his outdoor design. The fragrant aroma of sweet-smelling shortbread cookies filled the room. "Mmm," Cate murmured as she entered. "I'm ready to skip breakfast and go straight for the cookies!"

"Not if I have anything to say about it," Mrs. Fraser told her. "We've got a long day of work ahead, and you need your breakfast, Lady Cate!"

Jack chuckled, already seated at the table as well. "I've already tried that, Lady Cate. My attempt was a bust, too."

"There'll be plenty of time for nibbling on cookies while

we decorate. And I've already got milk warming for hot chocolate."

Cate smiled at her, already salivating for the tasty warm drink. "If you behave yourselves, there'll be a repeat performance when we decorate our private tree on Wednesday," Mrs. Fraser promised.

Cate shot Jack a glance, giggling. "I'm excited to decorate this weekend for the party. Although, I'm more excited to spend the day with everyone on Wednesday! I haven't decorated a tree with anyone other than Riley in a long time!"

"I'm excited for the cookies!" Jack answered, reaching toward the pan as Mrs. Fraser pulled it from the oven.

"Don't even try it," she warned, batting his hand with her oven mitt. "With that done, breakfast is ready!"

"Sit down, Mrs. Fraser," Cate ordered. "Let me get your oatmeal. You've done enough work this morning." Cate ushered her to the table.

"Oh, what nonsense!" Mrs. Fraser protested. "I'm capable of retrieving my oatmeal."

"I'm aware of how capable you are, but I insist," Cate asserted. Mrs. Fraser shook her head but allowed Cate to serve her. Cate retrieved her own bowl, and sat next to the woman.

They spent their breakfast discussing their weekend decorating plans. Everyone pitched in to clean up after breakfast before moving to the ballroom. Jack and Mr. Fraser had already placed bins of decorations from years past in the room, along with any new purchases. Cate brought the dogs with her, wanting to include them in the festivities.

They began on the trees in the main hall outside the ballroom. Cate reminded them to check their schematic to be sure the color scheme matched Mrs. Campbell's wishes. Jack commented they'd be up the entire night before the party redecorating if her plans were not met.

The morning work went quickly as they strung lights and garland on the trees, adding ornaments and a tree topper to finish. They admired the finished products before moving on to the next set of trees. Cate and Mrs. Fraser retrieved the cookies and hot chocolate while Jack and Mr. Fraser continued to string lights on the next two trees. They finished the two groupings of trees outside the ballroom before stopping for lunch.

When they returned in the afternoon, they decorated the trees inside the ballroom. The row of dull green Christmas trees standing in front of the windows overlooking the garden came to life with sparkling white and colored bulbs, silver, gold and plaid garland and snowflake ornaments. Riley and Bailey spent their afternoon playing tug of war with a large plaid bow the two pups had stolen from one of the boxes.

Cate stood back, admiring their work as the afternoon turned to evening. She hoped Mrs. Campbell would be pleased. The bright, sparkling trees transformed the ballroom into a winter wonderland. Tomorrow, while Jack drove to Edinburgh to pick up Molly, they would add details to the scene. Blankets of fake snow, wreaths, wrapped boxes, sleighs and more would be added to augment the already festive scene.

They finished for the day, gathering in the kitchen for a light meal of sandwiches prepared the day prior by Mrs. Fraser. With the growing excitement for Molly's arrival, Cate hoped she would sleep that night. The day's demanding physical work allowed her to nod off within minutes of her head hitting the pillow. The following morning, Cate felt well rested from a deep sleep.

After breakfast and a thirty-minute walk with the dogs, Cate began her Sunday by finishing details in Molly's room. Cate set out a few framed photos on the mantle, unpacked a few personal items, placing them around the room, and laid out a welcome gift basket on the bed. Pleased with her work, Cate hoped the added touches helped settle Molly into her new home.

Cate spent the rest of the morning adding more detailed decor to the ballroom with Mr. and Mrs. Fraser. They finished the decorating mid-afternoon, just in time to freshen up before Molly's arrival. Mrs. Fraser hurried below stairs to put the final touches on the special dinner she planned to welcome Molly.

Cate ushered the dogs downstairs and out for a quick walk. As she led them back to the front door, she spotted the estate car pulling down the drive. As Jack exited the car, Cate was unable to restrain Riley any longer. He bounded to the car, balancing on his hind legs to capture Jack's attention.

Cate approached the passenger door with Bailey as it burst open. Molly spilled out of the car, her excitement overflowing. "CATE!" she shouted, racing to her and throwing her arms around her. "I made it!"

Cate returned the hug. "Yes!" Cate exclaimed. "The time seemed to drag. It seemed like this day wouldn't arrive, but here it is! I've been excited for days! It'll be so nice to have you settled in the castle."

"I can't wait to get settled! I can't wait to start my new job! How about that, huh? I'm actually excited about work! It doesn't even feel like work!"

Jack retrieved Molly's lone suitcase from the car's trunk. Riley bounded toward Molly to greet her. Molly bent to pet both dogs before they entered the castle. She hugged her purse to her chest, following Cate into the foyer. "I'm so excited I could burst!" she exclaimed as she stepped into the entryway. "How are the decorations coming?" she asked.

"Almost finished!" Cate announced as Jack passed them on the way to deliver Molly's luggage to her room.

"I bet the place looks great. And thanks for waiting for me to get here to decorate the private tree, honey," Molly replied, placing her hand on Cate's arm. "It makes me feel like I'm part of the household already!"

"You're welcome. I'm looking forward to it. These trees have been fun to decorate, but I can't wait to decorate our tree! And I'm excited for Mrs. Fraser's hot chocolate and cookies!"

"Me too!" Molly giggled.

"Interested in taking a peek at the ballroom?" Cate inquired. "We have some time before dinner."

"Sure!" Molly agreed. "I can't wait to see it! Jack told me your two little rascals absconded with one of the bows yesterday."

Cate led Molly toward the ballroom, Riley and Bailey in tow. "They did, the little thieves," Cate admitted. "They had a fabulous time tugging on it until they tore it to shreds."

As they approached the ballroom, Molly gasped. "Oh goodness, it's beautiful!" she exclaimed, eyeing the trees. Even unlit, they appeared majestic and festive surrounding the doorway. Cate led Molly inside, striding across the room to turn on the tree lights. "OH!" Molly shouted from inside the doorway. "It's incredible! You've done a magnificent job! I'll bet Mrs… ah, what's her name, will be so pleased!"

"Campbell," Cate informed her, crossing back to admire the lit trees again. "And I sure hope so. Although Mrs. Campbell has a way of spotting any flaw, no matter how small. I'm sure she'll demand something be adjusted."

Molly laughed as Cate hurried across the room to turn off the lights. "Is she still on you about that snow machine?"

"She is. Jack is at his wit's end with her. She asked him again on Friday," Cate replied, closing the ballroom doors as they exited. "I'm surprised he didn't lunge at her."

"This place looks great with or without snow!" Molly stated.

"I agree!" Cate answered, leading her upstairs to the bedrooms. "Here you are, the Rose Room! I'll give you some time to unwind and freshen up before dinner."

"I'm too excited to unwind! I'm super excited to be back here! I feel so at home here, so I'm sure I'll be relaxed in an instant."

"I took the liberty of setting some of your things out," Cate responded, opening the door. "I'm sure you'll want to shift things around, but at least it's a start. I unpacked the clothing also, so you don't have to do it. Especially since you wanted to dive right in with work tomorrow! Are you sure you wouldn't rather take a few days to settle in?"

"I'm positive!" Molly answered, following Cate into the room. "Oh, wow! You made it so homey! You put my photos out! And my blanket! Oh!" Molly exclaimed, seeing the welcome basket on the bed. "Aww, Cate, you shouldn't have! This opportunity was enough. You didn't have to do this!"

Molly picked up the new cardigan Cate laid out with the welcome basket, hugging it to her chest. "This is beautiful!" she exclaimed. "Thank you! I love it!"

"You're welcome," Cate replied, hugging Molly. "I'm glad you like it. See you in about half an hour for dinner?"

Molly nodded. "Thanks. Oh! I almost forgot. I have something for you. Oh, it's buried in the luggage, I'll get it out and bring it to dinner."

"No rush," Cate noted. "See you soon!"

Cate escorted the two pups from Molly's room, closing the door behind her, and steered them toward her bedroom suite. When she emerged for dinner, she found Molly waiting in the hallway, a brown bag in hand. "Found the stuff I brought!" she declared, holding the bag up with a triumphant expression. "I'll give it to you downstairs. I brought something for everyone!"

They navigated to the kitchen. Molly received another round of welcome hugs as they entered the kitchen. Mrs. Fraser set the last dish on the table and they sat down to eat. As they ate their Scottish Berry Brûlée, a special dessert prepared for Molly's arrival, Molly passed out her gifts. She brought a special Christmas ornament for each of them. Jack and Mr. Fraser each received a bear dressed in a Scottish kilt. Mrs. Fraser received a teddy bear dressed in a plaid dress. Cate received a teddy bear dressed in an eighteenth century ballgown. "I figured we could hang them on the tree together!" Molly informed them. "I brought my own, too, see?" She brandished a bear wearing sunglasses and an American flag t-shirt.

A smile spread across Cate's face. "That's such a cute idea," Cate agreed. "Thank you, Molly. It will make a memorable ornament for a memorable Christmas."

Molly smiled. "Oh, I have one other thing for you," Molly replied to Cate. She withdrew a trinket box with a coat of arms on the lid from the bag. "This is from Maggie Edwards. You remember her, don't you? She worked for me. I ran into her a few times over the last semester. Remind me to tell you what happened with her, it's wild! Anyway, when I told her I was moving, she made a point of dropping this off for you. She came across it at her shop and thought it would be a perfect gift for you."

"Oh, thanks! It's beautiful!" Cate answered, gazing at the box. "Yes, I remember Maggie. I spoke with her before your last visit. She emailed me and said she ran into you! I promised her a visit!"

"Who's the mysterious Maggie? Some American celebrity?" Jack asked after a bite of his dessert.

"She was a student at Aberdeen College," Cate explained.

"She worked as a graduate assistant with Molly. She lives in the town neighboring Aberdeen. She's got a great little antique shop slash bookstore there."

"And a hunky new boyfriend to help her with it, too," Molly added.

"No more Leo?" Cate inquired.

Molly shook her head, swallowing some dessert and washing it down with a sip of water. "Mmm-mmm," she began as she drank. "Nope. No more Leo. Henry now. A gorgeous Aussie. Took her on an around the world adventure, finding her uncle who was kidnapped by grave robbers! It was crazy! Anyway, invite her over, she'll tell you all about it!"

"Ollie Keene was kidnapped by grave robbers?!" Cate shouted, shock in her voice. "What?"

"Yep," Molly assured her, nodding. "Went searching for Cleopatra's tomb and ended up on the wrong side of some nasty people. That's how she met Henry."

"That IS crazy!" Cate agreed.

"Wow! I never realized how exciting American life is," Jack chimed in. "Lady Cate, you must be so dreadfully bored here."

Cate sighed dramatically. "Yes, nothing EVER happens here," she joked, shooting a look at Jack who understood her meaning all too well.

"I, for one, am looking forward to an unexciting life," Molly responded, not understanding the full breadth of Cate's joke. "Although I don't imagine one can call life in a castle dull or boring!"

"I'm with you, Molly," Mrs. Fraser agreed. "A simple life is the best life!" She stood, clearing a few dishes from the table.

Without missing a beat, Molly rose, pitching in to clear the table. "I agree! Although I still maintain living in a castle is not what I call a simple life."

"You Americans really find castles fascinating, don't you?" Mrs. Fraser queried.

"Yep," Molly concurred. "I'll admit I love my new home!"

"And you're sure you want to start working tomorrow? Don't want a few days to settle into your new home?" Mrs. Fraser questioned.

"Nope! Cate already asked me, and I already declined. I'm ready to begin! Besides, you all have most of my things unpacked for me! So, I am settled in!"

The two ladies chatted about their upcoming day as they cleaned the kitchen. Cate, Jack and Mr. Fraser pitched in to finish clearing the table. After dinner, everyone retired to their separate spaces. Cate cuddled with her dogs on her chaise lounge under a thick blanket. Laptop in hand, Cate sent a quick email to Maggie thanking her for the gift, asking about her adventure across the globe, and extending an invitation to the castle.

After sending the email, Cate selected a movie to play, setting the laptop on a nearby table. Without thinking, her hand landed on the folder of articles about the theft. Cate grabbed it, thumbing through the papers again as the movie played in the background.

With Molly settled in the castle and most of the indoor decorating complete, Cate's mind returned to the mystery she hoped to solve. She grabbed a few sheets of blank paper and a pen. Given the late evening hour, she wouldn't get much done, but she could make a start on researching the time period. Cate wrote a few preliminary questions on the first blank sheet. She hoped the questions would guide her research when she had a moment to begin. Her questions included determining what family members lived in the house, if any guests were visiting for the holidays and workers who were new or who were dismissed around this time period.

Her questions would take a fair amount of research through personal correspondence, journals, photo albums, employment records and any other source she could find. With her work outlined, Cate set the folder aside, relaxing with her pups for the rest of the evening.

CHAPTER 4

Cate climbed from her bed, her muscles complaining with every motion. The decorating, while enjoyable, took a physical toll. With a groan and a frown, Cate popped the top on her bottle of acetaminophen and washed two capsules down with two gulps of water.

She stretched for a few minutes before enjoying a long, hot shower. She dressed for the day, already feeling some relief from her aches and pains. Both dogs still lounged in their beds, too lazy to move. Cate grinned at them as she pulled her boots on over her leggings. After kneeling down next to them, she stroked each of their heads and prodded them from their beds. The promise of a long walk roused Riley. At the mention of the special "w" word, he bounded out of bed, offering a small yip and dancing in a circle. Bailey, excited by Riley's excitement, leapt from his bed, joining the fray. Slowly but surely, Bailey was learning from Riley and reacting in similar manners. It was heartwarming to watch the progress he made every day, turning from frightened orphan to full-fledged family member.

Concern crept over Cate as she took a brief morning

stroll with the dogs before breakfast. Research was her top priority, and she wondered what progress she might make on finding anything beyond the basics. A second source of jitters stemmed from Molly's first day of work. While Cate expected no issues, nervousness over whether Molly would enjoy the position filled her. She desired Molly to enjoy her work and find the new position a welcome change, but worried she may find it more than she bargained for. Since Cate couldn't control Molly's feelings, her only recourse was to hope for the best.

Cate returned to the castle, ushering the two pups into the kitchen through the kitchen door. She found Mrs. Fraser and Molly busy readying breakfast as she stepped into the sweet-smelling kitchen. "Good morning, Lady Cate," Mrs. Fraser called from across the kitchen.

"Good morning," Cate answered, waving to both women.

"Good morning, Cate. Oh, Lady Cate," Molly responded, catching herself and glancing toward Mrs. Fraser with some trepidation. Mrs. Fraser nodded to her.

"Now," Mrs. Fraser informed Molly, "Lady Cate eats breakfast with us on Monday mornings, so there's no need to set the dining room. But on the other days of the week, Lady Cate takes her breakfast in the dining room."

Molly nodded, making a mental note of the schedule. "Right. Mondays with us, all other days in the dining room," she repeated.

"Yes," Mrs. Fraser confirmed as Cate seated herself at the already-set table. "Unless she requests otherwise." Riley and Bailey found a spot near the warm stove, curling up for a nap to prepare for their morning stroll after breakfast. "Oatmeal is the normal unless we're entertaining. In that case, we put out a bigger spread. Well, you'll see over the holiday. And Lady Cate uses brown sugar and raisins, so we keep the pantry well-stocked. On occasion, I'll put out other fruit if it appears good at the market. Blueberries, cranberries and the like."

Mrs. Fraser wasted no time in instructing Molly on the day-to-day workings of breakfast. Cate found it strange to listen to the instructions about how to prepare her breakfast. She glanced at the table in front of her, pursing her lips as Molly repeated Mrs. Fraser's instructions.

"Now, I use this server," Mrs. Fraser instructed, "when breakfast is served upstairs with guests. I fill a bowl for Lady Cate when she eats upstairs alone. When we eat here, we take it straight from the pot. Lady Cate insists!"

"I could save you the wash and take it from the pot every day, Mrs. Fraser," Cate offered, joining the conversation. "I'm capable of carrying a bowl of oatmeal from the kitchen to the dining room.

"Now, we'll have nothing of the sort, Lady Cate," Mrs. Fraser scolded. "And if you're going to change the routine, I'll not allow you to eat down here anymore!"

Cate bit her lower lip, glancing to Molly. "I'm starting to wonder who's really in charge here," Molly whispered as she set a bowl of brown sugar on the table in front of Cate.

Cate giggled. "Me too," she admitted.

Mrs. Fraser, a fan of tradition and propriety, preferred to maintain centuries-old traditions established for attending family members in a household such as this. Cate, an American, was unused to the attentiveness of a staff and, having lived a life devoid of such traditions, was still adjusting to them. She appreciated Mrs. Fraser's dogged determination to maintain the standards of serving a countess, but hated putting the woman out.

After her arrival, Cate and Mrs. Fraser had come to terms with their opposite views on running the household. Cate allowed herself to be pampered as a countess while Mrs. Fraser allowed Cate a few nontraditional customs such as regular, no-frills dining with the staff on a well-defined schedule. The balance they struck pleased both of them. Their relationship grew into a solid friendship and, with time, Cate was evolving to become accustomed to her new way of life.

"How was your first night in your new home?" Cate inquired of Molly as Mr. Fraser and Jack entered.

"Fabulous," Molly admitted. "Best night's sleep I've had since I was here last!"

"You'll have another good night's sleep tonight, I imagine," Mrs. Fraser teased. "I've got a full day planned for us!"

The statement didn't dampen Molly's spirits. She grinned at Mrs. Fraser as she gave the oatmeal one last stir. "I can't wait! This is all ready."

Cate grabbed her bowl from her place setting and approached the pot. One of her bargains for breakfast with the staff was serving herself first. Mrs. Fraser insisted, and no one dared approach the pot before Cate, lest they invite the wrath of Mrs. Fraser. Cate filled her bowl, followed by Jack, Mr. Fraser, then Mrs. Fraser and Molly.

They all sat around the kitchen table. "How are the preparations outside coming along?" Cate questioned as they ate.

"Splendid," Mr. Fraser assured her. "It will be a winter wonderland for the guests!" Proud of his garden design, Mr. Fraser beamed as he answered Cate's question.

"If only we had snow…" Jack joked.

Cate laughed, shaking her head. "If you've changed your mind…" she teased, letting her voice trail off.

"I know just who to call if I have," Jack answered.

Cate giggled, reminding Molly of the ongoing battle between the household and Mrs. Campbell regarding the snow machine.

"What is your dress like for the ball, Molly?" Mrs. Fraser inquired.

"Oh, bright, Christmas red!" Molly exclaimed. "It has a shawl collar, kind of almost off the shoulders, but not quite. And a big, red bow cinched with a glittery brooch on the side." She pointed to her right hip.

"Sounds very pretty," Mrs. Fraser replied.

"I splurged on it," Molly answered. "I wanted something flashy as a last purchase in Aberdeen. Then I made them mail it here. I'll bet that got around town with lightning speed!"

Cate chuckled. They continued to discuss a few additional party details before changing the subject.

"Will you be working on your research today, Lady Cate?" Mrs. Fraser inquired.

"Yes," Cate answered. "I'm moving on to another time period. Mid-1920s."

"I thought you were working on the 1850s?" Mrs. Fraser questioned.

"Yes, I was. However, something intriguing came up, and I'd like to follow up on it," Cate responded. "I'll return to the 1850s once I have this sorted out," Cate promised. "I've done a fair amount of work in that time period already."

"You don't say," Jack replied.

"Well, Lady Cate," Mrs. Fraser answered. "How you captured the era, the MacKenzies' very personalities, and made them come alive! I must say, the chapter I perused made it almost sound as though you were on the estate in those times!"

Jack choked on the water he was sipping at Mrs. Fraser's compliment. He sputtered a cough out as he regained his composure. Cate shot Jack an amused glance, suppressing a giggle.

"I'd believe it," Molly chimed in, none the wiser to Jack's reaction. "I'll bet Cate's a talented writer!"

"Oh, yes, almost like she's lived through it, so vivid."

"Almost…" Jack expressed.

* * *

Cate gathered several materials to begin her research, settling in the library with Riley and Bailey. She spread her work across the desk, setting out several blank sheets of paper along with her list of questions from the previous night.

First, Cate opened the family bible containing the family tree. She glanced through the script writing on the inside cover. The marking of the heritage, her heritage, still sent chills up her spine as she studied the long legacy of MacKenzies that had come before her. A smile crossed her face as she found Randolph's and Victoria's names in the tree. She traced her finger down the family tree to find the family members alive and living in the castle in 1925.

During this era, Rory MacKenzie, Randolph and Victoria's grandson, and his wife, Anne, inhabited the castle. Both in their thirties, they were joined in the castle by their almost eleven-year-old son, Oliver. Oliver was the father of Cate's benefactor, Gertrude MacKenzie.

The small family was low on Cate's suspect list as they stood nothing to gain from the theft. Short of Oliver playing a childish prank, she could think of no reason for them to have stolen the jewels. As far as Cate was aware, there was no insurance payment for them, so they stood to gain nothing from falsely suggesting they had been stolen.

Cate turned her attention to anyone else in the family who may have been on the estate during the theft. Rory's father and mother were both deceased by 1925. Cate stared at the large inkblot over her side of the family. She recalled finding it after arriving at the castle as she tried to research her connection to the MacKenzies. Fearful that there had been a rift in the family, Cate pondered if the inkblot had tried to erase her side of the family.

Cate still wasn't certain who was responsible for the destruction of the family tree in the bible. However, she had tracked down the information through her attorney's assistant, Gayle Pearson.

Cate found her own copy of the family tree after rummaging through her papers. This reproduction contained the information that laid under the inkblot. According to her research, or rather, Gayle's, Rory had a younger brother, Lucas. Lucas, Cate's great-grandfather, was six years his brother's junior.

Cate confessed to be unaware of any information regarding Lucas or his wife, Amelia. Had they lived in the castle, too? Or had they taken up residence somewhere else? Cate's limited self-history led to a plethora of questions she hoped to find answers to. While Cate hated to admit it, if they were on the estate at the time of the theft, they were suspects. Motives could be many. However, the one that stood at the top of the list was jealousy. Was Lucas motivated by envy to rob his older brother, Rory, of part of the inheritance that he would never receive? Cate hoped this wasn't the case. She felt guilty even entertaining the idea that her great-grandfather could be a thief. A thief she descended from. The idea made her skin crawl, and she hoped to prove it incorrect. Could this be the reason for the inkblot, Cate wondered?

With an abundance of reluctance, Cate created a new sheet titled *Possible Suspects*, and she placed her great-grandfather and his wife on it. They wouldn't welcome their first child, her grandfather, Charles, until later in 1925, according to her family tree. Based on his birthday, in the latter half of the year, she concluded pregnancy wouldn't have prevented them from traveling to visit family for the 1924 holiday season. While she had no confirmation, they may have been in the castle. Perhaps she could find conclusive evidence that they were not and remove them from the suspect list right away. Perhaps a Christmas card wishing happy holidays and suggesting they would not see the family or family home. Cate wrote a note to check for this.

Cate stared at her research so far. She grimaced as she read the only two names on her suspect list. She stared in disappointment as her mind continued to churn until two voices disturbed her musing. Mrs. Fraser and Molly made their way through the door.

"Just as I told you," Mrs. Fraser announced. "Lady Cate often takes her lunch in the library. She's usually here working."

Molly nodded, carrying the tray as Mrs. Fraser directed her toward the set up near the fireplace. "And how is the research coming along, Lady Cate?" Mrs. Fraser asked.

"Slow," Cate admitted. "I'm shocked it's time for lunch already! I must have let my imagination run away with me and time ran right along with it!"

"It appears you've done a good bit of work judging by the spread on the desk!" Mrs. Fraser quipped.

Cate laughed as she stood and gazed at the cluttered desk. "Or made a fine mess at least!" Cate approached the fireplace. "And how is the first day going?"

Molly smiled. "Great by my marker!" Molly glanced to Mrs. Fraser who nodded in agreement.

"Aye," Mrs. Fraser concurred. "She's a fast learner and a good worker. You made a fine choice in her, Lady Cate."

Molly beamed with pride at the woman's comments. "Anything else you need, Lady Cate?" she inquired of Cate.

Cate shook her head. "Nope. I'm all set! Have a great lunch, ladies!"

"Thanks!" Molly exclaimed, following Mrs. Fraser from the room.

Cate tossed a few logs onto the fire, then plopped into

one of the armchairs near the roaring fireplace. She glanced around for the two dogs. Not finding them laying near the fireplace surprised her. Her brow wrinkled as her eyes swept the room. Her eyes locked on them laying in front of the same bookcase she found them intrigued with a few days ago. It appeared to have captured their interest again.

"Riley! Bailey!" Cate called across the room. "What are you two doing over there?" Riley glanced to her, then returned his gaze to the bookcase. Cate shook her head. If she didn't already possess a research plan for the afternoon, she'd have tried again to find out what was so interesting about that bookshelf.

Instead, Cate was hellbent on searching employment records to add to her list of potential suspects. Cate felt guilty searching through employment records attempting to finger another individual, but she wanted the suspicion off her own family. Despite the suspicion belonging only to Cate, she still felt uneasy.

Cate finished her lunch and took the dogs for as long a walk as the chilly afternoon air allowed. The cold temperatures drove them back inside to a roaring fire, stoked and tended by Mr. Fraser while they were out. The dogs curled near it and Cate left them to their dreams while she searched the castle for employment records from the 1920s. After an hour of hunting, Cate stumbled upon records from the era. Pleased with her find, she gathered up the record books and hurried back to the warmth of the library's fire.

Nestled under a blanket in an armchair near the fireplace, Cate noted the name of each employee working when the theft occurred. When completed, her list totaled over twenty. Her next move would be to order the list based on people whose employment status changed within a few months prior to or following the theft. While likely unfair, Cate devised no other method to sort the list.

Cate created a column next to the list of employee names, noting their employment dates. She was about to dive into filling the column when the doors opened. "And as you can see, you'll often find Lady Cate STILL working at dinner time."

Surprised, Cate fumbled her timepiece open, noting the late hour. She rushed to gather her research into a folder, clearing and cleaning her space. "Oh, I've lost track of the time again!" Cate confessed.

"When you work, you really work!" Molly exclaimed, carrying the tray to Cate's location. She turned to Mrs. Fraser. "Sometimes I'd text her to make sure she remembered to go to lunch or class. When she was researching, nothing, and I mean NOTHING, pulled her attention away."

Cate laughed at Molly's synopsis of her work ethic. "Oh, I'll bet. Lady Cate's only been here a few months and already I can see how she throws herself into her work! If it weren't for us, I'd worry she'd not eat!"

"Or eat cereal," Molly joked. Mrs. Fraser groaned at the idea as Cate held in a chuckle, realizing Molly spoke the truth.

"My diet has improved by leaps and bounds since I've moved here," Cate admitted.

"I'm glad!" Mrs. Fraser replied. "Enjoy your dinner, Lady Cate!"

"Thank you. Enjoy yours, too."

Before eating, Cate cleared her area, dumping all her materials on the desk. She returned to the armchair near the fireplace, relaxing into it and pulling the tray onto her lap. When she finished eating, she took the dogs for a brief walk before settling in her sitting room with a book.

About an hour before she retired, a light knock sounded on her door. Startled, she hollered, "Come in!" She swung her legs over the edge of her chaise, assuming there was a problem that required her attention.

Molly's head popped through the door. "Hey, sorry to disturb you, may I come in for a minute?"

"Sure," Cate replied, "what's up? Is everything okay?" She started to stand.

"Oh, yeah, yeah, honey," Molly responded, waving her back down onto the chaise. "Don't get up. Everything's fine."

Cate plopped onto the chaise between the two dogs as Molly approached her. She perched on the foot of the lounge. She took Cate's hands in hers and said, "I just wanted to tell you how great my first day went and how thrilled I am that you offered me this job. And how happy I am that I accepted it."

Cate smiled at her. "I'm so glad, Molly," she answered.

"I didn't want anything more than that and I won't disturb your evening any further. But I wanted you to know how happy I am."

"I appreciate you telling me, Molly. I'll admit, while I hoped you'd love it here, I worried you wouldn't."

"And that's exactly why I came. I know you. I realize you're a worrier! Only you would worry that changing someone else's life for the better didn't make them happy!"

Cate chuckled. "No," she asserted. "I worried that I didn't change your life for the better. But I'm so glad to hear that wasn't the case!" Cate leaned forward, embracing Molly.

Molly wrapped her in a warm, friendly hug. "Well, I'm going to read and relax in my room. Mr. Fraser built me a cozy fire for my first night here, and I'm going to take advantage!"

Cate grinned at her. "Go put your feet up. Enjoy the Rose Room!"

"Oh, I plan on it, honey!" Molly assured her. "Goodnight, Lady Cate."

"Goodnight. Oh, you don't..." Cate began.

Molly waved her hand at Cate. "I do. Because it's proper, and I'm determined not to let those traditions die. There's really something magnificent about how Mrs. Fraser insists on the pomp and circumstance. Almost magical. I'm proud to be a part of this grand tradition. So, goodnight again, Lady Cate." Molly nodded her head toward Cate before striding from the room. Cate's eyes followed her across the room. Self-respect and confidence filled Molly's stride. Never a shrinking violet, Cate had been surprised during her last visit to see how battered Molly's ego had been. It appeared the change in her circumstances improved Molly's outlook. It pleased Cate to have been part of that change. Contentment filled her as she witnessed the happiness displayed by her dear friend. Cate smiled to herself, diving back into her book. She'd sleep well tonight, contented with all her friends close and happy within the castle walls.

CHAPTER 5

Cate awoke drenched in sweat, gasping for breath. Her heart thudded in her chest at a rapid pace. Her breathing, labored and ragged, made her lightheaded. Her hands trembled as she gulped for air attempting to calm herself.

As her breathing and heart rate slowed, Cate climbed from her bed. She paced the floor of her bedroom, eventually venturing out into her sitting room to collapse onto her chaise. What disturbed her sleep, she wondered? What caused her to awaken in such a state?

Cate laid her head back onto the chair's plump back. A dream, she mused. Yes, that was it! A dream had startled her from her sleep. She tried hard to recall the details. She pushed her mind to reach for any piece of information.

A party, she remembered. She was hosting a party in the dream. Cate stood in the ballroom, in a long sapphire-blue, princess-style evening gown. Randolph and Victoria greeted her with an embrace before taking their place for a waltz on the dance floor. After that, several guests swirled around her with a ceaseless amount of chatter. Her head swam with it as face after face passed in front of her, some smiling, others leaning in to kiss her cheek. Music filled the room, loud and discordant. Cate's head ached from the off-key noise. Incessant chatter, high-pitched laughter and a swirl of mixed perfumes filled the air. Something about the entire event overwhelmed her far beyond the general anxiety experienced by an introvert at social gatherings.

Needing to escape from the dizzying parade of guests and noise, Cate excused herself, fleeing from the ballroom and shutting herself inside the library. She gulped for air as she leaned against the library doors, composing herself. Riley and Bailey greeted her, racing toward her. She bent over, gathering both into her arms. Warm kisses raced across her cheeks. As Cate's nerves loosened from the tight knot they were balled in, Riley and Bailey pulled away. Both dogs spun to face the bookcase.

"What is it about that bookcase?" Cate inquired. The dogs raced to it, Riley yipping at it. Bailey followed suit, tossing his head back and howling in a panic at the bookcase. The dogs became more and more frenzied as Cate approached the bookcase. The windows blew open and an icy wind flew around the room. Cate rubbed her bare arms as she continued across the room.

Riley and Bailey continued their frantic barking, undisturbed by the windstorm in the room. Papers swirled in a whirlwind. Cate fought through them to the bookcase. As she neared the wall, the bookcase dissolved, fading away to blackness. A gaping hole yawned in front of her. Icy cold air gusted from the hole. Riley and Bailey ceased barking, backing from the hole, their tails between their legs. They turned and raced to hide under the desk.

Cate's brow furrowed as she followed their scamper across the room. A noise spun her back toward the hole in the wall. An unearthly groan emanated from the hole. Cate took a step closer to the void. Air wafted from the blackness, accompanied by another groan. This time, it sounded like a voice. "Hello?" Cate called into the darkness.

She stepped closer, squinting into the dark. As she took another step closer, a powerful gust of wind blew from within the cavity. The gale storm wind knocked Cate onto her backside. As she struggled to sit up, a voice growled from within, "BEWARE!"

Cate gasped at the recollection, realizing it was this ominous warning that had awakened her from the nightmare. Cate struggled to find meaning in the dream. After an hour she gave up. She chalked the dream up to her subconscious mind's reaction to the stress she experienced from the upcoming parties and her worry over Molly's arrival. Her mind must have pieced together details from the past few days to create a strange and terrifying experience.

Cate sighed, chuckling at herself. "What a foolish girl you are, Cate Kensie," she whispered to herself. Cate shook her head. She'd let her fear get the better of her as she had when she first arrived, imagining ghosts lurking in every hall. Embarrassed by her behavior, Cate dragged herself back to bed.

* * *

The sun had already made its appearance over the moors when Cate awoke. She slept in after her rough night. She leapt from bed, not wanting to be late for breakfast. Hurrying around, she dressed for the day before ushering the dogs from their beds and out for a quick morning frolic. She entered the dining room just as Molly and Mrs. Fraser appeared with her breakfast.

They exchanged good mornings before Cate settled in for her breakfast. Afterward, Cate made her way to the library, intending to continue her research on her list of potential suspects. As she entered the room, her eyes slid to the bookcase. She ogled it suspiciously, as though she expected to relive her dream during her waking hours. Cate shook her head at the bookcase, turning away from it and approaching the desk.

After a moment, Cate, unsettled despite her best attempts to shrug off the dream, decided a walk with the dogs was in order. It gave her an excuse to peruse the gardens off the ballroom and glimpse the progress being made on the outdoor decorations.

Cate spent the better part of her morning outside, despite the chill in the air. The garden was transforming into a winter wonderland, and Cate found it difficult to tear herself away from it. She circled through multiple times, each time finding something new that she missed before. Delighted with the progress, Cate sought Jack and Mr. Fraser to commend them for their hard work.

Cate returned to the library just as Molly delivered her lunch. "Thanks, Molly!"

"Long morning walk? I'm surprised you're not frozen solid!"

Cate laughed. "I couldn't tear myself away from the gardens. Mr. Fraser's design is magical. It's like a winter wonderland."

"Oh, I can't wait for the party!" Molly squealed. "Until then, I'm excited to decorate tomorrow!"

"Me too!" Cate answered. "I don't want to keep you from your lunch, enjoy it!"

Molly nodded to her as she disappeared through the door. Riley and Bailey stretched in front of the blazing fire, soothed by its warmth after their morning outside.

As Cate ate, she stared at the bookcase that was the source of her consternation in her dream. She bit into her pickle, her eyes narrowing at the bookshelf. After a moment, she rolled her eyes. "Cate, knock it off!" she scolded herself, earning a glance and a sigh from Riley. "It was a silly dream, nothing more. A bookcase does not dissolve away into thin air!"

"Talking to yourself?" Molly inquired, entering the room.

Startled, Cate almost dropped the tray right off her lap.

"I'm afraid I was," Cate admitted. "Just trying to make sense of my research."

"Needed expert advice, huh?" Molly joked.

Cate giggled. "Yep," she replied, handing the tray off.

After Molly exited, Cate approached the desk, plopping down on the desk chair. Determined to make more progress, Cate opened her folders, spreading out her notes. She glanced through the employee list. She flipped open the records, ready to track down their dates of employment. At the top of the list was Lachlan Reid, Jack's great-grandfather. Cate did not suspect he was the thief, she had only listed him since he was the estate manager in 1925, so they were aware of all of the players. Lachlan was Stanley Reid's father. Cate made a note to ask the elder Mr. Reid about any information his father may have passed along about the theft. She also noted Lachlan was not a suspect and his employment dates were not of interest since he worked most of his life on the estate. Cate would never dream of insulting Jack, Stanley or the memory of his family by suggesting he had robbed the MacKenzies.

Cate moved on to the remaining list of employees. She scoured the employment records back to front over and over, jotting down hire dates when available, dates of first payments, termination dates and dates of last payments listed. She cobbled together rough dates of employment for each of the people on the list. The project took her the entire afternoon.

Cate admired her handiwork as Riley pawed her leg. A smile spread across her face as she glanced down at the small dog. “Look, Riley! I got everyone’s dates! Are you proud of me?” Riley glanced quizzically at the paper Cate brandished in front of him. “Next step is to comb through these dates and determine if anything seems suspicious! For example, someone coming to work just before the theft, or leaving soon after.” Cate explained her process to Riley. His dark almond-shaped eyes stared back at her as though he understood. Since she adopted him, he had been her friend, confidante and sounding board. Despite his lack of advice in most situations, Cate still discussed her ideas with him as though he understood. “What do you think, Riley? Will I find anything interesting?” she questioned, setting the sheet down as she scooped him into her arms. Riley gave her a lap on the face. Cate laughed. “Thanks for the vote of confidence, buddy. I bet you’re dying for a walk! We have just enough time before dinner, let’s find your brother!”

Cate rose from the chair, carrying Riley with her. She roused Bailey from his peaceful nap near the fireplace. After dressing both dogs in a cozy winter coat and donning one herself, she led them outside for an evening walk before dinner.

Cate returned to the library just before dinner, snapping her laptop open to check her email before dinner arrived. She found one from Maggie Edwards.

Hi Cate... or should I say Lady Cate?! You’re welcome! As soon as I saw the trinket box, I thought of you! I was glad I caught Molly before she left for Scotland so she could take it over. Saved me a trip to the post office! I needed the rest after that exciting trip. I’m sure Molly told you my uncle Ollie (I think you knew him while you were at Aberdeen) was kidnapped. In the end, it all turned out for the best! Not only did we find Uncle Ollie, but we also found Cleopatra's tomb!!!!

I've never been on such a wild ride in my entire life! Henry was my rock through the whole thing! I can't wait for you to meet him! I hope I don't sound too eager, but I'd love to accept your invitation to visit! Maybe in the spring? I bet it's just beautiful there during that season. I bet it's just beautiful there in all the seasons!

I heard from Molly already. She sounds ecstatic about her new job! Gosh, I can't wait to visit and see you both! Let's talk about a spring visit if that's okay with you!

Enjoy the holidays! Maggie

Cate grinned at her laptop screen. Same old Maggie, she mused. Backward Cate always found Maggie's more extroverted nature alien, although she appreciated her forthrightness. Maggie had no qualms to accept her invitation and suggest a date. It pleased Cate to have Maggie take the lead. It saved her from an awkward evening of second-guessing whether to suggest a time frame to Maggie or ignore it in case she preferred not to visit but was being polite in "accepting." Cate's overthinking often drove her berserk.

She returned Maggie's email over dinner, agreeing to a spring visit. As Cate finished the email and closed her laptop, she leaned back in her chair, spooning another mouthful of Mrs. Fraser's soup into her mouth. The news about Ollie Keene was unreal! How much everyone's lives were changing.

Cate carried her tray to the fireplace, in a pensive mood. She finished her dinner as she watched the flames dance in the fireplace. After Molly retrieved her tray, Cate elected to relax in her sitting room for the evening. She gathered both dogs into her arms and exited the library. Before stepping through the door, she shot one last glaring look at the bookcase that cost her a good night's sleep the previous night.

* * *

Cate bounded out of bed, excitement filling her. Today, for the first time in years, she'd decorate a Christmas tree with people she considered family instead of alone. Of course, she never considered herself alone even before moving to Scotland. She'd had her trusty pal, Riley, with her through the holidays. Riley, however, did not often hold up his end of the conversation. It thrilled Cate to have others share in draping the tree in lights and ornaments. She also looked forward to the warm cookies and hot chocolate Mrs. Fraser promised. Cate wasn't sure if the tree decorating or the cookies excited her more, but either way she felt like a kid on Christmas morning. She could almost taste the buttery flavor of the cookies in her mouth already.

Cate skipped downstairs with Riley and Bailey in tow. The household planned to gather after breakfast and make a relaxing day of tree decorating. Cate brought an ornament she purchased for Riley's first Christmas with her. She'd tracked down a matching one online and had it sent to add to the tree marking Bailey's first Christmas. She'd also purchased several new toys for the two pups to find under the tree on Christmas morning. This Christmas would also mark the first time in years Cate would exchange gifts with others. She had excitedly shopped for unique gifts for everyone.

Cate was the first to arrive to the sitting room. Evidence of Jack's presence was obvious with the arrival of the live Christmas tree set up near the window. A smiled spread across Cate's face as she eyed the tree. After a spirited discussion weeks ago, Mr. Fraser and Jack had won

Cate over from a fake Christmas tree to a real one. Mrs. Fraser, who claimed she had no horse in the race, mentioned enjoying the scent of a real pine to help sway Cate's mind. Cate agreed, confessing she'd never had a live tree before.

"All the more reason to have one now!" Jack concluded after they decided.

Jack joined Cate in the sitting room, carrying two boxes of decorations with him. "Let me help you," Cate offered, relieving him of one of the boxes.

"Thank you, Lady Cate. I've got two more boxes to bring," he informed her as he set his box down.

Cate dumped hers near the tree. "I'll come with you," she proposed. "I can carry one of the boxes."

"At the risk of Mrs. Fraser having my head, okay. There's a light one you can carry. Besides, I'm sure I can't talk you out of it," Jack mentioned.

"You can't," Cate assured him. She followed him from the room, leaving the two pups sniffing the boxes like newfound treasure. "Oh, while I have you," Cate began as they traversed the hallways to the storage area.

"Oh, no," Jack complained. "I suspected you had an agenda." He chuckled.

Cate harrumphed. "I do have an agenda. It's helping you carry the boxes. And, to kill two birds with one stone, I figured I'd impart the information I found in my search for the missing jewels."

"Have you solved the case yet?" Jack asked, hope filling his voice.

"Afraid not," Cate admitted. "I've got a good list of suspects. I plan to try to narrow it down tonight. I created a list of everyone working on the estate at the time, along with anyone else who may have been in the house visiting for the holidays."

"Anyone look promising as a thief?" Jack questioned as they entered the storage room.

"I'm not sure yet," Cate dodged. "I spent hours yesterday collecting employment information for each employee whose name appears in the records. I tracked down all the start and end dates, more or less. I plan to check if anyone was a recent addition to the staff just before the theft, or if anyone quit shortly after."

Jack nodded. "Sounds like a solid plan. Do you suppose you'll find anything?"

Cate shook her head. "I doubt it, but it's a decent place to start. I assume it's an angle the police or family would have followed up on."

"Possibly," Jack admitted. "Or they may not have and you might get lucky." Jack shrugged. Cate nodded, agitation clear on her face. "Something else on your mind?" Jack asked as he handed her a small, light bin marked "Christmas decorations."

Cate shifted the box to balance on her hip. She frowned. "Rory MacKenzie, the master of the castle in 1925, had a brother, Lucas. He's my great-grandfather. Oh! Speaking of great-grandfathers, Lachlan Reid served as estate manager then. He's your great-grandfather. He's Stanley's father! I wonder if your grandfather has any information about the theft. Perhaps his father passed some stories to him."

"Uh-oh," Jack mumbled. "This is serious."

Cate's brows knit together. "What do you mean?"

"You're avoiding. When you avoid, there's something troubling you."

"I'm not avoiding!" Cate exclaimed.

"Oh, aren't you? I suppose that worried expression on your face came from telling me I may run into my great-grandfather."

"Well, you do hate time travel," Cate replied, shrugging.

"Cate, what's on your mind?"

Cate stared down the hall as they ambled its length. "Well..." Cate's voice trailed off.

"Caaaaaate," Jack prodded.

"What if Lucas MacKenzie was the thief?"

"Rory's brother? Your great-grandfather? Why would he steal from his own family?"

"Because he didn't inherit the bulk of the estate like his brother, Rory?" Cate conjectured.

"That's a stretch," Jack responded.

"It's not. Family jealousies can run deep. Rory inherits the castle, the title, the bulk of the fortune, most likely because he was born first. It must seem unfair in many instances."

"Are we sure Lucas inherited nothing?" Jack inquired.

Cate shrugged. "I'm unsure of the terms of the will, but I'd be surprised if he inherited anything substantial. Remember, he was my great-grandfather. My family wasn't wealthy. I'm not saying we weren't comfortable, we were. But we weren't millionaires."

"Okay," Jack answered, processing the information. "So, Lucas is jealous of big brother, Rory, for inheriting the fortune and steals some of the family jewels. Possible, but I'm still not convinced it's probable."

"Probable or not, we can't rule him out. He's a reasonable suspect. He has a motive..."

"Potential motive," Jack corrected.

Cate nodded, then continued. "He likely had means and opportunity, as I doubt they'd keep the family jewels under careful guard from family members."

"Okay," Jack agreed. "You've got a point. I agree he should remain on the suspect list for now. But why is it such a worry?"

Cate grimaced. "If Lucas turns out to be the thief... well,"

Cate paused, ceasing to walk and staring at her feet. "I've descended from a thief!"

"Oh, Cate," Jack admonished gently. "Is that what's got you worried? So what? It doesn't make you a thief! Besides, I think it's a long shot."

Cate shrugged, remaining unconvinced. "It would explain why my family was blotted out of the family bible. It may also explain the unsolved case. Perhaps Rory figured it out. To save face, he may have kept mum about it outside of the family, including to the police. But he blotted my side out of his life."

"We have no confirmation the blot occurred in Rory's time," Jack responded. "And isn't Lucas still listed? The blot only covers his children and their children and so on, right?"

Cate nodded. Lucas' name was still visible in the Bible. "Right," she admitted.

"It's quite a leap to assume Lucas is the thief. And even if he is, Cate, it means nothing now. What your great-grandfather may or may not have done has no bearing on you. You, Catherine Kensie, are a wonderful, caring, kind person." A smile crossed Cate's face. "For that matter," Jack continued. "Perhaps it was MY great-grandfather who was the thief. And, as you can see, even if it was, it has no bearing on how wonderful I am." He chuckled at his joke.

Cate giggled, too. "No," she agreed. "No bearing on your humility either. And, just to be clear, I considered your ancestor, but there'd be no reason for him to steal it and continue working on the estate."

"That's not true. Perhaps he had a similar reason of jealousy. Perhaps Pap is hiding those jewels somewhere at home for a rainy day. Perhaps he did it for the thrill. Perhaps Lachlan sold them and set up a trust fund I'm not aware of!"

"Oh, Jack," Cate responded, shaking her head. "Now who's reaching?"

"Well, perhaps it is a reach, but my point is let's not be judge, jury and executioner for your great-grandfather just yet."

Cate nodded, agreeing. "Okay, deal."

"Good, I'm glad that's settled," Jack answered as they approached the sitting room door.

"Oh, one more thing," Cate muttered, screwing up her face as she glanced up to him.

"Uh-oh," Jack groaned. "That expression is just as bad as the worried one."

Cate rolled her eyes at him. "We can't investigate until after the new year. But we could make a quick trip to the past after the Snow Ball to check the lay of the land."

"Ugh," Jack groaned. "And here I assumed I had at least two weeks off from time traveling!"

"Perhaps we can rule Lucas out as a suspect. I'd sleep a lot better if we could!" Cate flashed her best pleading glance to Jack.

Jack rolled his eyes at her. "Okay, okay," he agreed. "You tell me when and I'll go with you. For the sake of clearing your name and your sleep habits, Lady Cate."

Cate smiled at him. "Thank you," Cate answered. "I appreciate that and so do my sleep habits."

"It's for my well-being, too. I'll never win an argument with you."

They pushed through the doors, finding the rest of the group already sorting through decorations from the boxes. Molly and Bailey played tug-of-war with a frayed bow. Riley nosed through the boxes with Mrs. Fraser. Mr. Fraser worked to unravel a string of lights. Cate beamed at the Christmas card-like scene. No matter what she found investigating the theft, she would not allow it to dampen her spirits.

They spent the rest of the day stringing lights, hanging

ornaments, sipping hot chocolate and enjoying Mrs. Fraser's cookies. Cheese and wine were served in the afternoon as they relaxed and shared memories of Christmases past. To add the final touch, Cate climbed the step ladder and placed the star on top of the tree. Afterward, Jack lit the lights, turning the tree into a glimmering focal point of the room. Applause erupted from the group as they admired their handiwork.

Cate slept like a log that night. She awoke refreshed and ready to greet Mr. Smythe and Gayle, set to arrive later in the day. She even felt prepared to take on the Isla Campbell meeting scheduled this morning. With the party just around the corner, Mrs. Campbell would be brimming with enthusiasm.

With her busy schedule, Cate figured the day would race by. She climbed from her bed, dressing for the day as she hummed a Christmas carol. The dogs enjoyed a brisk walk after breakfast before she herded them into the library with a pair of bones courtesy of Mrs. Fraser. With the pups occupied, Cate met Mrs. Campbell at the front door, escorting her to the decorated sitting room.

"Oh, oh, doesn't that tree look marvelous!" Mrs. Campbell complimented.

"Thank you! We took a day as a household yesterday to decorate it together."

"Oh? You mean... with the... staff?"

"Yes! Jack, Mr. and Mrs. Fraser and our newest addition, Molly!" Cate noted as Molly entered with a tray of tea.

"Speak of the devil!" Molly joked, setting the tray down on the coffee table as Cate and Mrs. Campbell settled into their seats.

"Mrs. Campbell, you may remember Molly Williams, our newest addition to the castle. Molly worked at Aberdeen College with me."

"Oh, hello, Molly!" Mrs. Campbell greeted her, eyeing her from head to toe. "Welcome to the staff!"

"Thank you! I'm excited to be here!"

Mrs. Campbell studied her another moment before turning her attention to the tea tray. "Thanks, Molly. We're all set," Cate prompted, realizing Mrs. Campbell hoped to be rid of Molly to begin their meeting.

"Oh, right! Just give us a ring if you need anything else!" Molly disappeared through one of the doorways, leaving Cate and Mrs. Campbell alone.

"Charming girl," Mrs. Campbell commented, sounding as though she didn't mean it.

Cate poured her tea, handing it to her. "She's a wonderful addition," Cate agreed.

"I'm glad to hear she's working out. Well, we have a million details to discuss. Shall we begin?"

"Yes," Cate replied, opening her folder. They covered the remaining outstanding details, discussed the timeline for final setup and double-checked all the particulars. As they finished, Cate mentioned viewing the trees. "I imagine you'll be quite pleased when you see them. They're exactly what you wanted."

"I cannot wait to verify that! Oh, but before we go, I hoped to take a few minutes to discuss the upcoming VIP New Year's Eve party."

"Of course," Cate agreed.

"Oh, I realize we'll meet again twice before that event, but my nerves are getting the better of me!"

"Well, I'm sure you've got everything handled as always, Mrs. Campbell," Cate assured her.

"Yes, yes," Mrs. Campbell waved her hand in the air, glancing over her reading glasses at Cate. "Platitudes are comforting but," she began, pulling her glasses away from her face and shutting her eyes. "This party MUST come off without a hitch. It's so vital. This is the first time in YEARS the castle will entertain VIPs. There is NO room for error!"

"I understand..." Cate began.

"With all due respect, I'm not sure you do, Lady Cate," Mrs. Campbell interrupted her. "Peerage, lines of succession, et cetera. Americans tend not to be well-versed in these subjects. Word of parties such as these get around. We want them to get around the appropriate social circles and for the proper reasons. We want to be the talk of the town, for all the right reasons! We want everyone who is anyone to seek an invitation to Dunhaven Castle again!"

Cate smiled and nodded. "I'm coming to understand the importance, yes."

"Oh, I apologize if I sound overbearing. But Dunhaven Castle has been no stranger to elites in the past! And we want it to welcome them again! Why, I'm almost certain Dunhaven Castle has welcomed even a duke once or twice before!"

"How exciting!" Cate feigned.

"Oh, yes! To welcome a duke... oh!" Mrs. Campbell shut her eyes as though she was imagining the scene in her head.

Cate indulged her. The parties meant a great deal to the woman, and Cate allowed her to have her moment. "With the work you're doing," Cate commented, "I'm certain we'll welcome a duke again. Soon, I'll bet!"

"You're too kind, Lady Cate." They spent another forty-five minutes going over details for the VIP event. Afterward, Mrs. Campbell and Cate toured the ballroom and gardens outside. After a few minor adjustments, the decor satisfied Mrs. Campbell's picky tastes. Even the gardens received her approval after careful inspection. Mrs. Campbell promised to return prior to trucks arriving with the tables and chairs the following morning.

After seeing her off, Cate shut the door behind her,

leaning against it for a moment. "Exhausting, isn't she?" Jack queried, startling her from her musings.

"Yes," Cate laughed. "But at least she approved everything with minimal changes."

"But she couldn't resist mentioning that bloody snow machine one last time."

Cate laughed, glancing at her timepiece. "Almost lunch time. Good thing. I'm starving!"

"Party planning makes you hungry, does it?"

"It does," Cate admitted. "But first I'd better take the pups outside."

"Where are the poor little pups? Shut away from the party czar?"

Cate chuckled as she led Jack to the library. "Yes. Shut away in the library with a few bones courtesy of Mrs. Fraser."

She popped open the door, searching the room for Riley and Bailey. She spotted the bones discarded on the rug near the fireplace. After scanning further, she found both dogs in their new favorite spot.

"That's odd," Jack noted, spotting the dogs across the room.

"Not really," Cate admitted. "They have been interested in that bookshelf for days. I don't understand why. I've searched around the area and found nothing." Cate shrugged. "I'm going to have to follow up on it later."

"Let me know if you find anything," Jack requested.

"I will," Cate answered. "If I get a chance after the party, I'll give it a thorough search."

"Speaking of, anything else that needs taken care of before the party or before Mr. Smythe and Ms. Pearson arrive today?"

Cate shook her head. "No, we're all set!"

"Okay," Jack answered. "I'll meet you out front when they arrive to help with the luggage."

"Thanks! Come on, Riley and Bailey, let's go for a walk!" At the offer, both dogs bounded toward Cate. Cate indulged them in a walk both before and after lunch, feeling guilty for keeping them contained all morning. By mid-afternoon, they were tired enough for a quick nap before the rest of Cate's guests arrived.

The rest of the day flew by with Cate greeting Mr. Smythe, the estate's attorney and his assistant, Gayle, in the late afternoon and enjoying a dinner with her guests before they retired early, both tired from their long journey. Cate turned in early also, hoping to get a solid night's sleep before the final set up tomorrow. She slept soundly, her dreams filled with balls, dresses and entertaining royalty.

CHAPTER 6

Cate's alarm screamed through the morning air, startling her awake. Cate bolted upright, surprised she hadn't awoken before it as usual. She must have been more tired than she realized from the commotion in the house yesterday. At least she had slept, she figured, as she climbed from her bed, yawning.

She plodded to her en-suite bathroom to shower and dress for the day. She hopped outside for a few brief moments with the dogs before breakfast. Frosty morning air greeted her, and she snuggled deeper into her coat. It signaled a cold snap moving into the area. The latest weather pattern was predicted to bring snow with it, just in time for the party.

After breakfast, everyone met in the ballroom to await the arrival of the tables, chairs and other last-minute furniture items for setup. Mrs. Campbell arrived moments before the trucks pulled up. With everyone's help, they were unloaded by late morning and they completed the final setup by late afternoon.

Mrs. Campbell was pleased Cate invited her to stay for

dinner. Cate enjoyed entertaining her guests although she missed eating dinner with her household staff as was her norm on Friday nights.

Cate was returning to her suite with the dogs for a cozy night of reading when Jack caught her in the upstairs hallway.

"Lady Cate," he called, flagging her down. "Do you have a moment?"

"Sure, what's up?" Cate asked as Jack scooped Riley up for a petting. Riley offered an appreciative lick to the face as Jack scratched his ears.

"I just wanted to tell you when I checked on these little rascals earlier in the day, I found them staring at that bookshelf again."

Cate's brow furrowed. "I do not understand what keeps them so interested!"

Jack shrugged his shoulders. "I'm not sure either. I did a cursory glance over it. Nothing jumped out at me. The only reason I bring it up is because with the frequency that you've mentioned them interested in the same spot, we may want to have it looked into by an exterminator."

"An exterminator?" Cate questioned, grimacing.

"Yes, to ensure there are no vermin."

"Vermin?!" Cate queried further, a deeper frown setting into her delicate features.

Jack chuckled. "Yes, vermin, Lady Cate. Not very regal, but nevertheless, sometimes an issue in these old places."

Cate wrinkled her nose at the notion but nodded. "Perhaps after the party, no sense in worrying about it right now. We've all got enough going on. Besides, I haven't spotted anything, so, with any luck, it's just a minor problem, if that's the issue."

"Right, I agree. Hopefully it isn't the issue, but if it is, better to take care of it sooner rather than later. I'll call on

Monday to set up an appointment. It can't hurt to have it checked."

"Sounds like a plan. You can do it right after our trip to the past!" Cate exclaimed.

Jack rolled his eyes at her. "Don't remind me. I'd rather the vermin than the time traveling."

Cate made a face at him before they said their good nights. Jack returned Riley to Cate, and she and the pups disappeared down the hall into her suite. With the day's work, Cate slept well when she retired. Not even the mice of the castle roused her. When Saturday morning arrived, Cate awoke to a winter wonderland outside her window. Overnight, several inches of snow had fallen. It dusted the landscape in a pristine white blanket. Another few inches were expected today, but not before a sunny start. The sun crested the moors, creating a sparkling effect on the ground below. The white diamond blanket gleamed under the brilliant sun. It was a perfect winter scene for the party later.

Cate almost hated to step out into the unspoiled display and ruin it with footprints, but the dogs required their bathroom break before breakfast. Cate stood under an eave as she watched the dogs frolic around in the white powder. Aberdeen didn't receive vast amounts of snow, so the sensation was new to Riley. He seemed to enjoy it, bounding through mounds of snow with a goofy grin on his face. Both dogs nuzzled their faces into the cold, wet snow, pushing and rolling it around with their snouts. When finished, Riley wore a white beard of snow, clinging to his fur like glue.

As both dogs trotted back, Cate vowed to carry them into the castle and dry them before they made a mess of Mrs. Fraser's kitchen. The woman had the place gleaming in preparation for the caterer's arrival later today.

Cate, a dog under each arm, pushed through the kitchen door. "Oh my!" Mrs. Fraser exclaimed. "What have we here?"

"They were a little overzealous in the snow," Cate commented. "I don't want them creating a melted mess in here."

Mrs. Fraser lifted Riley from Cate's arms as Molly retrieved a towel. Together, they toweled off both dogs before allowing them to settle in front of the warm stove.

* * *

Cate donned her dress for the party. Her black velvet bodice met her flowing plaid ankle-length skirt with a large plaid bow. Cate smoothed the fabric of the skirt as she gazed in the mirror. "What do you boys think?" she asked Riley and Bailey. Both dogs, each sporting matching plaid bow ties, gazed at Cate, a quizzical expression on their faces.

Riley ventured over, sniffing at Cate's skirt, then cocking his head to the side and staring at her. Bailey, who didn't care for his new attire, rubbed at his face in an attempt to pull the tie off. Cate planned to take them to the party for the first hour before settling them in her room for bed. Now that Riley was at home in the castle, she hoped to include him in more events.

Cate ushered the two pups from the room, meeting Molly along the way. She scooped Bailey into her arms and Cate gathered Riley into hers. Together they made their way to the ballroom to await the guests' arrival. Mrs. Campbell arrived moments later, spending most of her time assessing the decor and making adjustments. She finished by giving a list of orders to the catering staff. After sending them on their way, orders in hand, she rejoined the group.

"Well, everything now seems in to be order," Mrs. Campbell noted. "Is everyone ready?"

Everyone nodded, dressed in their finest and ready to receive guests. Jack held Riley and Mrs. Fraser carried Bailey, leaving Cate free to meet and greet guests. "Are you sure the dogs will be... uh, that is, won't they be anxious through this?" Mrs. Campbell inquired.

"Oh, they'll be just fine. We'll put them to bed before the music and entertainment begins," Cate assured her. "It'll be fun for people to meet them."

"Oh," Mrs. Campbell glanced toward them, a disdainful look on her face. "I'm sure it will be."

Chimes sounded throughout the castle. "Ah, that must be our first guests arriving," Cate announced. "Places everyone!" Nervous chuckles escaped her as she departed with Mrs. Campbell.

The ballroom filled up within fifteen minutes of the first guest arriving. When Cate reentered, leaving her post at the front door guarded by historical society volunteers, a buzz of chatter filled the air. Several people grouped around Riley and Bailey and their caretakers, fussing over both boys. Riley, secure in Jack's arms, enjoyed the attention. Bailey played gracious host well as Mrs. Fraser encouraged him to "shake hands" with each guest.

Cate joined them, checking on both dogs before moving on to make her rounds around the room. She greeted each guest again, spending a few moments with each to discuss holiday plans, weather, hobbies and a myriad of other small talk options. Cate tried to make everyone feel welcome and ensure they were enjoying themselves. Despite her introverted nature, Cate found this party easier than the Halloween Ball, her first party within the castle. It appeared her hostess skills were growing. Cate felt proud.

After greeting all her guests a second time, she returned to her two best buddies. Cate suggested they depart for a good night's sleep. With Jack's help, she returned them to her suite upstairs, removing their bow ties and settling them in their beds. They returned to the party within a few minutes.

Mrs. Campbell stormed toward them as they reentered. "THERE you are!" she exclaimed as though she'd been searching for hours.

"Is everything okay?" Cate inquired. "We just stepped out to settle the dogs."

"I suppose it is now that I've found you. The orchestra is ready to begin."

"Oh, great!" Cate exclaimed. Mrs. Campbell nodded expectantly at her. Cate glanced around the room, unsure of the meaning behind Mrs. Campbell's stare. "Is there something else?"

"Of course, you should lead off the dancing, Lady Cate! Set the tone for the evening. Everyone will expect it of you."

"OH!" Cate exclaimed. "Oh, no, I don't think that's necessary. Oh, it's fine to just begin. I'm sure everyone will realize."

"Nonsense, Lady Cate," Mrs. Campbell dismissed, waving her hand in the air. "It wouldn't be proper at this event to allow the guests to 'join in' whenever they'd like. The lady of the house MUST lead the first dance!"

"Well..." Cate hesitated, seeking a way out of the situation. "Perhaps Mr. and Mrs. Fraser. They're a lovely couple and they'd do great starting the dancing off!"

"But THEY are not the Countess of Dunhavenshire!" Mrs. Campbell tittered.

"But I..." Cate tried again.

"Nonsense, nonsense. No excuses. Who will you choose as your dancing partner? Have you someone in mind?"

"Ah..." Cate floundered, eyes wide as she searched the room.

"Lady Cate," Jack chimed in, bowing extravagantly, "might I have the pleasure of the first dance?"

Cate chuckled at him, breathing a sigh of relief. "Yes," she answered, grinning.

"Well, I suppose he'll do," Mrs. Campbell added. "He's a

nice strapping lad. I hope you have good form. And don't step on her toes."

"I wouldn't dream of it," Jack assured her.

Mrs. Campbell offered him an annoyed glance. "I shall make the announcement, then you lead Lady Cate to the dance floor to begin."

"Thanks for the save," Cate whispered as Mrs. Campbell departed for the small stage where the orchestra was seated. "That threw me."

"You're welcome. I have a feeling the party czar is less than thrilled. If she had her way, you'd at least be dancing with someone equal in station."

"Or a duke," Cate chuckled, recalling Mrs. Campbell's earlier statements about entertaining above Cate's station.

Mrs. Campbell tapped on the microphone. "Oh, hello, is this on? Ah, yes it is! Good evening, everyone. Thank you for attending the first annual Snow Ball at Dunhaven Castle! I hope you are enjoying yourselves and are as excited to be here as I am. I'd just like to take a moment before we begin the dancing to thank Lady Catherine Kensie, Countess of Dunhavenshire, for offering her lovely home for the event." Cate held in a giggle, recalling it as less than an offer and more of a demand. "The gardens outside have also been decorated for your enjoyment, please take a moment to enjoy them if you need a breath of fresh air. They are quite the winter wonderland! We're about to get underway with our entertainment and dancing, so I won't take up much more time! So, without further adieu, our Lady Cate will start us off, escorted by Mr. Jack Reid. Please join in with her after she sets our tone!"

Jack led Cate to the dance floor after she encouraged Mr. and Mrs. Fraser to join in after they began.

Cate smiled at Jack as she placed her hand in his and her other hand on his shoulder. He gripped her waist, a nervous grin on his face. "I must confess, Lady Cate, I doubt I'll be as good a partner as Randolph MacKenzie, but I'll try not to step on your toes."

Cate chuckled as the music began. Her mind flitted to her nightmare of a few nights ago. She hoped the music didn't have the same dizzying effect it had in her dream. "Listen, I'm no dancer either," she admitted.

"You made it look so easy with Randolph!" Jack noted as the orchestra began.

"Randolph made it look easy. He was the one who had to drag me around the dance floor," Cate joked as they began to move to the music. They circled the dance floor once before others joined in. Mr. and Mrs. Fraser joined next. The ever-outgoing Molly had already found a partner in Mr. Smythe to join with for the first dance. Gayle partnered with a local business owner, and was followed by Mrs. Campbell and her husband. Several others joined in as the music continued. Cate relaxed as others joined them on the dance floor and she ceased to be the main focus of the group. The music, perfectly tuned, did not have any disorienting effects.

The song ended and everyone applauded. Despite enjoying the dance, Cate left the dance floor, relieved to have finished her duties as hostess. "We made it through without me breaking your toes!" Jack exclaimed in triumph.

"And I didn't trip you either!" Cate added. "Although I am pleased to be finished with that duty."

"My dancing's that bad, is it? And here I thought I won you over."

Cate chuckled. "It's not. And as thoroughly enjoyable as that experience was, I'd have preferred it without everyone gawking at us."

"Ah, I'll keep that in mind. Lady Cate prefers private dances." He smiled at her.

Their conversation ended as a gentleman approached and

asked for a dance with Cate. Cate obliged him, allowing him to lead her back to the dance floor. She spent the next several songs bouncing from partner to partner, though Cate found each experience enjoyable.

She left the dance floor to retrieve a drink, parched from the effort of the dances. Jack sidled up to her as she floated at the room's edge. "You say you're not a dancer, Lady Cate? You seem to be doing a fine job of it for the last hour or so, lassie!" he joked.

"I've had a good set of partners," Cate explained.

"Speaking of a good partner, Lady Cate," Stanley Reid began approaching his grandson, Jack, and Cate, "would you fancy a dance with a real partner?"

"A real partner?" Jack questioned. "She's already done that. Didn't you catch the first dance? We were on full display, Pap." He offered a playful clap on the older man's back. Molly approached the trio as they spoke.

"Oh, I saw it, that's why I'm offering her a real dance. Poor lassie with you and your two left feet dragging her around the dance floor."

"Two left feet, bah!" Jack replied.

"I would be happy to dance with you, Mr. Reid," Cate answered, chuckling.

"How about your two left feet dragging me around?" Molly queried, laughing.

"I'd be happy to," Jack answered, offering her his arm.

"Watch your toes," Stanley warned Molly with a chuckle as each couple made their way to the floor.

As the next song began, Cate marveled at Stanley's smooth moves on the dance floor. He grinned at her. "I told you I was a good dancer," he boasted.

"Very good!" Cate agreed. "Lots of practice?"

"I've had a fair amount," the older man admitted. "Enough to make that young laddie look like an amateur," he added with a wink.

Cate laughed. "Jack's not a bad dancer either," she responded.

"Learned everything he knows from me," Stanley claimed. Stanley spun Cate around, flinging her away from him before pulling her back. "But I kept a few tricks to myself."

"Poor Jack. You kept him in the dark on the best moves!"

"Aye," Mr. Reid answered.

Cate smiled at him. "Do you mind if I ask you a question not related to dancing?"

"I don't mind at all, lassie."

"I've been reading about the theft that occurred here at Dunhaven Castle. The one back in 1925. I was wondering if you had any information about it."

"Ah, the infamous theft. Yes, happened when my father was the estate manager here."

"Yes," Cate nodded. "That's right. Did he ever mention it or anything about it?"

"Aye, he mentioned it all right. Never solved it. Said it was a real shame someone stole those jewels. Beautiful pieces, a real loss to the family."

Cate nodded. "Yes, the pieces were beautiful. I'm surprised the police never solved the case."

"Looking into it, are you?" Mr. Reid asked, a twinkle in his eye. "One of the rips goes back to the year when the theft was discovered, doesn't it?"

Cate smiled and nodded. "It does. And I'll admit, I'd like to investigate it."

"Jackie fighting you tooth and nail?"

"You know him so well!" Cate admitted. "He isn't pleased, but he's willing to try at least."

"Progress!"

The music ended, and the two left the dance floor to finish their discussion over a cool glass of punch. Jack joined them. "Well, I wish I could tell you more, lassie, but I'm afraid there wasn't much information available to solve the crime."

"Ah, she's hit you up for information on the theft, eh, Pap?" Jack queried.

"Aye. We were discussing it while we floated across the floor. Did you see how it's done, Jackie?"

"Very funny, Pap. Now, is there anything you can tell us about this theft so Lady Cate can stop with her harebrained schemes to travel to the past?"

Stanley shook his head. "'Fraid not. No one ever found the jewels. It's still a mystery. And a terrible shame. My father told me the jewels were stunning."

"So, he did talk to you about it?" Jack inquired.

"Aye," Stanley responded, nodding again. "He shared this story with me once. I asked about it after reading it in an old newspaper article."

"And?" Jack prodded.

"And nothing. The jewels went missing after a New Year's Eve party. They didn't return the jewelry to the safe that night. Nothing out of the ordinary. Figured they would be safe. They never imagined a theft would occur!"

"No suspects?" Cate questioned.

"Oh, they considered everyone on the estate. But they never found the jewelry and never built a strong case against anyone. Dad said after a while Rory refused to speak of it any further. He assumed it was too painful since they were his grandmother's jewels that had been lost. No one ever brought it up again. The mystery faded into oblivion, just like the jewels."

Jack shook his head. "Damn. I hoped you had the inside track."

"Thank you for the information," Cate replied.

"Sorry I couldn't be of more help," Stanley lamented. "I'm afraid those jewels are lost forever."

"Oh! THERE you are!" Mrs. Campbell shouted above the din of the room, waving to Cate. A tall, thin gentleman followed her. "Lady Cate, please meet Lord Dickinson. He'll be attending our VIP event. He traveled early to attend the Snow Ball. He's fascinated with your home!"

"Oh, thank you," Cate voiced, smiling at the man as she shook his hand. "I'm pretty smitten with it myself."

"How charmingly American of you," he commented, bursting with laughter before whisking her away for a dance. Afterward, Mrs. Campbell cornered Cate to discuss the experience, gushing over the coup of having the likes of Lord Dickinson for not one but two events on the estate.

As the dancing wound down, Cate made another round through the party, chatting and conversing with each of her guests. The party started to wind down around midnight and Cate was overwhelmed with guests wishing to express their goodbyes and thank yous.

After the last guest had departed, Mrs. Campbell chattered to Cate about the rousing success of the event. With another event a little over a week away, she already had her next project to focus her excited energy on. Mrs. Campbell reminded Cate of their upcoming meeting on Friday. Only after Cate assured her she had not forgotten about the meeting did she judge it appropriate to depart for the night.

Cate found the rest of the group snuggled around the Christmas tree in the sitting room. She dragged herself into the room, slipping her shoes off as she sunk next to Molly on one of the loveseats. "Whew," she groaned. "I'm exhausted!"

"It was a lovely party, Lady Cate," Mr. Smythe replied, nursing a nightcap.

"Oh, I agree," Gayle echoed. "You're getting good at this."

Cate offered a weak smile. "I'm not sure about that. Mrs. Campbell is a pro at these things."

Mrs. Fraser guffawed at the mention of Isla Campbell's

name. "And she'll have this place rented out every chance she gets, I'm sure."

"Not if I can help it!" Cate commented. "While I love to share this castle with anyone who wants to enjoy it, I value my privacy!"

"It sounds like she plans to milk this for all it's worth," Molly agreed with Mrs. Fraser. "She hasn't stopped yammering on about having the 'upper crust' of society here."

"She's planning to put Dunhaven on the map, all right," Mr. Smythe added. "I must agree the VIP party was a splendid idea."

"She's full of those," Cate admitted. "Although, I have to say again, she's quite good at this and her ideas are well-planned."

"Except for the snow machine," Jack interjected.

Cate nodded, grinning at him. "Except for the snow machine, yes."

"Well," Gayle announced, standing. "I had a splendid time! And I am looking forward to the next party! But for now, I'm looking forward to stretching out in my bed. So, I shall say good night to everyone."

Mr. Smythe finished his drink. "Yes, I will also take my leave."

"You've both got the right idea," Cate admitted. Everyone agreed, exchanging good nights and retiring for the evening.

As Cate changed into pajamas, she reflected on the evening. Another successful event was under her belt. She even enjoyed herself, feeling less overwhelmed than she had at her first party. A smile crossed her face as she went over the night's events.

As she turned the bathroom light's off, padding across her room to climb into bed, she recalled her conversation with Stanley Reid. While he could not provide much information, something he mentioned rattled through her mind. The elder Mr. Reid commented that, after a time, Rory refused to speak of it. He surmised it was too painful a memory. Cate wondered about the validity of that statement. Perhaps there was another reason Rory MacKenzie refused to speak of it any further. Perhaps he learned the fate of the jewels and wanted the story buried lest the family name be impugned. Perhaps it was Cate's ancestor who was the thief. The idea blazed through Cate's mind as she struggled to sleep. Was she descended from a thief?

CHAPTER 7

A cloudy day greeted Cate as she stretched in bed on Monday morning. She leapt from her bed, nervous excitement driving her to rise and dress for the day. While she'd likely find nothing during their trip today, a sense of adventure still filled her as it did before every trip to the past.

Despite entertaining guests, Cate and Jack figured with the time difference between past and present, they could make the trip, peek around the castle in 1925 and be back before anyone missed them. For every fifteen minutes spent in the past, only one minute passed in the present. This allowed them to make a trip of even several hours without being missed for longer than a few moments.

The trick of time during time travel fascinated Cate, and she appreciated that anomaly, especially when entertaining guests. However, the reality also meant Cate and Jack often lived two days in one. During their last adventure solving the murder of a footman in 1856, Cate and Jack spent hours in the past, returning less than thirty minutes after they departed in the present time. The trips often left both of them exhausted.

This should be an easy trip, Cate surmised. It should take less than an hour. She hoped to poke around, determine what bedrooms were being used, get a general feel for the mood of the castle at the time and select points for her to explore in her time for clues. They would return to the 1925 holiday season. If Cate could determine if her grandparents were or were not staying at the castle, perhaps she could rule them out as suspects.

After breakfast, Cate took the dogs for a long morning walk to tire them out. Jack suggested they travel late this morning just before lunch. Most of the household, both past and present, should be occupied, allowing them to slip back and forth between eras unnoticed.

Cate met Jack in the library around ten. Riley bounded toward Jack, leaping into his arms as he approached. Bailey pranced across the room, interested but not quite as sold as Riley on Jack's appeal. "Good job, laddie!" Jack praised the little pup as he caught him mid-leap.

"He's really taken to that new trick you've taught him," Cate mentioned.

"Aye, he has. He's a good little laddie, aren't you, Sir Riley?" Riley answered with an appreciative lap on Jack's face. "And you're a good laddie, too, Mr. Bailey," Jack assured the other dog, giving him a pat on the head.

"Are you ready?" Cate queried, her brow raised, a twinkle in her eye. "I set the clothes out from the 1925 trunk in the usual place for you earlier. I think they'll fit! I left them in your usual spot. All we have to do is change!"

"Nay, but I don't suppose I have a choice."

"Don't be a stick in the mud," Cate warned. "This is the easiest trip we'll make! No talking to anyone. No stories to tell."

"Speaking of stories. What is the cover story this time? In case we need it. Oh, please, let's not make me a lawyer. The last time we pulled that number I ended up almost getting a man sent to death row."

"First, you didn't almost get him sent anywhere. Randolph did that on his own. And second, you ended up getting him released and the case against him dismissed. And third, we don't need to say you're a lawyer this time. People traveled more during the 1920s than the 1850s."

"Hmm," Jack pondered a moment, setting Riley on the floor. "True, but it makes most sense to continue the charade of being family. It gives us the best access to the family and the house. Although, on this trip, there is no reason to say we're staying in Dunhaven. They had cars then! We could be traveling from town to town!"

"Good point. We don't need to be traveling for business. So, there's no reason for you to be a faux lawyer. Instead, we could be on vacation!"

"On vacation? The last time we spent weeks coming and going. Is that wise? Vacations are usually short term."

"Hmm," Cate murmured. "What about…"

"Land deals!" Jack exclaimed. "We're traveling in the area to consider properties for clients. I'm a land agent, seeking properties for wealthy clients whose information I cannot disclose because of confidentiality."

Jack puffed his chest out at the suggestion. Cate pursed her lips. "It should work. Many estates had fallen on hard times before and during this era. It would make sense."

"Perfect. That's our story then. While in the area, I decided to look up my distant MacKenzie cousins and pay a call on them. This is my lovely secretary, Cate."

Cate's jaw dropped. "Secretary?! Come on! Why do you always get to play the relative?"

"Because even in the 1920s, an American cousin sounds fishy. And what else would you be? Oh, you could be my wife again," he added, winking.

Cate shook her head, considering the options. "I'll take wife. Even in the 1920s, a secretary traveling with her boss would look too forward. It might raise too many eyebrows. I'll have to dig up that fake wedding band again, I suppose."

"Okay, Cate. Shall we change and meet in your sitting room at eleven?"

Cate nodded. "Yes. I plan to leave the dogs there, too. The rip exists in the bedroom so they should be safe, and it'll be easy to tell which era we're in when we open the bedroom door."

"Oh, that reminds me, before we go," Jack began. "I called the exterminator this morning. He's going to stop by tomorrow. I realize it's the day before Christmas but better sooner than having vermin running about all over the castle days before the VIP party."

Cate wrinkled her nose. "I agree. Tomorrow's fine. Okay, I'll see you soon!" Cate ushered the two dogs to her suite. They settled near the fireplace, playing with a few toys Riley pulled from his toy bin. Cate disappeared into her bathroom, doing her best to pull her hair into an acceptable style for the 1920s. After she was satisfied, she pulled on her day dress, which fell just below her knee and featured a drop-waist characteristic of the period. She paired it with t-strap pumps, also common for the era.

Cate glanced in the mirror, fussing with her hair until a knock sounded at her sitting room door. She rushed to the door, opening it and waving Jack into the room. He entered, wearing his British wool suit Cate selected for him. "These clothes are much more comfortable than the last getups, but they still leave something to be desired," he complained.

"These are MUCH more comfortable than the 1850s hooped skirts. I am not complaining in the slightest," Cate responded.

"Yes, it appears much less unwieldy. If you fake a fainting

spell, I can easily drag you around the castle!" Jack joked, referencing one of Cate's stunts in a previous time traveling adventure. "Ready to get this over with?"

"Just a minute," Cate replied, dashing from the room. She returned a moment later. "Now I am." She shoved a gold band onto the ring finger of her left hand. "Can't forget my fake wedding ring!"

"No, we can't forget that!" Cate gave each pup a pat on the head and a kiss goodbye. "I must say, Lady Cate, I'm flattered you picked posing as my wife over my secretary. What a boost to my ego!"

Cate rolled her eyes at him. "Let's get going. That is, if you can fit through the door with your boosted ego." She laughed.

"Okay, okay," Jack agreed, following Cate into the bedroom. Jack placed his hand around Cate's as she clutched the timepiece in her hand. Together they rubbed the watch's face with their thumbs. The timepiece's second hand slowed, signifying interaction with the time rip. Within moments, the second hand crawled across the face, barely moving. Cate glanced at the engraving on the watch case as she closed it. *Always keep an eye on your time.* She recalled the admonition, calling her attention to the time differential. The timepiece kept the wearer's present day time, its secondhand crawling along to show the slowed passage of time in the era from which they traveled.

Cate eyed the room. "We made it!"

Jack pressed his hands over his chest in various areas. "I guess so."

Cate pointed across the room. "The dog beds are gone," she noted. "We're in 1925!"

"Stop sounding so excited about it," Jack responded, creeping to the door. He inched it open, peeking into the sitting room. "All clear," he announced.

"Let's go!" Cate answered, pushing past him into the sitting room.

"Cate!" he hissed.

"What? No one should be in this wing. Gertrude used this bedroom well after the 1920s. If the ancestors in this era kept to the plan, they kept this room and hallway clear since a time rip leads to this year."

"Still, we should be careful!" he warned, hurrying to catch up and pass her. He approached the doors leading to the hallway. He twisted the knob inch by inch, easing the door open and peering into the hallway. "Clear," he whispered. He shut the door again. "Cate, are you sure about this?"

"Yes!" she exclaimed just above a whisper. "It's two days before Christmas, the house is likely abuzz with Christmas preparations. Any holiday guests should have already arrived. Let's just have a peek around."

Jack wiped a bead of sweat from his brow. "Okay, okay. Let's get this over with." He opened the door, entering the hall.

Cate strode down the hall. She turned the corner into another wing of bedrooms. In an instant, she turned back, shoving Jack around the corner. She held her finger up to her mouth. She nodded her head to the other hallway as she signaled to peer around the corner.

They both leaned around the corner, staying as hidden as possible. A couple disappeared into a bedroom halfway down the hall. Cate and Jack overheard raised voices, though they could not make out the words. Within a few moments, the man emerged, storming down the hallway. A moment later, the woman appeared, sniffling and wiping her nose with a handkerchief before shoving it up her sleeve. She sighed before heading in the opposite direction from their hiding spot with a determined step.

Cate narrowed her eyes, glancing to Jack. He shrugged his

shoulders in response. She motioned for them to continue down the hall. Cate noted the bedroom the couple used, planning to check it for any clues when she returned to her time.

They reached the end of the hallway and Cate sped down a back set of stairs. She hurried along the corridor toward the main staircase. Jack raced behind her. "Cate," he breathed, "where are you going?"

"To attempt to identify that couple. They must have been headed down here. Perhaps to the sitting room or the library. Let's see if we can overhear a conversation!"

They spent a few moments skulking around the common areas of the castle. They found nothing. A lone woman read in the library, her feet propped on an ottoman. The slit between the doors allowed no other information about who else may be in the room, if anyone. They spotted the man from the bedroom scene walking outside alone. Another woman sat in the sitting room, working on needlepoint.

"Shoot!" Cate groused, stamping her foot as they hid around a corner near the main staircase.

"Sorry, Cate," Jack uttered. "No conversations to overhear. Let's head back."

Dejected, Cate nodded in agreement. Jack led her down the hallway to the backstairs. They ascended the staircase, turning into the hallway containing the 1925 couple's bedroom, on their way toward Cate's suite. Halfway down the hall, a footman rounded the corner from the hallway containing Cate's suite. Jack and Cate stopped dead as did the other man. For a brief moment, they stared at each other, each party hesitant and questioning. Time seemed to stand still. Cate's eyes went wide, her jaw hung open in shock. She glanced to Jack as the man called, "Oi! Who are you two?"

Cate grasped Jack's arm, tugging him in the opposite direction. "Hey! You two stop right there!"

Cate raced around the corner, Jack in tow. She ran full speed, veering around another corner. "Quick!" she shouted. "To the back hallway!"

They ran headlong down the next hall, approaching the windowed corridor overlooking the back gardens. Cate skidded to a halt, out of breath and puffing. She grabbed Jack's hand, placing the time piece in his palm. After placing her thumb on his thumb, she wrapped her hand around his. She forced his thumb to rub the face. "Come on, come on!" she implored as the second hand speeded up.

"There you…" the footman shouted as he rounded the corner. Within seconds, he disappeared before their very eyes as they slipped back to the present time.

"Oh!" Jack gasped, grabbing his chest as he collapsed against the windowsill.

Cate breathed a sigh of relief, propping herself against the neighboring windowsill. "That was close."

Jack issued her a troubled glance. "THAT'S what you call close? That man almost caught us! We disappeared right in front of that man's eyes! Thank goodness you remembered this hallway is a universal return point."

Cate nodded. "Yeah, or we'd be toast!"

"We already are, aren't we?"

"What do you mean?" Cate inquired.

"That footman got a good look at us. He'll recognize us if we go back."

"Only if we go back this month," Cate reminded Jack. "If we travel in January, he wouldn't have seen us yet. The year resets. Since he saw us in December of 1925, and we'd be traveling back to January of 1925, he hasn't seen us yet. We're in the clear to investigate after the new year."

"Oh, right. I never keep that straight."

"Good thing I do," Cate grinned.

"Oh, yeah," Jack said, his voice still shaky. "Good thing. Now we're clear to take our life in our hands again."

"Next time we won't skulk around. We'll just sneak from the house and 'visit' with the family!"

Jack rolled his eyes. "Oh, is that all?"

"Very funny."

"So, we're agreed no more trips to the past until after the new year at least?"

Cate nodded. "Agreed. We can't chance getting caught again and we can't introduce ourselves to anyone. We're chained to the present until after the new year." Cate sighed.

"I prefer to call it safe until after the new year," Jack countered.

"Well, on the bright side, it gives me over a week to plan our next trip! Now," Cate said, standing, "time to change!"

"First suggestion I agree with in this whole situation!"

Cate chuckled. "You okay? Need a hand?"

"My heart is just settling to normal rhythm," Jack admitted. "One day you'll be the death of me, Lady Cate." Jack stood, heaving a deep breath and wiping a bead of sweat from his brow.

"I certainly hope not!" Cate replied, giggling. They threaded their way through the back hallways, avoiding her company and returning to their respective bedrooms to change. As Cate removed her 1920s frock, she reflected on their journey. Who was the couple they spotted in the hall? Was it her ancestors, Lucas and Amelia? Their presence on the estate in late 1925 would suggest they had been invited back the following holiday season. Which led Cate to surmise there hadn't been a falling out. Or had that been when Rory discovered they were the jewel thieves and refused to speak of the incident further? Too many questions stirred in her mind. Those questions piled on top of the close call would make for a sleepless night later, Cate assumed.

She considered the chance meeting. Jack and she had been in the wrong place at the wrong time, stumbling upon the surprised footman. Her palms dampened with sweat as she recalled their race through the hallways to escape since the lone footman barred their pathway to the rip point.

A long sigh escaped her as she folded the dress and set it aside in her bedroom. Their first visit to 1925 was a bust. They gained no information. They couldn't visit again until after the new year. Cate sank to her bed, perturbed by the situation.

After a moment, she rose, unable to solve anything and unwilling to sit still and fret. Instead, she decided to visit the room they had spotted the couple in after lunch. If she was lucky, perhaps she would find a clue to their identity. If she was even luckier, perhaps she'd find the missing jewelry. Cate chuckled to herself as she rounded up the dogs for a pre-lunch walk. She wasn't that lucky. Then again, she did inherit a castle…

* * *

After lunch, Cate enjoyed a long walk with Gayle and Mr. Smythe around the property. They parted ways for an afternoon respite. Cate seized the opportunity to search the bedroom she flagged during their visit to the past.

At first glance, the bedroom didn't appear to hold any secrets. Cate spent her time poking around any hidden areas she found. She peered under the bed, shining her cell phone's flashlight into every nook and cranny. She searched through drawers, most of which were empty. She slipped her hand between the mattress and box springs, feeling around blindly for any scrap of evidence. She found nothing.

Cate sat back on her haunches, sighing. She glanced around the room again. Undeterred, she made another search, this time peering behind furniture, checking underneath drawers, pressing decorative features on the walls and anything else to find a secret compartment or hidden message.

She finished, hands on her hips, glaring at the room with narrowed eyes. It told her nothing. She hadn't expected to find much, but she was still disappointed. She trudged back to her bedroom to freshen up before dinner, frustrated.

* * *

Cate gasped, shooting up to sitting as she caught her breath. Her heart raced and sweat beaded across her forehead. Another nightmare, she recalled. A shaky hand reached for the clock, checking the time. It was two in the morning. Cate collapsed back into her pillows. She closed her eyes, but after a moment, they snapped open again. She couldn't sleep yet, not with the memory of the nightmare running through her mind.

She recalled the details, allowing her mind to process it in an attempt to calm herself. Cate entered the library, intent on doing work. She carried dozens of folders in her arms, brimming with papers. She struggled through the door. Riley and Bailey greeted her on the other side. As she entered, the two dogs burst into a barking fit. Riley's shrill howl mixed with Bailey's raucous baying. The sound startled Cate and she lost her grip on her research materials. The folders fell to the floor, their contents dumping in a chaotic array in front of her.

"Shoot!" Cate mumbled, stooping to collect the papers. She glanced toward the dogs as they continued their ear-piercing ballad. As she raised her eyes to them, her jaw dropped open. The source of their panic obvious, Cate shot up to standing, her eyes unwavering from their target. A gaping hole stared back at her where a bookcase had been. She swallowed hard, digging deep to find the courage to approach the dogs and shoo them away from it. As she stepped toward them, a gust of wind blew through the room, rustling the spilled papers. The air smelled of dampness and must. She continued a few more steps, now fighting the growing windstorm. The contents of the dumped folders swirled around the room in a dizzying eddy. Cate held her arms in front of her face, shielding it from the flying papers that threatened to slice her cheeks with their razor-sharp edges.

The sweeping wind reduced Cate's eyes to slits. An odd sound met her ears, causing her to open her eyes wider and lower her arms. She stared into the black abyss yawning in front of her, straining to make out any sound. Then it hit her like a wall of water. An unearthly disembodied voice warned her to beware. She clapped her hands over her ears, squeezing her eyes tight as she doubled over. Her heart pounded, her pulse raced, and she held her breath. Then she awoke.

Cate shook her head at the dream's memory. She concluded she was nervous about what the exterminator would find. She rolled over, staring at the moonless sky. Even with the stars, the sky seemed as black as the gaping void in her dream. She shivered, reminded of the phantom voice emanating from the hole. She was glad the exterminator was coming today. Perhaps then she could put one mystery to rest.

CHAPTER 8

Cate paced the floor of the library, waiting for the exterminator to arrive.

"You're going to wear a hole in the floor, Cate," Jack warned.

"I can't help it," Cate answered. "I had another dream about that bookcase. I can't wait to get these results!"

After the exterminator arrived, Cate continued her nervous traipsing about the room, anxious to hear the man's report. After two hours of poking around the library and other various locations in the castle, the man, whose uniform name tag read Duncan, noted a few things on his clipboard, then glanced to Jack and Cate.

"Well, what's the verdict?" Jack questioned.

"Everything appears in order. No signs of infestation, droppings or anything of the sort," Duncan answered, his Scottish accent thick.

"Really?" Cate queried. "Nothing?"

"Don't look a gift horse in the mouth, Lady Cate. I, for one, am glad we don't have mice or bugs."

"It appears you don't. I've no idea what's intriguing the

little rascals. I've found nothing. Which is excellent given the size and age of the castle. I placed a few traps around, just in case. I can return on Friday to check on them. If there's nothing in them, I'd say you're all clear."

"Well, I suppose it is good news," Cate admitted, pleased her new home wasn't being overrun by vermin.

"Yes, it is," Jack agreed. "Friday is fine." He reached out to shake the man's hand. "You can leave your bill with me and I'll show you out when you're ready."

Duncan retrieved his bag, stowing his clipboard inside after tearing off the top sheet and handing it to Jack. He slung it over his shoulder and reached for Cate's hand. "Lady Cate, enjoy the rest of your day."

"Thank you," Cate answered, shaking his hand.

Duncan turned to Jack and said, "Lead the way, Jackie."

Cate chuckled at Jack's nickname, one used by his grandfather and evidently his former high school classmates. Jack appeared a few moments later, stuffing the paperwork into his estate folder. "Well, barring any finds in the trap, we don't have to worry about any creepy crawlies in the castle."

Cate nodded in agreement. "Thank goodness! That's not a subject I'd like to discuss just before lunch!"

"Me too! I'd hate to have my lunch ruined. I'm starving!"

* * *

After lunch, drizzly rain kept everyone indoors. Mr. Smythe had brought two jigsaw puzzles to pass his holiday. "A lovely puzzle, wouldn't you agree?" he asked Cate as she admired the picture on the box. "Reminds me of a winter in Dunhaven in olden times with the horse-drawn sleigh and the snow-covered streets!"

"A little too many snow-covered everythings," Gayle

quipped, not as happy with the one-thousand-piece puzzle as Mr. Smythe.

Cate imagined Mr. Smythe's assessment was correct, figuring the town looked similar to this in bygone eras. She glanced outside the window. Cold rain drizzled from a gray sky, washing away the snow. Cate lamented the loss of the white powder, but a Christmas Day storm promised a white Christmas again by mid-morning.

"Whew," Gayle sighed, hands on her hips. "Cate, I dare say we need you to more than dabble if we plan to finish this puzzle before we depart!"

Cate laughed, staring at the partially built puzzle, consisting of an outer ring of edge pieces and a blank center. Gayle attempted to build the horses, sleigh and its passengers but didn't have much luck.

"Mmm, yes, this is thoroughly challenging," Mr. Smythe agreed. "But we're up to the challenge! If we begin with the snowy pieces..."

"Begin with the snowy pieces?" Gayle cried. "Why that's ALL the pieces!"

Cate snapped her book shut. "Okay, I'll play," Cate replied, inching closer to the table. She began on an unoccupied corner, starting with the snow-covered ground.

Hours later, with cricks in their necks, they left the puzzle in favor of dinner. It remained half finished, but they had made significant progress on the snow-covered ground, much to Mr. Smythe's delight.

After their evening meal, which they shared as a group with staff and guests alike, they gathered again in the sitting room, lit only by the roaring fire and lights from the Christmas tree. They enjoyed each other's company, swapping stories of Christmas' past before bed. The easy evening relaxed Cate, allowing her to fall into a tranquil sleep.

Christmas morning brought snow from the day's first

light until mid-morning. After playing in the snow, Cate settled Riley and Bailey near a warm fire in the sitting room. The household met to exchange gifts over a light, catered meal.

Out of everyone, Riley and Bailey received the most. "We may need to put another room on the castle for all these toys," Cate joked, eyeing the spread under the tree after the gifts were unwrapped.

"Those two cuties are too fun to buy for," Molly commented.

"I agree," Gayle chimed in. "And I deleted a few items from my cart before I purchased, I'll have you know."

"I preferred edible presents," Mr. Smythe responded, handing each dog a treat. "You only need to store those until they are eaten."

Cate offered a wry smile at Mr. Smythe's practicality as she sipped her hot chocolate.

"Aye, they'll be out of those in no time," Mrs. Fraser confirmed. "Those two rascals are always begging for a treat."

"Reminds me of someone," Stanley, who had also joined them for Christmas, joked as Jack snagged another cookie from the cookie tray.

"Those laddies take after the perfect specimen," Jack retorted. "And why pick on just me. Lady Cate's been sneaking cookies all day!"

"Lady Cate is allowed because she is the lady of the house," Mrs. Fraser answered.

"Hey!" Cate exclaimed. "Stop counting my cookies!"

Molly grabbed another cookie from the tray and refilled her hot chocolate. "Yikes, I hope you haven't been counting mine." Gayle agreed, nodding her head.

"Okay, okay," Jack said, holding his hands up in defeat. "Stop picking on me, ladies, I haven't been counting anyone's cookies!"

"You need to keep a better eye on him, Stan," Mr. Fraser suggested with a chuckle. "Jackie's going to get himself in trouble one of these days with those girls."

"Don't worry." Mrs. Fraser patted Stanley's hand. "I've got my eye on him. The moment he steps out of line..."

"Please, don't continue," Jack answered. "I've learned my lesson. And weren't we talking about the laddies and their love for treats?" Jack poured a few more from the bag, handing them out to Riley and Bailey.

"Nice deflection," Cate responded.

"How about a few Christmas carols?" Mr. Smythe suggested. He seated himself at the piano to accompany the singing. The group passed the rest of the afternoon with hot chocolate, cookies and Christmas carols.

Dinner brought a fantastic feast courtesy of the catering company Mrs. Fraser contracted. The amount and variety of food left everyone full and sluggish. They gathered again around the Christmas tree in the sitting room for a lazy evening.

Cate climbed into bed, satisfied with her first Christmas in the castle. The gifts she received brought a smile to her face, each for its own unique reason. However, Cate felt as though she needed no gifts this Christmas. Her new home was gift enough.

The next day, Cate joined her guests and staff for a day of post-Christmas shopping in town. It allowed her staff an additional day of rest since the group dined in town for both lunch and dinner after enjoying a quiet morning on the estate. They enjoyed the town's picturesque, charming nature and the post-Christmas sale prices. Molly joked she may need to request a raise after her purchases, many of which were gifts she planned to send home. A nice reminder to her sister of her new life, she stated.

They returned to the castle in the early evening. Cate

dumped her packages in her sitting room and retrieved the dogs for an evening walk. She contemplated her upcoming day. A meeting with Mrs. Campbell topped her to-do list. Preparations for the upcoming VIP New Year's Eve event must begin after clearing away the Snow Ball set up and decorations.

The past few days had been idyllic, a wonderful relaxation after the bustle of the party. Ready to take on the next event, she climbed into bed for a solid night's sleep before her planning and work meeting tomorrow.

* * *

Cate sat at the library desk. A blank cursor stared back at her. The penning of her chapter on Douglas MacKenzie, the castle's first proprietor, stalled. She pawed through her notes, searching for information to add to the chapter. As she searched, the words blurred on the page. Cate blinked a few times, trying to clear her tired eyes. She stared at her notes, finding them incomprehensible. Letters jumbled together into meaningless nonsense.

Cate shook her head, shutting her eyes. When she opened them, the words on the page appeared to be moving. Disgusted, she shoved the papers away from her, realizing the movement was not words but bugs. The insects scattered in all directions, hiding from the light in any dark corner they found on the desk.

Cate pushed back from the desk, standing and retreating a few steps away. While she contemplated what to do, a breeze rustled her hair. Cate snapped her head in the wind's direction, surprised to find an open black hole in place of one of the bookshelves in the room. Cate's pulse quickened as she stared at the hole. Despite her better judgement, Cate approached the opening, trying to make out anything within. She spotted nothing except blackness.

Cate stood at the edge of the opening. Cool air drifted from the space hidden by the bookcase. She peered into the darkness. A musty smell filled the air inside. "Hello?" she called. A roaring sound barreled toward her. It filled the air around her, sounding like a train barreling ahead of rushing waters. Cate retreated a step as a new sound filled the air. Light and fluttering, Cate barely detected it after the barrage of noise moments earlier.

She shrieked and held her arms to cover her face as papers flew out of the space like bats from a cave at dusk. The black hole continued to spit papers into the library at a terrifying rate until the room's floor was no longer visible.

Cate swallowed hard as the last few pages drifted through the air before settling in a lazy dance to the floor below. One paper wafted near Cate as it sailed through the air, landing at her feet. Black lettering, bold and thick, appeared on the upside-down page. Cate reached for it, turning it over to read it.

As she turned the page, the black letters turned scarlet red and dripped from the page. In horror, Cate threw it down, realizing the letters were written in blood. A chill shuddered through her body as the image of the single, blood-red word burned in her mind: BEWARE.

* * *

Cate clutched her pillow, moaning in her sleep as she writhed in bed. She bolted upright, holding back a scream. Her eyes darted around the room as panic filled her. She spotted familiar things: her wardrobe, a chest of drawers, two sleeping pups in their beds, a moonless sky beyond a draped window. As her heart rate slowed, Cate caught her breath and sighed, running her fingers through her hair. She glanced at the clock. It read 1 a.m.

She collapsed back onto the pillow behind her. Another nightmare. This one more terrifying than the last. Cate's tired mind attempted to rationalize her dream, determining the bugs were a remnant from the exterminator's visit. The indiscernible words were a metaphor for her stalled research while she entertained guests. After a while, she gave up, deciding not to pursue the impossible task of rationalizing what her subconscious mind cobbled together.

Instead, she tossed and turned for another hour, still too unsettled to fall asleep. She chided herself for her foolish behavior, but even still, she found herself unable to relax. She climbed from her bed, pacing the length of her sitting room. After several laps, she wandered from her room into the hall. Without realizing, she wound her way through the halls to the library. She hesitated for a moment, hovering at the room's entrance. Still unsure, she ventured one step into the room, then a second. On her third step, a random groan emanated from the centuries-old castle, sending her scrambling out of the room and up the staircase.

As Cate clung to the banister as she caught her breath, her mind scolded her childish behavior. She felt like a youngster who, afraid of what may lurk in the darkness, raced up the basement stairs before anything captured them. Still, nothing compelled her to return to the lower level to explore the library.

Instead, she ambled down the hallway toward her bedroom. As she rounded a corner, she bumped into a dark figure. She bit back a scream, stumbling back several steps as she swatted at the dark figure looming in front of her.

"Lady Cate?" Jack whispered. "Cate! It's me!"

"Jack?" Cate queried.

"Aye," Jack replied, his face lighting up as his cell phone's light lit the dim hall.

Cate placed her hand on her heart, breathing a sigh of relief. "Oh, thank goodness," she gasped.

"Who did you imagine it was?" Jack questioned.

"Oh, I don't know," Cate answered, fluttering her hand in the air to dismiss her foolishness. "A ghost?"

"A ghost? Is that what has you roaming the halls in the wee hours of the morning, lassie? Searching for ghosts?"

"I'm ashamed to admit it but, sort of," Cate replied. The dim light hid the rising red color on her cheeks. "What are you doing roaming the halls in the wee hours of the night?" she added, changing the subject.

"Investigating a noise," Jack responded. "Must have been you. Or perhaps that strange man with the cobwebs on his clothes and menacing red eyes I passed on my way here."

"Very funny, Jack," Cate replied, crossing her arms and shaking her head.

Jack grinned at her, his smile appearing more smirky in the cell phone's dim light. "Now, what's all this about searching for ghosts?"

Cate rolled her eyes, mostly at her own behavior. "I had a nightmare. I feel foolish now, but I got up to search around for anything unusual."

"Unusual?" Jack questioned, then added, "why don't we talk about it over a warm cuppa to settle your nerves?" Cate hesitated. "I know where Mrs. Fraser hides the cookies," he said, sweetening the deal.

"Sold," Cate replied.

They made their way to the kitchen where Jack set about making two cups of tea. He set a steaming teacup in front of Cate and an open tin of Mrs. Fraser's best shortbreads.

"Now that I've plied you with tea and cookies, will you tell me what odd thing you were searching for at 2 a.m.?"

"I told you," Cate said, trying to swallow a mouthful of cookie first, "I had a bad dream. I couldn't sleep after it, so I went to the library - that's where my dream took place - to figure out what caused the nightmare. Stupid, really," she admitted, rolling her eyes.

"What was your dream about?" Jack inquired, biting into a cookie as he leaned across the kitchen's island toward Cate.

Cate sipped her tea before launching into her tale. "I was in the library trying to work on my research. I stared at my papers, but nothing made any sense. It was like I couldn't read any of my notes. I tried to clear my eyes, but when I glanced at the papers again, bugs covered them. I backed away from the desk, trying to decide what to do when I noticed a gaping hole where one of the bookcases used to be."

"Gaping hole? Where THE bookcase is? The one the dogs are so interested in, you mean?"

Cate nodded. "Yes, THE bookcase. Only the bookshelf wasn't there anymore, instead it was just a big black hole. For some dumb reason, I approached it and yelled down the hole and then there was a loud noise and papers flew out of it. They were everywhere, flying around the room like crazy! One of them landed near my feet and when I picked it up it said 'beware' in blood."

"'Beware' in blood, huh?"

Cate nodded again. "Yep," she confirmed, munching on another cookie.

Jack nodded his head, his lips tightening to a line. "Well, this is an easy one to solve, Lady Cate. I've already pinpointed the meaning of your dream."

"You have?" Cate inquired, her eyes growing wide.

"Mmm-hmm," Jack murmured, bobbing his head up and down.

"What is it? What does it mean?"

"It means you, my dear Lady Cate, have been watching too many movies about ghosts."

"Ah!" Cate scoffed. "That's not funny! And I haven't been watching any ghost movies for the record."

Jack chuckled at her reaction. "Oh, come on, Lady Cate, it's quite funny. But on a serious note, I don't imagine it's anything to worry about. Your mind is likely processing the events of the past few days. The dogs' reaction to that bookcase, the exterminator, your inability to work on your research with all the excitement in the castle. It makes sense, right? Getting nowhere on your work, bugs, the bookcase."

"What about the paper that says 'beware' in blood?"

Jack shrugged. "Perhaps beware of letting the party czar talk you into more parties." He grinned, a twinkle in his eye.

Cate stared into her teacup, not buying his explanation. "Aw, Lady Cate, I was only teasing you," he continued, taking her hand in his.

Cate offered a weak smile. "Yes, I realize that, but I'm not convinced it's as simple as you're making it."

"Listen, dreams rarely have any real meaning. Only to those strange folks on TV who want to take your money for them to tell you some mumbo jumbo about how it means your life will change or you'll come into money."

"This is the third dream I've had about that bookcase, though," Cate admitted.

"Have all of them been the same?" Jack questioned.

"Not identical. But they all have had a gaping black hole where the bookcase is, and two of them have warned me to beware."

Jack pondered it for a moment. "I still don't imagine it's anything to worry about. You've been anxious about the bookcase since the dogs reacted to it. The dreams are your subconscious trying to parse through your apprehension."

Cate sighed, still far from accepting Jack's simple solution. However, the tea, cookies and conversation alleviated her nerves. She stretched and yawned. "Maybe you're right."

"Of course, I am!" Jack exclaimed. "I'm always right!"

Cate flashed him an amused smile. "Even if you're not, I feel much better. I'm ready for bed!" She yawned again, shuffling to the sink with their teacups. "Better wash these first before Mrs. Fraser finds them in her sink and we get in trouble for messing up her pristine kitchen!"

"You're right," Jack agreed. "You wash, I'll dry." He pushed the cookie tin back into its hiding spot high on a shelf behind a basket, then grabbed a tea towel to dry the cups and saucers before putting them away. "There, no evidence, not even a crumb."

Cate nodded in approval. "We'd make great burglars. Not a trace of us!"

Jack walked Cate to her suite. "Good night, m'lady," he said with an extravagant bow.

"Good night, Jack. And thanks," she replied, smiling at him. She disappeared into her sitting room, crossing it and climbing into bed. She pushed the replay of her dreams and their conversation regarding them from her mind, determined to sleep.

* * *

Still groggy, Cate dragged herself from her bed the next morning. While she'd slept after her tête-à-tête with Jack, the hours of interrupted sleep left her drained. She groaned as she slogged into the bathroom, showering on autopilot. The steamy shower helped her to wake up. She toweled off, applied her makeup, pulled on her clothes and greeted her dogs, ready to take them for a morning pit stop prior to breakfast.

After breakfast, Mr. Smythe suggested they move the

puzzle table to the library so he and Gayle could continue work on the puzzle while Cate used the sitting room for a pre-party meeting with Mrs. Campbell. Gayle suggested settling Riley and Bailey with them, too. If they were lucky, Mr. Smythe mentioned, they would finish the puzzle today and could try for a second one-thousand-piece puzzle depicting fireworks over the London Eye on New Year's Eve. Gayle groaned at the challenge, but Mr. Smythe seemed thrilled by the prospect. Cate left them to their puzzle-building, returning to the foyer to await Mrs. Campbell.

* * *

At 9:15 a.m., Mrs. Campbell's car blazed a path down the drive. Cate, prepared for the fifteen-minute early arrival, met Isla at the door. "Oh, Lady Cate! I am still buzzing with excitement from the Snow Ball. I've received nothing but compliments!"

"As well you should, Mrs. Campbell. You did a fabulous job with the planning!"

"Thank you! Even the snow cooperated, and we didn't need the snow machine. I am so glad that wasn't an issue!"

"As am I," Cate admitted.

"Now," Mrs. Campbell said, plopping on the loveseat, dropping her folders on the cushion next to her, "this upcoming event is QUITE different. We must be prepared for the dissimilarity, so the event comes off without a hitch. There is, again, no margin for error. Some of the country's most affluent, upscale figures will be in attendance."

Cate nodded. "You have outdone yourself with the guest list."

Mrs. Campbell pinched her face into a curt smile. "Speaking of the guest list, are you certain your staff wants to attend?"

"Yes, they are looking forward to it!" Cate assured her.

"Of course," she responded, sounding dejected by the answer. "I only wanted to be sure they weren't uncomfortable. The guest list can be overwhelming!"

"I'm certain they will handle it with ease and grace."

Mrs. Campbell offered another pithy glance to Cate. "If you're sure. Let's move on to discuss final menus and flow of the party. We begin with a seated dinner in the dining room." Mrs. Campbell went over the details of the party, having it planned minute by minute as far as Cate could tell. Cate was surprised she hadn't suggested talking points at each juncture for Cate.

Mrs. Campbell shared the seating chart, pointing out the intricate details of how the guests were seated. Mrs. Campbell, adept in the intricacies of how dinner parties at estates of this position must be conducted, had expertly placed individuals according to their station and to maximize conversation flow. Despite her at-times boorish nature, it pleased Cate to have someone so well-versed leading the planning efforts.

The party was an ambitious undertaking, however, for the guest list, a party of this degree would be expected. Cate guessed most of the guests turned down other offers to attend this party, probably out of curiosity since it had been years since the castle entertained VIP guests.

After reviewing the details, Cate and Mrs. Campbell met Jack in the ballroom to go over changes to the decor. Thankfully, there were few, however the trio removed the linens from the Christmas party and placed them in Mrs. Campbell's trunk. The plaid linens, while perfect for the Snow Ball, were "unsuitable" for the New Year's Eve party. They would be switched for gold and silver, which would arrive the day prior to the party.

They made a few adjustments to the placement of the

tables and chairs before Mrs. Campbell was satisfied. After perusing the dining room and commenting on the decor for the event, Mrs. Campbell decided they had covered everything. She bid Cate farewell just prior to lunch, reminding her of their next scheduled working meeting on Monday.

Cate pushed through the doors to the library, exhausted by her lack of sleep and morning meeting. Gayle waved Cate over to show her the progress on the puzzle. Mr. Smythe surmised they would finish this afternoon.

Cate greeted the two dogs lounging near the fireplace. After rousing them from their slumber, she suggested a walk before lunch for them. Riley leapt to his feet, excited to go.

"Oh, that reminds me, Cate," Gayle mentioned, glancing up from the puzzle. "Both pups were intrigued with that bookcase. They stared at it for a good part of the morning, smelling and pawing at it." Cate followed the line of Gayle's finger. She pointed to the bookcase that filled Cate's nightmares.

Cate did her best to fluff off the comment. "Yeah." She shrugged. "They seem very interested in that. Enough that Jack called an exterminator. He found nothing. Guess they're seeing things!"

"Guess so!" Gayle chuckled, returning to fitting her piece into the puzzle.

"I'll see you both in the dining room as soon as I take these little rascals for a short walk!"

"Have fun, Riley and Bailey!" Gayle called as they left.

Cate walked the perimeter of the castle with the dogs before lunching with her guests. In the afternoon, they retreated to the library. Mr. Smythe's sole mission centered around the puzzle's completion. He preferred to begin the second puzzle fresh the next morning. Cate chuckled at his work ethic as he pushed Gayle to focus. Cate, flanked by

Riley and Bailey, settled into an armchair near the fireplace, laptop in hand.

Cate opened her book document, intent on penning a few words in her latest chapter. Instead, she became distracted by the bookcase across the room that haunted her dreams. She stared at it, eyes narrowed over the top of the laptop.

The light conversation concerning the puzzle faded into the background as she replayed her dreams in her mind. Her head sunk back into the chair behind her as she ruminated. In each dream, a gaping hole replaced the bookshelf. An idea struck Cate. She snapped the laptop shut, setting it aside, and strode to the bookcase.

Riley and Bailey were quick to follow her, glancing between the object and Cate as though trying to communicate something.

"Everything all right, Cate?" Gayle inquired.

Cate nodded, glancing back at them. "Yes. Just curious to determine what Riley and Bailey find so interesting about this bookshelf. They've been at it for two weeks!"

"I'm sure it's nothing," Gayle assured her.

"It must have a smell that intrigues them. Perhaps another dog," Mr. Smythe suggested.

"Yes, it's probably something simple," Cate agreed. "But I'm not making much progress on my work, so I figured I'd distract myself."

"You could finish this puzzle," Gayle commented.

"And steal the joy of finishing the job away from you? I wouldn't dream of it!"

"I'd live," Gayle whispered, shielding her lips from Mr. Smythe with her hand.

"I heard that," he murmured, his eyes never leaving the puzzle.

Gayle made a face at Cate before letting a giggle slip and turning her attention back to the puzzle. Cate returned her gaze to the bookshelf. She peered at it, studying it from top to bottom. With some hesitance, she approached it closer. She read a few book titles from the shelf. The books, some of them aging, were beautifully bound.

Riley and Bailey stayed behind Cate, settling to the floor, peering at Cate as she studied the contents. She sniffed the air near the shelf, not noticing any scent. Although, Riley's and Bailey's noses were far more adept at detecting odor than hers. At random, Cate pulled a few books from the shelves, flipping through them before replacing them.

After thirty minutes, Cate gave up, gleaning no information from her cursory search. She returned to her armchair and forced herself to write a paragraph in her book. After many deletions, rewrites and edits, Cate was satisfied with the work and closed her laptop for the day. She opted to take the dogs for another walk after reviewing the progress on the puzzle. By her estimation, Gayle and Mr. Smythe would finish by the time she returned from her walk.

Outside, Cate and the dogs made the trek to the loch. Ice ringed its edges. Leafless trees waved in the distance, their bare branches reaching toward the cloudy gray sky. A light drizzle drove them back sooner than Cate expected. She returned to the library to witness the triumphant finish of the thousand-piece winter scene jigsaw puzzle. Mr. Smythe snapped a picture with his cell phone for posterity prior to dismantling the puzzle to ready the table for tomorrow's venture.

They followed dinner with a nightcap and Cate turned in early, exhausted from her previous sleepless night.

CHAPTER 9

Saturday brought a bright, sunny, cold day to Dunhaven. Cate, wrapped in a warm coat, gloves, scarf and hat, spent a good bit of her morning outside walking with Riley and Bailey, both sporting their tartan coats. Gayle and Mr. Smythe joined her for part of her excursion before returning to the castle to begin their second puzzle.

Cate's mind hovered between her two mysteries as she circled the property. Days away from the new year, the theft crept ever closer. With no clues, Cate was no closer to solving it than she was when she discovered the mystery. She'd found nothing obvious in the employee records to suggest any staff member was involved. Still, she had some work to do inspecting the records to discover if any interesting anomalies existed. She grimaced, concluding her ancestors remained the prime suspects.

Her mind flipped to the bookshelf in the library. She'd taken a closer glimpse at it yesterday. Nothing stood out. The shelves held a variety of books. Nothing seemed of particular interest to her. She found no evidence of bugs or other creatures that may have stirred the dogs' interest. Were her dreams about the bookcase purely driven by stress? A desperate attempt for Cate's mind to process the busy time at the castle? Or were they a warning? But of what?

Cate's mind whirled as she tried to piece together a reasonable theory with no information beyond the interest of her dogs and a few nightmares. Cate glanced down at the two pups, nosing around a nearby bush. "I don't suppose either of you is willing to discuss your interest in the bookshelf?" she questioned.

Riley glanced up at her, his head cocked to the side. His eyes twinkled as though he held a secret. "Yes, little Mr. Riley," Cate added, reaching down to scratch his chin. "What has gotten you so interested in that one spot?"

Riley gave Cate's hand an appreciate lick, then returned to sniffing the ground. "I guess neither of you is talking, huh?"

"Talking to ourselves, Lady Cate?" Jack questioned, rounding the corner and approaching Cate from the rear.

Cate jumped, startled by his sudden appearance. "Oh! You startled me!"

"On edge? And now talking to yourself. Tsk tsk, Lady Cate. If you're not careful, you'll be in a looney bin soon."

"I was talking to the dogs," Cate informed him.

"Oh, I see," Jack responded. "Talking to the dogs, eh? Did they answer?"

"No, they didn't, thank you," Cate replied, dryly. "They refused to discuss the bookshelf in the library."

"Are you still on about that bookshelf, lassie? The exterminator said it's right as rain. Nothing found in the traps either when he stopped yesterday. We're in the clear."

"In the clear from vermin, yes," Cate agreed.

Jack's brows scrunched together, and he glanced sideways at Cate. "What other possibilities were we considering?"

Cate shrugged. "Nothing in particular. But the dogs were at it again yesterday, according to Gayle. SOMETHING has got them bothered. And then there are my nightmares. Three of them, all similar, all revolving around that bookshelf."

"And likely stemming from your overwrought mind. Between the parties and the guests, your quiet little country life is upside down."

"I enjoy having Gayle and Mr. Smythe here," Cate contended.

"Yes, but as enjoyable as you may find it, it's still quite a change to your normal, quiet routine. That coupled with the dogs' interest and your mind is concocting all sorts of strange manifestations."

"Perhaps," Cate mumbled. "Or perhaps it's a warning."

"A warning? Of what?" Jack questioned.

Cate shrugged again. "I'm not sure, but this seems more meaningful than just something my excitable mind cooked up. The dogs' reactions paired with the 'beware' messages in my dream can't be coincidence or conjecture."

"But beware of what, Cate?" Jack inquired as they returned to the castle, with Riley and Bailey leading the way.

"No idea. But why would my brain add a strange detail like that?"

"Once I dreamt my teeth fell out, but look," Jack responded, grinning, "they're still all here! Who knows why our subconscious minds do what they do!"

They arrived at the castle door, pushing through into the warm kitchen. "And what is our subconscious mind doing?" Mrs. Fraser inquired, catching the tail end of Jack's comment.

"I'm afraid mine is scaring me," Cate admitted sheepishly. "I've had a few nightmares in the last week and can't seem to decide if they're just a creation from my stressed mind or a warning."

"A warning?" Mrs. Fraser questioned, stopping dead and staring at Cate. "Why, Lady Cate, whatever of?"

"Same question I had," Jack responded. "My conclusion was a warning not to agree to any more parties with the party czar."

Mrs. Fraser chuckled. "Well, I daresay that's why your mind is frenzied. That woman would drive a saint from heaven to cast off his halo and swear like a devil."

Cate giggled at their mutual dislike of Mrs. Campbell. Molly nodded at Mrs. Fraser. "I agree. I've only met her a few times, but she puts out an unpleasant vibe."

"She isn't my favorite person either, however, she's a pro at party planning. And I must admit, the parties are a positive thing for the castle in my opinion. This place deserves to be a showpiece, admired far and wide!"

"Aye, I can't argue with your last statement, Lady Cate," Mrs. Fraser agreed. "But your health comes first. If you're fretful because of the parties, we'll have to do something to fix that! Tell you what, I'll make you a special tea after dinner tonight. You'll sleep like a baby."

"I appreciate that, Mrs. Fraser," Cate responded. "But really, I'm fine, don't trouble yourself."

"'Tis no trouble at all! I'll have it ready with the dessert."

"Thank you! Well, I won't say no to a good night's sleep, that's for certain," Cate answered.

"As well you shouldn't," Mrs. Fraser agreed. "Now, off you go to get ready for your lunch. Leave the pups with me, I've got a few bones for them."

Cate nodded, leaving Riley and Bailey to receive their treat from Mrs. Fraser. She ascended the stairs, heading for the library. She found it empty. Next, she tried the sitting room. There she found Mr. Smythe and Gayle setting out pieces of their latest jigsaw puzzle. They had built the edge, and they worked to group pieces together to fill in the middle.

"Here you are!" Cate greeted them, plopping next to Gayle on the loveseat. "You've made quite a good start." She added, gazing at the progress.

"Yes!" Mr. Smythe exclaimed. "Building the edges is the first step toward success!" Cate deemed this the most excited she'd ever witnessed the man.

"Seems like an appropriate time to break for lunch," Cate suggested.

"I agree," Gayle commented. "I am famished."

"I suppose it's a good time. We'll start the fireworks section when we return," Mr. Smythe responded.

They left the puzzle behind, eating lunch in the dining room before separating, with Cate going to the library to complete some work while Gayle and Mr. Smythe returned to the sitting room for their afternoon puzzle session. Cate settled into the chair behind the desk. She spread her notes over the desk's surface, opening her laptop in front of her.

Cate took a deep breath as her document loaded, glancing over her notes. After a moment, she stared at the blinking cursor marking the spot her next character would be placed. An eerie sensation passed over her and she shivered. The scenario too closely resembled the events of her latest nightmare.

She glanced over her shoulder to the bookshelf. She turned back to her laptop, adjusting herself in the chair. She cleared her throat, placing her hands on the keyboard. After squaring her shoulders and tightening her jaw, she raised her eyebrows and typed the word "The." After a long few breaths, she typed "castle." Her creativity ran out after those two words. She sighed, her shoulders drooping.

Her eyes flitted around the room, perusing everything but her work. Her gaze finally settled on the bookshelf. She slammed the laptop shut and stalked across the room, staring at the bookcase. She scanned the shelves again. The bookcase, built of dark, stained, solid wood, contained decorative accents around the edges. Cate pushed on the bookcase. It didn't budge. Next, Cate tried pulling on the bookshelf. Again, nothing.

Cate stood back, frowning at the bookshelf. She felt around the edges, pushing and pulling the decorative pieces. No movement, no clicks of secret panels opening, nothing. Cate sighed. "That always works in the movies," Cate bemoaned.

A notion crossed Cate's mind. Perhaps there was a fake book that triggered a secret panel or prompted the bookshelf itself to open. "Only one way to find out!" Cate stated aloud.

She began with a middle shelf, expecting the trigger, if it existed, to be there. Starting on the left, Cate pulled each book out, removing it from the shelf. She piled them near the armchair on her left. The number of books forced Cate to split the stack into two before she ended up with a wobbly tower of books that threatened to collapse.

With the shelf empty, Cate examined it closely. She ran her hand across every available surface of the shelf and its surrounding area. She brought her eyes level with the shelf, inspecting it for any anomalies. She examined every aspect of the shelf. Nothing stood out to her.

She moved to the shelf below. Book by book, she emptied the shelf, creating another two stacks on the floor. Again, she examined every inch of the shelf, her fingertips probing the entire surface. Nothing generated any reactions.

Cate stood, glancing at the growing mess around her. As she stared at the piles of books, Cate worried she would forget where they were on the shelf. Before continuing, Cate retrieved several sheets of paper from the desk and a marker.

She put a note on each stack marking the shelf number and side of the shelf where the books originated.

After logging the locations for her current piles, she knelt on the floor, tackling the bottom shelf. One by one, she removed and stacked the books next to her on the floor. Halfway through, Jack popped his head through the door, knocking. "Lady Cate?" He glanced around the room, not finding her where he expected at the desk.

"Yeah?" Cate answered, placing a note on top of her newest stack.

Jack stepped into the room, his brow furrowing, his face contorting into a questioning expression. "This is a new spin on your research," he commented.

"I'm afraid I wasn't getting very far on that," Cate admitted. "I typed two words and one of them was 'the.'"

"So, you decided to tear apart the bookshelf instead, huh?" Jack inquired, sidling up to her, still staring at the mess spreading out around her.

Cate stood, dusting her hands off. "Pretty much," Cate conceded. "I tried to open it or determine if there was a secret panel or something, but so far, no luck. Now I'm removing every book in case it triggers a hidden mechanism. Or in case the books are covering a trigger point."

Jack nodded, pulling his mouth into a thin line. "Well, I suppose I'll leave you to it. I just wanted to make sure there wasn't anything else that needed taken care of before the next party."

Cate shook her head. "No. We'll just have the linens to do when they arrive Monday and the balloon drop will need set up the day of the party. But Mrs. Campbell has her own crew of 'experts' setting that up."

"Okay, great." Jack glanced around at the piles of books. "Well, if you need any help here..." His voice trailed off as though he was unsure he wanted to offer help.

"I'll be okay," Cate replied, stooping to the bottom shelf to continue her work.

"Where are you putting this stack?" Jack inquired, kneeling next to her.

Cate smiled, handing a book to him. "Put it next to that one," she answered, pointing to the most recent stack.

"Got it," Jack replied. Together, they created an assembly line to remove the books and shuttle them to a stack. When they cleared the shelf, Cate examined it. "Anything?" Jack questioned as he marked the stack of books.

"Nope, nothing," Cate responded with a shake of her head.

"Four more shelves to go. Top shelf next or move to the next empty shelf?"

"Let's move to the top. We'll keep those books closer to the shelf to make it easier to remove them."

"Good plan, Lady Cate," Jack replied, pushing one of the library's ladders to the bookcase. "I'll do the climbing and hand the books down to you."

"Okay," Cate agreed. "I hate to send you up the ladder but…"

"But I'm more used to a ladder than you. We can't have Lady Catherine Kensie falling and breaking her leg mere days before the VIP party."

"True," Cate replied, nodding, "Mrs. Campbell would never forgive either of us."

"No, she would not," Jack added, climbing the ladder and pulling the first few books from the shelf. Cate reached high overhead, grasping the books between stretched hands. "Got 'em?"

"Yep," Cate breathed, straining a bit to juggle them as she lowered them to the floor. "Maybe less next time, though," Cate requested with a wince.

"Okay," Jack responded. "No problem."

Jack handed the books down two by two and Cate stacked them as close to the shelf as she could with the other stacks. She marked the two stacks as Jack climbed down from the ladder. "I figured you would want to scour that shelf yourself for a mechanism."

"You figured right!" Cate answered, mounting the first step of the ladder. She climbed to the top, inspecting the shelf. The smooth wood showed no flaws or imperfections consistent with a hidden mechanism. Still, she ran her fingers over every inch. She probed the sides of the bookcase, the top and any decorative elements at the top.

"Anything?" Jack called up to her. He peered at Cate from below.

Cate shook her head. "Nope," she answered, deflated. "Three more to go!" She climbed down off the ladder, sending Jack back up for the second shelf from the top.

"Looks like there might be some interesting volumes in that stack," he said, ascending the ladder.

"Hmm," Cate murmured, glancing down at the piles. "I will check them out as we put them back." She accepted the first set of books Jack handed her, beginning a new pile. Their work area was growing crowded. Cate placed this stack a few steps away. She shuttled the books away from the shelf, scurrying back and forth until the shelf was empty.

They switched places, with Jack waiting below as Cate ascended to the newest empty shelf for a careful inspection. Again, she found nothing. Two shelves remained, and Cate's hopes dwindled with each book they removed. Careful inspection of the last two shelves offered no clues, hidden mechanisms or anything else of interest.

Arms crossed, Cate stared at the empty bookcase. Disheartened, she sighed. In one last effort, Cate pushed and pulled the now-empty bookshelf, hoping it may move after being relieved of its load. "Help me push," Cate appealed to Jack, grunting as she leaned her full weight into the shelf.

Jack obliged, pushing and pulling the shelf with Cate. They pushed forward, side to side, and pulled back. The shelf didn't budge. "I doubt this solid old bugger is going anywhere," Jack said, giving the bookcase a pat.

Cate sighed again, frowning at the bookshelf. She threw her arms in the air, letting them slap her legs as she lowered them. "Nope, you're right. I must have been wrong." She shook her head in disbelief. "I was sure we'd find something. Sorry I wasted your time."

"It wasn't a waste, Lady Cate. Should we return these to their rightful place?"

Cate checked her timepiece. She shook her head. "It's getting close to dinner. We've managed to waste the entire afternoon! I'll tackle it tomorrow. Thanks for your help!"

"We'll tackle it tomorrow morning. I helped make this mess, I'll help you clean it up."

Cate chuckled. "More like I forced you to help make the mess. You can have your Sunday off." Cate waved her hand at Jack, declining his offer.

Jack shook his head, standing firm on his overture. "Nay, Lady Cate. I'll help you. We'll tackle it tomorrow morning. I'll still make dinner with my grandfather. This won't take that long."

Cate smiled a thank you at him. "Okay, if you're insisting, I'll not turn you down twice. Thanks."

He nodded to her. "Of course, m'lady," he responded, giving her a deep bow.

Cate rolled her eyes at his theatrical display. "You're such a ham." She giggled. "Well, I better run the dogs out before dinner."

"Okay. Meet you tomorrow morning around nine?"

"That sounds perfect!"

Cate navigated below stairs, finding Mrs. Fraser and Molly abuzz with activity as they made final dinner preparations. Riley and Bailey gnawed on bones near the warm stove. "You two seem quite content with those bones," Cate said, ruffling the fur on the tops of the heads.

"Aye, perfect angels, they've been, Lady Cate," Mrs. Fraser answered, ladling soup into a tureen.

"Did you make a lot of progress on your book, Lady Cate?" Molly inquired.

"I made a lot of progress on books, but not mine. Jack and I ended up removing all the books from the bookshelf Riley and Bailey have been so interested in. We found nothing," Cate continued, shrugging, "but it took the better part of the afternoon."

"What were you hoping to find?" Molly questioned as she bustled around the kitchen. She seemed to be fitting in well. For less than a week on the job, it appeared as though she'd been working these kitchens for years.

"Nothing in particular, I guess," Cate admitted. "I'm not sure what I expected. But the dogs are unrelenting with their interest in that shelf. That coupled with a few nightmares I've had about it made me curious enough to examine it."

"Nightmares?" Molly queried further.

"Yes," Cate responded with a sheepish nod to her head. "I had a few bad dreams about that stupid shelf. So, my overzealous mind concluded the shelf held some secret."

"It's not a reach in a big old castle like this. You never know where a secret passage might be hiding!" Molly replied.

Mrs. Fraser considered the statement. "Nothing comes to mind about that library. Course hidden nooks and crannies exist in a few areas, but not there that I'm aware of."

"Well, we made a thorough test of that hypothesis and you are correct, Mrs. Fraser. There is nothing there."

"At least now you know and can put that to rest," Mrs. Fraser answered with a nod of her head.

Cate nodded in agreement. "Okay, boys," she said, turning to Riley and Bailey. "How about a walk before dinner?"

* * *

As the sun crested the moors, Cate stretched, working out the kinks in her arms, legs and back. Her sore muscles complained with every movement, but after a few extra moments in bed, Cate's grumbling muscles obliged her and moved her to her bathroom for a steamy shower. After a long, hot shower, Cate's loosened muscles no longer protested. She dressed for the day, ready to clean up the mess she created in the library.

How foolish of her, she chided herself. Not everything was a mystery for her to solve. Some dreams were just that, dreams. Perhaps Riley and Bailey spotted a shadow on the bookcase and imagined something was there.

Cate stepped into the chilly morning air with the two pups. She bundled deeper into her knee-length coat, glad they would only require a few minutes outside. Pleased to return to the warmth of the house, Cate climbed the stairs, arriving in the dining room with Mr. Smythe and Gayle.

Gayle exclaimed over breakfast that she had convinced Mr. Smythe to accompany her into town for a shopping trip. They'd lunch in town but planned to be back for dinner. While Mr. Smythe itched to get back to his jigsaw puzzle, he agreed to the break.

Cate saw them off as she took the dogs for their morning walk around the property. Cate returned to the castle in time to meet Jack in the library for their morning task.

"Good morning, Sir Riley!" Jack exclaimed as Riley leapt into his arms. Bailey trailed behind him, accepting a chin scratch from Jack. "And good morning to you, too, Mr. Bailey." Jack stood again, glancing to Cate. "And a hearty good morning to you, too, Lady Cate."

"Good morning!" Cate answered. "Ready to help me clean up my folly?"

"I am," he assured her, setting Riley on the floor. "I built a fire for good Sir Riley and Mr. Bailey to curl up by while we work."

"They'll enjoy that," Cate replied, as Riley approached the fireplace and curled into a ball near it. "Where shall we start?"

"Top," Jack suggested. "I'll climb the ladder while I'm still fresh! Then, when we're good and tired, we can sit on the floor and work."

Cate nodded and waded through the stacks of books to the two marked "TOP SHELF."

"We'll work right to left," she instructed. She handed him the first book on the stack marked "RIGHT SIDE." Before handing it off, she fanned the pages, holding the book open to the floor.

"What are you doing, speed reading?" Jack quipped.

"No, just checking the books to see if there's anything interesting stuffed inside," Cate informed him, thumbing through the next book before handing it up to Jack.

"You're really intent on finding something, huh?"

Cate shrugged one shoulder, trying the next book. "While we have the books down, it doesn't hurt to check. I'm no longer convinced anything is here but…"

"But you're convinced something is here."

Cate chuckled. "No. I just remain skeptical that the dogs' reaction and my dreams are meaningless."

"Fair enough. We'll find out soon enough if your hunch is correct," Jack noted.

Cate continued her cursory search of each book before

handing it up to Jack. The careful examination of each book slowed the work, however, Cate persisted. They finished the first stack. Cate's fastidious review of each book slowed the process. Cate glanced up to the half-filled top shelf, realizing this task would take them all morning.

"Sorry," Cate apologized, her eyes flitting to Jack for a moment as she searched the next book.

"No apology needed," Jack assured her. "I've got all morning."

"I didn't intend to take up your entire morning though," Cate replied.

"I don't mind, Cate," he responded. "I'd rather do it now than have an encore."

Cate tried to move faster with this stack. However, several small books made the process tedious. They finished the stack, finding nothing. Cate sighed under her breath, her hopes deflating with each book. Jack descended two steps on the ladder, ready to restore the next shelf.

Cate moved to the first stack for this shelf. She searched the first book, then shuttled it to Jack. The process was slowed by Cate's shuffling back and forth to reach the stack. They wrapped up the second shelf with five more to go.

"One more then I'll need a breather," Cate informed Jack.

"Sounds good to me," Jack answered. He climbed off the ladder, pushing it away. He could reach the remaining shelves while standing on the floor.

Since he no longer required the ladder, both Jack and Cate searched through books before filling the shelf. The task went faster with two of them tackling each stack. Three shelves in and they had nothing to show for it but sore fingertips and dusty hands.

Cate collapsed into a leather armchair near the fireplace. Riley lifted his head, eyeing her through narrowed eyes.

Satisfied everything was well, his head dropped back to the rug below him with a deep sigh.

"We'll make quick work of those last four shelves," Jack assured her. "Between the two of us, we'll tear through those stacks."

Cate nodded without answering.

"Too tired to answer?" Jack questioned.

Cate gave him a weak smile. "No. But with every book that passes, I feel more and more foolish."

"It wasn't all for naught, Lady Cate!" Jack encouraged.

"No?" Cate queried. "How do you figure?"

"It gives me something to tease you about for years to come. That makes it worth it in my book, pun intended!" He issued a devilish grin aimed her way.

Cate offered a wry look in return. "You're right," she responded. "That makes it all worth it." Cate paused for a few long breaths. "Well, I suppose we should get back to it."

"Okay," Jack groaned, pulling himself from the chair.

They approached the next two stacks, sorting through the books, checking them one-by-one and replacing them on the shelf. They moved on to shelf number five. Four books in, Jack thumbed through a book, shaking it upside down. A yellowed envelope fluttered to the ground from between the pages. Excited, Cate dumped her empty book on the shelf and raced to retrieve it.

"What is it?" Jack inquired. "Note written in blood warning you to beware?"

Cate grabbed it, turning it over in her hand, searching for any markings. "I'm beginning to worry you may quit your job in favor of stand-up comedy," she quipped.

Cate joined Jack with the envelope. "There's nothing on the envelope. No address or salutation."

"Anything inside?"

Cate opened the aging envelope. Two handwritten papers

had been folded and stuffed inside. Cate unfolded the pages. Black cursive handwriting filled them. Jack peered over Cate's shoulder as they read the note. Cate swallowed hard, her eyes widening as she read each line. She shuffled to the next page, scanning the text scrawled on it. When she finished reading, she twisted to face Jack, her mouth hanging open, aghast.

"Cate, don't jump to any conclusions," Jack warned.

"Don't jump to any conclusions?!" Cate exclaimed. "Did you read it?"

"Yes, I read it. And I already realize the scenario your hyperactive mind is creating."

Cate sunk into one of the armchairs, the letter still in her left hand. Her right hand propped her chin up as thoughts raced through her mind. Hypotheses were created, accusations were produced, and conclusions were formed in seconds. The warnings made sense. But they hadn't been calling her to investigate, but rather warning her to stay away. Warning her she wouldn't like what she found if she kept searching.

CHAPTER 10

Jack tugged the papers from between her fingers, folding them and setting them aside. "Cate," he said, perching on the edge of the armchair nearest her. "We don't know what that letter refers to. It could be to anyone about anything. It could mean nothing."

"And it could mean everything," Cate countered.

Jack shook his head. "You're jumping to conclusions. Even if you're correct, it has nothing to do with you. Let's put it aside, finish the work here, sleep on it and discuss it tomorrow."

"But…"

"But nothing," Jack responded. "We both read it. We both interpreted it differently. It's vague. Leave it, let's discuss it tomorrow." Jack paused for several breaths. "Plus, there's only a few more days until we can investigate the theft. Then we'll figure out if this has any meaning for ourselves."

Cate brightened at the prospect of time travel. Jack bringing up time travel, anticipating the trip, not complaining or disagreeing marked progress, even if he was only doing it to humor Cate and get her mind off the disturbing note.

Cate nodded her head in agreement. "Okay. But only because you promise we can investigate at the first opportunity." She pointed her finger at him, adding volume to the words as she spoke them.

"I promise!" Jack answered, right hand on his heart, left raised in the air. "Now let's get at these shelves. I've got a dinner date!"

Cate giggled. "I do NOT want to keep you from your date!"

"No," Jack replied, standing and pulling Cate up. "You'll never hear the end of it from Pap if you do."

Cate left the note laying on the coffee table as she and Jack continued their work. Despite the findings already made, they continued to check each book for anything it may contain. Book by book, shelf by shelf, they finished the task.

As Cate placed the last book on the shelf, Jack breathed a sigh of relief at being finished. Riley, who had joined them as they knelt on the floor working on the bottom shelf, leapt to his feet. Cate assumed he, too, was excited to be finished with the task. Instead, the little dog narrowed his dark, almond-shaped eyes, glaring at the bookcase. After a moment, he backed up two steps and emitted a long, high-pitched howl.

His boisterous bark awakened a sleeping Bailey who climbed to his feet, racing to Riley's side. He glanced at the bookcase as Riley continued to back away, still barking. Bailey joined in the fray, adding a raucous yipping to Riley's yapping.

Cate's brow crinkled as she regarded the dog's strange reaction. "Riley! Bailey! Hush!" she instructed. Cate shushed them a few more times before they quieted. Cate shook her head at them. Riley, still vigilant, sat on his haunches, ready to leap into action at the first sign of distress or danger. Bailey stood at his side. He stared at the bookcase, his mouth opening and closing, ready to bark at a moment's notice.

"Perhaps it's the books they hate," Jack mentioned.

Cate twisted back to the bookshelf, eyeing it. After a moment, she shrugged her shoulders. "I don't..." she began. She stopped short, her brows knit together in confusion. She put her hand out in front of her, moving it around.

"What is it, Cate?" Jack asked, his eyes toggling between her and the bookcase.

"Air," Cate stated.

"Air?" Jack questioned.

"Yes, here. Put your hand here," Cate instructed. She waved her hand to pinpoint where he should place his. "Do you feel it?"

After a moment, Jack shook his head. "No, I..." He paused. "Wait, yes! A draft, slight but there." He glanced around the room. All the windows were closed and many of the curtains drawn to help keep the cold at bay. None of the curtains rustled, signifying no air leaking from the windows.

Cate climbed to her feet. She raced to the desk drawer, pulling it open. She retrieved a box of matches kept there.

"Good idea, Lady Cate," Jack announced, as she knelt next to him. Cate struck one of the matches, holding it in front of her. It flickered, the flame blowing away from the bookshelf. Cate waved the flame out and crawled closer. She peered at the edges of the shelf, running her fingers around its frame.

"There's definitely air coming from this bookcase. The question is: why? What's behind it?"

"Let me have a look," Jack suggested. Cate sat back on her haunches, allowing him to access the bookcase. Jack pawed at the edges of the shelf. He shook his head. "You're right, there's air coming from here."

Cate nodded. "That's what's driving the dogs crazy. There must be some scent on it. Outside, perhaps?"

"How is the outside air getting here? This isn't an outside wall," Jack responded, still staring at the shelf.

"Leaky chimney? The chimney for this room doesn't abut this bookcase. Is there another chimney from another room?"

Jack shook his head. "Not that I'm aware of. There isn't a chimney anywhere near this bookcase."

Cate tightened her lips in speculation. "Perhaps there's something there we don't realize. Maybe an old chimney. Perhaps there were renovations that left behind remnants of a previous iteration of construction."

"As far as I recall, the library hasn't changed. In fact, it appeared almost identical when we were here in 1856."

"Yes, I agree. If there were changes, they weren't perceptible. Are there plans for the castle we could consult?"

Jack nodded. "Yeah, there are. I'll dig them out as soon as I get back from dinner with Pap and we can check them out tomorrow."

"Okay," Cate agreed. She checked her timepiece. "Oh, speaking of, you better get going or you'll be late!"

"Mm, yeah," Jack responded, checking his wristwatch. "Damn, I'd prefer to solve this now!"

Cate grinned at him. "Enjoying sleuthing on the mysterious case of the leaky bookshelf, are you?"

"No," Jack countered. "But I'm concerned about what air is leaking from where. In an old place like this, we don't want any minor problems to turn into major ones that may become expensive to fix."

"Oh, all business as always, huh? And here I assumed you were ready to crack a case and find a secret passage lurking behind here, brimming with jewels and treasure."

"I doubt that, Lady Cate. Likely just some strange issue

that will need fixing before we've got a freezing cold library, or worse, a flooded one." Jack climbed to his feet. Cate followed suit. "We'll look at it first thing in the morning," he promised.

"Okay."

"Until then," Jack warned. "Don't let your imagination run wild, okay? No pirate treasure or ghost's gold."

"You're no fun!" Cate cried with a laugh.

"No, I'm not," Jack agreed. "And I like me just fine that way." He dusted his hands and gave a parting ruffle to each dog's fur. As he spun to leave the room, he spotted the letter on the table. He snatched it on his way toward the door.

"Hey! Where are you going with that letter?" Cate questioned.

"Oh, you saw that, huh?" Jack inquired, spinning to face Cate, a sheepish grin on his face.

"I did," she replied, one eyebrow raised at him.

"Figured I'd take it with me so you couldn't read it over and over and obsess over it."

Cate stalked to him, pulling the letter from his hands. "I won't obsess. But I will read it again. A few times. And take some notes. Jot down some ideas."

"Obsess over what it means," Jack concluded for her.

"I won't obsess, I promise. I'm not even going to read it again until later. I'm planning to spend the afternoon puzzle building with Mr. Smythe. I figured I'd give Gayle a break, take her place."

"Ah, that sounds like a perfect way to spend the afternoon. Let your brain solve a safe, innocent, straightforward puzzle."

Cate nodded. "Exactly." She folded the letter, placing it back in its envelope and setting it on the desk. "Say hello to your grandfather for me."

"Will do, Lady Cate. See you tomorrow morning." Jack

stepped to the door. As he bowed extravagantly, he said, "M'lady."

* * *

Cate spent the afternoon bent over the Fireworks over London jigsaw puzzle. Gayle nearly tripped herself fleeing from the puzzle table and grabbing a book to spend the afternoon reading. As Cate worked to build the London Eye with a bursting red firework over top, her mind wandered to the letter retrieved from the mysterious leaky bookshelf. She'd promised not to dwell on it, but her mind could not let it rest. Still, she pressed on, helping Mr. Smythe complete a good amount of the puzzle before dinner. In his estimation, they would finish the puzzle tomorrow just in time for the New Year, the party and their imminent departure. It was obvious he couldn't be more pleased with himself. Cate considered it the first time in seven months of knowing William Smythe that she'd ever seen him enjoy himself outside of work. Wonders never cease, she reflected.

After dinner, Cate curled up with a book in her sitting room. She'd tucked the letter into the pocket of her cardigan earlier and removed it, placing it on the side table in her sitting room when she retired to her suite. Now, as she tried to focus on the words filling the page in front of her, the small yellowed envelope beckoned to her like a siren to a seaman.

Her eyes drifted sideways, staring at its frail, aged countenance, its yellow-white color a stark contrast to the deep, rich wood of the table. Cate shook her head, returning to her reading. No, she chided, she would not dwell on it. Not before bed. Otherwise, she'd be treating herself to a night full of postulating, theorizing, fretting and sleeplessness.

Cate read another sentence. The words passed through

her brain as though it didn't exist. Two sentences later, Cate found herself staring at the small, unmarked envelope. She hadn't a clue what she'd read, her mind unable to retain any of the context. Cate snapped the book shut, trading it for the envelope. After sliding the thick papers out, she glanced at them. Despite the words they held, there was something extraordinary about holding something so personal from another era. Another individual, one within her family, had held these pages, written their thoughts. The written word was rare in this day and age. People rarely wrote hand-written notes or letters anymore, relying on the speed and ease of typed communication.

Cate turned the pages over in her hands, noting the feel of the paper, the stylized cursive handwriting, the thick, black ink, the care and time put into folding the pages. Even given the note's contents, Cate appreciated the nearly century-old piece of history she held in her hands. If the note hadn't suggested something vile, she'd have been giddy to reread it multiple times.

Regardless of Cate's opinions on it, the note existed. It recorded history. Her history. With a big sigh, Cate re-read the note, painful as that history was to acknowledge. The letter contained no salutation, it began in a frank and curt manner.

I include no salutation for you know who you are and I cannot bear to write your name. I can barely bear to acknowledge that you exist. What you have done to me, this family, your OWN family is a travesty. You should be ashamed, regardless of the excuses you gave for your abhorrent behavior.

What you have stolen from this family is far more precious than you realize. Or perhaps more precious than you wish to acknowledge. While you believe it is "due" you, it is not.

My husband warns me not to let my anger get the better of me, but I am so filled with rage and loathing toward you, I wonder if it is even possible for me. Perhaps my husband is of a better disposition than I am, however, it may be, perchance, that he is better suited at hiding his true feelings. Although, those feelings run more to heartbreak than anger.

There is nothing more to be said. But know with your theft, you have robbed this family of more than valuable keepsakes. You have stolen trust, faith and loyalty also.

Should we ever meet again, and I sincerely hope we never do, I would cross the street rather than look at you. If you ever return to this household, I will have you arrested at once, regardless of my husband's inclination to turn a blind eye to your wicked ways.

I wish you all the happiness I'd wish unto my worst enemy.

I hope your bounty smothers you and crushes your very soul under its weight.

Anne MacKenzie

Cate heaved a sigh after reading the emotionally charged letter. Anne, Rory's wife, displayed strong feelings for someone. While she never sent the letter, the words contained within showed her level of anger and frustration with the unknown recipient. Cate scanned it again. The words "stolen," "theft" and "robbed" leapt off the page. These couldn't be coincidental. Anne's letter must refer to the theft of the precious family heirlooms.

The other unmistakable component was the reference to the thief's origins. Anne claimed the person robbed their own family, implying a family member had been the culprit. This brought a frown to Cate's face. Rory's immediate family consisted of his wife, child, parents and his brother, Lucas. Of course, there were cousins, distant or otherwise. However, Anne's reference to being "due" something would put the family connection at a close relative. Cate had a sinking feeling her original fear and suspicion was correct.

Lucas MacKenzie, her great-grandfather, had stolen the jewels. The letter seemed to confirm her suspicions. She was descended from a thief. One willing to rob his own family.

* * *

Cate startled awake, glancing around the dimly lit room. She swallowed hard, getting her bearings as her sluggish brain raced to awaken. Riley and Bailey lay near the fireplace, sound asleep. Cate had drifted to sleep pondering and fretting over the meaning of Anne's letter. The pages, now strewn across the floor after falling from her limp hand, reminded her.

Reaching down, Cate scooped the papers off the floor. She glanced at them, a forlorn feeling sweeping over her. Her ancestors were thieves. No wonder someone blotted them out from the family bible. Now Cate owned the castle. Anne MacKenzie was probably rolling in her grave.

Cate folded the note and tucked it back into its envelope. She set it on the side table on top of her discarded book. As she swung her legs over the side of the chaise, intent on retreating to her bed, the memory of a dream flooded back to her.

The dream had awakened her with a start. Her confusion upon waking distracted her, but now it all came rushing back. Another nightmare about the bookshelf. Generations of the family surrounded her in the sitting room. They introduced themselves with bewildering speed. When Rory introduced himself and Anne, Cate explained she descended from Rory's brother, Lucas. Anne MacKenzie dropped Cate's hand, an expression of disgust on her face. Cate recalled the letter, the emotions expressed by Anne. Generations worth of gaps between her and her great-grandfather had not quelled the fury the theft stoked within her.

She spun, stalking away from Cate, her face a mask of rage. She whispered in the ears of Victoria and Randolph. Shocked expressions crossed their faces. They gasped, their eyes flitting to Cate.

The information branched through the generations of the family. Everyone gaped at her, their eyes glaring with acrimony and distrust. Cate backed away, speechless, unable to explain away anything. She closed the sitting room doors behind her. Tears streamed down her face. She ran to the library, seeking the comfort of Riley and Bailey. She trusted her two dogs would not turn their backs on her.

As she entered the library, a strong gust of wind blew the doors from her grasp. Her eyes narrowed as her hair twisted in the air. She stepped further into the room, seeking the source of the wind. She studied the windows, all closed.

She glanced across the room, her eyes widening. A gaping hole stood where the bookshelf used to be. Cate marched toward it. With Riley and Bailey nowhere to be found, concern filled her they had stumbled into the void. "Riley! Bailey!" she called.

A booming voice answered back, stunning her and causing her to fall backward. "BEWARE!"

Cate shuddered at the memory of the dream, specifically at the disembodied voice shouting its ominous warning. She shook her head. What was it about that bookshelf that haunted her? Perhaps she would find out when she and Jack checked the plans for the castle.

It would need to suffice. Cate needed sleep. It was already after midnight and Cate's snooze on the chaise left her cramped with a crick in her neck. Besides studying the castle plans, most of the setup for the New Year's Eve party must be completed today. Cate needed all the energy she could muster. After carrying each pup to their bed, Cate dragged herself to her own, climbing in and stretching out. By shifting her shoulders back and forth, she eased the kink in her neck. The rhythmic motion lulled her to sleep.

* * *

Cate met Jack the following morning before Mrs. Campbell was scheduled to arrive. He carried a cardboard tube, pushing the library door open for her to enter first.

"Those the plans?" Cate inquired.

"Aye," Jack confirmed.

Cate cleared a space on the desk. "Let's see what's behind that bookcase, shall we?"

Jack popped the top of the tube, extracting the plans and spreading them across the desk. The blue pages contained detailed drawings of the castle. Cate stared at the crisscross of lines, marks, numbers and words. The plans were disorienting even when one lived in the castle.

Cate searched for a space matching the library. Jack found it first, pointing it out. He'd had no trouble reading the plans. "Here's the library," he noted. "Windows here, door here, fireplace here." He tapped locations on the drawing. "That would put our bookcase right about here." He tapped another location twice.

"So, what's behind it? Secret passage? Hidden chamber?" Cate questioned.

"A hallway," Jack responded.

"What?" Cate queried. "There has to be something between the hallway and the bookcase!"

"Nope." Jack shook his head. "There's nothing on the plans." He shuffled through a few other pages containing the schematics for the other floors. "Nothing above it or below it that would lead to air leakage."

Cate wandered to the bookshelf, her finger on her lips.

"Something is causing the air flow," she murmured, deep in reflection.

"No chimneys, no outer walls, no pitch changes in the roof." Jack shuffled the papers again. "Nothing I can identify to cause air flow."

Cate continued to stare at the bookshelf. "What is your secret?" Cate inquired of it.

"I'm not sure it holds one, Lady Cate," Jack replied. "There's nothing behind it."

"Are you sure they noted secret passages and rooms on those plans?"

Jack nodded. "These are updates of Douglas MacKenzie's original plans. Copies of his personal copy. He included all the secrets of the castle on his plans to make sure they were built to his specifications. A lot changed during the last renovation. Some of those secret spaces were converted to bathrooms to update the castle."

Cate meandered back to the desk. Jack pointed out a few "secret" rooms, now bathrooms. Cate grimaced. Jack rolled the plans up and stowed them back in the tube. "Sorry, Lady Cate. No secret pirate gold for you."

"Darn," Cate answered, snapping her fingers. Something nagged at her in the back of her mind, but she pushed it aside. The plans told a different story than her imagination created. Facts didn't lie or exaggerate, unlike her overly inventive mind. "I guess that's that," Cate said with a shrug as Jack slid the top back on the document tube. "Meet you in the ballroom?"

Jack nodded. "I'll see you there as soon as I return these to the office."

They parted ways, with Cate collecting Mrs. Campbell from the front door before escorting her to the ballroom. Cate, Jack and Mrs. Campbell spent the rest of their morning making final adjustments to the layout, setting out the linens and finishing adjustments to the decorations.

* * *

Cate slept in on the last day of the year. The promise of a late night chock full of hostess duties meant she'd need to log the extra sleep. Cate spent a lazy day trying to relax before the party. With the party beginning with a late evening sit-down dinner, she had plenty of the day to enjoy with her guests.

Much to his delight, Mr. Smythe finished his puzzle, snapped a picture for posterity and dismantled it, careful to break apart the pieces so the next player could "enjoy the full experience." The castle would be too quiet after they left, Cate mused. Cate would miss their quiet presence after their holiday stay. Still, Cate hoped her time travel adventure would distract from missing her guests.

When late afternoon arrived, Cate began dressing for the evening's event. As she slipped into her gold-sequined, trumpet-style, floor-length gown, thoughts crowded into her mind. Last New Year's Eve, Cate was holed up in her small apartment in Aberdeen with Riley. She'd bought a mini-bottle of champagne and chocolate covered strawberries to ring in the new year with sweatpants and sweets. In a well-worn Aberdeen College sweatshirt, athletic socks and a messy faux-bun created with an old scrunchie, Cate parked herself next to her pup with a bowl of popcorn. She'd fallen asleep on her couch before midnight, a romantic holiday-themed comedy streaming on TV.

Cate chuckled, reminded of how different her life had been then. Fast-forward one year and Cate stood staring into a floor-length mirror within her bedroom suite in a gold-colored evening gown, her hair coiffed in a chic updo, evening make-up complete with smoky eyes and red lips.

The suite alone surpassed the size of her apartment by a hundred square feet at least. The remaining castle dwarfed the apartment building she'd called home. Cate, too, had changed, morphed into a new version of herself.

She stared into her own blue eyes, noting the changes both physical and mental. She recalled her awkwardness at social events. Now a countess, she didn't have the flexibility to shy away from social settings or shut herself off from the world. While she still enjoyed her privacy, Countess Cate was becoming more at ease with entertaining, becoming accustomed to playing the role of gracious hostess.

She smoothed her dress a final time before slipping on her shoes. Her mind shifted gears, from her own journey less than a year ago to the events of almost a century ago. As she buckled the ankle strap, she imagined her counterpart one hundred years ago, doing the same thing. Anne MacKenzie, then the Countess of Dunhavenshire, was likely dressing for her own New Year's Eve party. Perhaps donning a floor-length ballgown like Cate or perhaps a shin-length dress with a drop-waist. Had she worn her hair up or in the popular finger waves of the time? Cate imagined she wore a headband, popular during the Roaring '20s. She'd donned some of Victoria MacKenzie's jewels, removed from the safe for the evening. Which necklace had she chosen to wear and which was left in her room for the evening, Cate wondered?

When she attended Victoria's Halloween Ball in 1856, Cate had borrowed Victoria's sapphire necklace. Victoria, gifted a new ruby necklace by her husband, Randolph, had worn it as a perfect match to the color of her ballgown. Which was Anne wearing tonight? In either case, both of them would be gone by morning. Stolen away in the wee hours of 1925.

Cate glanced to the timepiece she wore around her neck. Mere steps away was the rip that could take her to 1925.

After the clock struck midnight, she could travel back to the moment the jewels were stolen. Perhaps she should. Perhaps after her own party wound down, she should convince Jack to travel back and catch the thief red-handed.

The memory of her last attempt to catch someone red-handed flashed through her mind. While trying to solve a murder, Cate ended up being tossed into the loch and nearly killed. She escaped thanks to Jack's good timing. He fished her out before she drowned.

No, she thought, perhaps catching the thief red-handed was a bad idea. Besides, who would she say she was when the confrontation occurred? Would she admit to Anne and Rory she was a time traveler from the future, there to stop the robbery? Rory would realize the truth, but would Anne? That was assuming she could stop the thief without meeting an unfortunate end. Surely someone willing to steal was willing to do other nefarious things. She'd also have no guarantee they'd arrive in time to stop the thief. Anne MacKenzie said she retired for the evening around 1 a.m. The theft occurred sometime between then and when Lady MacKenzie's ladies' maid noticed the jewels missing around eleven the following morning. If her party lasted longer than the MacKenzie party of the past, they could miss the theft. Then again, if the theft occurred later in the morning, they could be hanging around the halls for hours, increasing their odds of being discovered.

Cate shook the silly idea from her head as she slipped the timepiece beneath her dress. She'd have to let the theft happen and investigate it from there. Cate crossed her bedroom to the sitting room. Sprawled near the warm fireplace, both pups laid chewing bones provided by Mrs. Fraser. Cate approached them, stroking their backs with each hand. Riley lifted his head from his prize, giving her a quick sniff. "Yes, I'm all dressed up, buddy. Not my usual leggings, huh?" Riley stood on his hind legs, reaching for her face with his tongue. "Thank you for the kiss, but I'm not going anywhere. Just downstairs for a party. You hold down the fort with your brother, Bailey. I'll be back as soon as I can!"

Cate gave the two dogs another scratch before leaving them to their bones and heading downstairs. Mrs. Campbell was already ringing the doorbell when Cate arrived at the foot of the stairs. Jack opened the door after a wolf whistle. "You clean up nicely, Lady Cate," he said, grinning.

"As do you," Cate returned the compliment as Mrs. Campbell pushed through the door, her black formal gown's sequins shimmering with each step.

"Oh!" she exclaimed, stopping short mid-step and leaving Jack unable to close the door. "Don't you look elegant, Lady Cate. How befitting the golden gown is on our newest Countess."

"Thank you," Cate answered, looping her arm through Mrs. Campbell's to lead her to the sitting room where pre-dinner drinks were being served. Mr. and Mrs. Fraser, along with Molly, were already present. "And your dress is also lovely. What beautiful detailing with the subtle shimmer of sequins."

Mrs. Campbell tittered. "Yes, well, I succeeded in finding something suitable for the occasion without being overdone."

Jack followed them into the sitting room as Cate offered a drink to Mrs. Campbell. She took a small sherry. "Oh, Jack, shouldn't you be at your post?"

"My post?" he asked, sipping his scotch.

"Yes, aren't you filling in as butler this evening?"

"Oh, no!" Cate exclaimed, a giggle escaping her with her words. "One of the waitstaff we hired is handling that. Jack just happened to be in the foyer when you arrived. He's a guest tonight, remember?"

"Oh, yes," Mrs. Campbell replied, her voice brusque. "How could I forget?"

"In case your memory is failing you," Jack chimed in. "This is my grandfather, Stanley Reid. He's also a guest tonight."

"Yes, I do remember Stan. Good to see you again. Forgive me, I had quite forgotten about Lady Cate's guest list with so many other details swimming through my mind."

"Of course, Mrs. Campbell," Cate responded. "I just mentioned earlier this week the fantastic job you've done in putting together these events. Everyone on my guest list has been most excited to attend."

"I'm sure," Mrs. Campbell noted, her voice still dry. Mr. Smythe and Gayle arrived moments later, requesting a drink from the waitstaff and joining in the conversation. Soon afterward, guests began to arrive, were shown in for cocktails and introduced. Conversation flowed well around the room with guests mingling with each other for light conversations. Cate met several lords and ladies, even a fellow countess, although her husband, the count, was no longer alive. An up-and-coming industry titan who was recently knighted by the Queen also was in attendance.

Cate's head swam with details of who was who, who knew who, where they were from and why that mattered. She wondered if she'd really grown into her role of Countess, as she'd thought she had only an hour ago. As Cate struggled to keep up with the witty banter, dry British humor and dizzying array of intricate peerage, the dinner announcement was made.

Cate breathed a sigh of relief as the group headed for the dining room. Her everyday, no-frills dining room had been transformed into a scene from a movie. Crisp, white linens covered an intricately set table. Lit candles beamed from the center where pine sprigs and cones surrounded them. The place settings were delicately laid, perfectly spaced, and the silverware gleamed. Cate wondered if she had wandered onto the set of *Downton Abbey* by mistake.

"Oh gosh, it looks so great in here. I feel like royalty," Cate overheard Molly say to Mrs. Fraser.

"Aye," Mrs. Fraser agreed. "Dunhaven Castle has entertained many a gentleman and lady through the years."

"Yes, even a Duke here and there!" Mrs. Campbell exclaimed with pride as she pushed past the women into the ballroom, leading a lord something-or-other to a place setting next to Cate's. As everyone was seated, Cate spied her staff near the far end of the table. She smiled forlornly to the group, separated from her by what seemed like miles of table. Molly waved to her, chattering to Mr. and Mrs. Fraser, gesturing to the decor. The elder Mr. Reid chatted to the woman sitting to his right. If Cate recalled, she was the daughter of one of the VIPs. She giggled at whatever Mr. Reid told her, his hands gesturing in the air.

Everyone seemed to be enjoying themselves. Cate made a short speech thanking everyone for attending prior to the meal being served. Mrs. Campbell had arranged a meal fit for a king, with seven courses. The food never seemed to end. The meal, lasting several hours, concluded well into the night, leaving less than two hours before midnight.

After dinner concluded, drinks and music flowed in the ballroom until midnight approached. As Cate eyed the time passing, she pondered the MacKenzies of 1924. With only minutes left before midnight, they hurled toward an unstoppable event. While not as devastating as the murder that occurred sixty-some-odd years earlier, it still would leave a scar. Its effects would ripple through time.

As the moment approached, champagne flutes were distributed, and the crowd counted down the final few seconds until the clock chimed midnight. Balloons cascaded from the ceiling. Gold and silver globes showered down around them, floating across the floor as people exchanged hugs, kisses, handshakes and well-wishes for a happy and healthy new year.

A loud cannonade of sound drew the revelers to the back gardens. "Oohs" and "aahs" rose among the group as fireworks exploded overhead, showering the onlookers with colored lights. Despite the chilly air, almost every guest lingered outside for the entire show. An explosion of applause resounded after the final firework sparkled overhead.

The party wound down around 1 a.m. with most guests saying their goodbyes about twenty minutes past. By quarter to two, everyone had departed, including Mrs. Campbell, promising to contact Cate "very soon" about the next event. Cate joined her staff in the sitting room for one final toast to the evening's success before everyone retired, exhausted from the evening.

Cate climbed into bed around 3 a.m., two exhausted pups nestled in their beds below. As she drifted to sleep, Cate wondered if the jewels were already stolen in 1925 or if the nightmare had yet to unfold.

CHAPTER 11

Cate lounged in bed the next morning, enjoying a late sleep-in. She stretched out in bed before venturing out, choosing her bathrobe instead of dressing before leaving her room. Cate bundled the robe tighter around her neck as the cold struck her when she let the dogs out for a few moments.

Despite her late rise, no one else was awake. She ushered the dogs back to her suite after their breakfast, tiptoeing through the halls with the cold breakfast she'd retrieved for herself from the refrigerator. Cate settled on her chaise, balancing her bowl of fruit and cereal on her lap as she pulled a blanket across her legs. Riley and Bailey leapt onto the chaise, nestling into the blanket on either side of her.

Cate ate her breakfast, her mind wandering to the events of 1925. In two hours, Anne's maid would discover the missing jewelry. The house would be turned upside-down, the guests and staff would be questioned, and a full police investigation would be launched. During that investigation, something would come to light that would cause Rory to refuse to speak of the incident and Anne to pen the letter sitting on her side table. But what?

It had to be that a family member had stolen the jewelry. This wouldn't be the first time the MacKenzie family covered up a dark secret. Emilia MacKenzie, Randolph's younger sister, died birthing her first illegitimate child. The family listed her death as caused by influenza and kept her child locked in the tower room. While Randolph loved the child, she had been kept a secret, a blemish on the family name.

A jewelry theft from a family member would possibly evoke a similar response. Cate imagined the family Bible, the ink splotch over her side of the family. She envisioned Anne staring at her branch of the family, enraged. With a contemptuous expression, Anne poured ink over that branch, blotting them from her memory and the family.

Cate planned to continue her investigation into the staff today, but all signs pointed to her great-grandfather, Lucas. Cate sighed, her spoon rattling around the empty bowl on her lap. The effect echoed the thoughts rattling around her brain.

She set the bowl aside, laying her head back. Tempted to read the letter again, Cate rolled her head to the side, staring at the small envelope. Her fingers reached out and touched the envelope, the texture rough on her fingertips.

The grainy texture mirrored the harsh words contained inside. Cate swallowed hard, pulling her hand away. The enmity and acrimonious language disturbed Cate. She didn't blame Anne for her reaction. Cate understood her emotion of betrayal. She experienced something similar when her tenure-tracked request had been denied by her old workplace. She'd felt the same sense of betrayal, the same wish to lash out. This betrayal, from a close family member, must have stung even worse than hers. But she refused to read it again. She'd dwelled on it enough. Jack was correct.

She must focus on changing things. The theft had occurred, but could she solve the mystery? Could they find the missing jewels and return them? Was it possible to do this before anyone was any the wiser about the thief's identity? Or, at least, could the strained relationship between the family members be salvaged if the jewels were returned?

Cate was determined to answer these questions. She returned her bowl to the kitchen, washing, drying and putting it away. It appeared no one else had ventured down yet. The stack of bowls set on the island remained untouched, six spoons still splayed next to them. On her way back to her suite, she stopped in the library, picking up her research folder.

She paused for a moment before exiting the room, eyeing the bookshelf. The bookshelf, the source of the disturbing note, still held a secret. At least in her mind it did. Even after finding the note, it still haunted her dreams. The air escaping from behind it must signify something. She refused to believe it resulted from a loose shingle or leaky chimney. Her mind maintained something else caused this.

But what, her analytical side mused. The plans showed nothing behind the bookcase. No secrets lurked on the other side. Cate sighed, frowning at it before she departed, heading for her sitting room.

Cate met no one in the halls as she made her way back to her suite. Everyone was enjoying a long, luxurious sleep, leaving the castle quiet. Cate's anxious mind put a stop to her sleeping ability. The theft that occurred on this day nearly one hundred years ago filled her mind the moment she awoke. She'd soon be able to investigate in person, and she wanted a solid understanding of who Jack and she should pay close attention to.

Cate snuggled under her blanket, opening her folder. She shuffled through the papers, locating her suspect list and her staff list. She studied the list of names, searching for any clue that may hint toward them being a thief.

No one had left the employ of the MacKenzie family immediately following the theft. However, Cate reasoned a quick departure of an employee would call suspicion, so the thief, if they were a member of the staff, would probably stay long enough to cast away any suspicion from themselves.

Several staff members had been employed long before the theft and remained so long after the theft. Cate placed check marks by the names of staff members who had years of employment both before and after the incident. They would be low on the suspect list. It wasn't probable that a loyal staff member would steal from the family they served, nor that they would stay around to continue their job afterward.

The remaining list consisted of five individuals. Two maids, a groom, a footman and an under-butler. Cate noted their arrivals and departures. Most of them had arrived at least a year prior to the theft, except the footman. William Barrow, the footman, had arrived nine months prior to the theft. Their departure dates were all within one year of the theft. Alice Huxley, a scullery maid, left the employ of the MacKenzies four months after the theft. The other maid, Bertha MacIntyre, worked until September 1925. William Barrow ceased to be listed in the employment register around the same time as Bertha. The groom, Thomas Gould, was last paid by the estate in June. And the under-butler, Charles Forsythe, departed in May.

Cate noted these five staff members on her suspect list. She placed them below her great-grandfather's name. The evidence gathered thus far continued to support a case against him. She listed her reasons for suspecting them next to their names. Near Lucas' name, she wrote *Motive: limited inheritance, Evidence: Anne's angry letter, Opportunity: ? Was Lucas at the castle then?*

Next to the staff's names, Cate jotted a note that their arrival or departure suggested they may be connected to the theft. It was weak, but it made Cate feel better to include it.

Perhaps she could find out more about the staff prior to her journey to the past with Jack. Cate doubted much information was kept about them, but perhaps she could dig up something to help eliminate one or more of them or provide more evidence to include on her suspect sheet.

Cate climbed from her comfy perch and dressed for the day. Thoughts tumbled around her mind like clothes in a dryer as she dressed and pulled on her boots. As she took the dogs out for a walk around the property after bundling both herself and both pups in winter coats, her mind created fantastical theories about the culprit's identity. Her logical side shot down every one of them, concluding the prime suspect continued to be Lucas MacKenzie.

Dejected, Cate entered the castle through the kitchen door, shaking her cold coat off. "Up and about already, Lady Cate?" Mrs. Fraser inquired. She stood in the kitchen, a plaid bathrobe wrapped around cozy flannel pajamas.

"Yes," Cate confessed. "I've already enjoyed my first walk of the new year with the dogs."

"I took full advantage of my sleep-in! I don't mind getting up early, but I will admit the luxury of a long, lazy morning was welcome." Mrs. Fraser fixed two bowls of cereal and fruit.

"Need help carrying them up? Or can I bring a cup of tea to you with your breakfast?" Cate questioned.

"Nay, I've got it, Lady Cate. But thank you." The woman disappeared into the hallway. Cate noted three bowls remained. One other person had claimed their cold breakfast. Cate wasn't certain, but she guessed it was William Smythe.

Her guess was confirmed as she stripped off the dogs' coats. Mr. Smythe, already dressed in a casual outfit, wandered into the kitchen, placing his bowl in the sink and setting about washing it.

"Good morning, Cate," he said in his usual tone. If Cate hadn't known she wouldn't have guessed he'd had a late night.

"Good morning. I hope you slept well and enjoyed a late morning," Cate answered, picking up a towel to dry the bowl and spoon and put them away.

"Yes," he responded. "And I plan a leisurely day. I spotted a detective novel in your library and with any luck, I will polish it off in one day! If I manage it, this shall have been one of the most successful leisure trips I've ever taken! If I'm needed, I shall be in my room."

"I won't hold you back," Cate promised. "Enjoy your book!" Mr. Smythe gave her a curt but genuine smile before disappearing down the hall. Cate marveled at the man. He considered completing two thousand-piece jigsaw puzzles and polishing off a detective novel the definition of a successful trip. What a unique individual. Although, with the long hours the man put in, these activities represented leisure to him.

Cate ushered the dogs upstairs to her suite. The rest of the household still slumbered, and she intended to retreat to her room with the employment and household records for 1925 to determine if she could discern any additional information about her newest suspects.

Cate retrieved the records along the way and fished out the two bones Mrs. Fraser had provided for the pups the night before. A pleasant fire warmed the sitting room when she returned. Mr. Fraser must have built the fire while Mrs. Fraser fetched their breakfast. Cate appreciated the simple gesture, which brought a measure of warmth and calm to the room. She settled the dogs with their bones near the fireplace.

Cate settled on the floor near the dogs. She laid out each item in a semi-circle around her, setting her note sheets and pen in her lap. Cate picked up the employment ledgers first, studying them in depth around the dates when each employee departed. She scanned the pages for notations, differences in payments, anything that may suggest a reason for leaving.

There were no special notes listing reasons for departure for any of the five employees Cate flagged. Cate didn't expect there would be. She hoped to get lucky, but luck was not on her side. She tossed the book aside, sighing and staring at the pile of other records she'd retrieved. She'd spend her afternoon digging through these, looking for a needle in a haystack.

As she contemplated the work ahead of her, a quiet knock sounded at the door. "Come in, it's open!" she shouted. She shuffled through paperwork as the door opened. As she glanced up, she spotted Molly slipping in.

"Good morning, Lady Cate," Molly greeted her, joining her on the floor. "Or, gosh, afternoon, I guess!"

Cate chuckled, setting the papers on the floor. "Good day," Cate decided on. "Did you sleep well?"

"I did," Molly responded, stretching. "What a party!"

Cate nodded, raising her eyebrows. "Yes," Cate answered. "Last year for New Year's Eve, I was asleep before the ball dropped. How life changes."

Molly agreed, nodding. "Last year, I was married," she lamented.

"O-Oh," Cate stuttered, her voice dropping to a whisper. "Molly, I'm sorry. I didn't mean…"

Molly waved her hand in the air, interrupting Cate. "No, no. I didn't mean that as a bad thing. I wasn't reminiscing of better times. I was recalling a WORSE time."

Cate offered a tight-lipped smile, grabbing Molly's hand. After a few breaths, Molly continued, "That's part of the reason I came here today. It's been a couple of weeks since I arrived. I just wanted to let you know how happy I am you offered me the position and I accepted."

Cate gave her a fuller smile, her face brightening at Molly's admission. "That party was like a fairytale. And I'm LOVING the job here. I get to cook and bake, which is one of my favorite things to do. I live in a CASTLE! The grounds here are beautiful. It's like I'm living a dream."

"The only problem is that nasty boss you have," Cate quipped.

Molly burst into laughter, throwing her head back and holding her stomach. "Yes, her. She's just terrible. She makes Jeff look like a saint." Molly wiped a tear from her eye as she collected herself. "Oh my," she said with a final chuckle. "In all seriousness, though, I love it here. THANK YOU for offering me this position." She grabbed Cate's hand, squeezing it.

"I'm glad it's working out for you, Molly. It's a big change. I love it here, but that doesn't mean it's for everyone. Scottish country life is quiet. Some people would hate it here. I'm glad you don't! And I'm glad you told me. You know me, I'd worry about your acclimation otherwise."

Molly nodded. "I realized that," she replied. "That's why I wanted to tell you how I felt. I'm in love with my life now. For the first time EVER. And I mean that. I wasn't this happy even when I was a newlywed." Molly sighed, staring into the fireplace. "In retrospect, I suppose I realized then Tom and I weren't right for each other. But I just kept on clinging to that idea that we were." She shook her head. Her eyebrows raised, and a smile brightened her face. "But everything worked out, everything is corrected. Perhaps I had to suffer through that to realize where I was supposed to be. Otherwise, maybe I'd not have had the courage to move to a new country."

"That's a good attitude to have," Cate agreed.

"It's easy to look at it that way when it's the best decision of my life!"

Cate pulled her into a hug. "I'm so glad this worked out and we're both happy here!"

Molly squeezed her back in the embrace. After they let go, Molly stared at the mess on the floor. "Research?"

Cate nodded. "Yeah. Figured I'd spend a lazy day in front of the fire sorting through some records for my book."

"Only you consider this a lazy day," Molly chuckled. "I remember finding you sprawled at a library table many a day like this at Aberdeen."

"It's mindless work to do while I'm still sleepy," Cate admitted.

"Did you get any sleep?" Molly inquired.

"Yes, I did. But I was awake early. Residual energy from the party, I guess," Cate responded with a shrug.

Molly gave her a coy smile. "You are turning into quite the countess."

It was Cate's turn to roar with laughter. "Oh, right. I'm such an outstanding partier."

"I'm serious!" Molly contended. "You are the picture of grace. Composed, polite, kind and beautiful."

Cate blushed at the string of compliments. "Thank you," she replied in a hushed tone.

"Your dress last night… stunning. So elegant, so perfect."

"Thanks," Cate answered, color rising in her cheeks from

the compliment. "Your dress was great too. You looked like you came right off a magazine page!"

"I sort of did," Molly admitted. "I bought a knock-off of a dress a celebrity wore on the red carpet! I will not ask for a 'Who wore it best' poll, but…"

"Well, I'd vote for you! You looked like a million bucks! And those shoes were to die for!"

"Ah," Molly corrected. "A million pounds here. Oh… wait, that sounds bad." Molly chuckled at her own joke. Cate giggled, too. "Anyway, you are really the definition of aristocratic breeding, even if you didn't grow up in it!"

"You may be going too far," Cate countered. "But I appreciate your sentiments. I've really grown up since I've come. It's been easy though, like you said. I'm living most people's fantasy."

"No one deserves it more than you, Cate."

"Speaking of fantasies," Cate said after a pause, changing the subject. "I emailed Maggie. She'd like to visit in the spring. So, looks like we'll be entertaining again in a few months!"

"That will be fun! She'll LOVE this place. What with that antique shop? She'll be exploring your house like it's an auction. May want to check her suitcase before she leaves, in case she tries to smuggle anything to her shop," Molly joked.

Cate laughed. "I'll hide the silverware," she giggled.

Molly pulled her phone from her pocket as she chuckled at Cate's joke. "Here's the picture I snapped of us last night," Molly said, swiping at her phone. "We should send it to Maggie. I'm going to have it printed and framed." Molly faced the phone's display toward Cate. Cate studied the screen, recalling posing for the selfie with Molly. Their smiles beamed back at her. Their arms around each other, cheeks together, they appeared the vision of happiness.

Molly's assessment was correct. The photo documented a great memory.

"Aw," Cate exclaimed. "Can you print one for me too? I'd like to frame it and put it on my mantle. I love it! Our first holiday!"

"Sure thing! When I was scrolling through my pictures from last night, I fell in love with this one. Well," Molly said, slapping her hands on her thighs. "I'll let you get back to it. I just wanted to express my gratitude again and make sure you realized just how happy you made me."

Cate smiled at her. "I'm so glad! And you don't have to keep thanking me. I'm just as grateful you're here. So, thank you for taking the job! You were always a good friend to me while I was at Aberdeen College, glad I could return the favor."

Molly pulled Cate into a tight hug. "Have fun with your restful work." She giggled as she climbed to her feet, shaking her head at Cate's version of relaxation.

Cate's eyes followed her as she exited the room, pulling the door closed behind her. The exchange left Cate contented and upbeat. She dove back into her work with renewed enthusiasm.

She spent the entire afternoon and early evening pouring over the records. She took two brief breaks to take the dogs for a quick walk and retrieve sandwiches from the kitchen. During one trip, she ran into Gayle, who was also using the day to relax with a book in the library. It seemed everyone was enjoying their lazy vacation day.

As Cate munched on a cold roast beef sandwich, she poured over a personal accounts book. Number after number floated past her eyes. Dress expenses, personal investments, allowances. Cate's eyes glossed over. As week after week, month after month passed, Cate began to doubt she'd find anything. When she reached August, she considered giving up. She figured since she was over halfway finished, she'd press on and finish the book.

As Cate worked through the September records, she found an entry that almost made her drop her sandwich. Riley's head popped up, hoping for a bite of the roast beef if it landed on the floor. Cate caught it before it hit the floor. She stowed the sandwich on its plate on the table near her as she peered more intently at the entry that caught her eye. Listed in the register book was the entry *Wedding Gift - Mr. and Mrs. William and Bertha Barrow*. The names seemed familiar. She shuffled through her papers, locating the suspect list she'd made. She scanned it and found William Barrow and Bertha MacIntyre. It couldn't be a coincidence. William and Bertha departed in the same month. And in that same month, the MacKenzies of 1925 gave one William Barrow and his new wife, Bertha, a wedding gift.

Cate smiled. The two staff members had likely met, fallen in love and married, leaving the estate for another opportunity after their marriage. This lowered them on the suspect list, given the obvious reason they departed. Cate noted it, pushing them to the bottom of the list and placing a large question mark next to them to signify her doubtfulness as to their guilt.

The list was narrowing. Unfortunately, her ancestors remained at the top. Still, she'd made good progress. Satisfied with her work, she snapped the register book shut. She and Jack would have a good start on their investigation. They'd concentrate on the individuals on this list when they returned to 1925 to investigate.

Cate cleaned up the mess she'd created, returning all her sources to the office files. She used the rest of the evening to relax with a movie.

Cate rose early the next morning. Breakfast would be

served early to accommodate Mr. Smythe and Gayle's early departure. Cate met them in the dining room.

"Good morning," Cate greeted them as she entered.

"Good morning, Cate," Gayle responded. "I was just mentioning to Mr. Smythe how sad I am to leave. It was a lovely visit with two lovely parties included."

"I'm so glad you enjoyed it. I'll miss you both, but I'm glad you enjoyed your stay."

"Most enjoyable!" Mr. Smythe agreed.

"Did you finish your mystery novel?" Cate inquired.

"Yes. Quite a good whodunit. I polished it off early last evening. So that's two puzzles and a novel I've completed. Not a bad take for this trip in my estimation. A perfect holiday," Mr. Smythe replied.

"I'm so glad you consider it a success," Cate answered.

"I consider it a success despite those tedious puzzles," Gayle added, chuckling.

"Those puzzles keep your wits sharp!" Mr. Smythe assured Gayle.

"Molly seems to be settling in well," Gayle replied after a quick eye roll at Mr. Smythe.

"Yes," Cate agreed. "She is. I spoke with her yesterday and she mentioned how at home she felt and how much she loved the new job."

"Mrs. Fraser seems quite pleased with her," Gayle added.

Cate nodded. "Yes, they get along well and Molly loves working in the kitchen as does Mrs. Fraser."

"She seems a valuable addition to the staff," Mr. Smythe agreed. "I'm so pleased it worked out so well."

"And your new addition, Bailey, seems to have settled right in, too!" Gayle mentioned.

"Oh, yes!" Cate exclaimed. "He's really coming around. And Riley is delighted with his new friend!"

"That little pup is a darling," Gayle said, referencing Riley.

"Thank you," Cate answered. "He loves life, that's for certain!"

"He seems thrilled with his new yard!" Mr. Smythe added.

"With the parties over, how will you fill your time?" Gayle questioned.

"Oh," Cate reflected on her mystery before answering, "I'm sure I'll find something to fill my time!" She paused a moment, then added, "Plus, I'm certain Mrs. Campbell will soon have the next party lined up!"

Gayle chuckled at Cate's comment. "Well, I, for one, am sad they are over. And look forward to another!"

"I look forward to having you back at the castle soon. But you don't need a party to plan a visit. You are both welcome anytime. Please just let me know when you'd like to stay, and we'll arrange it!"

"How generous of you, Cate," Gayle replied.

"I've had such a lovely time, I may take you up on that sooner rather than later."

"Please do! I'm glad you found your time here relaxing and pleasant!"

They finished their breakfast, continuing light conversation before Cate saw them off about an hour after. Cate offered a wistful wave as they pulled down the drive, sad to see her guests go. She consoled herself with a long walk of the property with her dogs. Despite the chill in the air, Cate settled on the banks of the loch for a few moments of quiet reflection.

"Well, Riley and Bailey, tomorrow we'll start exploring the theft. What do you expect we'll find?"

Riley stared back with quizzical eyes while Bailey offered a small whine. "I'll admit," Cate continued, "I'm not as excited to tackle this mystery as I was the last one. I'm a little nervous about what I'll learn about my ancestors."

As if in response, Riley climbed onto Cate's lap, settling in with a kiss to her cheek. Bailey cuddled next to her. Perhaps the dogs sensed her apprehension and hoped to assuage any trepidation on her part. Cate wrapped her arms around both pups. "You're right. No matter what I find, it'll be okay. But I'm still nervous. Don't tell Jack though," she confided to them, winking at them.

"Don't tell Jack what?" Jack inquired, appearing behind her.

Cate shook her head. "Nothing, just vetting some ideas out loud to the dogs." He settled on the ground next to her.

"Did they have any worthwhile commentary?"

"I'm afraid not," Cate told him.

"Perhaps you should try a human audience."

"That's not a bad suggestion," Cate admitted. "It might provide more feedback than a kiss on the cheek."

"So, let's have it," Jack said.

Cate sighed before plowing in to her latest research. "Well, I spent yesterday researching employment records and noting anything unusual or suspicious."

"And?"

"And… it appears my ancestors are still the most likely suspects. I found five staff members whose departures were within a year of the theft. Hardly damning evidence against them, but enough to consider them above others who stayed on for years."

"Seems fair enough," Jack commented.

"Of those five, it appears two of them left the MacKenzie employ because they married."

"Each other?"

"Yes. At least, it seems so. A maid and a footman departed the same month. Also during that month, I found a note in the private ledger entry stating an amount was paid out of that account for a wedding gift. The first and last name matched the footman, and the first name matched the maid."

"Okay, that seems a fair assumption then," Jack agreed, nodding. "So that leaves us three staff members whose departures still make them suspicious."

"Yes," Cate replied. She provided Jack with the information about the remaining staff members.

"All right," Jack answered when she finished. "Those are the folks we'll concentrate on when we begin our investigation tomorrow."

Cate nodded in agreement. "Wow, Lady Cate quiet about time travel? Not brimming with excitement? Are you ill?"

Cate giggled. "I'm not. I'm just still nervous about proving my ancestors are thieves. Solving the mystery if that is the end result seems..." Cate's voice trailed off, unable to finish the sentence.

"We have no confirmation they are the thieves. Let's start with an open mind. Perhaps we'll be proving they AREN'T thieves!"

"Open mind, right," Cate repeated.

"We have no confirmation that letter from Anne MacKenzie refers to this incident. It could be anything!"

"That's a stretch, but you're correct. We have no confirmation the letter refers to the theft."

"Of course, I'm right. I'm always right," Jack added with a wink. "I'm also freezing. I'm heading back."

"Me too," Cate replied, accepting Jack's hand to pull her to standing. "I guess we'll find out soon enough if you're right!"

"Care to make it interesting? Put a little wager on it?" Jack joked.

"What? Twenty bucks I don't descend from a line of thieves?" Cate inquired.

"Twenty pounds maybe. You live in the UK now, remember?"

"Right. Okay, twenty pounds says my ancestors committed the crime."

"You're on!" Jack replied, thrusting his hand at her. Cate grasped it, shaking on the deal.

Cate, Jack and the two pups returned to the castle, warming themselves near the kitchen stove. "Are you planning to clean up the ballroom today?" Cate questioned Jack as Mrs. Fraser and Molly finished lunch preparations.

"Yes. We're starting inside. We'll take two days with that, then move outside. The weather's supposed to improve next week. It will be easier to clear the gardens in the milder weather."

"I'd like to help with the interior at least. I'll meet you after lunch in the ballroom," Cate suggested.

"It's not necessary, Lady Cate," Jack responded. "But I'm sure I can't talk you out of it."

Cate shook her head. "Nope. I got us into this, and I'll help to get us out. At least with the interior decorations!"

"Drawing the line at the outside work?" Jack queried.

"I am. Your version of milder weather is still cold for me!" Mrs. Fraser put the finishing touches on Cate's tray, which Cate picked up before Molly could. "I've got it, Molly!"

Molly glanced to Mrs. Fraser, who nodded at her. "Often Lady Cate is too ambitious, and we let her carry her own tray."

Cate offered a wry smile at Mrs. Fraser as she called the dogs to follow her upstairs. She lunched in the library, studying notes from her book at the desk while she ate. The dogs remained quiet, napping near the fireplace, tired after the long morning walk.

Despite their quiet demeanor, Cate still eyed the bookcase across the room with suspicion. Distracted from her work, Cate approached the bookcase. No air flowed from it today. She began to question whether or not she and Jack had experienced the air flow from behind the bookcase. Were they mistaken? Nothing in the castle plans pointed toward any structures behind the bookshelf that could cause such a phenomenon. Perhaps they were barking up the wrong tree in searching.

No, Cate concluded with a shake of her head, the dogs noticed the phenomenon as well. That was what called their attention to the issue to begin with. Surely the dogs were not mistaken. Their senses were superior to Cate's human ones. Plus, the match implied air flow also. No, an air leak existed behind this bookshelf. There was no doubt.

Cate checked her timepiece, reminded that she would use it tomorrow to begin unraveling another mystery on the estate. It was already a few minutes past one. Jack and Mr. Fraser would be in the ballroom working, having finished their lunch fifteen minutes earlier.

Cate rushed to clean up her paperwork on the desk. She exited the room, glancing back at the two dogs, sleeping on the area rug near the fireplace. As she did, something caught her eye. Her brows knit together as she performed a mental calculation, glancing between the hall and the library.

She was pulled from her mental machinations by Molly, who skirted past her into the library. "Excuse me, Lady Cate. Something wrong?" Molly inquired, retrieving the empty tray.

"Oh, no," Cate assured her. "Just considering if I should move the dogs to my sitting room or leave them napping here."

"Well, you know what they say, Lady Cate," Molly began.

Cate nodded. "Let sleeping dogs lie," they said in unison.

Cate closed the doors behind them as they both departed, parting ways with Molly heading downstairs to the kitchen and Cate heading down the hall to the ballroom. "Sorry I'm late," she announced, entering the ballroom.

"You're not late, Lady Cate," Jack assured her as he and

Mr. Fraser attempted to fold a table linen. "You can't be late to a job that's not required."

Cate chuckled, more at their attempt to fold the linen than Jack's joke. "Why don't you let me take over the linen folding and you can dismantle the tables and move them?"

"Aye," Mr. Fraser agreed. "I'm afraid Emily would faint dead away if she spied our folding abilities."

Cate laughed louder at this admission. "I agree. Don't worry, my lips are sealed. I won't give away your secret."

"Thank you, Lady Cate," Mr. Fraser replied. Cate laid the tablecloth back on the table, straightening it then set about folding it into a neat square. She placed it in a nearby bin provided by the linen company. Cate continued around the room, folding table linens, napkins and runners as she went, dragging the bin behind her. Jack and Mr. Fraser followed behind her, deconstructing tables and setting them aside for the rental company to pick up.

With that work finished, they folded chairs, stacking them against the tables before finishing for the day. They planned to remove the decorations from the Christmas trees tomorrow and dismantle those to return to storage.

Cate returned to the library to collect the dogs for a pre-dinner walk. Both dogs were excited to see her after her absence, showering her with kisses and wagging tails. Cate finished her day with a relaxing meal and a movie in her sitting room.

Time travel pervaded her thoughts, crowding into every corner of her mind. She and Jack planned to travel to 1925 the following afternoon, hoping to introduce themselves to the family and gather some preliminary information.

The movie on Cate's laptop played on without Cate hearing it. Her mind ran wild with excitement and nervous anticipation. Cate doubted she'd sleep tonight. Still, she would try. After closing her laptop, Cate took the dogs for one final walk before crawling into bed and squeezing her eyes shut in her best attempt to go to sleep.

She tossed and turned for hours, practicing greeting family members from an era gone-by. She rehearsed feigning shock at the unfortunate news of the theft. Midnight came and went, leaving Cate still wide-eyed and worried. She dozed off somewhere between one and two in the morning.

CHAPTER 12

Tears streamed down Cate's face. She wiped at them with the back of her hand, feeling ridiculous and childish. As silly as it sounded, she was glad to still have Molly, the Frasers and Jack staying in the castle. Their presence, despite asleep and rooms away, calmed her frayed nerves. She'd slept only two hours before the nightmare woke her.

Her hands still trembled from the experience. But her heart rate and breathing had settled into a normal rhythm. The stress must be playing tricks on Cate's mind, she assumed. Cate recalled the dream, trying to process it.

It centered around the bookcase in the library again. A black hole filled the spot where the bookshelf once stood. Cate approached it as wind swirled around her, blowing from the void. Eerie, haunting sounds emanated from the space. Cate peered into the blackness, unable to see anything.

She grabbed a nearby flashlight, training the light into the hole. At first, she spotted nothing. Then a light beam blinded her, glaring back as though she'd turned the flashlight into her own eyes. As she squinted against the light, she lowered her flashlight, discovering a mirror in front of her.

She stared at the mirror, careful not to shine the light in such a way as to blind herself. Something was odd about the reflection. Cate glanced down at her attire. She wore a simple ensemble of leggings, a tunic and cable knit cardigan. Her brows scrunched together as she returned her gaze to the mirror. Cate's reflection wore a low-necked blue and gold-striped gown with a skirt opening to show her petticoat, a style traditional of the late 1700s. Her hair was piled high on her head with curls trailing down her neck.

The reflection stared back at her, tears streaming down her cheeks. Her mirror image's mouth opened and closed as though trying to impart some words to Cate. A shadow passed over the mirror and her reflection glanced behind herself as did Cate. She snapped her eyes back to the mirror after finding nothing lurking behind her. Her reflection continued to search behind her as darkness crept across the mirror.

Within moments, an ear-piercing shriek shattered the silence surrounding Cate. The noise, emanating from her mirror reflection, splintered the glass in the mirror. It crumbled, littering the floor with shards of glass. Cate peered at the pieces, noting movement in them. Hands trembling, Cate lifted a shard from the rubble, watching a tiny portion of the scene she witnessed in the full mirror moments ago continue to unfold.

Fireballs rained from an unknown source, landing and exploding with a spray of flame and earth. Cate's reflection passed by, racing away from the unknown attacker. Cate watched for another few breaths before she dropped the shard.

The ground shuddered beneath her and a deafening noise tore through the room. Cate's ears rung from the sound and she pushed herself up to sitting from where she had fallen when the foundations of the castle shook. Disoriented, Cate tried to stand, but a second explosion knocked her off her feet again as it blasted through the castle's exterior wall.

Cate crawled to the window, gazing out at the hellish landscape. Black clouds blocked out the sun. Fires raged across the grounds. Bolts of lightning streaked across the sky. Cate's eyes widened as a large fireball hurled straight toward her.

The dream ended before she was struck but still prompted her to bolt upright, her chest heaving and heart pounding. Tears flowed from her eyes as she clutched her bedsheets. The realization set in that it had only been a horrible nightmare. Cate recovered, gulping down a few deep breaths while chiding herself about her foolish reaction, allowing a dream to disconcert her this much.

Still, Cate's mind remained troubled as she eased back into the pillows. She'd never struggled with nightmares before. This continued obsession from her subconscious mind regarding the bookcase baffled her. What was her mind trying to impart?

Or was this preoccupation with the bookshelf a misdirection, a trick of her subconscious mind. Was she focusing on an easy target while her mind attempted to wrap around other stressors? Perhaps her uneasiness about her ancestor's involvement in the jewel theft was causing this. Perhaps she remained fixated on the bookcase because it held the secret unsent letter from Anne MacKenzie highlighting the family member's involvement in the episode.

Still, Cate pondered, staring out of the window at the moonlit sky, this seemed rather extreme. And why the strange clothes? If the center of her stress was the theft, why was she not dressed in clothing from the 1920s. Instead, she saw herself in clothes from a much older period. What was the connection?

Cate shook her head, returning her gaze to the ceiling above her. Perhaps she was crazy for even trying to make sense of her nonsensical dream. Often, there was no explanation, no reasoning or sense. Perhaps her overstimulated mind pasted together a variety of things to create the scenario, and it held no meaning.

Cate tried to convince herself of that idea. She repeated to herself that it was just a dream, that it had no meaning. Like a child afraid of the dark, Cate placated herself with these platitudes until she fell asleep.

Cate crawled from her bed the following morning, yawning as she plodded her way to the bathroom for a shower. Still tired when she emerged, she hoped the wintry morning air would awaken her. She gathered the dogs, taking them out before breakfast. After breakfast, she left them chewing fresh bones with Mrs. Fraser in the kitchen and made her way to the ballroom to finish assisting with the dismantling of the party decorations.

She yawned as they pulled ornaments from the tree and placed them in bins to be put away for another year. "Late night, Lady Cate?" Jack inquired as she yawned a second time.

Cate shook her head before answering, weighing how much to say. "Something like that," she decided on.

Jack peered down at her from the ladder he stood on to reach the top of the gigantic tree in the ballroom. "Uh-oh, I feel like there's more to the story."

Cate stared ahead, her mind churning about not only her

dream but their upcoming trip to the past. "Cate?" Jack questioned when she didn't respond.

"Wound up about the visit to the past later, I guess," she answered, shrugging. Jack narrowed his eyes, staring at her. "What?" she asked, shrugging again. Jack didn't respond, handing her another ornament without averting his gaze. "Okay, okay," Cate caved. "I had another nightmare about that stupid bookshelf."

"The bookshelf again?" Jack queried, climbing down from the ladder while juggling a few ornaments.

Cate sighed. "Yes, the stupid bookshelf again."

"Same thing? An open hole there?"

"Yes and no. Same thing with the gaping hole there. But then it took a weird turn. In the hole was a mirror. But when I glanced at my reflection, it wasn't me. I mean, it was me, but I wasn't dressed in the clothes I was wearing. I had on a dress characteristic of the late 1700s. Then I noticed my reflection was crying. She glanced behind her and I thought I saw something, so I did the same. Then the reflection of me started screaming, and then the mirror broke into pieces. But in the broken shards, I could still see what was happening to my reflection. There was fire everywhere. Then the next thing I knew, I was on the floor and my ears were ringing. The whole castle shook all over. I crawled over to look out the window and fire surrounded us all over the property. It was like a hellscape. It was horrible." Cate shook her head again, her brow furrowing as she recalled the terrifying dream.

Jack listened to each detail before speaking. "I'm not discounting how awful that must have been, but I wouldn't put too much stock in it, Lady Cate. We all have nightmares. As unpleasant as they are, they rarely mean anything."

Cate nodded in agreement. "Yes, I realize that. That's what I kept repeating to myself last night. But..."

"But?"

"But I keep experiencing these dreams. They're getting harder and harder to discount as nothing when they continue to crop up."

Jack nodded at her. "Yes, I understand that. Perhaps it has something to do with the investigation we're about to embark on. Maybe once we get a better handle on it, they'll die down."

"I hope so," Cate replied. "We can't begin soon enough."

"Ah, there's the Cate I know!" Jack grinned. "Excited to time travel!"

Cate chuckled, returning his smile. "Yes, despite it all, I'm excited," she admitted.

They spent the rest of the morning boxing decorations and dismantling artificial trees. Mr. Fraser had made good progress on some of the trees leading into the ballroom. They helped him finish them before lunch.

"We'll haul these up to storage this afternoon, Jack," Mr. Fraser suggested as they broke for lunch.

"Sounds good. I'll meet you here as soon as I finish the estate business with Lady Cate after lunch," Jack fibbed. Jack and Cate's estate business involved a trip to the past to begin their investigation of the jewelry theft. With the time differential that existed when they time traveled, they could spend hours in the past and only be "busy" for less than an hour in the present. No one would be any the wiser about their absence.

Cate opted to lunch in the dining room, attempting to avoid the library. Despite Jack's assurances, Cate preferred not to encourage her subconscious mind with more fuel. She consumed her lunch in record time, excitement growing for her trip to the past. She hurried upstairs, dressing in a tailored ladies' travel suit for the occasion. Jack appeared in a men's traveling suit, knocking at her door within thirty minutes of lunch.

Cate greeted him with a grin in her cloche hat. "Ah, Lady Cate, your mood has improved, I see."

"It has!" she agreed. "I must admit I'm excited to go. And you're right, whatever the outcome, it has nothing to do with me. It may be a disappointment, but I'm grateful for the opportunity to immerse myself in the culture." Cate closed the door to her sitting room behind them. "The Roaring Twenties!" Cate exclaimed, waving her arm from left to right as though the words hung in the air. "What an exciting time to go to. The world was changing, modernizing and having a fabulous time doing it! Flappers, Jazz..."

"Gangsters," Jack commented.

Cate stopped dead. "In America!" she corrected him.

"Still too close for comfort," Jack responded.

Cate rolled her eyes at him. "Come on, let's go," Cate waved him into the bedroom, holding out the timepiece.

"I'm glad you've gotten over your angst," Jack responded, wrapping his hand around hers. Together they rubbed the watch face. Within seconds, the second hand slowed. It continued to stall until it crept along, keeping time in the present, not in the past.

When the second hand reached its slow crawl, Cate glanced around. "We're here," she pointed out, referencing the missing dog beds.

Jack adjusted his collar. "So we are," he answered, wiping a bead of sweat from his forehead.

Cate stepped to the doors, flinging them open to the sitting room. She crossed the room, Jack following behind her. "Wait up, Cate," he whispered as they crossed the room. "We're going down the back stairs at the end of the hall, correct?"

"Correct," Cate responded. "Then sneak around the

corner and head straight to the main entrance. Fingers crossed we're well received!"

"Fingers and toes. I'm crossing everything I've got," Jack quipped. "Last time was a spectacular fail. We were caught in our backstory almost right away!"

"It should be easier to blend in this time," Cate noted, as they cracked the door to peer into the hall. "The Twenties are much less formal than the 1850s!"

"At least there'll be no waltzing," Jack replied. "All clear. Let's go." Jack pulled the door open, and they hurried down the hall, disappearing in the stairway at the end of the hall. They descended and exited the castle unseen.

Rushing around the corner, they slinked past the front windows, ducking when needed to reach the front door. Jack lifted the lion's mouth door knocker. "You sure?"

"Positive," Cate responded, recalling the last time Jack asked her this. They stood outside the castle in 1856, and Cate had felt anything but sure. This time her confidence was bolstered. Not only by their previous experience, but also because the time period was far closer to their time than the previous. It should make blending in easier than when they traveled to 1856.

Still, nervous butterflies flitted around Cate's stomach as the door opened. "May I help you?" a large man with a deep voice inquired.

"Mr. and Mrs. Jack MacKenzie to see Rory MacKenzie. I'm a distant cousin."

The man raised thick eyebrows, questioning, "Are you expected?"

Jack shook his head. "We didn't send a letter, as we weren't sure if my schedule would allow us to visit. Lucky for us, it did! So, we took a chance!"

The man frowned but stood aside. "Please come in. I will

announce you to Count and Countess MacKenzie." The butler ushered them into the sitting room.

"He didn't seem pleased," Jack noted as the doors closed behind them.

"No," Cate admitted. "I hope Rory and Anne are friendlier."

"You and me both or our investigation may be finished before we start it."

The doors swung open, interrupting their conversation. A tall man entered the room, his athletic form hidden under a men's day suit. Thick, dark, curly hair topped his head and piercing blue eyes, deep set in his face, stared at them. He had a friendly countenance. There was no mistaking him as a MacKenzie. Cate saw the resemblance between this man and his grandfather, Randolph.

"Cousin Jack," the man greeted them, holding his hand out as he stepped toward them. "Rory MacKenzie."

Jack took his hand, giving it a long, firm shake. "Jack MacKenzie, distant relative. Very distant. Pleasure to meet you! And this is my wife, Cate."

"Mrs. MacKenzie," Rory said, turning his attention to her.

"Lord MacKenzie," Cate returned, taking his hand in a light handshake.

"Lord MacKenzie was my father. I'm Rory," he answered. "My wife, Anne, should be along any moment, I'd expect. What brings you to Dunhaven?"

"Land," Jack answered.

"In the market for a castle?" Rory asked with a chuckle.

Jack laughed. "Not quite. But I'm in land management. I search for properties that might interest my clients. They hire me to do their legwork. We were in the general area and hoped to stop in. I wasn't sure how long my business would take. Some of the clients can be picky."

"How fortunate your latest clients allowed you time to visit us. Are you able to stay long?"

"Given the conclusion of my last land deal, we were hoping to take a vacation in the Scottish countryside for a week or two. Perhaps discover some of my heritage."

The doors reopened, and a woman entered. In a day dress, she wore her dark hair swept into a low bun at the nape of her neck but full around the face. "Ah, please meet my wife, Anne," Rory introduced them. "Anne, this is a cousin of mine, Jack MacKenzie and his wife, Cate."

"Pleased to meet you," Jack and Cate echoed to the woman.

"Have you ordered tea yet?" Anne inquired of Rory.

"Not yet." Anne traveled to the wall, pulling a cord to ring for the butler. "Won't you both have a seat and we can get better acquainted? Anne, Jack was telling me they plan to vacation in the countryside for a week or two after the conclusion of a successful land deal."

"How lovely," Anne answered, taking a seat opposite Jack and Cate who had settled on a loveseat. The frowning butler entered the room and Anne ordered tea from him, calling him Benson.

They made small talk regarding the castle and neighboring town until Benson returned with a tea tray. "Excuse me, m'lord," Benson said, clearing his throat. "Might I have a brief word outside."

"Please excuse me for just a moment," Rory said as Anne poured and offered tea to Cate, then Jack.

Anne asked how Cate enjoyed Scotland, realizing her accent was American. After Cate answered, assuring her she found the country charming, Anne informed them that Rory's brother, Lucas, was staying at the castle for the holidays. She assured them he and his wife would be interested to meet Jack and Cate. Cate's pulse quickened at the mention of his name. Not only her great-grandfather, Lucas was also her top suspect. As Cate attempted to settle her racing pulse, Rory returned. Anne gazed at him with questioning eyes.

"My sincerest apologies, you've caught the household in quite the uproar, I'm afraid," Rory explained.

"It's my turn to apologize," Jack responded. "We took a chance on visiting and with no notification, appear to have caught you at an inopportune time."

Rory waved his hand in the air, dismissing Jack's concern. Anne glanced to the floor before making eye contact with Jack and Cate. "We've suffered an unfortunate incident," she admitted.

Jack pressed his hand to his chest. "Oh, there's no need to rehash any details on our account."

"You'll read about it in all the local papers, sure enough," Rory assured him.

"Yes, it's a tawdry story that's quite captured the town's interest, I'm afraid," Anne admitted. "Following our annual New Year's Eve party, some of the family's more precious jewelry pieces were stolen. Quite the story in these parts, a brazen theft right from under the family's nose."

"The police are still mucking about the estate, searching for the culprit."

"How terrible," Jack feigned shock. "Have they any leads?"

Anne shook her head. Rory responded, "No. The police have done nothing thus far but wave their hands and inconvenience my holiday guests."

"Yes," Anne agreed. "The poor Richardsons were scheduled to depart today and have been asked to stay for several more days. I daresay any future guests may shy away from us with this fiasco."

"Don't fret over it, Anne, fair-weather friends are not friends."

"I understand. However, I feel terribly responsible. It was

I who suggested we secure the jewelry the following day rather than immediately following the party. Careless of me, I realize."

"Anne, it was not your fault," Rory assured her.

Anne pressed her lips together, tilting her head as though considering the idea. Then she shook her head as though dismissing it. "My apologies for seeming curt, but if you'll excuse me, I'd like to lie down. I am not feeling at all well."

Jack stood as Anne rose from her seat. "Not at all, Countess MacKenzie. I hope you recover soon."

"Thank you. And please, call me Anne." Anne left the room as Cate took another sip of her tea.

"Again, apologies," Rory said as the doors shut behind Anne. "Anne has taken the theft quite badly. It upsets her to no end."

"Understandable," Jack answered, reclaiming his seat next to Cate. "Ah, if you don't mind me sticking myself where I don't belong, my wife, Cate, is quite the amateur sleuth. Perhaps she could help solve the case. She's even helped the police in solving a murder once."

Rory's eyebrows raised, glancing to Cate. "Really?"

"Yes," Jack answered for her, placing his arm around Cate's shoulders. "Cleared an innocent man's name!"

"Bravo, Mrs. MacKenzie," Rory responded.

"Please, call me Cate," Cate answered. "And thank you. I seem to have a knack for mysteries. I'd love to assist in any way I can. Especially if it can help ease Anne's nerves. Poor lady."

"Oh, but I wouldn't dream of asking you to spend your travels lurking around the depths of our castle in search of lost jewels."

"I can't imagine a trip more interesting or memorable for my Cate," Jack responded with a loud laugh. "It's the least we can do for showing up on your doorstep unannounced."

"No, no. Do not trouble yourselves about that. We're happy to have met you and hope to entertain you more than once over your stay here. I suppose if you'd find the challenge entertaining, I've no objections," Rory agreed. "Typically I'd decline your kind offer, but poor Anne has herself tied in knots over this. Perhaps you'll be more effective than these bumbling detectives The Yard has sent." Rory rolled his eyes.

"I've never met a mystery I couldn't solve, so I hope to have the jewels back in your possession in short order!" Cate exclaimed.

"Tell you what, why don't you stop by tomorrow? The detectives will return in the mid-afternoon. You can discuss the details with them over afternoon tea," Rory suggested. "Unless you have plans for the day already."

"That sounds perfect. We've no solid plans for our stay as yet," Cate informed Rory.

"Well, then allow me to get onto your schedule again before it fills. If you'd join us for dinner on Monday, you can meet more of the family. My brother Lucas and his wife, Amelia, are staying with us."

"How charming, that sounds lovely, thank you," Cate answered, glancing to Jack.

"Yes," he added, "a most gracious invitation. We would be happy to join you. Is 6 p.m. appropriate to arrive?"

"Yes, that should be perfect," Rory answered. "Are you staying in town?"

"No," Jack informed him. "We're in neighboring Canberry."

"Ah," Rory answered. "That seems a bit of an inconvenience for you. What with the traveling back and forth. Why not stay with us?"

"We couldn't possibly inconvenience you that way," Jack replied.

"Inconvenience? Hogwash! Your wife has just offered to help solve the theft, and I've pressured you both into being here over the next two days! The least we can do is offer you a room." Rory seemed as personable as his grandfather, Randolph.

"There's no guarantee how long this may take, we'd prefer not to take the chance of wearing out our welcome," Jack dodged.

"Nonsense! Have your luggage sent for, you'll stay here." Rory strode to the wall, pulling the bell alerting the servants.

"Oh..." Jack's voice faltered as he searched for words to rescue them from the situation. Cate's jaw dropped open as she glanced wide-eyed at Jack. She shrugged as Benson entered the room.

"Benson, Mr. and Mrs. MacKenzie will be staying with us going forward. Mrs. MacKenzie is an amateur detective and has taken on our missing jewelry case. Prepare a room for them. Perhaps the suite at the end of the unused hall. It should allow Mrs. MacKenzie sufficient privacy and room to conduct her investigation."

"Yes, m'lord, very good." Benson disappeared from the room to handle Rory's request.

"This is very generous, Rory," Jack said, standing. "But please, there's no need to send for our luggage. We'll return for it, stay the night in Canberry and return tomorrow following lunch."

"If you're sure," Rory replied. "Whatever you judge is best."

"Well, we should be off," Jack announced, glancing to Cate who set her saucer and teacup down on the coffee table and stood. Jack extended his hand to Rory. "I can't tell you what a pleasure it was to meet you, cousin."

"The pleasure is all mine," Rory assured him, grasping his

hand. "And quite a stroke of luck! I hope your wife can assist us."

"I've no doubt she can," Jack answered. Cate said her goodbyes. Rory walked them to the front door, seeing them out. Cate and Jack walked down the drive, silent at first.

As they passed a row of hedges, Jack cut in behind them, making the circle back to the castle. "Should we..." Cate began.

Jack raised his hand to halt her speaking. "Later," he grumbled. Cate bit her tongue as they approached the castle. Using a back entrance, they snuck inside and crept unseen to what would become Cate's bedroom. Without a word, they used the timepiece to return to the present.

Once returned, Jack dropped the time piece, wandering away while exhaling a loud breath. He doubled over, hands on his knees.

"Should we talk about it?" Cate inquired.

Jack snickered. "Talk about what a bad turn the situation just took."

Cate sighed. "Or how we're planning to pull this off. I mean, staying at the castle?" Cate paced the floor. "There's no way we can be present for everything, meals, family time, the works."

"And there was no avoiding it. He didn't give us a choice. I had to accept."

"Yes, I know. You didn't have a choice."

"No, at least I bought us some time until tomorrow."

"I hope it's enough to figure this out."

"Look, Cate, perhaps we should just quit while we're ahead. Never return, just leave things go," Jack suggested.

"What?" Cate glanced up sharply at him. "No! No way!"

"Cate," Jack cautioned, "this is way beyond what we can pull off. We can't go missing from the castle in either time and we can't keep dancing back and forth between past and present. We'll run ourselves ragged between the time added to our days and the constant costume changes."

Cate nodded her head. "I agree. This presents us with quite the sticky wicket." Jack remained silent. "But I don't agree that we can't find a way around it."

"You're being a little too optimistic."

"And you're being too pessimistic. We'll figure something out. We have until tomorrow afternoon. If we don't find a solid solution, my vote is we go back and take things as they come. It's not like we can't return if things get too difficult. We'll be in the castle! It'll be easy to slip away and head back."

Jack dropped his head back between his shoulder blades. "Oh, Cate," he groaned, shaking his head, "I'll never understand how your mind works."

"What?" Cate questioned. "I'm just pointing out that it's not the end of the world. We may be able to pull this off after all. And if we can't, so what? We just come home! And we're already in the castle to do that!"

"You're right about that. At least we'll have easy access to the time rip. Okay, I'm convinced. We'll go back tomorrow as planned. You speak with the police and we'll figure things out from there. If worse comes to worst, we can always feign sightseeing or some other nonsense to get us out of family obligations."

"That's the spirit!" Cate replied, grinning at him. "Plus, things have taken an interesting turn in terms of suspects. Who are the Richardsons? Could they have reason to steal the necklaces?"

"I suppose we'll find out, won't we?" Jack answered.

"We will! Well, I suppose after I change, I had better pack us a few suitcases that we can carry with us tomorrow."

"Suppose so," Jack answered with a sigh.

They parted ways to change and, after an afternoon walk with the dogs, Cate spent the remaining time before dinner packing for their stay at Dunhaven Castle in 1925. Cate filled the luggage with multiple items for each of them, ranging from day clothes to evening wear. Her background as a historian assisted her in selecting the items they would need to fit in during this era. They could then leave the suitcases in the past, adding to their ruse of staying at the castle. Cate hoped they could pull off the subterfuge. Despite her trepidation about identifying her ancestor as the culprit, she still hoped to solve the mystery.

CHAPTER 13

Cate bounded from her bed with a mix of excitement and anxiety filling her. She cursed having to wait until afternoon to travel. She attempted to spend most of her morning keeping busy, either with trekking around the property with Riley and Bailey or working on her research. She spent her work time in the sitting room, still avoiding the library. While she felt foolish, she explained it away to herself and Mrs. Fraser as a need for a change in scenery to motivate and assist her in making progress.

The move failed to effect much change. Her progress remained slow, her mind distracted by her upcoming travel. After lunch, Cate hurried to her room, dressing for the trip. She fussed with the finger curls she put in her hair, trying her best to style them like Anne's. She changed clothes to a 1925-appropriate outfit and waited for Jack's knock at her sitting room door.

Cate perched on the edge of her chaise, gazing at the two pups who chased each other around, play-fighting over a toy moose. She blew out a long breath, catching Riley's attention.

He pranced over to Cate, sniffing her clothes then staring at her as though demanding an explanation.

Cate smiled at him, ruffling the fur on his head with her fingers. "What do you think, Riley? Do I look like I belong in the Roaring Twenties?"

Bailey joined them while Riley eyed Cate. "Care to give your opinion, Bailey?"

Neither dog offered their thoughts. "I guess I'm a little early," Cate admitted, drumming her fingers on the chaise's seat. "Jack and I got ourselves into some hot water yesterday and I'm not sure how we're going to handle it, so I'm a bundle of nerves." Riley cocked his head to the side. "Yes," Cate continued, "I'm not sure how we're going to handle this, but I'm determined to try."

A knock sounded at the door. "That must be my partner in crime now!" Cate announced to the pups. They stared at the door as Cate hurried to open it. Jack entered and Riley raced toward him.

"Hello, Sir Riley," Jack called as Riley leapt into his arms. "Have you talked Lady Cate out of her crazy plan?" Riley offered a lick of Jack's cheek in response. "I'll take that as a no. How about you, Bailey?" Jack asked the other pup who stood at his feet.

"It's a no," Cate assured him.

"I figured as much," Jack admitted. "So, it's up to me, I guess. Cate, are you sure about this? Rory seems… savvier than Randolph."

Cate shrugged. "He may be, but he seemed friendly enough. If things go wrong, we come back and we don't return. Simple as that."

"I have the impression it will not be 'simple as that' when it comes down to it."

Cate shrugged, playing innocent. She led him to the bedroom. "I've got suitcases packed. We can leave them there to keep up the ruse we're staying. That should help with our cover up."

Jack blew out a breath. "I should have said we were staying in Dunhaven," he lamented.

"No, the other town was a good call," Cate replied. "That's what gave us away to Randolph. We said we were staying in town and no one in town knew us."

"Yes. But we landed ourselves in a world of trouble, anyway."

Cate shrugged. "At least we've not gotten ourselves caught yet! See, we're improving!"

"I REALLY need your optimism, Lady Cate," Jack quipped. "Well, I suppose if we're going to do this, we may as well go." Jack held out his hand for the timepiece.

Cate grinned at him. Despite the danger, excitement brimmed in her. Instead of the timepiece, though, she offloaded a suitcase into his hands. She grabbed her own along with another case, jostling them into one hand's grasp. Then she offered the timepiece. Jack sighed, closing his hand around hers and they activated the mysterious mechanism controlling the time rip. As the second hand slowed to a crawl, Cate and Jack slipped back into another era.

Cate glanced around the room, confirming it was devoid of her personal effects. "We're here," she breathed.

"For better or worse," Jack replied. "I hope we can sneak out with these things without any trouble!" Jack waved the suitcase in the air.

"It's not too heavy. I can still hurry," Cate assured him.

"Give me yours," Jack insisted. Cate opened her mouth to protest, but the expression issued by Jack stopped her. She handed the suitcase off, keeping her train case. "Okay," Jack answered with a nod of his head. "Here we go." They exited the bedroom, crossing the sitting room. Jack eased the door open, peering through the crack. He held a finger to his lips, motioning with his head toward the hall. Cate nodded, understanding his signal to mean someone was in the hallway. They waited a few moments in silence, Cate holding her breath, afraid even the sound of light breathing may give them away. After a few moments, Jack peered through the opening between the doors again. This time he offered a thumbs up to Cate. They proceeded down the hall, hurrying to reach the stairway. They scrambled down and were able to exit the castle.

As they circled toward the front entrance, Jack wiped a bead of sweat from his brow. "Too heavy?" Cate quipped, motioning toward the suitcases.

"This whole situation is too heavy," Jack bantered. They reached the main entrance and Jack used the door knocker to summon Benson. The butler showed them into the sitting room, assuring them he would have their luggage placed in their room.

Cate and Jack waited. Jack's leg bobbed up and down. Cate placed her hand on his knee to steady it. "Sorry," he apologized, "I'm nervous."

"You don't say," Cate joked.

He wiped at his brow again. "I can't believe you're not," he commented.

"I didn't say that. I'm just better at hiding it."

The doors to the sitting room swung open and Rory entered. "Jack, Cate," he greeted them, approaching with his hand out. Jack rose and shook his hand, then Rory embraced Cate. "Glad you made it. I didn't hear a car." He glanced to Jack.

"Oh, we walked from the property edge," Jack explained.

"Ah. Carrying luggage? Your American wife must be made of strong stuff!"

"That she is," Jack assured him.

"Well, allow me to show you to your room. You'll find it suitable, I'd imagine, to continue your work."

Rory motioned for them to exit the room. They stepped out into the hallway and waited for Rory to lead them upstairs. "Thank you again, cousin, for offering the room. It is very generous of you to welcome us this way."

"Not at all," Rory commented as they made their way up the main staircase. They traversed the halls with Rory leading them to the hallway they had just navigated to sneak from the castle. As he marched down the hall toward the room they had just come from, Cate hoped the surprise on her face was not apparent. Could he be placing them in the exact room she used nearly a century later?

Cate glanced to Jack, who gave a slight shrug to acknowledge the strange situation. Sure enough, Rory led them to Cate's suite's doors. He opened them, stepping inside and motioning for them to enter. "I hope you'll find this suitable."

Cate swallowed, stepping into the room and pretending to the best of her ability to act as though it was the first time she saw it. "It's lovely!" she exclaimed.

"Yes," Jack agreed.

Rory closed the doors behind them. "And I believe best suited to your travels back and forth between here and your own time."

Cate's stomach somersaulted, and she glanced to Jack, wide-eyed.

"Ahhhhh," Jack began, unsure what to say.

"You are time travelers, aren't you?" Rory pressed.

"Time travelers?" Jack repeated as though unfamiliar with the concept. He creased his brow, playing confused.

Cate followed his lead. "What an interesting concept. Most entertaining!"

Rory chuckled, narrowing his eyes. "Let's not play coy," he insisted. "I'm not outraged at your presence. Quite the opposite, I'm thankful. If you can help solve the mystery and set Anne's nerves to rest, I should be grateful."

Cate swallowed hard. She glanced to Jack and, with a shrug, said, "Okay, you caught us. We can't tell you much else, but yes, we aren't from this time."

Rory nodded, a smile on his face. "I knew it," he announced. "My instincts were correct."

"But how?" Jack questioned.

"Two things," Rory explained. "First, your names. Jack and Cate MacKenzie. When I was a boy, my grandfather told me a fantastical tale about two time travelers that saved his life. He told me one day I'd understand more about the story, but when I was a child, the legend of these two time traveling heroes filled my imagination. Their names: Jack and Cate MacKenzie."

Jack rolled his eyes at their foolish gaffe of using the same names as when they had visited Rory's grandfather, Randolph MacKenzie's era in 1856.

"And the second thing?" Cate inquired.

Rory paced the room in front of them. "I'll admit, after hearing your names I was suspicious, but I wasn't sure until you told me the second piece of information." He spun to face Jack. "You, Jack, mentioned Cate helped solve a murder and saved an innocent man's life. That coincided with my grandfather's story. I put the pieces together and bet you were the same two who'd helped him."

Cate and Jack shared a glance. "That makes it official then," Jack declared.

"Official?" Rory queried.

"Yes. We are officially the worst time travelers ever."

Rory burst out laughing. "It can't be easy maintaining your cover when the castle's proprietor is aware of the secret. Oh, on that note, my brother, Lucas, is unaware of the astonishing secret protected within these walls."

"Understood," Cate answered, nodding. "We don't plan on spreading that information. We were only hoping to help solve the mystery."

"And again, I am most grateful. I'm afraid Anne's taken the loss badly. She feels responsible for the loss of the keepsakes. They were my grandmother's jewels. Oh, but you probably realize that. You were acquainted."

Cate nodded again. "Yes. In fact, I wore one of the necklaces to the Halloween Ball she hosted."

"How fascinating. I must admit, I'm not as adventurous as my great-great-grandfather, Douglas, nor as you, Jack and Cate. I don't do much time traveling."

"It's not all it's cracked up to be," Jack admitted.

Rory offered a small chuckle. "If I am correct, this room leads to this year. So, you may use it as a conduit to shuttle back and forth between times. This should make your comings and goings easier."

"Yes, it will. Thank you," Cate answered.

"Well, with that settled, I'll leave you to discuss your plans before the police arrive. They plan to be here midafternoon. You may speak with them then about the investigation. I shall tell them to provide you with any information you request." Rory strode to the doors leading to the hall. "Oh," he mentioned, turning back, "will you be dining 'in town' this evening?"

"Yes," Cate replied. "But we will still join you for dinner tomorrow if the offer still stands."

"It most certainly does. I shall tell Anne that you plan to take in sights in the area whilst here, that will explain your absences without trouble."

"Thank you, Rory," Cate answered with a smile.

Rory exited the room, closing the doors behind him. Jack collapsed onto the chaise lounge, exhaling loudly. "Oh, you've got to be kidding me!" he exclaimed after a moment.

Cate sunk onto the chaise next to him, her hands clasped as she leaned on her thighs. "We really are the worst time travelers ever, aren't we?"

Jack gave her a sidelong glance. "Yes, we are. We are oh-for-two on these trips."

"Using the same name was not that smart in retrospect."

"No. We should have made up different names. Like Hank and Beth MacKenzie or something."

Cate wriggled her nose. "Hank and Beth?"

"Yeah, Hank and Beth."

Cate shrugged. "Oh well. At least, it worked out. Rory was extremely accommodating. And it only makes our work easier!"

"Lucky us!" Jack retorted, his voice thick with sarcasm.

"Now all we have to do is prove my great-grandfather isn't a thief. Then we can chalk this up to another successful venture!" Cate stood. "Come on. Let's see if the police have arrived."

"Ugh," Jack grumbled but climbed to his feet. "My heart is just returning to normal speed."

Cate giggled at him. "Oh, come on, you need some excitement in your life!"

Jack and Cate traversed the halls, arriving in the foyer as Rory escorted the police from his study. "Ah, how fortunate! This is the woman I was speaking of," Rory informed the officer. "I'd appreciate it if you'd fill her in on any details. Her reputation at solving crimes is most exceptional. You can speak in the sitting room."

The officer studied Cate up and down with a grunt. "Follow me," he barked at her.

Cate and Jack began to follow the man through the doors when he stopped short. "You too?" he questioned, jabbing a finger toward Jack.

"If you don't mind," Jack responded.

The officer rolled his eyes. "Anyone else in the family who'd like to discuss the private details of the case?"

"No, thank you, Officer MacCullough," Rory replied, a perfect example of non-reactionary British breeding.

With another roll of his eyes, Officer MacCullough led them into the sitting room. "Shall we sit?" Cate requested, motioning toward the setup near the fireplace.

"I suppose so, Mrs., ah, MacKenzie was it?"

"Yes, that's correct. Catherine MacKenzie, Cate for short. This is my husband, Jack." Cate extended her hand to shake his, as did Jack.

"And how are you related to Lord MacKenzie?" the officer asked after grazing her hand with his in a limp handshake.

"My husband is a distant cousin," Cate explained.

"I see. Well, Lord MacKenzie asked that I share the current information about the case. Before I do so, I want to make it clear, Mrs. MacKenzie, that I prefer you do not interfere with the investigation. This is serious police business."

"I don't plan to interfere, but, as Lord MacKenzie may have mentioned, I'm good at mysteries. I'd like to assist. Poor Lady MacKenzie is beside herself."

Officer MacCullough offered another eye roll in response before continuing, reading from his tiny notebook. "I suppose you've heard the story, but here it is again. The jewelry was removed from the safe on 31 December. Lady MacKenzie selected the piece she would wear for the party and left the other piece on her dressing table. When she returned to her room following the party, the other piece of jewelry was still there. She removed her necklace and earrings, setting them next to the others in their case. She retired around 1 a.m. and when she dressed the following morning at eleven, the jewelry was discovered missing."

"Thank you for the recap, I am aware of that. What of the investigation?"

With a sigh, the officer flipped a page and continued to read. "We interviewed everyone. No clear suspects emerged."

"That's it?" Cate questioned, aghast.

"Yes, Mrs. MacKenzie, that's it. We're working with very little information here. Most people were asleep during the robbery. No one has a clear motive. For all we know, someone snuck in, grabbed the jewelry and ran off!"

"While that's a theory, I'm not sure how plausible. This would imply someone knew that Lady MacKenzie would leave the jewelry on her dressing table and could navigate to her room to retrieve it while she slept."

"Thank you for that adept analysis, Mrs. MacKenzie, but it doesn't rule out the possibility."

"No, it doesn't, but it makes it more likely that the culprit is right under our noses in the house."

The officer appeared vexed, as though his patience with the amateur detective was wearing thin. "We've interviewed everyone. Nothing's stood out. We continue to check on the statements we've taken, verify details and so on, but nothing has pointed to anyone."

"No leads? Not even a conjecture?" Cate questioned.

"We have no solid leads, Mrs. MacKenzie. If you ask me, I'd say her ladies' maid did it. The opportunity the young woman had alone makes her the primary suspect."

"That's rather prejudicial, wouldn't you say?" Cate queried.

Officer MacCullough let out a sigh. "Nothing else points to anything solid. Often hunches provide the best avenues in my experience."

Cate narrowed her eyes at him, guessing his experience was not all that vast. After a moment, she nodded. "Thank you, Officer MacCullough, for the information."

He nodded to her and turned to leave. As he reached the doors, he faced her again. "Oh, and just a reminder, Mrs. MacKenzie, I don't want you interfering in my investigation." With that, he pulled the doors open, exiting the room.

"Well, wasn't he just a big bowl of sunshine," Jack commented after he left.

Cate nodded in agreement. "He does not seem pleased about us butting into his case."

"What case? The man's done less investigating than you have, Cate."

Cate chuckled. "You may be right. And his theory that it's Murray, Anne's maid, is absurd. Based only on conjecture with nothing substantiated."

"I didn't remember her name appearing anywhere on your suspect list," Jack admitted.

"No, it doesn't. Although, I may be wrong," Cate answered with a shrug.

"I doubt it. His entire case is based on the fact that it was convenient for her to have stolen the jewelry. Yet I'm sure he has no answers about how she's disposing of it or why she's never had sticky fingers before. Certainly this isn't the first time she's handled pricey items for her ladyship."

"I agree. The case is weak. I doubt it's her." They were silent for a moment. "I don't know what we expected to be honest," Cate admitted. "We already realized the case goes unsolved. So, it isn't any wonder the police have zero theories."

"No, you're right. Looks like we have our work cut out for us then. The police won't be of any help."

"Yes. Well, perhaps we should take our leave for the day. It's almost time for the dinner gong and we're supposed to be 'dining in town' tonight. We should disappear to our room and return to our time."

"Okay, Cate," Jack agreed, happy to return to the present.

They navigated to the room. Before leaving, they unpacked a few items from their suitcases to make the room appear lived in. Cate also rumpled the bedsheets so the maids would find the bed "slept in" when they tidied the next morning. With their work complete, they returned to the present.

When they returned, Cate reminded Jack that despite Rory's invitation to dinner Monday, their dinner plans were tomorrow, Sunday. In 1925, January 5 was a Monday. Jack thanked her for the reminder before leaving to change.

After changing and eating dinner, Cate spent her evening writing notes about their journey. She tried to include all relevant details she had gleaned from the police detective, which had been few. His supposition about the maid seemed more a guess than a theory. Still, Cate noted the direction the investigation seemed to be heading.

She compared her new findings to the notes she had made prior to the trip. The new information did nothing to augment her current hypotheses regarding the guilty party's identity. The maid didn't even appear on her list of probable suspects. And Cate wasn't about to add her name, either. The notion made little sense. It was only a step away from the old "the butler did it" theory. The only names she added to the suspect list was that of the mysterious Richardsons. She wrote a note asking who they were and if they could have any motivation to have committed the theft. It was around this time that many families found themselves unable to keep up their lifestyles. Perhaps the Richardsons were one of these families. Perhaps a jewel heist would provide enough funds for them to maintain their home. It was a wild theory, but no less probable than the theory of the maid committing the crime.

Cate sighed, staring at the note sheets spread in front of her. Try as she might, willing them to provide more information failed. Frustrated, she stuffed them back into her folder and tossed it on the nearby side table. Her head sunk back onto the chaise. Perhaps she would find out more information tomorrow at dinner. She would meet the rest of the family then. She'd also meet the Richardsons. Perhaps then she could shore up or dismiss the case against them.

CHAPTER 14

Cate awoke the following morning with her mind in a knot. Her two trips to the past had clarified nothing. Instead, they'd only added two names to her list. Two names, she reminded herself, that did not represent family members, at least not to her knowledge. She'd added the Richardsons to the list, but Anne's damning note spoke to their innocence. In Cate's blind desire to make the criminal anyone but her ancestor, she'd listed them on her suspect sheet the previous evening. But now, in the cold light of day, Cate questioned her decision to do so. It was likely unfair, but she'd leave it for now.

Cate wandered the property with the dogs after breakfast. Her investigation weighed on her mind. With no leads from the police, she'd be going it alone. So far, she'd not made much progress. With any luck, meeting everyone at dinner would provide some enlightening information. But what information could she glean from light conversation over cocktails or at the dining table?

Cate's mind attempted to concoct a plan for retrieving information. However, she couldn't see a way to fish for information without being obvious, especially without knowing the players involved, their personalities and how they might react to her. Furthermore, Cate's introverted nature made her a less-than-proficient conversationalist.

Cate imagined scenario after scenario in which she might elicit information from someone without being obvious. She sighed as she stared out over the loch, frozen at the edges. None of these conversations would occur the way her mind created them. No amount of preparation would help her. Tonight, she would have to wing it.

Cate returned to the castle. She used the time after lunch to search for any details about the Richardsons of 1925. She searched through any resources from the time including photo albums for a hint of information. Cate found none. She was left to wait until their dinner engagement.

To fill the time, Cate opened the manuscript for her book. She focused long enough to type a description of Rory and Anne MacKenzie into the document. Pleased with her ability to complete even a small amount of work, she saved the document and closed her laptop. After checking the time, she realized it was nearly time to return to the past. They planned to dress for dinner in 1925 with the clothes Cate packed. However, Cate changed into a suitable dress before they departed.

Jack met her in the late afternoon, sneaking into the castle so as not to run into the castle's other occupant, Molly. He had already changed into period-appropriate clothing before they made the trip back.

"Whew!" Jack exclaimed, wiping sweat from his brow as 1925 settled around them. "I was so afraid we'd appear in front of a maid."

Cate glanced around the room. The bed was made, and the suite tidied. "If I'm not mistaken, they'd tidy the room in the morning, so we must be careful if we pop back then."

"Well, I suppose we should change for dinner," Jack admitted. "Would you like to go first?" Jack inquired, offering her the use of the bathroom.

"Thanks," she answered, pulling a dress from her suitcase. Cate entered the bathroom, fixing her hair into an updo. She touched up her makeup with the few supplies she brought with her. After slipping out of her day clothes, she pulled on the dinner gown she selected for the evening. The beige dress was heavy, the bodice made up of silver beading. Frills cascaded to the floor from the drop waist and flutter sleeves caressed her arms. Cate finished the look with a choker, popular in this era. She pulled on her shoes and emerged from the bathroom.

"Your turn," she announced.

"Wow, that's some dress!" Jack replied as he grabbed his evening clothes.

"Thanks," Cate beamed. "I thought it was rather pretty, too!"

Jack's process went much faster than Cate's. She waited for him in the sitting room, pulling on her elbow length black gloves. He emerged from the bedroom, pulling at his collar. "Could they make these any stiffer?" he grumbled.

"Stop complaining, you look great!" Cate answered, standing.

"That has less to do with the clothes and more to do with my stunning good looks, Lady Cate," Jack quipped, flashing her a grin.

"And your humility," Cate retorted with a wink.

"Aye, humble to a fault, that's me," Jack said, broadening his grin. He offered Cate his arm. "Shall we?" Cate accepted, and they sauntered to the sitting room where the family and their guests met for cocktails before dinner.

When Cate and Jack entered, Anne and Rory were

already present. Another couple sat on the loveseat across from Anne. The man rose as Cate and Jack came in.

"Ah, there you are. You see, Anne, I told you they'd be dining with us," Rory said as they entered.

"Oh! Yes, I was worried when you weren't at any of the earlier meals. I wondered if the nasty business with the police put you off."

"Not at all," Cate assured her. "We've been taking in some sights around the countryside."

"Yes," Jack added. "We left early this morning. We are early risers."

"Please allow me to introduce you to my brother, Lucas, and his wife, Amelia," Rory announced, guiding them to the other couple in the room. "Lucas, this is our distant cousin Jack MacKenzie and his wife, Cate."

Jack shook hands with Lucas and Amelia, who remained seated. "A pleasure," Lucas replied as he shook their hands. Cate swallowed hard as she gazed into the eyes of her great-grandfather. She searched them; the momentous moment tainted by her conjecture about him being a thief.

He smiled at her as she continued to stare longer than she should have. "And how are you related to us, cousin Jack?" he asked of Jack when Cate tore her eyes away, sitting down next to Amelia, her great-grandmother on the loveseat.

"Oh, ah, I'll attempt an explanation, though I'm never good at familial connections of this nature," Jack stalled. "My great-great-great… or is it great-great…"

The appearance of another couple interrupted Jack's attempts at an explanation. "Good evening," the older man greeted them. On his arm, a much younger wife.

"Ah, good evening Bryce." Cate noted the first name, Bryce Richardson. She'd search any records she could find on him when she returned. Rory made introductions, presenting Cate and Jack to the Richardsons. Cate learned

Bryce's wife's name was Eleanor. Stories like Eleanor's were familiar to Cate as a historian. Eleanor, also an American, was a "dollar princess." New money who married into British nobility. Eleanor gained a title and status while Bryce gained a fortune to keep his estate running. It was unlikely that these two had stolen the jewelry unless they had suffered some recent misfortune that resulted in the loss of Eleanor's money. Judging by the jewelry Eleanor sported, a large ruby necklace, rings on many fingers and a cascade of sparkling bracelets, this wasn't the case.

Cate surmised she could cross the couple off her suspect list. At least, she surmised, it made conversation with Eleanor easier since it thrilled the woman to no end to have found another American to talk to.

During dinner, Jack's connection to the family came up once again. Jack, looking like a deer caught in headlights, stared at Lucas as he commented, "Jack, you never finished your explanation of how you're related."

"Didn't I?" he answered, his brow furrowing as though confused. "Oh! How thoughtless of me. Well, as I began to mention, we share a…"

"Great-great-great-great-grandfather," Rory finished for him. "I believe you missed one of those greats earlier, Jack. Yes, Douglas is our common relative. Jack descends from Finlay's brother."

"Oh, yes, quite distant then," Lucas responded.

"Quite," Jack answered, nodding.

"But still carrying the MacKenzie name," Lucas added. "How interesting! How close and far we all are."

"Yes," Rory agreed. "And how fortunate to have met our relative. We are pleased you are staying with us."

"Yes. I hope to get to know you better," Lucas commented.

"Will you be staying on long?" Cate inquired.

"Lucas and Amelia planned to stay through next weekend," Anne informed her. "This dreadful investigation has stranded Bryce and Eleanor here. Oh, how we've ruined your plans."

"Think nothing of it, dear lady," Bryce assured Anne. "Paris will still be there in a few days' time."

"And how exciting to be caught up in a real mystery!" Eleanor exclaimed.

"How gracious you both are," Anne replied.

"It sounds as though we'll have the opportunity to get acquainted," Lucas followed up. "I understand you'll be staying at least a week."

"Yes," Jack assured him. "And we'd like to spend some time getting to know everyone."

Dinner conversation continued discussing various small talk items. Afterward, Cate departed with the ladies to the sitting room, allowing the men to enjoy a brandy and cigar. Cate made polite conversation, hoping to have a discussion with Lucas.

After twenty-five minutes, the men joined them in the sitting room. Cate touched base with Jack before circulating around the room to speak with others. She made her way to Lucas after speaking with Rory for a few moments.

"Jack and I are both pleased you were here for the holidays. When we chanced stopping by, we hoped to meet at least Rory. We were so fortunate to meet you both!" Cate began.

"I'm pleased to have been here to meet you also," Lucas responded.

"Do you often spend the holidays here?"

"We have since our marriage, yes. Amelia enjoys winter on the estate over the hustle and bustle of the city."

Cate nodded in understanding. "It is charming here. I see the appeal."

"So, you are enjoying our little hamlet? How does it compare to the States?"

"I am enjoying it very much," Cate answered. "Life seems so very settled here."

"Do you find us very quaint compared to life there?"

"Not at all. A refreshing change!"

"Where are you from there, Cate?"

"Just outside of Chicago," Cate answered. "What about you? Where do you call home?" Cate sipped at her sherry, a bundle of nerves as she tried to glean information from Lucas.

"London, at the moment," Lucas responded.

"At the moment?" Cate inquired.

"Yes. We spend most of our time there, anyway. We spend the Christmas holiday in Dunhaven and we summer at Amelia's family estate."

"Oh, how lovely," Cate commented. "The English countryside is enchanting. I'm sure the summers are truly restful."

"Indeed," Lucas agreed. "Amelia's family's country home is most charming."

"Will the property come to you?" Cate pressed, hoping she didn't overstep.

"No," Lucas admitted. "Amelia's inheritance is most generous but does not include the country estate. That will go to her brother, who will also inherit the title of Earl."

"How interesting. I hope you don't find me too forward, but I've little idea about how these things work here. In America, we have no restrictions on passing property to daughters. I understand that to be entirely different here."

"Oh, it is. Land can be passed but not title. And the title only goes to one person. As with myself and my brother, Rory. He inherited Dunhaven Castle, along with the title of Count of Dunhavenshire. As second-born, I did not."

"This is so fascinating to me. Lines of succession do not

exist in the States. I imagine this may lead to some… jealousy in some families. With assets being split and titles being passed to only one son."

"Oh, it can cause quite the uproar in some families, you can be sure!"

"Hmm, it seems to have caused no strife in yours. What a wonderful testament to your parents."

"Oh, none at all," Lucas assured her. "Father provided well for each of us, I've nothing to be jealous of. And to be frank, the burden of care of the castle and the county is better laid on my brother's shoulders than mine. He was always more serious than I. I was a dreamer!"

Cate smiled at him. "And are you still?"

"I'll admit, I've quelled most of my childish fantasies, but I still enjoy the freedom afforded me by being the younger brother." He winked at her.

Cate chuckled. "There's nothing wrong with that. It is fortunate that you enjoy your role. Many people would allow displeasure to build inside them over it. I find it frustrating. A person can change many things, but family is not amongst them."

"Very true, Cate. And family is too important to spend life bickering with. What about your family? Do they miss you terribly with your move here? I assume with Jack's business you reside in the country?"

Cate nodded. "We do, yes, at the moment. We, too, are a bit of two rolling stones. We haven't settled just yet."

"Perhaps you'd prefer life in the States nearer to your family?"

"I have no family," Cate mentioned. "My parents passed when I was younger, before I met Jack. I have no siblings."

"Oh, how tragic for you," Lucas lamented. "It must have been very jarring and frightening to be orphaned at a young age."

Cate offered a closed-mouth smile. Her great-grandfather summarized her true feelings when her parents died in the tragic and unexpected car accident. Strange, how he read her reaction to her father and his own grandson's death so well.

"I've upset you," he continued, reading her expression. He set his drink down, placing a hand on her arm. "My sincerest apologies. Do you need to sit down?"

Cate shook her head, shaking the feelings from her heart as well. Enough time had passed that, despite the temporary sadness that swept through her, she could recover without descending into an emotional wreck. "No, no," she responded, waving her hand at him, "I'm fine. It has been several years. But your description is accurate."

Lucas nodded, giving her a pitying expression. After a moment, he suggested they change the subject. Cate and Lucas chatted for several more minutes about the country and a few recommended attractions Cate and Jack may like to visit while staying at the castle. Cate thanked him for the suggestions before continuing to circulate the room.

After another hour, Cate and Jack announced they would retire for the evening. They promised Anne to join them for dinner the following day, informing her they'd be off on another day trip to some of the sights Lucas suggested.

They traversed the halls to their room, changed from their evening clothes to something more suitable to appear in the following day prior to dinner. As Jack changed, Cate again mussed the bedsheets and laid out a few items around the room to give the appearance of a couple staying there. When they finished, they used the timepiece to return to the present time.

Jack gave his customary sigh of relief when they returned. "Glad to be home?" Cate inquired.

"Yep. I'm always nervous when we time travel. I'm with Rory on this, not adventurous."

Cate giggled at his faint-heartedness for time travel. She checked the timepiece. It was only late afternoon. Despite the hours they'd spent in 1925, only minutes had passed in the present. "Would you mind comparing notes after we change?" Cate inquired of Jack.

"Not at all," Jack replied. "I'm curious to hear what you learned. I spotted you talking to Lucas."

"And you must share the secrets you learned during the cigar and brandy men-only session," Cate chuckled, rolling her eyes.

"Oh, no, no, no, Lady Cate," Jack chided, waving his finger at her. "Those secrets of the universe can never be shared to someone outside of the male gender!"

Cate offered him a wry glance as he backed out of the room, winking at her. "Meet you in the library in a few," she said.

Cate sped through changing, then gathered the dogs and headed for the library. When she arrived, Jack was already lounging in an armchair near the fireplace. Riley raced over to leap onto his lap for attention. Bailey trailed behind, staying on the floor.

"Hello, Sir Riley!" Jack greeted him. "And Mr. Bailey, too!"

"He's starting to come around," Cate noted as she sunk into the chair opposite Jack's.

"Aye," Jack agreed. "He is. Poor little fellow, he's so shy, but he's learning from his big brother that there's nothing to be afraid of. Aren't you?" Jack ruffled the fur on Bailey's head. "So, what did you learn from Lucas? Did he confess to the crime?"

"No," Cate answered with a shake of her head. Her brows wrinkled as she went over their conversation in her mind. "And to be honest, it would have surprised me if he did it."

"Really?" Jack questioned. "Isn't he your prime suspect?"

"He was. He is." Cate shrugged and sighed. "I don't know anymore."

"What about your conversation with him leads you to think he may not be our guy?"

Cate pondered the question. "Well," she began, piecing together her thoughts on the subject. "Several things. First, one would assume the motivation for a theft is money. Assumedly the thief will profit. It appears that Lucas isn't in need of money. Unless he's squandered it all and is putting on a good show. Or his motivation is wanting to make Rory unhappy. But that doesn't seem to be the circumstance. He stated his father left him a generous inheritance, as did Amelia's father. He also admitted he preferred not to be lord of the manor. He considered it a burden and regards his brother's personality as better suited for the role."

Jack raised his eyebrows as he digested the information. "Sounds as though he was reasonably open with you. How d'you elicit that information?"

"He mentioned Amelia's family holds the deed to a country home that they summer at. I asked if the property would pass to Amelia. When he said it didn't, I feigned ignorance in the ways of how British property and titles pass and allowed him to explain that they typically go to the first-born sons and titles cannot pass to daughters. Then I pretended to consider the information and concluded that this may cause strife within many families. I tried to guide the conversation to determine if there was any hint of jealousy between my great-grandfather and my great-uncle."

"No hints?"

"None. He seems to hold to the belief that family is most important, and it's senseless to spend life arguing with them."

"Anything else?"

"He was very kind when we spoke about my parents' deaths. I'll admit I found that conversation bizarre considering we were speaking of his grandson's death. Anyway, his general nature doesn't seem to coincide with a jewel thief."

"So, is he officially off the suspect list?"

"No," Cate admitted. "Perhaps he's a fantastic liar. Perhaps all his familial sentiment and openness about his feelings regarding his brother's inheritance are a cover."

"He didn't strike me as a liar. He seemed very genuine when I spoke with him. Even during our secret man meeting," Jack responded.

Cate chuckled at Jack's last statement. "You're really not going to tell me what went on during the secret meeting, are you?"

"Lady Cate, I'm bound by centuries of tradition and trust not to. What is discussed over brandy and cigars after the ladies have left is privileged information. Like a confession or attorney-client privilege."

Cate rolled her eyes at him. "Well, as long as it doesn't affect our investigation, I'll leave you to your secrets. My other reason for not removing him from the list is Anne's letter. She clearly calls out a family member. Perhaps it pertains to this theft, perhaps not, but it's our biggest clue. And Lucas is the only family member present."

"Again, she never references the jewelry or anything specific. It could refer to anything."

"What are the chances a letter that discussed being robbed and something being stolen refers to something outside of the major jewelry theft at the estate."

"I'm not a statistician," Jack replied.

"I don't think you need a doctorate in statistics to realize the event is unlikely."

"Okay, okay, but given the information you just shared, I'd try to keep an open mind as we proceed. Don't get stuck on that one bit of information."

"You're right. And like I said, I'd be surprised. If Lucas is the thief, he's also an exceptional liar."

"Perhaps it's Amelia," Jack suggested. "Anne may consider her family being her sister-in-law."

Cate considered the new idea. "Maybe," she responded. "What would Amelia's motivation be? It appears she was also well-provided for. They aren't wanting."

"Perhaps she is motivated by jealousy? Lucas may not have wanted to be king of the castle, but perhaps Amelia wanted to carry a title."

"It's a possibility," Cate agreed, "although something doesn't scan to me."

"Why's that?"

"Amelia would have realized it was unlikely for Lucas to inherit the castle. If she wanted a title, she could have married a man sure to receive one."

"Perhaps she didn't have any offers," Jack suggested.

"Perhaps," Cate conceded.

"But you don't believe that," Jack added.

"No, I don't. But you have a point. Both she and Lucas need to stay on the suspect list. However, we'll keep an open mind about other suspects."

"You've still got a few staff members on your list, right?"

"Yes, and the Richardsons, however, they don't seem likely either. First, they aren't family, so Anne's letter doesn't make sense. And even if we disregard that, unless they've lost a great deal of money quickly, they probably aren't doing it for the cash. Plus, if you noticed the amount of jewelry on Eleanor, I doubt they're hurting."

"That could be fake. And how do you know they've got a fortune?" Jack questioned.

"Eleanor is American. It's probable she's a dollar princess."

"A what?" Jack queried.

"A dollar princess. She was an American heiress. Eleanor married Bryce to gain a title and a place in society. He married her to salvage his estate from financial ruin. It happened quite a bit just prior to the twenties. Given their age difference, I'd say that's what happened."

"Interesting," Jack responded, rubbing his chin. "So, with the infusion of cash, it's not likely they are broke."

"No, unless he made some poor investments. However, that doesn't seem to be the case. I know people can present the illusion of wealth, but with their frequent travels, I'd say it's more than an illusion. I'll try to spend some time with Bryce and Eleanor at dinner tomorrow and see if I can extract any information."

"Okay, good plan."

"I don't agree, but it's the best we've got. The only thing I'm certain of is that Anne's ladies' maid didn't do it."

"Certain?"

Cate nodded. "Yes, she'd been with Anne since she was a child. She was a maid in her parents' household who became a ladies' maid to Anne as she aged and married Rory. She's had plenty of opportunities to steal from both families and never did. Why would she do it now?"

"Did they have some kind of argument? Is Anne looking to replace her?"

"No," Cate answered with a shake of her head. "According to Anne, she feels terrible over the position the girl is in. She's adamant that Murray did not steal from her."

"Ah, did you learn this in your secret girls only meeting?"

"I did. Unlike you, I'm willing to share the secrets of the universe despite centuries of tradition."

"Well, then I suppose we continue on checking out the other guests and the few staff members we've got on the suspect list," Jack stated.

"Yep, that's about all we can do," Cate agreed. "You're off the hook until around four tomorrow afternoon, I guess."

"All right, then. I suppose I'll head home and enjoy life in the present."

Cate nodded as Jack stood. "Enjoy the rest of your day off."

"I will. See you tomorrow." Jack ambled to the doorway, turning back before he left. "Oh, I almost forgot. Have you had any more dreams about the, you know?" he questioned, pointing to the bookshelf.

"No," Cate responded. "I haven't. Hopefully it was just a fluke caused by the drafty castle."

"I hope so, too," Jack answered with a smile. "Good night, Lady Cate. Sleep tight, don't let the bookshelves bite," he called as he proceeded down the hall.

"Very funny," Cate shouted after him. She sat for a few more moments in the library pondering the case or lack thereof she was building. Finding no additional information after going over the conversations in her mind, she chose to retire to her room. She gathered Riley and Bailey and exited the library. Despite no more disturbing dreams, Cate had no desire to remain in the library.

CHAPTER 15

Cate stared at the cursor on her screen. Her mind was as blank as the document's page in front of her. She'd spent most of her morning searching for information on the Richardsons. She'd found a few news articles mentioning them and one announcing their marriage. Based on the information in the article, her guess was correct, Eleanor was a dollar princess. The infusion of cash into Bryce Richardson's estate allowed him to keep the house until his son sold it later in the century. They did not appear to be suffering from a lack of money. Cate concluded they could be removed from the suspect list.

After lunch, Cate spent the few hours before she and Jack planned to travel back to 1925 working on her book's manuscript. She found she possessed neither the interest nor the concentration needed to make any decent headway. Instead, she gaped around the sitting room, searching for anything to divert her attention from the task at hand. She'd chosen to work in the sitting room again, remaining apprehensive about spending time in the library. It was foolish of her, she realized, but her instincts still preferred to avoid the room until her subconscious mind stopped obsessing over it.

Cate closed the document on her laptop. Anything she wrote today she'd likely delete the next time she worked, so there was no sense in wasting time. Instead, Cate browsed around a few shopping sites and checked her email. She found a few personal emails and sent responses to each sender. When she finished the last response, she checked her timepiece. She had enough time to walk the dogs before changing for her trip to the past.

After the walk, Cate paced the floor of her sitting room with time to spare even after changing. Time seemed to stand still as she waited for Jack to arrive. Finally, a soft knock sounded at the door. Cate raced to open the door, waving Jack inside.

"Anxious?" he asked with a chuckle.

"Very," Cate admitted. "I hate waiting all day."

"Okay, let's get going then," Jack replied as they entered the bedroom.

They used the timepiece to activate the time rip, sending them back to 1925. Cate glanced around the room, noting it had been tidied. A note on the night table bearing her and Jack's names caught her eye. She dashed to it, tearing it open.

"Who is it from? What does it say?" Jack asked, peering over her shoulder.

"It's from Rory. He says they have canceled formal dinner. Anne is too upset because... oh my gosh!" Cate exclaimed with a gasp. "Murray has been arrested and charged with the theft!"

"With what evidence? Where is the proof of her guilt?"

"I'm not sure, he doesn't mention anything else. He says to seek him out when we arrive to discuss the situation."

"This is a good thing," Jack commented.

"A good thing?" Cate questioned, spinning to face him.

"Yes, I won't have to wear the monkey suit tonight," Jack responded with a grin.

Cate grimaced at him. "It's not that bad!"

"It is! You try wearing a starched collar all night! It has rubbed my neck raw!"

"The beaded dress isn't exactly the height of comfort, you know," Cate informed him. "But comfort aside, I rather like the monkey suit."

"Yes, it makes me look rather dashing, doesn't it?"

"I appreciate the value placed on formality in eras like this. People were fervent about customs and traditions. Things like dinner took on special meaning."

"If you had money," Jack pointed out.

"Yes, I suppose you're right, but my romantic side clings to the pomp and circumstance of it all."

"My romantic side clings to my plaid pajama pants and a well-worn hoodie," Jack quipped.

"Funny. Well, no need to change. Should we look for Rory?" Cate queried, waving the note in the air.

"Guess so. Let's find out what's going on so we can adjust our plan."

Cate and Jack left the bedroom, navigating to the office where they supposed Rory may be working. Despite the late hour, since there was no need to change for dinner, they found him there.

"Ah, Jack, Cate, please come in. You received my note, I trust."

"We did. How terrible for Anne and Murray!" Cate replied.

"Yes, I'm afraid Anne is taking it badly. Hence the canceled dinner. I hope we haven't inconvenienced you in that way. I can have a tray sent up."

"Not at all," Cate replied, "we don't need a tray. What

evidence do the police have that prompted the charge against Murray?"

"Little, it seems. She has the best means and motive according to Officer MacCullough."

"That's no reason to charge the poor girl," Jack chimed in.

"I agree," Cate concurred.

"Despite both my and Anne's protestations, Officer MacCullough continued forward with the arrest. I'm afraid there's little to be done."

"I'd like to speak with her," Cate replied, pacing the room. "We'll go as soon as we've finished speaking."

"To what end?" Rory questioned. "Murray maintains her innocence. I'm not sure what details she can provide to you to assist."

"Perhaps none," Cate admitted, "however it may do her good to realize more than you and Anne are on her side."

"I'm sure she will appreciate your support, yes," Rory agreed.

"Is there anyone you suspect, Rory?" Cate questioned.

"Suspect? No, there isn't anyone. This turn of events shocked me, to be honest. It gives me chills to conclude a thief lives among us."

Cate's heart dropped as she considered at the top of her suspect list was Rory's own brother. Poor Rory could barely accept that there was a thief within his household. How shocking would it be to realize the thief was a member of your own family? No wonder Anne wrote the scathing letter. The disappointment they both experienced must have been soul-shattering.

Cate reminded herself she hadn't yet solidified the case against Lucas. Perhaps she'd be proven wrong, though she didn't see how. "What about the Richardsons?" Cate questioned. "Is there any reason to suspect them?"

"Bryce and Eleanor?" Rory inquired, his voice incredulous. "You must be joking!"

Cate shrugged. "I'm not accusing them. But we've got to eliminate some people to zero in on the correct person."

"Their reputation is above reproach. And what would be their motive?"

"Financial?" Cate posed it as a question.

"With Eleanor's fortune, I shouldn't expect they'd need money."

"So, her fortune is intact? It's not been lost?"

"Lost?"

"Yes. No gambling problems or bad investments?"

"None that I am aware of. And those tales do get around."

"Okay," Cate said, giving up on that line of questioning, "so we can clear them of any suspicion."

Rory nodded in agreement. "I'm quite at a loss, Cate. But I do appreciate your help with this. Thank you for trying."

"There's no need to thank us," Cate responded. "We're happy to help." Cate glanced to Jack. "Well, I suppose we should head to town. If we learn anything worth passing along, we'll share it with you before we return to our time."

"Thank you. Can I send you in a car? Make the journey a little less taxing?"

Cate considered it. "If it's no trouble, that would be preferable."

"No trouble at all!" Rory responded, pulling a cord on the wall to call Benson.

Within moments, a servant arrived at the door. "Yes, m'lord?"

"Ah, Forsythe, please arrange a car for Mr. and Mrs. MacKenzie to go to town. They're visiting the police station. Have Williams wait with them and bring them back." Cate recalled the name. Charles Forsythe was the under-butler and on the suspect list. She side-eyed him, trying to assess his character with a glance. His dark hair was slicked down to his head and his mouth seemed set in a permanent scowl. Did his dark eyes hold secrets behind them, Cate wondered?

"Very good, m'lord. I'll make the arrangements at once. I shall have Williams bring the car 'round to the front." The under-butler gave a slight bow and left.

"What happened to Benson?" Cate questioned when the man departed.

"He's likely busy attending to ensuring meal trays are delivered. Forsythe is our under-butler."

Cate nodded, recalling the detail from her research. "Well, we'll leave you to your work," Cate said. She and Jack departed. "I just need to collect my coat upstairs. I'll bring yours, too." Cate hurried up the stairs, navigating the halls to her room and retrieved the coats they wore when they arrived. She pulled hers on, fastening it before returning to the foyer with Jack's.

By the time he'd donned his, the car arrived in front of the house. Cate and Jack exited, climbing into the backseat and confirming their destination with the chauffeur. He pulled the car near the station and informed them he'd wait there until they were ready to return.

Cate and Jack crossed the street, entering the building. "Jack and Cate MacKenzie to see Lillian Murray," Jack told the clerk at the desk.

"One moment," the clerk replied, disappearing into a back room. He returned, saying, "I'm afraid Miss Murray isn't permitted visitors."

"We're not visitors," Cate insisted. "Please speak with Officer MacCullough. I'm sure he'd inform you we have permission to see her."

The clerk offered an annoyed glance to Cate. "Mr. MacKenzie," he began, "please understand…"

"My wife is correct. If you'll check with MacCullough, you'll find we are not mere visitors."

"Sir, I..."

"No!" Jack exclaimed, raising his voice a bit. "I'll not hear excuses. Now I've explained as has my wife that we're approved to see the prisoner. Please arrange our visit at once!"

The man appeared startled but complied. "Wait here just a moment," he answered. He disappeared again, then returned. "Right this way." He signaled them to follow down the hallway. Cate and Jack were familiar with it, having traversed these halls almost seventy years ago when freeing Randolph from prison.

"Good going," Cate whispered as they followed the clerk down the hall.

"Thanks. Same to you for scoring the car ride!"

Cate raised her eyebrows, smiling at him. The clerk showed them into the same room they had met Randolph in, instructing them to take a seat.

"Weird, huh?" Cate inquired, as they sat down.

"Definitely," Jack agreed. "I hold such fond memories of this room."

"I'll bet," Cate chuckled. The door opposite them opened, and a woman appeared, her hands in handcuffs. The woman's hair hung around her face, having long since escaped the low bun she'd placed it in. She wore a haunted expression, the shock of the situation apparent in every worry line. She sunk into the chair across from them, making no eye contact.

"Hello, Lillian," Cate began once they were alone.

The woman didn't respond. Cate's heart broke for her. She reached across the table, taking the woman's hand in hers. "Lillian, we're very sorry this happened to you, but we don't believe you are guilty. We're here to help."

The woman raised her tear-filled eyes to Cate's. Confusion crossed her face. "Help?" she questioned.

"Yes," Cate reiterated. "We believe you are innocent. We want to help, to prove your innocence."

Lillian's brow furrowed, and she slid her eyes between Cate and Jack. Tears spilled down her cheeks, and she clung to Cate's hand with both of hers as she wept. Cate and Jack allowed her the moment of emotional release. Cate rose from her seat, approaching the woman and wrapping her in an embrace. "Shh, Lillian, it's all right." Cate stroked her hair as the woman's sobs eased.

Jack pulled Cate's chair around the table, allowing her to sit next to Lillian as the woman composed herself. He offered her a handkerchief. Lillian accepted it, drying her eyes. "I'm ever so sorry, Mr. and Mrs. MacKenzie," Lillian said, choking down her sobs.

"It's fine, Lillian. We understand," Cate assured her.

"It all happened so fast," Lillian choked. "I was preparing Lady MacKenzie's dress for dinner when the police burst in and took me into custody."

"It must have been very traumatic for you," Cate agreed.

Lillian nodded. "It was not me," she insisted. "I didn't take the jewels!"

"No, I'm sure you didn't. And we plan to prove it."

Lillian sniffled, glancing between them. "I'm afraid I can't pay you."

"We don't want any payment," Cate informed her, shaking her head. "We just want the guilty party caught."

"And we don't want to see an innocent person accused," Jack added.

"Right," Cate confirmed. "Now, if you're up to it, Lillian, could you tell us anything you remember about the night before and the morning after the theft?"

Lillian nodded, swallowing hard and composing herself.

"Lady Anne... er, Lady MacKenzie," she corrected, "retired around one in the morning. I tended to her. She informed me to place the jewelry on her dressing table and leave it for the morning. I did as she instructed." A sob escaped her. "If I'd only taken them to the safe for Mr. Benson to put away right, then..." her voice trailed off.

"No," Cate asserted, "you did nothing wrong. This isn't your fault."

She nodded. "I put them on the dressing table and placed her dress over the chaise to be inspected and cleaned the next morning. I left and retired for the evening."

"Did you place the jewelry in its case?"

"Aye," Lillian responded. "I placed it into the velvet bag."

Cate nodded. "And the bag was placed on the dressing table?"

"Aye," Lillian said with a nod.

"Did you see or hear anyone as you returned to your room?" Jack inquired.

"Nay," Lillian answered. "Not a soul."

"Anything unusual when you returned to your room? Odd noises? Doors closing later than they should have?" Jack inquired.

"None that I recall, sir," the maid answered.

"And the next morning?" Cate questioned.

"I went to her ladyship's chambers to retrieve the dress for cleaning. It was then I noticed the dressing table empty. I asked Lady MacKenzie if she'd returned the jewelry herself or asked another servant to do it. She said no, and we searched her room, figuring maybe they'd fallen onto the floor or the like, but we didn't find it. It was then they called for the police."

"Okay, Lillian. Thank you for the information," Cate answered. "Can you recall anything else uncommon about that night? Anything at all, whether or not you presume it's related. Anything that wasn't within the normal operations of the household?"

Lillian pondered a moment, her brow furrowing in thought. She shook her head as though to signal a negative response. Then she sat straighter. "What is it, Lillian?" Cate encouraged her.

"Might be nothing. But that night, Lord MacKenzie's valet took ill. Mr. Benson ordered him to bed right after the staff dinner. Said he'd tend to Lord MacKenzie himself if he had to."

Cate considered the information. "So, Lord MacKenzie's valet went to bed for the night, leaving someone else to tend him. Yes, that might be useful. Thank you, Lillian." Cate glanced to Jack who nodded. "Okay, we're going to go now. We'll try to visit tomorrow or the next day. If you think of anything else, hold on to it or write it down and we'll follow up on it."

Lillian nodded. She squeezed Cate's hand, offering a tight-lipped smile to her. "Thank you ever so much, Mr. and Mrs. MacKenzie. It means so much to me that someone is willing to help. I know Lord and Lady MacKenzie to be on my side, but it lifts me to no end to have more folks believe in me."

Cate squeezed her hand back. "Take care, Lillian, and try to get some rest. We'll try to have you out of here as soon as we can." Cate and Jack stood to leave. As Cate moved to skirt the table, Lillian leapt from her seat, throwing her handcuffed arms around Cate in a tight hug. Cate returned her embrace. When Cate pulled back, she saw something new in Lillian's teary eyes: hope.

Cate and Jack exited the police station, crossing the street to the car. They refrained from speaking until they were alone in the castle's foyer. Even then, Cate held up a finger to silence any conversation. "Let's find Rory and give him a brief update, mention no names, then regroup when we're alone," Cate whispered.

Jack nodded in silent agreement. They proceeded down the hall to Rory's office, finding it empty. "Try the sitting room?" Jack queried. Cate nodded, and they backtracked, checking the sitting room. They found it empty. "Now what?"

Cate pulled the ribbon on the wall. "Let's ask Benson," Cate suggested.

They waited a few moments until Benson appeared in the sitting room doorway. "Yes?" his deep voice questioned.

"Oh, Benson," Cate answered. "Have you seen Lord MacKenzie? He asked us to speak with him upon our return, but we've not been able to locate him."

"If I'm not mistaken, he is with Lady MacKenzie. She's taken ill, shock from the events of today. I'm sure you understand. Shall I disturb him?"

"No," Cate answered, shaking her head and strolling to the desk in the room. "Please don't disturb him. I'll leave a note you can deliver to him when convenient." Cate scribbled a note onto the paper there, folding it in three and handing it to Benson. He placed the note in his breast pocket.

"I shall deliver it when we speak next. Is there anything else you require for the evening? A tray from the kitchen for dinner, perhaps?"

"No, nothing, thank you," Cate replied. "We plan to retire for the evening."

"Very good, Mrs. MacKenzie. I shall see you are not disturbed."

"Thank you," Cate answered. She and Jack returned to the bedroom and used the timepiece to return to their time.

"Same drill?" Jack questioned. "We've got some time before dinner."

"Yep," Cate answered. "See you in a few." Cate changed

and gathered her notes and her two furry friends. She entered the library, finding Jack in his usual spot.

"Oh, what a mess we have on our hands, Lady Cate."

"Indeed," Cate agreed. She slumped into the chair next to him. Cate opened her folder, spreading the materials across her lap. She uncapped her pen, preparing to jot down notes as they spoke. "Okay," she muttered, pen cap between her teeth. "Lillian Murray has been accused and arrested. But we're sure she didn't do it." Cate shuffled the papers around, finding her suspect list. She stuck the pen cap on the pen's end and continued. "We can cross the Richardsons off. They didn't do it. We've got multiple reasons to remove them, agree?"

Jack considered it. "Okay, agree."

"What's your hold-back?" Cate asked, noting his hesitation.

"Nothing, just weighing how sure I am."

"And?" Cate inquired.

"I'm sure enough. According to Rory, they have no money problems and their reputation is above reproach. I can come up with no motivation for them to steal from Rory and Anne. I'm certain the police would have searched for the necklace and they didn't find it with them."

Cate nodded. "Rory's right about their money. They keep their estate until his son sells it much later, so that seems right." Cate scratched them from the list. "Okay," Cate murmured, scanning the list, "there's no one else we can remove right now."

"Anyone we should add?"

"The valet, perhaps," Cate conjectured. "And Benson."

"Benson?!" Jack exclaimed.

"I don't actually imagine he did it," Cate replied. "But according to Lillian, on the night of the party, the valet was too ill to attend Rory and Benson sent him to bed and said he'd take his place if no one else could attend Rory."

Jack screwed up his face. "How do you figure that makes either a suspect? The valet was sick, and Benson filled in."

"The valet's illness seems convenient. What if he faked it to steal the necklace later but have a good alibi?"

"Point taken. Okay, add the valet. But why Benson?"

"What if Benson poisoned Rory's valet, so he was out of commission, sent him to bed and attended Rory so he was nearer to Anne's bedroom to steal the jewelry?"

"Hmm, that's quite a theory."

"Again, I doubt it's correct, but let's list Benson with a big question mark. The other thing I'll note is he said he'd attend Rory if he needed to, but we don't know if he did or someone else did."

"Who else would have?" Jack questioned.

"A footman… or Forsythe, the under-butler. He'd be the more likely one."

"And he's on your suspect list."

"He is," Cate answered, circling his name. She wrote *Find out who attended Rory on New Year's Eve* on her note sheet. "Anything else?"

Jack pondered for a few moments. "No. Lillian didn't have much information to offer."

"No, she didn't." Cate sighed. "But we've got a few leads to follow. When should we return to do that?"

"Tomorrow afternoon? Right after lunch, perhaps?"

"Sounds great. I'll try to catch Anne for afternoon tea. Perhaps she'll open up more one-on-one."

"I suppose I'll drink a brandy and smoke a cigar in the sitting room," Jack joked.

"Might be a good time to meet your ancestor, Lachlan. You haven't run into him yet," Cate pointed out.

"No, I haven't. I'm not sure how I feel about that."

"What do you mean?" Cate questioned.

"My grandfather's father. It's just odd. Although, I suppose it's the same for you. You mentioned the strangeness of discussing your parents' deaths with your great-grandfather. The poor man was discussing his own grandson's death and never even realized it."

"No, and it is odd. But also monumental, unforgettable."

"I can imagine," Jack agreed.

"If you do meet him, enjoy it." Cate paused a moment. "We really are lucky. No one else gets to meet their ancestors. The people whose decisions were responsible for their very existence."

"It truly is a gift. I'm starting to comprehend the appeal you've always recognized." Cate smiled at him. "Don't give me that look, Lady Cate. I'm still not completely keen on this whole thing."

Cate laughed. "Well, I suppose we must keep trying until you are!"

"I was afraid you'd say that. And on that note, I'm going to leave you to your notes." Cate began shoving her papers back into the folder. "No more theorizing tonight? I'm shocked."

"Oh, I'm going to do plenty of theorizing," Cate promised. "But not in this room!"

"Oh?" Jack questioned.

"Still not keen on the creepy library with its unexplainable, leaky bookshelf."

"Lady Cate, I didn't realize you were such a 'fraidy cat."

Cate frowned at him. "Neither did I! But after that last dream," Cate uttered with a shrug, "I'm just uneasy every time I'm in here."

"Well, you have plenty of other rooms to use, I guess," Jack quipped as they walked from the room.

"I've no shortage of those," Cate replied, shooing the dogs into the hallway as she shut the door.

Following dinner, Cate retired to her suite, curling up on her chaise with her notes spread. She'd focus on the other servants in her discussion with Anne tomorrow. They were the only remaining suspects outside of her great-grandfather. As unfair as it was, she hoped against hope to find something to ease her suspicion of her ancestor.

CHAPTER 16

The following morning, Cate stared at her suspect list again. Fresh eyes offered no aid in solving the mystery. Today they would visit 1925 in the early afternoon, hoping to catch the household for afternoon tea. Cate planned to discuss the staff with Anne. She'd glean any details she could hoping to make a definitive decision on some of the suspects on her list.

Cate shoved the list into her folder, setting it on her side table. She returned to her laptop, pushing herself to continue work on her manuscript. Despite her distracted mind, Cate made some progress on her book. Pleased with herself, she shut the laptop and took the dogs for a walk to the loch before lunch.

Again, Cate found herself practicing for conversations that, in all likelihood, would never occur. She determined creative ways to solicit information from Anne without singling any particular person out. Cate returned to the castle, buzzing through her lunch in record time. She returned to her room and dressed for the trip back. When she finished, Cate checked the time piece. She had plenty of time to spare prior to Jack's arrival. Cate sunk onto her chaise, reviewing the suspect list for the umpteenth time. No new information leapt out at her.

Jack arrived right on time. Cate folded the suspect list and shoved it in her pocket. "Ready?" Jack asked, entering the room.

"I am," Cate answered. "Ready to get more information!"

"Okay, let's go."

"Wow!" Cate exclaimed. "You're raring to go today!"

"I'm getting used to this," Jack answered. "It's weirdly becoming normal." Jack shook his head. "Wow, I can't believe I just said that. Never imagined I'd utter the phrase time travel is becoming normal."

Cate chuckled. "I'm glad you're getting used to it. Soon you may even admit it's fun!"

"I wouldn't go that far, Lady Cate," Jack cautioned as he wrapped his hand around hers. They activated the timepiece and arrived in 1925.

Cate approached her suitcase, rummaging through it. "What are you doing?" Jack questioned.

"I want to change. I wore this yesterday," Cate responded.

"Oh, right, I forgot."

Cate selected another dress and disappeared into the bathroom. She emerged in her new dress, folding the other one and returning it to her suitcase. Jack had also selected another outfit, swapping places with Cate to change. When he returned, Cate suggested he find Rory.

"Yes, I plan to needle any information I can from him."

"Okay, good. I'll do the same with Anne. Afterward, we should visit Lillian at the police station. I don't want her becoming despondent. She was so upset yesterday."

"Yeah. Poor woman," Jack replied. "I hope we can help her."

"Me too. Well, let's get to it."

Jack and Cate emerged from the suite and made their way downstairs. They found Rory in his office. Cate inquired as to Anne's whereabouts, informing Rory she hoped to take afternoon tea with Lady MacKenzie. Rory agreed it would be an excellent idea since Anne still harbored many emotions over the arrest of her ladies' maid.

Cate left the men to talk and followed Rory's directions to Anne's room. She knocked at the door but received no response. Cate tried again, but still received no answer. After trying the doorknob, Cate found the room unlocked. She pushed the door open a few inches, sticking her head through and scanning the room. Anne lay on her chaise, staring into the fire in the nearby fireplace.

"Anne?" Cate whispered. The woman didn't respond. "Anne?" Cate tried again, this time raising her voice louder.

"Oh!" Anne answered, snapping her head to look at Cate. "Oh, Cate. I'm sorry, I didn't hear you. Please come in. Although I'm afraid I won't make for much company."

"That's all right," Cate assured her, entering the room and closing the door behind her. "Rory informed us about the predicament with Murray. I'm so sorry to hear about that. What a terrible mess."

A tear fell to Anne's cheek. Her hand rushed to wipe it away. "Yes," Anne replied, attempting to steady her voice. "The poor girl is in quite… a predicament." Her voice broke as she finished the statement.

"Oh, Anne," Cate replied, putting her arm around her shoulders. "Please try not to fret."

Anne wiped at her tears again, sniffling. "Silly, I realize. The girl is a servant. However, I believe she is earnest in what she says. She insists she is innocent."

"It's not silly," Cate reassured her. "I also believe she is being truthful. And I do not consider your worry for her silly."

"Thank you," Anne answered, patting Cate's hand. "Yes, Murray is quite a confidant. Almost a friend, actually. She came with me from my father's home, she's been with me quite a long time."

"Which is why I regard the police's current course of action with great suspicion. No doubt if Murray planned to steal from you, she's had many other opportunities to do so. Why now? They have nothing to suggest any motive on her part."

"No, I quite agree."

"I'm not sure if Rory confided to you, but Jack and I are investigating on our own. I hope to help clear Murray's name."

"He did not, but thank you."

The two were silent for a moment. "Perhaps you'd like to take some afternoon tea in the tearoom," Cate suggested. "It may lift your spirits."

"Oh, what a terrible hostess I am. I'm sorry, Cate. However, I'm not sure I'd provide good company."

Cate was about to respond when a knock sounded at the door and it popped open. "Knock knock!" Amelia called in, peeking into the room. "Oh, Cate! Hello!"

"Hello, Amelia," Cate answered.

"I didn't realize you were in here. I came to retrieve my sister-in-law for tea."

Anne offered a brief smile. "Thank you, Amelia, but as I just explained to Cate, I'm not very good company this afternoon. Why don't you two go along without me?"

"Nonsense!" Amelia replied. "Getting out of this room is exactly what you need. Now, come along, let's work on improving your mood."

Amelia's optimism seemed infectious. Anne offered a wider smile. "All right, you've convinced me. Just allow me to fetch my shawl. The tearoom is sometimes cold at this time of year."

Amelia nodded as Anne disappeared into her bedroom. Cate smiled at Amelia. "Great job convincing her. She was adamant about not leaving the room when I tried."

"It's the best thing for her," Amelia responded.

"I agree," Cate concurred.

"Poor thing! What a terrible mess this all is."

"Yes," Cate answered.

"First the missing jewelry, then her ladies' maid accused. I don't suppose it's true, but if it turns out to be, it's a terrible abuse of trust."

"I don't expect it to be true either," Cate responded as Anne emerged from her room.

"Ready?" Amelia asked in a cheery voice.

The ladies made their way downstairs to the tearoom and within fifteen minutes were served hot tea with finger sandwiches and scones. Amelia kept the conversation light and flowing. Her sunny disposition made things easy.

"Well, Cate, tell us about yourself," Amelia encouraged as Anne poured tea.

"There's very little to tell, I'm afraid. I'm not that interesting a person," Cate admitted.

"Nonsense! How did you meet Jack?"

"We were seated together at one of my aunt's dinner parties," Cate fibbed, sticking to the backstory they created before their first time traveling excursion.

"I see," Amelia responded. "And how do your parents feel about your moving to another country? They must miss you terribly. Do you visit often?"

"My parents passed away before I married Jack," Cate responded.

"How sad, what of your siblings? Do they miss you, particularly since your parents are gone?"

"I haven't any siblings," Cate said. "Therefore, the move was easy. It allowed Jack to stay near to his family, and since I have none, there was no worry about mine. What about you, Amelia?"

"I've two older brothers," Amelia said with a roll of her eyes.

"I'll bet that was a challenge growing up!" Cate exclaimed.

"Quite. Always teasing me about my dolls and the like. I prayed for a sister every night."

"Were you very disappointed when you didn't receive one?" Cate queried, biting into a cucumber sandwich.

Amelia glanced to Anne. "No, because I received one." She reached to Anne, grasping her hand.

Cate smiled at the gesture. "How lovely."

"Indeed," Amelia agreed. "When I married Lucas, I could not have asked for a better sister-in-law. We are like sisters despite there being no shared blood."

"I am lucky to count you among my family, Amelia," Anne agreed.

"Do you have other siblings, Anne?" Cate inquired.

"Yes, three. An older sister and two younger siblings, a sister and a brother."

"Are you very close with them?"

"Only with my younger sister," Anne responded. "We are close in age. A surprise we got along so well. One tends to find sisters that close in age sparring over dresses, men and so on, but Clara and I get along well."

"What a pity you've no siblings, Cate. Did it bother you very much growing up?"

"No," Cate admitted following a moment of introspection. "I suppose I didn't know any different. When my parents passed, though, I'm sure it would have been easier to bear with siblings."

"But then you met Jack. How fortunate. It is obvious he adores you," Amelia declared.

Cate smiled at her. "Yes, funny how life works."

Their conversation continued, discussing winters at Dunhaven, Amelia's summer estate, travel and other small talk items. Cate's mind whirled as the women conversed, trying to piece together their relationship and ferret out any reason for Amelia to have committed the theft. At the conclusion of their tea, Cate could find no reason that Amelia would have committed the crime. Was Amelia good at covering up a secret jealousy of Anne, or was she not the guilty party?

Deflated, Cate waited in the foyer to meet Jack whom Forsythe had been sent to retrieve. When he returned with Jack in tow, he asked them to wait in the sitting room before proceeding to town. Lady MacKenzie requested them to carry a note to Murray.

As they settled on the loveseats near the fireplace, Jack inquired if Cate had uncovered any information.

"Not really," Cate admitted, her voice lowered. "Although, it appears Amelia genuinely cares for Anne. Unless she is a fantastic liar, I can't imagine she's our thief either. Did you find anything of interest?"

"Get ready to be impressed. I found out who filled in for Rory's valet on New Year's Eve. And it wasn't Benson!"

"You did! Great job! Who was it?"

"Forsythe, the under-butler."

"Forsythe," Cate repeated, removing her suspect list from her pocket. She hurried to the desk and noted the new information on her sheet. "I'd say we can cross off Benson then. He was a long shot, anyway. And if he wasn't playing valet, then the theory that he poisoned the valet in order for his presence upstairs to be accounted for is no longer valid."

"I agree," Jack answered. "And put a question mark near

Amelia since, given your experience with her, we can't find a motive for her either." Cate complied, and they studied the reduced list. "That leaves three servants at the top of the list."

"Yes," Cate agreed. "The groom, the scullery maid and the under-butler. But this list calls into question our largest piece of evidence. The letter from Anne."

"We aren't even sure that letter concerns this investigation."

"We need more information about these three. Perhaps we should ask Rory after our visit with Lillian." As they considered the list, Forsythe returned, note in hand.

"I've had the car brought 'round for you. Here is the note from Lady MacKenzie."

"Thank you, Forsythe," Cate responded, accepting the note. She and Jack proceeded to the front entrance, finding the chauffeur waiting for them just outside the door. He drove them to the police station, again waiting for them outside.

Cate and Jack entered and secured a visit with Lillian Murray. Cate reiterated their support of the woman and reassured her that Anne also believed her version of events. They passed along the note and were pleased to find that it brought Lillian some measure of comfort.

"We're still working on searching for clues and information," Cate asserted.

"Thank you," Lillian responded.

"How are you holding up?" Cate questioned. "Are they treating you well enough?"

Lillian sniffled. "They continue to drag me from my cell all hours of the night. They ask me over and over to repeat my story or encourage me to admit to my wrongdoing. But I didn't do it! I cannae admit to something I didn't do."

"And you shouldn't have to," Cate agreed. "We will discuss

the matter with the police. You shouldn't be harassed like this!"

"Oh, please, don't put yourself out on my account, Mrs. MacKenzie. 'Tisn't any trouble. I'll survive it."

"It's nonsense!" Cate exclaimed. "You're exhausted. Their continued harassment will take a toll on you. They hope to coerce you into a confession to make their jobs easier. It's unacceptable."

"I'll admit, I would enjoy a night's peace even if it is in a jail cell."

"We will speak to them on our way out," Cate assured Lillian. "Now, was there anything else that you've remembered since we spoke last?"

Lillian shook her head. "No, I searched my brain, but I came up with nothing. I'm sorry."

"Don't apologize," Cate insisted. "We have generated some leads we will continue to work on. I hope to have some good news for you soon."

Lillian offered a slight smile. "Thank you again, Mrs. MacKenzie. And please, if you see Lady MacKenzie, thank her for her kind note and apologize on my behalf for the trouble."

"I will." Cate squeezed Lillian's hand and offered her a smile before leaving.

As they made their way down the hall, Cate told Jack, "We must speak with someone about her treatment."

"Aye, that's terrible. Poor girl."

"I'll ask to see Officer MacCullough," Cate suggested.

They approached the clerk's desk and Cate requested a meeting with the officer. "Just a moment." The clerk sighed, disappearing into another room. He reappeared, motioning for them to follow him. "This way."

Cate and Jack followed him into a room filled with desks.

Officer MacCullough sat at one of them, reviewing a document. "Thank you," Cate said, storming toward the officer.

"Officer MacCullough," she began. "I demand you cease at once with your poor treatment of Lillian Murray. The girl is being badgered at constantly."

"I beg your pardon, Mrs. MacKenzie?"

"She's being awoken all hours of the night and harassed. That, Officer MacCullough, is coercion and is grounds to have any information you receive from her thrown out of court."

"Are you now an attorney, Mrs. MacKenzie?"

"I am well-versed in matters of the law enough to know what you are doing is borderline illegal."

The man rolled his eyes. "Mr. MacKenzie, control your wife, please!"

"Control my wife?" Jack exclaimed, stepping in front of Cate. "I'll do no such thing! She is correct. I've a background in law, though I've given up my practice. But if I must resume practicing law to see Miss Murray is given fair treatment, I will. You are not to question her unless I or another attorney is present. Any straying from this and I shall sue you and this entire police department." Jack wagged his finger at the man. "Don't tempt me, Officer MacCullough. Your so-called investigation is shoddy and full of questionable practices. It would be an easy case, a laddie fresh out of law school could win it with his eyes closed."

"I've a right to conduct my investigation as I see fit, Mr. MacKenzie. And if I..."

"No, that's where you're wrong, sir. You've not the right to conduct it as you see fit, only as the law allows. Now, I shall return tomorrow and if I've heard you have put Miss Murray through the same machinations she's undergone in the last twenty-four hours, I will go to the judge myself and see that you lose your badge!"

Officer MacCullough set his face into a scowl. "Fine, Mr. MacKenzie. But if your wife keeps poking her nose into my investigation and I'm stopped from finding out the truth… so help me, I'll…"

"You'll what?" Jack queried, his eyes narrowed at the man. After a few breaths of silence, Jack added. "As I thought. Good day, Officer MacCullough."

He grabbed Cate's arm, dragging a stunned Cate from the police station and to the waiting car outside. They drove home in silence, not wanting to give too much away in front of the driver. When they entered the foyer, Cate stopped Jack from proceeding to find Rory. "Wow!" Cate exclaimed in a hushed tone. "That was some speech!"

"That's what he gets for telling me to control my wife. The jerk." Cate offered him a wry smile. "What? The man clearly has a problem with women. Consider how he's treating poor Lillian."

"It is awful. They hope to pressure her into a confession and wrap up the case with a nice bow."

"They have no interest in solving the case, only closing it," Jack agreed.

"I didn't realize you were going to resurrect your law career," Cate teased.

"Neither did I, but it seemed an appropriate time to dust off my law degree."

Cate giggled. "Perfect timing."

"So, shall we find Rory?"

"Yes. I'd like to ask him a few questions about the staff members."

"He should be in his office still," Jack stated. "Oh, by the way, I met Lachlan. And yes, it was staggering."

Cate smiled at him, happy he met his great-grandfather. They reached Rory's office and Jack knocked at the door.

"Come in!" Rory called, writing a note in his ledger. He glanced up. "Ah, Jack, Cate, how is Murray?"

"Holding up," Cate responded. "Despite some poor treatment at the hands of the police."

"Oh no," Rory said, frowning. "How terrible. Is there anything we can do?"

"I've spoken with Officer MacCullough," Jack chimed in. "I hope the behavior won't continue. They are trying to coerce a confession from the girl using any means possible."

"Oh, I do hope the behavior stops now that you've brought it to Officer MacCullough's attention."

"So do I. We'll check back tomorrow."

Rory nodded at them. "In the meantime," Cate added, "I was wondering if we might ask you a few questions?"

"Of course," Rory agreed, setting his pen down. "What is it you wish to know?"

"Lillian maintains her innocence and I believe her. But someone within this household stole that jewelry. Is there anyone who you'd suspect, even if in the slightest?"

"Why, no, no one. As I mentioned, the event shocked me."

"Can you recall anything out of the ordinary in the days prior to the theft? Or in the days that followed? Any unusual behavior, unexplained disappearances, anything?" Cate questioned further.

Rory shook his head. "Not that I am aware of. Benson would have better information on staff whereabouts, but surely you don't suspect…"

"Rory," Cate interrupted, "someone stole that jewelry. Either a guest in your house or a staff member. We must use whatever we can, no matter how small the clue, to determine who that was."

"Perhaps if you speak with Benson…" Rory began, seeming to be at a loss with the conversation.

"All right," Cate agreed. "We'll follow up with Benson. Would it be suitable to speak with him now?"

"Yes. I'll ring for him," Rory said, strolling to the wall cord and pulling it.

"Thank you. We'll meet him in the sitting room to discuss the matter," Cate suggested.

"Very good. And thank you."

Cate and Jack exited the room, traversing the halls to the sitting room. "He's in some serious denial," Jack said as they entered the room.

"Yes," Cate answered. "He'll be heartbroken if it turns out to be Lucas. He can barely fathom it being a member of his household staff."

"He looks at the world through rose-colored glasses."

Cate nodded in agreement. "Yes, he's a bit sheltered in his view of the world."

The doors opened, interrupting their conversation, and Benson strode in. "Mr. and Mrs. MacKenzie. Lord MacKenzie informed me you are working on investigating the theft. Lord MacKenzie said you have some questions you wish to ask me. A terrible business, this."

"Indeed," Cate answered. "Yes. We are hoping to aid Lillian Murray in proving her innocence."

"I shall answer anything. But…" he paused. "Never mind," he said after a moment. He shook his head.

"What is it, Benson?" Cate inquired.

"Nothing, Mrs. MacKenzie. I was only concerned you may believe me to be the culprit. I have worked hard to keep my reputation above reproach, ma'am. I hope you don't find my comments out of turn but…"

"Not at all," Cate assured him. "And no, we did not ask to speak with you because we believe you are the thief. Lord MacKenzie suggested we speak with you because you would know the staff whereabouts better than he."

"Ah, very good, Mrs. MacKenzie, and I am most grateful you've found no issue with my character."

"Benson, was there anything unusual that you noted in the days just prior to or just following the theft? Any odd behavior or unusual requests? Any staff members requesting time off, for example?"

Benson pinched his brow in concentration. "No, none that I can recall."

"What about the night of the theft? Lillian Murray told us Lord MacKenzie's valet was taken ill?" Jack inquired.

"Yes, Mr. Calhoun took a sudden turn following the staff meal. I sent him to bed."

"Any chance he was faking his symptoms?"

"None. The man was white as a sheet. He retched all over the staff dining hall floor. Poor Alice, the scullery maid, had to clean it up. I don't expect he moved out of his bed after that."

"I see," Cate replied. "And who filled in his role?"

"Forsythe. I intended to do it, but he offered since I had several other things to attend to."

"Mr. Forsythe hasn't been with the household long, has he?" Cate questioned.

"Mmm, the better part of a year," Benson responded.

"Did he come with references?" Cate inquired. "He seems young to be an under-butler."

"I did not review his references. I am not sure, Mrs. MacKenzie."

"Who did?" Cate queried, finding it odd the butler and head of the staff did not handle the hiring of his under-butler.

"Lord MacKenzie himself, Mrs. MacKenzie."

Cate's forehead wrinkled as she processed the information. That was odd. Why would Rory handle the hiring of the under-butler? He'd have approved Mr. Benson's recommendations, but he'd not have taken it upon himself to go through the intricacies of hiring lower staff.

"Is there anything else you can tell us that you deem may be relevant?" Cate asked after a breath.

"No," Benson replied after a moment. "I am shocked this occurred, to be honest. My theory is the thief snuck into the castle in the wee hours of the morning and absconded with the jewelry, never to be heard from again. At least that is what I hope happened."

Cate smiled at him. He, too, preferred not to suspect a member of his own staff. He presumably felt any fault within the staff reflected on his own character. A good butler, Cate surmised. "Thank you, Benson. I hope we have this sorted soon and you are correct. Lord MacKenzie prefers to imagine none of his guests or staff are thieves."

"And what do you think, Mrs. MacKenzie?"

"I'll reserve any comment until I have all the facts at my disposal," Cate answered.

"Very wise, Mrs. MacKenzie. Is there anything else?"

"No, Benson, nothing. You may go."

"Another dead end," Jack commented after the butler departed. He ran his fingers through his hair in frustration.

"Perhaps, perhaps not."

"What do you mean? Did I miss something from that conversation?"

"The fact that Rory hired Forsythe."

"So?"

"It's rather unusual in a staff this size that Rory would have a direct hand in the hiring of a staff member like the under-butler. The butler, yes, his valet, yes. But an under-butler? I'm surprised he took that on himself. Mr. Benson should have been the one to interview and go over his references."

Jack considered it for a moment. "It could mean nothing.

There are a million reasons Rory could have hired Forsythe. Perhaps he offered him a job as a favor to a friend, or he stole him from another wealthy friend because he liked his attention to service or something."

"There is one way to find out," Cate replied.

"Ask Rory," they said in unison. Jack led the way down the hall to Rory's office.

They knocked at the ajar door, entering after Rory called for them to come in. "Jack, Cate, did you speak with Benson? Was he of any help?"

"We did," Cate answered. "We're still sorting through what he's told us. We had one follow up question for you, though. Benson mentioned that he didn't hire Forsythe, the under-butler, but that you handled the hiring. Was there a particular reason for that?"

"Surely you don't suspect Forsythe?" Rory questioned.

Cate kept her expression and response neutral. "I didn't say that, but I found the detail odd. We're just following up on anything that seems irregular."

"There's really nothing to it," Rory explained it away, glancing at his desk as he waved his hand in the air. "He came recommended from a friend. He needed a position and I provided it. I took him on in London when I was on business there. Benson wasn't with me, otherwise he'd have handled it." Cate nodded, parsing the information. "I can assure you his character is above reproach."

Cate nodded again, adding a smile. "Thank you, Rory. That answers my question."

"Unless there is something else, I'll return to my ledgers," Rory responded.

"No, nothing. Good night, Rory."

"Good night."

Cate and Jack left Rory to his work, returning to the bedroom and their own time. It remained early afternoon despite the hours they'd spent in 1925. Cate paced the floor from the moment they returned. "Did that seem strange to you?" she queried Jack, going over the conversation in her mind.

Jack shrugged. "He seemed to have an explanation for why he handled the hiring."

Cate shook her head. "Before he gave the explanation. His initial reaction to my question."

Jack pondered it a moment. "I guess he seemed evasive."

"He didn't answer it. He immediately jumped to the conclusion that we may suspect Forsythe."

"Which we do," Jack added.

"Correct, but we didn't say that. His reaction seemed odd."

Jack considered it again. "You could make that case. Although it's a bit of a stretch."

"A stretch?" Cate questioned.

"His reaction wasn't THAT odd."

"No, it wasn't bizarre but… it struck me as a strange response. Again, it's nothing major, but nothing we've learned so far has been major. We're piecing together a puzzle with only the nubs of each piece instead of whole piece."

"Rory judges Forsythe's character to be irreproachable. How good a judge of character is he, do you imagine?"

Cate pondered it a moment. "No idea," Cate answered, throwing her arms in the air in frustration. "If we went by Rory's estimation, then Mr. Benson's theory is correct. Some unknown sneaked into the house, pocketed the jewelry and escaped."

"Come on, Cate, you don't honestly believe that, do you?"

"No, I don't," she said after a pause. "It's a ridiculous theory. So that leaves us with the fact that Rory has misjudged someone."

"Perhaps it's someone he doesn't know well enough to judge." Cate nodded, not in agreement but not having anything else to add. "I guess I'll change and get back to work. Don't sweat it, Cate, we'll figure it out."

"Yeah," she murmured, still consumed by her thoughts.

Jack strode to the door, turning back before he exited. "Hey, Cate?"

"Yeah?"

"Let it rest for the night. We'll start fresh tomorrow."

Cate nodded. She spent the rest of the afternoon attempting to read a book. Perhaps Jack was correct. She was overtaxing her mind, and it was getting her nowhere fast. After dinner, she settled to watch a movie. The movie played on in the background as her mind churned through all the information they learned, or lack thereof. She came to no new conclusions.

CHAPTER 17

The next morning, Cate set her open laptop in front of her on the floor of her sitting room. She spread her notes around her. Riley and Bailey gathered around her, curious about what she was doing. Cate stared at the papers, willing them to provide her with more information.

"What do you think, boys?" she inquired of her furry friends. "Who is the guilty party?"

Riley and Bailey stared at her, each with dark, questioning eyes. "Nobody strikes you as the culprit?" Cate frowned. "Me either. Let's review what we know so far." Riley laid down in front of her, as though waiting for the presentation to begin. Bailey remained on his feet, staring at Cate. "The suspects still on the list are Lucas and Amelia, my great-grandparents. Why are they still on the list? Anne's letter provides damning evidence against one or both of them, assuming her letter refers to this theft, which we can't confirm. But it's safe to assume that." Cate paused, considering the information again. "Yet neither of them seems to have any motivation to commit this crime. They both appear to care for Rory and Anne. Though it's possible they are faking. So, we can't cross them off the list."

Bailey took a seat as Cate continued to her next group of suspects. "Rory assured me the Richardsons are innocent. Although, Rory's judgement may be questionable. However, they have since left the estate so we've no way to continue investigating them. And, to be honest, boys, they had no motivation. That leaves us with the staff. I've flagged the groom, the scullery maid and the under-butler.

"The groom and scullery maid were likely nowhere near the area, nor did they have any reason to be. Although, I suppose I should check on their alibis. Forsythe would have had opportunity, but what is his motive? If Rory employed him as a favor, would he return that favor by robbing him? Perhaps."

Cate sighed. "I suppose it could be anyone of them or another staff member not listed. I have no idea! This investigation is going nowhere! I have the sinking feeling we may not solve this. Which means poor Lillian Murray may never clear her name. Ugh! What are we missing?" Cate sunk her head in her hands.

After a moment, she recovered, grabbing her laptop. She typed in the names of each servant, one-by-one, beginning with the scullery maid. Alice Huxley didn't generate many results, but after a good deal of scouring the Internet, Cate found a death notice. The woman had died at sixty-three, having worked her way up from scullery maid to assistant cook at Dunhaven Castle.

Next, Cate tried the groom, Thomas Gould. Thomas had married in 1932 to a woman from London. He'd lived until seventy, fathering five children. Nothing of note jumped out to Cate.

She tried the last name on her list, Charles Forsythe. Cate combed through every resource she found, however, none matched the time frame to fit with the man living on the estate in 1925. She searched news articles and death notices, finding none that fit.

She sighed, slamming her laptop shut. Another dead-end. Riley, who had fallen asleep as Cate searched the web, lifted his head to eye Cate. "Nothing new to report, buddy," she stated. He lowered his head back to the carpet below.

A knock sounded at her door. "Come in, it's open!"

"Hi, Lady Cate! Lunch is served!" Molly announced, carrying the tray to her coffee table. "Wow! Look at all that work. How do you keep everything straight?"

"I'm afraid I'm not keeping much straight on this subject," Cate answered.

"Is this for your book?"

Cate nodded. She hated lying, but she couldn't explain. Plus, it wasn't exactly a lie. She'd likely write about this in her book. "Thanks, Molly!"

"You're welcome. Just remember who serves you your lunch when you're a famous author!"

"I'd never forget!"

Molly smiled at her, almost bumping into Jack as she tried to exit the room. "Oops! You have a visitor! Hey, make it snappy, lunch is ready downstairs!"

"Will do," Jack promised. "I just have a quick question for Lady Cate."

Molly exited, leaving them alone to talk. "What's up?" Cate asked, climbing to her feet.

"I wanted to make a suggestion."

"Okay?"

"Let's head back and check the staff alibis after lunch. It might turn up nothing, but perhaps we can find some clue that will lead us in one direction or another."

"Wait. Is this Jack Reid suggesting we time travel?"

"Very funny, Lady Cate. You should take your act on the road. The Comedian Countess."

"Okay, I won't look a gift horse in the mouth. Let's try it. It won't hurt to ask each of them."

"I'm assuming you have gotten nowhere?" Jack scanned the mess spread across the floor.

"No," Cate admitted. "I'm getting nowhere, just staring at the same information. I even Googled the staff members, but I found nothing. I don't know what I expected to find, but..."

"Googled them? Did you find anything at all? It's not like they were on social media in 1925!"

"Just death notices. Although I couldn't find one for Forsythe. But we have no idea where he went after he left Dunhaven, so I may just be missing it."

"Well, perhaps we'll find something this afternoon. Meet you at one?"

"Sounds good. Now you better get down to your lunch before Molly and Mrs. Fraser have a fit!"

"Okay, see you soon, Cate."

Cate settled in, polishing off her lunch as fast as possible. She left her tray, cleaned up her notes and retreated to her bedroom to prepare for their trip. At 1 p.m., she overheard a commotion in the sitting room as both dogs scurried to greet Jack at the door. "Come in!" she hollered. "Your fan club awaits!"

"Hello, hello!" Jack greeted the dogs as he came in the door. He entered the bedroom, carrying Riley with Bailey trailing behind him. "Are you ready, Detective Cate?"

"I am," Cate assured him. "And my fingers are crossed that we find something. Although, what are the chances of that? The police didn't."

"The police probably didn't even ask the staff, judging by Officer MacCullough's detective skills."

"Good point," Cate admitted.

"Speaking of, we should go to the police station. Make sure Lillian isn't being mistreated."

"Okay," Cate agreed. "It might take a bit to question all the staff. Do you want to split our efforts? You go to the police station while I question the staff?"

"I hate to split up, but it might be easier that way. We'll discuss our findings when we're back."

Cate nodded. "Okay, sounds like a plan. Let's go." Cate held out the timepiece. Together, they used it to slip back to nearly a century earlier. After arriving, Cate and Jack sought Benson. Jack requested a car to town while Cate inquired if she could question the staff about their whereabouts on the night of the theft. Benson approved both requests, telling Cate to use his office to speak with each staff member. He then left her, taking Jack with him to retrieve a car for his trip to town.

Cate scanned the staff list Benson provided her. Most of them were finishing up their lunch when Cate arrived. Benson had asked them to stay until Cate had spoken with them. Cate called the first few kitchen maids, asking them where they were between the hours of 1 a.m. and 11 a.m. For the first several hours, they all reported being asleep. Most of them shared a room with someone else, and neither party recalled hearing the other slip in or out during the night. The scullery maids spent the rest of the morning in the kitchen.

Cate moved on to the cook, whose story was similar. She then worked her way through the maids and footmen. No one's stories drew any red flags. All reported being asleep until early morning, when they began their chores. They worked in pairs which provided them with solid alibis.

Cate moved on to Charles Forsythe. She found him in the silver storage room, pulling several pieces from the shelves to be polished.

"Sorry to interrupt. Do you have a moment?" Cate inquired.

"Yes, Mrs. MacKenzie. It's no interruption. I am checking the silver pieces used over the holiday have been properly polished."

"We can speak here if you prefer so you may continue your work."

"If it's convenient and no trouble to you."

"No trouble at all."

Cate asked the standard barrage of questions. She received the answers she expected. Mr. Forsythe's only difference was he did not share a room with another staff member. A privilege of being the under-butler. Other than that, his story matched the other staff members: he was asleep until early morning, when he arose to begin his duties. Several people saw and spoke to him that morning. Cate thanked him for his time, checking his name off her list.

She then moved on to her last group of people. She interviewed the grooms. Nothing in their stories seemed suspicious. The last name on her list was Rory's valet. He had been mending an overcoat and finished as Cate searched him out. "May I have a moment to ask a few questions?" Cate asked.

"May I return this upstairs first?" he questioned.

"It won't take but a moment," Cate assured him. This was the second time the man avoided her request. "Can you return it after?"

The man dithered a bit before nodding his head. "All right, Mrs. MacKenzie."

"Thank you. If I'm not mistaken, you took ill the night of the theft, is that correct?"

"Yes, it is."

"And did you spend the entire night in your room?"

"No," he admitted.

Cate glanced up from her note sheet. "No?" she verified.

"No. I was not in my room from 3 a.m. to four-thirty."

"May I ask where you were?"

"My stomach still experienced fits. I didn't want to keep my roommate awake, so I came down here. I returned around four-thirty and fell asleep until seven. Then I arose and began my normal work."

"Who is your roommate?"

"Thomas, the groom."

"Did anyone see you downstairs?"

"No, I'm afraid not."

"Was Thomas abed when you left?"

"Yes, I believe so. I didn't check for certain."

"And when you returned?"

He nodded. "Yes. Again, I believe so. It was dark, and I didn't check."

"Thank you, Mr. Calhoun. That's all."

The man left the room. Cate checked her notes. Thomas Gould mentioned Robert Calhoun being his roommate, but he omitted hearing him leave. Was Calhoun that quiet? Or was Thomas Gould not there to realize he'd left? Robert Calhoun specifically mentioned he did not check and was not certain that Thomas was in the room. Thomas Gould was a name on her suspect list. Was he the thief?

She climbed the stairs, navigating to the sitting room. She collapsed on the loveseat there to wait for Jack's return. Her mind swirled with questions. She attempted to piece together a situation in which Thomas Gould was the thief. After building the case against him, she played devil's advocate, trying to poke holes in her theory and identify weak points. Next, she tried to create a scenario in which Robert Calhoun stole the jewelry. He had no solid alibi and admitted being out of his room. But why admit it when he easily could have lied and stated he was in his room the entire night? Perhaps he was afraid Thomas Gould realized his absence and reported it. Or perhaps he admitted it to throw investigators off the scent. To appear upfront and honest, when he was the thief.

Jack's entrance into the room interrupted Cate's thoughts. "Well?" Cate asked, standing.

"She had a good night. They left her alone. They still won't release her, but at least we've succeeded in assuring they won't harass her into a confession."

"Good," Cate said. "One thing settled. For now."

"No hits on the servant query?"

"Nothing solid, but something interesting."

"What's that?" Jack inquired.

"Our sick valet admitted to being out of his room between three and four-thirty."

"Really? Did he say why? Maybe tell you he was stealing a few necklaces?"

"Nothing quite that definitive," Cate answered with a chuckle. "He said he was downstairs in the servants' dining hall. Said he was sick and didn't want to wake his roommate. No one saw him. No one can corroborate the story."

"What about the roommate? Can he at least confirm the times? That he was gone from three to four-thirty?"

"That's interesting, too. His roommate is Thomas Gould."

Jack raised his eyebrow. "One of our suspects."

"Yes," Cate replied. "And he never mentioned the valet's absence. So, either he didn't know, or he's lying."

"To protect Calhoun?"

"Or because he didn't realize he was gone because Thomas Gould wasn't in the room but rather was stealing the jewelry. Robert Calhoun couldn't be sure Thomas Gould was in bed when he left or when he returned. He said the room was dark, and he didn't pay attention, he assumed he was there."

"Hmm. That's the first solid lead we've had. Two people without alibis during the time the theft may have occurred."

"I wouldn't say solid, but it's something!"

"Yes. Let's concentrate on those two. Perhaps we can dig something up on where Thomas Gould gets himself off to and trace things from there."

"Okay, I'll research it tonight. Should we plan to return tomorrow morning? Perhaps float any information we have past Rory?"

"You want to speak with him now?"

Cate shook her head. "No. We don't have much. I'd rather try to find something more substantial. Rory doesn't want to believe one of his staff did it. We'll need something significant to convince him."

"Okay, let's go home then."

Cate agreed, and they returned to the bedroom, slipping back to the present. Jack sighed with relief as they returned. "It's good to be home. At least we made some progress on this trip though!"

"A little," Cate admitted. "I'll keep searching, maybe we can make something stick. And at least Lillian is having an easier time."

"Yeah. Shame I couldn't have her released."

"Losing your legal skills?"

"Well, I haven't applied them for almost seventy years! I'm rusty." Cate chuckled at his poor joke. "I'll try again tomorrow."

"You're a good guy, Jack Reid," Cate replied, grinning at him.

"And you are quite a lady, Lady Cate," Jack responded, bowing to her. "Text me if you find anything in your research."

"I will," Cate promised.

She set up camp in her sitting room for the rest of the

afternoon. She performed an Internet search for both men's names, searching for any information available on them. There wasn't much, but she pieced together that Rory's valet passed away in his late sixties in a neighboring village. He'd owned a small farm there he'd purchased after leaving the life of service with money he'd saved. Cate noted it, wondering if he'd used money from selling the stolen jewelry to purchase it.

Thomas Gould, the groom who'd left Dunhaven Castle months after the theft, died years later in London. He'd owned a restaurant there in partnership with another man, an Italian. The restaurant was well known for its pasta. How did Thomas afford to buy the restaurant? Was his fortune changed by stolen items?

Cate continued to search for more information about either man's change of fortune. She also consulted the household records to determine if she could glean any additional details from them. Cate worked through dinner, scouring every resource she could find.

After hours of work, she tracked down information on Robert Calhoun's land purchase. The land was owned by the MacKenzies. Cate noted it, wondering if Rory had given the man a break on the price after years of loyal service.

She continued on to search for information on Thomas Gould's restaurant. As she searched, her eyes became heavy. Despite the early hour, Cate fought to stay awake. The extra hours being crammed into her day were catching up with her.

Cate let her head drop back onto the chaise for a moment. Within seconds, Cate drifted to sleep. She startled awake. Darkness surrounded her. She must have fallen asleep and stayed asleep for a few hours. Outside, only starlight shined in the sky. She reached to the lamp, flicking it on. Nothing happened. She tried again but met with the same result. The power must have gone out, she surmised. Cate searched the drawer of the table for a flashlight, finding none. She stumbled from the chaise into her bedroom, feeling her way to her night table. She kept a flashlight in the drawer for just such occasions, although she hadn't needed it since her arrival.

Cate flicked it on, and its dim light shined onto the wall in front of her. The clock on the night table was unlit, confirming further her theory on the power outage. She checked her timepiece. Midnight. No sense in worrying about the power failure at this hour. She didn't want to wake anyone for the problem. Instead, she'd go back to bed and hope to sleep.

She headed back to the sitting room to collect Riley and Bailey. Before she called them to go to bed, her sitting room doors blew open. A chilly wind circulated the room. Cate shrugged her cardigan tighter around her shoulders as she crossed the room to determine the source and close the doors. As she grabbed hold of both door handles, Cate heard a noise. It began as a deep growl and seemed to originate from somewhere down the hall. She strained to listen. As she turned her ear toward the sound, it changed. "CATHERINE," a deep voice growled. Startled, Cate leapt back a step. The voice's owner was unknown, and Cate did not recognize it as belonging to anyone she knew.

Cate took a deep, steadying breath. "You're going batty, old girl," she told herself aloud, trying to remain calm. Her heart thudded in her chest so hard it echoed in her ears. "It's an old house, there are lots of noises," Cate continued, "you're imagining things."

She grabbed the door handles again, intent on closing the doors and going to bed. As she pushed the doors shut, the sound occurred again, this time, louder. "CATHERINE!" the voice roared as though displeased by being ignored.

This time the sound was unmistakable. Cate was incapable of talking herself down. This noise was not the random groaning of an aging castle. It was a voice. Someone called to her. Who? Cate shined the flashlight beam down the hall, her pulse quickening. "Who's there?" she called.

She took a tentative step into the hallway, shining the beam around. It failed to penetrate the length of the hall. Cate swallowed hard and took another few steps. "Hello?" she called again into the darkness. "Jack? Mr. Fraser?" Though she realized the voice did not belong to either of them, she hoped by some strange set of circumstances they were in the castle.

A wave of fear passed over Cate as a chill filled the air around her. Something was not right. She would text Jack despite the time of night. She could not shake this foreboding feeling. Cate retreated a step, continuing to keep her eye on the end of the hall. After a few steps backward, she turned and ran toward her suite like a child running up their basement stairs from the monsters they presumed hid in the darkness below.

As she reached the doors, they slammed shut. Cate turned the doorknob, pushing against the door, but it didn't budge. She pounded against it, pushing with her shoulder, but it was shut tight. Cate turned her back to the door, leaning against it as she lamented the fact that her cell phone lay behind the doors, preventing her from texting Jack. She'd search for Molly. She should be asleep in her bedroom at this hour.

As her mind parsed through ideas of what do to next, the floor shook, winds blew through the hall and the voice spoke again. "CATHERINE!"

Cate held her hands over her ears, squeezing her eyes shut. She slid down the door behind her to a sitting position. "Stop!" she shouted back. Silence fell over the castle and the air calmed. Cate removed her hands from muffling her ears.

Another noise sounded throughout the castle. Jack's voice called to her. "Cate? Lady Cate?"

"Jack!" she shouted in response. She climbed to her feet. Cate raced down the hall toward Jack's voice.

"Cate!" he called again.

"Jack! I'm here," she answered, turning the corner toward the main staircase. Jack's voice sounded again below, though he seemed further away. "Jack!" she yelled again. "Don't move, I'm coming to you!"

Cate hurried down the stairs, arriving at the foyer. She splayed her light around the area, searching in all directions for a sign of Jack. "Jack?" she called into the darkness around her.

"Lady Cate!" his voice answered from her left.

"I'm here! Stay where you are, I'll come to you!" she shouted back. Cate traversed down the hall. Light shined from the library. Jack must be inside. Cate hurried toward the room. She entered, toggling off her light. The power was on in this room. Lamps were lit across the room.

Jack stood near the bookshelf. He stared at it, his back to her. "Jack! There you are!" Cate exclaimed. "The power is out everywhere but here!"

He did not respond, nor did he move. "Jack?" Cate questioned. She stepped toward him. "Jack?" She received no response. "Jack," she said again, growing irked by his lack of response. "This isn't funny." She paused. "Come on, I'm serious. Some weird stuff has been happening and I'm a little scared." She closed the gap between them, tapping him on the shoulder. "Jack?"

The figure twisted enough for Cate to realize this was not Jack. He grasped her arm, pulling her in front of him. His other arm squeezed around her waist, pulling her against him and leaving her no room to escape. She wriggled in his grasp but could not pull away.

"Hello, Catherine," the man hissed.

"Who are you?" Cate choked through tears.

She received no response. The bookshelf in front of her dissolved away, leaving only a black void. Her captor pushed her toward it. "No!" she screamed, struggling against him. She dug her feet into the floor, but he pushed her as though she were only a doll. "NO!" She shrieked again. As blackness closed around her, she cried for help, but none came.

CHAPTER 18

Cate shot upright, sweat beaded on her forehead and her heart pounded. Tears streamed from her eyes and she gulped for air. She glanced around her surroundings. She was sprawled on her chaise in her sitting room. The side table lamp lit the room. Fresh tears fell as Cate realized she'd only been dreaming. She clutched at her blanket as her heart slowed. She wiped her tears with the back of her hand, once again feeling foolish.

Cate collapsed back onto the chaise behind her. Why were these dreams so taxing on her, she wondered? She was well beyond the age where nightmares should cause this much stress. Stress, yes, perhaps that was the cause, Cate surmised. These would disappear once she'd solved the mystery of the jewelry theft, she assured herself.

Cate reached for her phone to check the time, finding it was only ten. She also found a text message from Jack. After toggling her text app open, she read his message: *Find anything interesting?*

Cate wondered if it was too late to return the text. Perhaps it was, but she decided to anyway, hoping the distraction would calm her nerves. She typed back: *Maybe... found both of our new suspects made larger purchases after leaving the estate... not exactly a smoking gun but maybe enough to look into further*

Cate set the phone down on her lap. Despite the normalcy around her, Cate's nerves were still unsettled. Her phone's text alert made her jump. She fumbled with the device to open the text from Jack: *Interesting... we should follow up on it tomorrow... I was wondering where you were... thought you fell asleep on me*

Cate smiled at the message and responded: *Yes... we should... and I did, sorry... fell asleep and had another nightmare... ugh :(*

Within a minute, Jack returned a text: *That stupid bookshelf again?!*

Cate responded with an affirmative and waited a few breaths before the next text arrived: *Sorry, Lady Cate... I hope we solve this mystery soon... you need a good rest! Do you think you can sleep now?*

Cate pondered the question. Tiredness surged through her, the reaction to the nightmare only lent toward her fatigue. She responded: *Yes... I think so*

Jack replied: *Good. You can tell me all about the latest version of your nightmare tomorrow... for now, get some rest. :) Good night, Lady Cate.*

Cate replied with a similar sentiment before toggling her phone off and gathering the dogs for bed. After a short trip outside, she retired, able to fall asleep despite her frightening experience.

The sun creeping over the moors awakened Cate the following morning. She rose with a groan, cursing the nightmare for having spent her energy. Still, she was eager to follow up on her leads gathered from her day of research.

Cate passed the morning searching for any other information she could find about the purchases made by the valet and the groom. She found Thomas Gould purchased and opened his restaurant only a few months after leaving Dunhaven Castle. Cate noted the information, finding it suspicious. Where did he get the money to purchase a restaurant so soon after working as a groom?

Cate moved her staff lunch from Wednesday to today since she had spent the day researching yesterday. After lunch, Cate requested a few moments to speak with Jack concerning some estate business.

They proceeded upstairs and Cate started to climb to the next floor to change and return to the past. Before she could ascend the stairs, Jack grabbed her arm. "Wait," he said. "Do you want to talk about your nightmare?"

Cate stepped back onto the landing with a shrug of her shoulders. "It's becoming more of an annoyance now than anything. Silly, really," she admitted. "I wake up with my heart pounding, sometimes in tears." Cate shook her head. "I feel ridiculous. Like a child."

"It's not silly. Nightmares can happen to anyone. Was it the same thing as before?"

"This one was different, but it still involved the bookshelf."

"What happened?"

"I was in my sitting room. I must have been asleep because the dream started when I woke up. The lights were out. I thought the power was off. I was on my way to bed when the doors to the room blew open. I went to close them, and someone called my name. They continued to call me. I walked down the hall to determine where it was coming from and the doors to my sitting room blew shut. I tried to open them, but I couldn't. While I was figuring out what to do, I heard your voice calling me. I followed it and you were in the library. Or at least I thought it was you, but it wasn't. It was someone else. They grabbed me and the bookshelf disappeared, and they shoved me into the black hole. Then I woke up." Cate shrugged. "I don't understand what my obsession is with the bookshelf, but something about it bothers me."

"Hmm," Jack mused aloud, "I still think this is stress. We found the note you're fixated on in a book on that shelf. That's why your mind is dwelling on it."

"I'm hardly fixated on it, but I think it's an important clue!"

"Either way, it came from the bookshelf. Your mind is associating that with all the stress of assuming your great-grandfather is a thief."

Cate nodded. "I hope that's it. There's only one way to determine that: to solve the case. Let's go try!"

"Okay, Lady Cate. I'll change and meet you in your suite."

Cate nodded, and they climbed the stairs, parting ways to dress for the time period they'd soon find themselves immersed in. Jack knocked at the sitting room door as Cate pulled on her second shoe. "Come in!" she shouted. Jack entered as Cate fastened the buckle and stepped into the sitting room to meet him. "Ready?"

"Yes. Do we have a plan? Talk to the two servants again? Or Rory?"

"What about Forsythe or Benson? They'd have the most information about the servants. Perhaps we should consult with them and determine if we can find any additional information that clarifies the future purchases they made. Thomas Gould, the groom, purchases his restaurant soon after leaving Dunhaven, which is only a few months after the theft."

"Interesting timing," Jack noted. "Perhaps he had the funds to make such a large purchase from a little black-market jewelry sale."

"I'm wondering the same thing. That puts him square at the top of our suspect list!"

"All right then, we have our plan. Away we go," Jack stated, holding his hand out for the timepiece.

They arrived in 1925 and exited the bedroom, descending below stairs to find Benson or Forsythe. Benson's office was empty, but they found Forsythe in the mending room. Cate knocked at the door jamb. "Mr. and Mrs. MacKenzie," Forsythe answered, standing. "Is there anything wrong? May I help you?"

"I was hoping to have a few more minutes of your time," Cate responded. "We've a few questions about two staff members you may be able to assist with."

"I'd be happy to. Please, let us use Mr. Benson's office for privacy." He ushered them down the hall to the office, closing the door behind them. "How did your inquiry go yesterday, Mrs. MacKenzie? I hope it proved fruitful. Murray's situation has upset us all."

"All of you but one," Cate replied.

Forsythe's brows knit together. "But one?"

"Whoever is the real thief. They probably don't care."

"Ah, I see your meaning. And you suppose one of the staff is the culprit?"

Cate shook her head. "I don't suppose anything just yet. But there were questions raised yesterday that bear following up on."

"I shall assist you in any way I can," Forsythe assured them.

"Thomas Gould and Robert Calhoun share a room, is that correct?" Cate inquired.

"Yes, that is correct," Forsythe confirmed.

"And Robert Calhoun was the ill staff member the night of the theft?"

"Correct. Mr. Benson sent him to bed following our dinner. The poor man was ill."

"According to Mr. Calhoun, he remained ill. And in the wee hours of the morning, he exited his room and came to the servants' dining hall so as not to wake his roommate."

"Interesting, I assume no one can confirm his story."

"No, which leaves two of the servants without an alibi during the hours the theft occurred."

"I see. That is concerning. Do you suspect one of them?"

"I'm not well enough acquainted with either to accuse them and their lack of alibi is no proof of guilt. Perhaps you can tell us more. Is there any reason to suspect either? Perhaps a financial issue that may have prompted them to do something so desperate?"

"We're not looking to accuse anyone, we just want the truth," Jack added.

Forsythe remained silent for a moment. "I'm not aware of anything, but if you'll give me a day, perhaps I can track down some information that may help confirm or refute any suspicion against them."

"All right," Cate replied with a nod. "That would be most helpful. Thank you."

"Shall we agree to meet here around this time tomorrow?"

"Yes, we'll see you then, thank you."

"Yes, thank you," Jack added. "Would you be able to arrange a car for a trip to town?"

"Yes, I shall do so at once, Mr. MacKenzie. You may wait in the sitting room; I'll have the car brought 'round."

"Thank you," Jack answered.

Cate and Jack departed the office, climbing the stairs to the main floor. "Going to check on Lillian?" Cate inquired as they entered the sitting room.

"Yes, I think we should."

Cate nodded in agreement. "I hope she's had another peaceful night. Well, as peaceful as possible in a jail cell."

"Me too, otherwise I'll have to flex some legal muscle," Jack quipped, flexing his own muscle in a ridiculous pose.

The car passed the window, rolling to a stop outside the front door. "There's our ride," Cate said, standing from the loveseat. They proceeded to the car and into town.

The clerk's shoulders sagged as they entered the police station. "I'll get her, go ahead back," he waved them on as they approached the desk.

"Thank you," Jack answered, proceeding down the now-familiar hall to the interrogation room. They settled into the uncomfortable chairs as they waited for Lillian. A uniformed officer led her into the room, handcuffed.

"Hello, Lillian," Cate greeted her as she sat down. She reached across to take her hand. "How are you holding up?"

"All right under the circumstances, Mrs. MacKenzie, thank you."

"Have they let you rest?"

"Mostly, aye," Lillian nodded.

Jack stared at her until she made eye contact. "Lillian, has something happened?"

She shook her head, averting her gaze.

"Lillian," Cate prodded, squeezing her hand tighter, "you can tell us anything. It's important you are honest with us so we can help you."

"Have you made any progress?" Lillian queried.

"A little," Cate admitted. "We're following a few leads, but we have nothing solid yet. Lillian, don't avoid the question. If the police have mistreated you, you must tell us. Jack can handle them to be sure they don't trouble you further."

"I'm a terrible burden, complaining when you're already doing so much to help," Lillian replied, a tear rolling down her cheek.

"You're no burden, Lillian," Jack assured her. "I've a legal background and if they've done anything since our last visit, even talked to you without someone else present, we should know."

Lillian glanced between them both. "They questioned me again," she responded. Jack groaned. "They didn't harm me, only made me answer questions again."

"They've no right to do that," Jack stated. "I'll see that you're not bothered again. Stay here with her, Cate." Jack stood from his seat and stormed from the room.

Cate squeezed Lillian's hand. After a breath she said, "While we wait, perhaps you can give me some information on two of the servants in the house."

"I'll help in any way I can, Mrs. MacKenzie."

"We've learned there are two servants without alibis. We're not suggesting they are guilty, but we are following up on any leads like this. The two are Thomas Gould and Robert Calhoun. Do you know much about either?"

"Mr. Gould, no, I'm not well acquainted with him. But I've spent some time with Mr. Calhoun. Our schedules are often similar, being that we serve Lord and Lady MacKenzie. So we've spent some time together mending and the like. Surely you don't suspect Mr. Calhoun. I can't imagine him stealing from his lordship. He has a heart of gold."

"As I mentioned, we're not pointing the finger at anyone, but he was alone for a time the night of the theft."

"He was ill in his room."

Cate nodded. "Yes, but he left his room in the wee hours of the morning so as not to wake his roommate. He went to the servants' dining hall, but no one saw him there. That left both Mr. Calhoun and Mr. Gould alone for almost two hours."

Lillian furrowed her brow, considering the information. "Do you imagine Mr. Gould could have done it in that time?

Oh, how cruel I must sound. I hate to accuse him, but I'm innocent and someone had to do it!"

Cate shook her head. "You don't sound cruel. And you're right. Someone did it. We have to explore every avenue!"

Jack's return interrupted their conversation. He brought with him Officer MacCullough and another uniformed officer. "Remove the handcuffs," Jack instructed.

"Just a moment," Officer MacCullough replied, holding his hand up. "There are terms Miss Murray must be apprised of."

Cate glanced between Jack and MacCullough, confusion on her face. "By all means," Jack responded.

"Miss Murray, your attorney, Mr. MacKenzie has arranged for your release. During this time, you may not leave town for any reason. You should confine yourself to the estate..."

"Ah," Jack began, interrupting him.

"Calm down, Mr. MacKenzie, I said should not must. You are still our primary suspect, Miss Murray. You'd do well to remember that." He motioned to the officer. "Go ahead." The officer stepped forward, unlocking the handcuffs and removing them. "You're free to go, Miss Murray. For now." The officer turned on his heel and strode from the room, the uniformed officer trailing behind him.

"Come along, Lillian, you'll sleep in your own bed tonight. You can ride back with us," Jack said, helping her to her feet.

Lillian stood as though in a daze and Cate wondered if she may collapse. She hoped Jack had a firm hold of her arm. Cate rose in the event Lillian fainted. The woman stood in silence for a moment before throwing her arms around Jack's neck. Tears streamed down her face and she squeezed him tight.

After a moment she pulled back, wiping at her face. "Oh,

I'm so sorry, Mr. and Mrs. MacKenzie. I realize how untoward that was, but I never pretended to be a high lady! If I possessed any less grace, I'd have kissed you right on the cheek! I'm ever so grateful for this. My own bed tonight, I can't tell you how that feels!"

"You're welcome, Lillian. Remember, we've got an uphill battle still to fight. But at least you'll be able to get proper rest."

"Can we go? I've no desire to stay in this place another minute." Lillian laughed.

"Of course. After you," Jack agreed, motioning Lillian to precede him. He offered his arm to Cate. She grasped it, giving it a squeeze as they stepped into the hall. She beamed at him.

"I do not understand how you do it, Jack, but you are an amazing attorney!"

"A legal genius, you might say."

"You very well may be! One thing's certain: you're that girl's hero!" Cate exclaimed.

"And I nearly scored a kiss for it, too!"

"Is that the price tag for bail these days?" Cate queried.

"The smile on her face and yours was enough payment for me, Lady Cate."

They emerged from the police station. Lillian glanced up to the gray winter sky overhead, smiling at it with tears in her eyes. "Never expected to see it again. Oh, Mr. MacKenzie, I cannae thank you enough. But there is one issue."

"Issue?" Jack questioned as they crossed the street.

"I'm afraid I cannae afford your services. I've nothing to pay you with," Lillian confessed.

"Don't you worry about that. This is pro bono," Jack assured her.

"Pro bono, sir?" Lillian questioned before climbing into the car's front seat next to the driver.

"No charge, Lillian. No charge. Don't worry about it."

"Oh, but I couldn't, sir!" Lillian objected.

"Yes, you can, and you will," Jack assured her, easing her into the car and closing the door. "And I don't want to hear any more about it," he added, as he slid into the backseat next to Cate.

Lillian smiled at him but said no more as the car pulled away from town, heading toward Dunhaven Castle. Lillian offered another smile to both of them as the car swung onto the drive leading to the castle and eased to a stop outside the front door. Jack and Cate let themselves in the front door, bringing Lillian with them despite her protestations about using the inappropriate door.

"Just this once won't hurt, Lillian," Cate assured her. She took her to the sitting room. "We'll inform Lord MacKenzie you're back, wait here."

Cate followed Jack to Rory's study, where they found him reviewing paperwork for nearby land holdings. "Jack, Cate, any news?" he asked, glancing up from his paperwork.

"Yes," Jack informed him. "I've managed to get Lillian released from jail for the time being while the case is still open. She's not permitted to leave town, but at least she can return here and sleep in her own bed."

"Released? However did you manage that?" Rory questioned, astounded by the news.

"I've a background in law. The treatment she was receiving was beyond questionable and would ruin most of their case against her. It was in their best interest to release her pending the conclusion of the investigation."

"Have they any new information?"

"No," Jack responded. "They have pursued little beyond hounding Miss Murray for a confession."

"Poor girl," Rory murmured, tossing his paper onto his desk. "I'm glad you got her released. Is she here?"

"Yes," Cate chimed in with a nod, "I've asked her to wait in the sitting room. I wasn't sure if you or Anne would like to speak with her before she returns to her quarters."

"I am certain Anne would like to see her, yes," Rory answered, pushing himself up to standing. "I shall inform her at once."

"We'll wait with her until Anne arrives," Cate stated.

"Good."

They separated from Rory, who ascended the main stairs to inform and retrieve Anne. Jack and Cate continued across the foyer to the sitting room. Lillian sat perched on the edge of the sofa as though afraid to touch it. "Lord MacKenzie is retrieving Lady MacKenzie. He's sure she'll want to see you before you go to your room," Cate informed her. She sat next to Lillian on the sofa.

Moments later the doors to the room burst open and Anne rushed in, followed by Rory. "Murray!" she cried, rushing to the girl's side. "It's so good to have you back!" Lillian stood as Anne reached her, grasping Lillian's hands in hers. "Are you well?"

"I am, m'lady, yes," Lillian assured her.

"Oh, thank you for arranging this, Jack," Anne gushed, turning to reach for Jack's hand. She gave it a squeeze.

"You're welcome."

"Will this trouble Murray further?" she questioned.

"I'm afraid the case isn't closed yet but we're working to find more information so Lillian can put this behind her. Unfortunately, she's still the top suspect."

"Oh, how dreadful," Anne lamented.

"She won't be for long if we have anything to say about it," Cate asserted.

"Thank you both for your help on this. We are most grateful," Rory added.

"Yes, quite," Anne followed up. "Now," she continued,

turning toward Lillian, "I suppose you should go straight to bed."

"I'm all right, m'lady," Lillian assured her again. "I can attend to you before dinner if you aren't put off by my situation."

"Nonsense," Anne answered. "However, formal dinner is not being held this evening because of the uproar in the house. You can begin tomorrow if you feel up to it."

"I shall. I am most eager to work again, m'lady," Lillian stated.

"Then I shall see you tomorrow morning to dress for the day. Have you informed Benson of your return?"

"Not yet, m'lady. Mr. and Mrs. MacKenzie instructed me to wait here and speak with you first."

"Quite right of them. We shall inform him now and see that he is aware of the rest you require after your ordeal." Anne approached the call bell cord on the wall and rang for Benson. He appeared moments later and, after a brief conversation, led Lillian to the servants' quarters to speak with the head housekeeper before returning to her room.

"Again," Anne said once they were alone, "thank you both so much for arranging her release. I do hope she is troubled no more with this."

"You're welcome, Anne," Jack answered. "Well, we will leave you to enjoy the rest of your evening. We have dinner plans in a neighboring town."

"I hope you enjoy them," Rory said, smiling at them. They took their leave, heading upstairs to their bedroom.

"Ready to head back?" Cate queried when they arrived.

"Yes," Jack answered. "More than ready."

"I'll bet! You need a break after all your legal maneuvering," Cate joked.

"Oh, yes," Jack assured her. "I've exhausted my legal

muscles with all that flexing." Jack struck his strong man pose again, eliciting a giggle from Cate.

"Okay, come on, then, let's get you home so you can rest." They activated the timepiece's mechanism, drawing them back to the present time.

Jack gave his now customary sigh of relief after returning. "Boy, I hope Forsythe gives us some good information tomorrow. I'd like to wash my hands of this mystery and my legal career."

"Me too. Should we go with the same plan? Head back following lunch?"

"That'll work. That seems to be an opportune hour to speak with Forsythe."

"Okay. I'll keep working on finding information until then."

* * *

Cate spent the next several hours in a fruitless search for information on their two prime suspects. After dinner, she continued but gave up after an hour when she hit her thousandth dead end. She opted to stream a few episodes of a comedy show to ease her mind before bed. She found it did little to stop her brain from parsing through questions, scenarios and concocting more theories.

An hour before she turned in, her phone chimed to signal a text message. She found a message from Jack: *I hope you don't have any nightmares tonight, Lady Cate*

Cate smiled at the message, agreeing with the sentiment. She responded: *Me too... hit a dead end on my research here... hope Forsythe has some news tomorrow!*

Jack typed back: *Me too... I'm doing my homework over here.*

Cate wrinkled her brow in confusion, responding: *Homework?*

Jack returned a photo message showing his laptop streaming a police procedural show. Then responded: *Get some sleep, Lady Cate, see you tomorrow :)*

Cate chuckled at the picture, then toggled off her phone display after wishing Jack pleasant dreams and finished two more episodes attempting to lull her mind into a restful state. She retired for the evening, sleeping without interruption after her extended day and restless prior night.

CHAPTER 19

A bundle of nerves, Cate spent the morning distracting herself with her manuscript. She drummed her fingers against the table rather than adding meaningful content. But despite her distracted mind, she added two thousand words to her document before lunch.

Cate sped through her lunch and changed for their trip back. She sat waiting for Jack in her sitting room, drumming her fingers on the chaise's side as she waited. Giving up on that, she paced the floor as her mind spun out of control, wondering what information Forsythe would provide them.

"What do you think, boys? Will we solve this mystery today?" Cate inquired of the two dogs.

Riley eyed her, his head cocked to the side in a quizzical display. "Yeah, I doubt it, too, Riley," Cate admitted. "But perhaps Forsythe will give us some clue that will allow us to catch a break!"

Riley gave her a small yip after her last comment.

"I'll take that as a 'yes,'" Cate answered as a knock sounded at her door. "Come in!" she called.

"Hello, Lady Cate and her loyal subjects," Jack announced as he entered the room. "Ready?"

"Beyond ready. Let's go so I can stop pacing the floor and fretting about what we might discover."

"Okay, let's head back then." They entered the bedroom and slipped back to the bygone era. "Here we are, let's go straight to Forsythe. I'm dying to hear what he has to say."

"You and me both!" Cate exclaimed as they hurried from the room to the servants' area. When they arrived, Jack peeked into Benson's office, finding both Benson and Forsythe inside.

"Ah, Mr. MacKenzie," Benson greeted him. "Thank goodness you're here."

"Oh?" Jack replied, confused by the greeting.

"Yes," Benson continued, skirting his desk and approaching them. "Lord MacKenzie asked that I bring you to him at once should I run into you. There has been a problem with the police and given your law background, he'd like your expert opinion on the matter."

"Oh," Jack muttered, "a problem?"

"Yes, please follow me. A dreadful business, this," Benson added at the end.

"Oh, but…" Jack began.

"Go," Cate said, squeezing his hand. "And good luck."

"Ah… okay," Jack replied with a shrug, following Benson down the hall. He glanced back at Cate with a shrug, flashing his crossed fingers to her.

Cate pushed the door closed behind them, turning to Forsythe. "Is this an opportune moment to speak?" she questioned.

"Yes, though, with the uproar, I only have a few moments to impart my news."

"News? So, you found something?" Cate questioned, her voice raising to match the excitement coursing through her.

"Possibly," Forsythe answered. "I questioned the staff very casually about both men. Mr. Calhoun seems to have garnered a stellar reputation with the staff. Most consider him to be above reproach, and I found nothing untoward in his background or character." Cate nodded, and he continued. "But… Mr. Gould has a bit of a different reputation."

"Oh?" Cate inquired.

"Yes. Seems he enjoys alcohol more than he should. And he also enjoys cards. Last week during a regular card game that occurs in the stables, he imbibed quite a few drinks and told everyone he'd soon have enough money to open a restaurant. He confessed it to be a lifelong dream of his. No one could determine how he'd come up with the money for the venture, especially after he mentioned the location of the business he'd like to start."

"Where?" Cate asked, playing innocent.

"London!" Forsythe exclaimed, raising an eyebrow. "I'm certain you are aware of how expensive a venture of that nature would be!"

"I see," Cate murmured, deep in thought. "Yes, I understand your meaning. Thank you for the information. It's most helpful."

"Of course, Mrs. MacKenzie. If I learn anything else, I shall pass it along to you. I imagine this may have some bearing though, given the claims he made about coming into money."

The door to the office burst open. "Mr. Forsythe, you'd better come quickly," a maid said.

"Thank you, Forsythe," Cate said to end the conversation. She preceded him through the door and ascended the stairs to the main floor as he continued in the opposite direction to the servants' hall. Cate heard shouting coming from the sitting room. She hurried toward the room, slipping inside and into a firestorm.

Jack and Rory stood with Officer MacCullough and two other uniformed officers. Jack shouted at them, "... ludicrous! Nothing more than a scare tactic! You're upsetting the household for no good reason."

Officer MacCullough sighed. "As I've explained multiple times, I have a warrant to search the girl's room again. Your opinion on the matter, while noted, is meaningless."

Jack snatched the paper from the officer's hands, scanning it. "Fine," he retorted, tossing it back at the man, "but don't linger longer than needed and keep yourselves to only her space. I shall observe the search."

"Fine," the man answered with a grunt. "Boys..." He shoved a finger toward the upstairs, signaling for them to proceed with their search.

Cate joined Jack as they followed the police. She offered a questioning glance his way, eyebrows raised. "They want to search Lillian's room... again," Jack whispered.

Cate nodded in understanding as they climbed to the top floor housing the servants' quarters. The police charged down the hall to Lillian's room. The housekeeper waited outside. Lillian stood inside the door, wringing her hands. Cate approached her, putting her arm around Lillian's shoulders.

"Search it all," MacCullough grumbled to the other two officers, scanning the sparse furniture in the room. The other two officers each headed to separate corners, beginning their search. They tore drawers from the wardrobe, dumping their contents on the floor. Clothes were torn from hangers and tossed in a heap after they were poked and prodded to search for hiding spots. A small tin keepsake box clattered to the floor, startling Lillian and Cate after its contents were littered across the floor.

"Officer MacCullough, instruct your men to be more delicate, they are frightening the ladies," Jack warned.

The man grunted at them. "Perhaps the ladies should wait outside," he suggested.

"I will not be told where I can wait," Cate groused at him.

"Try to be a little quieter, boys," the man acquiesced, sounding anything but genuine in his request.

They continued their search, peering behind the furniture. They ended by stripping the beds and tossing the mattresses onto the floor. Nothing was found.

"Satisfied?" Jack questioned.

"Hardly," Officer MacCullough responded. He approached Lillian, who shook from witnessing the entire experience. "Where are you hiding them, girl? Sold them already?"

"I have done nothing!" she cried.

"That's enough!" Jack barked, stepping between the officer and Lillian. "You conducted your search, that is all your warrant allowed. Now leave."

"I have every right to question the suspect!" MacCullough maintained. "And if you interfere again, I'll take her back into custody."

"You'll do nothing of the sort. You've turned up no evidence to warrant her arrest. Just because you suspect her does not mean you can do as you please. You've had her in custody for over forty-eight hours. In that time, you've turned up no evidence to support your theory. At this juncture, any action on your part to remand her into your custody is harassment. Any judge will agree."

"You're preventing me from doing my job, Mr. MacKenzie. Any judge will see that!"

"I'm not. If you were doing your job, you'd be considering other suspects instead of railroading my innocent client. You've no proof Miss Murray did anything. In fact, at each turn, you are presented evidence of her innocence that you discard! And while you continue to pursue this dead end, the real thief is getting away with a crime! No, Officer MacCullough, what the judge will see is an incompetent policeman who is failing to do his job."

MacCullough huffed at Jack but backed down. "This isn't the end of this, Mr. MacKenzie," he answered after a breath, wagging his finger at Jack.

"I should hope not. It would be best if you actually caught the thief," Jack called as Officer MacCullough led the other officers from the room.

"Wow! Great job, Jack!" Cate whispered after they cleared the room.

Lillian glanced around the room. "Yes, thank you, Mr. MacKenzie…" she paused. "I had better clean up." She reached to pick up the tin memento box. A whimper escaped her lips as she began placing her strewn keepsakes back in the box.

"Let me help," Cate offered, kneeling down and gathering items of clothing from the floor.

"Oh, no, Mrs. MacKenzie, please. I've got it, it's mine to take care of. You've done enough for me."

"This will take a while, Lillian. You need help! It's no problem," Cate assured her.

"Cate's correct," Jack chimed in, heaving one mattress back onto its frame. "This is too large a job for one person."

"You are both too kind," Lillian murmured as they continued the cleanup. They had the room restored in ninety minutes. "Thank you ever so much, both of you," Lillian said.

"You're welcome, Lillian," Cate responded, squeezing her hand.

A gong sounded. "That'd be the dressing gong. We finished just in time," Lillian replied.

Cate nodded, taking it as their cue to leave. "Is there anything else you want to do before we go home?" Jack inquired as they traversed the halls to the bedroom.

Cate shook her head. "No. We can discuss the information Forsythe gave me once we get back."

As they rounded the corner to the hallway continuing to their suite, they spotted Anne coming toward them. "Oh, there you are!" she exclaimed as she caught sight of them.

"Hello, Anne," Cate greeted her.

"I was just looking for you. Rory said the police had left, and I assumed you returned to your suite."

"No," Cate informed her, "the police left quite a mess behind. We helped Murray clean it up. It would have been impossible for her to restore that room herself."

"How kind. The reason I was seeking you out was to invite you to dinner. With the household restored, we're returning to serving formal dinner. Won't you please join us?"

"Oh, well, we were..." Jack began.

"Oh, please. I've been such a terrible hostess thus far. I'd like to rectify that. I'd prefer not to take no for an answer."

Cate glanced to Jack. "Well, I suppose it would be nice to dine with the family again," Jack responded.

"Wonderful! I shall see you in the sitting room for cocktails soon, then!"

Anne stepped past them, rounding the corner and disappearing down another hallway on her way to dress for dinner. Jack held his arms out with a shrug. "Sorry," he confessed. "I didn't see a way around it."

"Me either," Cate admitted. "It's fine. And it's a nice chance to spend time with my family. Sort of."

"They are your family," Jack insisted. Cate offered him a smile. "Guess I'm back in the monkey suit for the night though."

Cate giggled as she perused her suitcase. "Yep. But like I said, I like the monkey suit." Cate selected a dress, heading for the bathroom to ready herself for dinner. She pulled on the evening dress, again heavily beaded with gold beads and sea-foam-colored frills making up the bottom. She switched places with Jack, pulling on her shoes as she waited for him to change. As she waited, she added a headband, crossing it across her forehead as was the style in the era.

"Wow, you really look the part, Lady Cate," Jack said, emerging from the bathroom in his so-called monkey suit. "You look great!"

Cate struck a pose. "Thank you!"

"Don't say it."

"Don't say what?" Cate questioned.

"I'm dashing, I already know." Cate shook her head at him. "Shall we?" He extended his arm to her. She accepted it and they made their way to the sitting room.

Anne, Rory, Amelia and Lucas were already gathered there. "I hope we haven't kept you waiting too long," Cate apologized as they entered the room.

"Not at all, we've only just gotten here ourselves," Rory informed her.

"I'm so glad you could join us," Anne added. She seemed in much better spirits than Cate had seen her before.

"Indeed, now we may all congratulate you on the fine work, Jack," Lucas chimed in.

"Oh, it was nothing."

"No, no, it was quite something," Anne argued. "Lillian is so indebted to you, as are we all!"

"Yes, fine work," Rory added.

"I wasn't aware you practiced law, Jack. I thought land was your business," Lucas mentioned.

"It is now. I haven't practiced in years, but when the situation called for it, I used my old career to our advantage."

"Lucky for us you did, particularly for Miss Murray," Rory commented.

Benson announced dinner, and they filed into the dining

room for the meal. Conversation continued about Jack's legal maneuverings before turning to other subjects. Cate enjoyed the evening, becoming more relaxed with the family than she had been before.

She and Jack "retired" shortly after dinner, returning to their own time after changing from their evening clothes. When they arrived home, Jack noted they had enough time to discuss the events of the day prior to their next dinner.

"Yes, we should have time before second dinner," Cate commented with a giggle.

"Okay, meet you in the library in a few," Jack said.

They parted ways, meeting again after changing into their regular clothes. They sunk into their usual seats as the dogs settled nearby, both weary from living through the hours that had passed in 1925 despite it only being forty minutes in the present.

"The double life is catching up to me," Jack admitted with a groan.

"Haha, yes. Estate manager by day and land acquisitions and lawyer… also by day," she answered with a laugh. "You're doing great though! That was some tough talking with Officer MacCullough today. Watching those legal dramas is really paying off!"

Jack burst into laughter. "Yes, I've learned quite a bit. Everyone's always yelling and threatening. It seems to work."

"What a mess this is," Cate lamented. "Poor Lillian. I'm convinced she's innocent yet that Officer MacCullough will not leave her alone!"

"The man's convinced he can close the case against her."

"Why?" Cate questioned.

Jack shrugged. "I'm not sure. Though it may be a case of pure laziness. He doesn't want to bother investigating if he expects he can wheedle a confession out of the lassie. It makes his job easier."

"That's awful," Cate grumbled. "Doesn't he have any sense of justice or fair play? Or even any pride in his work?"

"Doesn't seem like it. Anyway, was there anything interesting from Forsythe?"

"Yes," Cate responded with a clear affirmative. "He asked around about both men. In Robert Calhoun's case, he found nothing untoward. Everyone seemed to agree he was a nice guy and there wasn't anything questionable about his past or present or any shady dealings."

"That doesn't seem like much help, but I suppose it knocks him down a few pegs on the suspect list if we have no motive and no reason to believe he could or would do something of this nature."

"Right. But the more interesting bit was about Thomas Gould," Cate continued. "He likes both alcohol and gambling more than he should. And he's been bragging to his gambling buddies that he's going to be out of service soon and owning his own restaurant in London."

"Hmm," Jack mused. "That's interesting. Is it just idle chatter, do you imagine? Or is there something to this?"

"I'm not sure. Forsythe seemed to believe there may be something to it. Possibly because he let it slip while he was inebriated. Forsythe all but came out and said he stole the jewelry to finance his new career."

"So, Forsythe thinks he's guilty."

"He didn't say as much, but he certainly implied it, yes."

"What do you think?"

Cate was silent for a moment, parsing her thoughts. "I think it's enough to consider him as a suspect and move him up to the top of our list. It's not an open and shut case, but the circumstantial evidence against him is building. First, he has no alibi. And he never mentioned the absence of his roommate. So, either he lied to protect Mr. Calhoun, or he had no idea Calhoun left the room because he wasn't there.

Second, he's been bragging about coming into some money, enough to start a restaurant in an expensive city."

"Yes, the evidence does point toward his guilt. We just need some proof. We can't mention this to MacCullough yet. He'll never go for it, even with the mounting circumstantial evidence, without direct proof."

"I wonder if he'd go for it if the man were standing with the jewelry clutched in his hand," Cate quipped with a roll of her eyes.

"No doubt he'd still try to blame Lillian Murray somehow."

"Funny but not," Cate responded with a chuckle. "So, we've got ourselves down to two primary suspects."

"Still keeping Calhoun on the list?" Jack inquired.

Cate shook her head. "No. Still keeping Lucas on the list."

"Lucas? With what evidence?"

"Anne's letter." Jack let his head sink back into the chair behind him at her comment. "Jack, we can't ignore that letter! What else could Anne's letter have been referring to? What other type of theft would have gotten her so upset she wrote something like that?"

"Okay, okay," Jack answered, holding his hands up in surrender, "Lucas and Thomas Gould."

"The only way I can figure to solve this is by proving one of them is innocent."

"Or both of them are innocent."

Cate grimaced. "Which sends us right back to square one."

"No," Jack countered. "We'd have ruled out at least two people. Progress, see."

"Yeah, progress, right," Cate commented, sarcasm thick in her voice.

Jack checked his watch. "Almost time for second dinner. You joining us servants in the servants' hall tonight?"

Cate nodded. "I am, yes." She stood, glancing around the room in search of her furry friends. Her eyes rested on the bookshelf across from her. She narrowed her eyes, continuing to stare at it. Something nagged at her.

"Don't start with that bookshelf again, Lady Cate," Jack warned, noting the direction of her gaze. "You'll start your nightmares up." Cate shook her head. "Don't shake your head at me, lassie, you will so."

"No, I didn't mean that," Cate corrected. "But something is nagging at me. Something's off."

Jack glanced between Cate and the bookshelf. "You mean besides the horrible nightmares that thing's causing you?"

"Yes. She strode to the door, opening it and glancing into the hallway. She stepped into the doorway. Her gaze flitted between the two spaces. "Does this space look right?" she inquired after a few moments.

"Huh?" Jack questioned, screwing up his face. He glanced around it. "Looks fine to me? Has the cleaning company done something strange? Misplaced something?"

"No. Not that, the dimensions. Shouldn't it be... bigger?"

"Bigger?" Jack queried, still not following her thought process.

"Come stand here and take a peek," Cate instructed. Jack joined her in the hallway. "Now, we're aware of how deep the bookcases are. But consider their placement compare to where the wall is in the hall. Doesn't it look like they should be a few feet further back toward the hall?"

Jack glanced between the hallway and the bookcases a few times. "Eh, maybe?"

"Well," Cate added, standing against the wall for emphasis, "consider the wall being here and the bookcases coming out into the room this far." She stepped forward to illustrate. "Now look in the library. Those bookcases would be a few extra feet deep given where they are."

"Okay. I see what you mean," Jack conceded. "What are you implying?"

"That the room's dimensions are incorrect. There is something behind those bookcases! Like a secret passage."

"Or pipes," Jack commented. "There's no passage listed on the original plans or any other. But when indoor plumbing was installed, perhaps that was the space they were put into. This wall," Jack said, placing his hand against the hallway's wall, "may have been moved out to accommodate plumbing."

Cate considered the idea. "Hmm," she mused. "Then why wasn't it marked on the plans."

"Mistake? Last minute change? Careless error? Someone forgot. Could be any number of reasons."

"You may be right," she conceded, "although that's not very fun."

"I find indoor plumbing quite fun, Lady Cate."

"Funny, funny. Oh well, so much for my big discovery. Ready for dinner?"

"Yep."

"Come on, you two rascals," Cate called to the dogs. "Let's go get our dinner!"

CHAPTER 20

"Good morning, Lady Cate," Jack greeted Cate as she rounded the corner toward the back garden.

"Good morning. I see your fan club found you," Cate noted, eyeing the two small dogs grouped around Jack's feet as he petted them.

"Aye, they did," Jack responded.

"Kind of cold to be working out here, isn't it?" Cate inquired.

"It's not too bad. I won't be out long; I'm just noting a few things to plan for spring."

"Spring," Cate repeated with a smile. "That word sounds wonderful!"

"Aye. You've not experienced a spring in Dunhaven yet. You came almost at summertime."

"Yes," Cate agreed. "I'm looking forward to spring here."

"And then we celebrate your one-year anniversary with us," Jack replied.

"I know. I can't believe it. Almost a year already! Where has the time gone?"

"To 1856 and 1925, that's where."

"Uh-uh," Cate argued. "You can't count that! We get extra time to do that."

"Oh, right. Yes, you'd think your year would have taken longer, what with our thirty-six-hour days and all."

Cate chuckled. "Speaking of our thirty-six-hour days…"

"Same plan as yesterday? Head back after lunch?" Jack replied before she could finish her statement.

Cate nodded. "Yeah, that sounds good."

"What's the plan? Speak with Gould? Or perhaps Benson or Forsythe again?"

Cate shrugged. "My plan is bolder than that."

"Bolder? Oh, Lady Cate, I don't like when you say things like that."

"Yes, I know. But we've got to do something! We can't just keep asking people what they think might be true. We need proof!"

"How can we get proof? Or don't I want to know?"

"You don't want to know," Cate concluded.

"Now I HAVE to know."

Cate sighed. "Okay," she said, holding her hands up. "But don't say I didn't warn you. I want to sneak upstairs and take a peek in Gould's room."

"WHAT?! Cate, are you mad?"

"No," Cate countered. "But it may give us a clue. Perhaps he wrote a note mentioning he has the jewels, or someone replied to a request to sell them. Or perhaps the jewelry itself is hidden up there."

"And perhaps we'll get in big trouble if we're caught."

"Oh, that's simple."

"It is?"

"Yeah, don't get caught. You be my lookout; I'll do the searching."

"Ugh," Jack lamented.

"Jack! We're getting nowhere and soon that Officer

MacCullough is going to come back with some other request. As good of a fake attorney as you are, there may come a point where you can't help Lillian with your fancy but fake legal mumbo-jumbo!"

Jack sighed. "You're right. I hate it, but you're right. If we don't come up with proof soon, there may be no stopping MacCullough from pinning this on Lillian."

"Okay, so we're agreed?"

"Agreed. See you after lunch for the daring plan."

Cate nodded with a smile. "Okay, see you then!"

Cate spent the rest of her morning working on her book's manuscript. With the belief that only pipes were behind the library's bookshelves, Cate decided to brave it and work there. She answered a few personal emails during lunch before returning to her suite to dress for the trip back.

Around one, Jack arrived, and they slipped back to 1925. "I am not looking forward to this at all," Jack complained after they arrived. "Do we know which room is theirs?"

"No," Cate answered. "But I have a plan to ascertain that information. I'm going to ask Forsythe in the name of following up on our clues."

"Okay. Well, it's your show," Jack said, motioning for her to precede him.

They navigated below stairs, seeking Charles Forsythe. They found him in Benson's office selecting a wine for the evening dinner. "Excuse me, Forsythe," Cate said, knocking at the door.

"Mrs. MacKenzie! May I help you?"

"Do you have a moment? I had a few questions about our discussion yesterday I'd like to follow up on."

"Yes, please come in," Forsythe responded. "Oh, hello, Mr. MacKenzie."

Jack nodded to him in greeting as Cate closed the door. "I've informed Mr. MacKenzie of the information you passed along to me yesterday. This coupled with the fact that for several hours Mr. Gould is without an alibi has brought up a few other questions."

"I'll help in any way I can," Forsythe assured them.

"Could you tell us the location of Mr. Gould's room in the hallway?"

"The location?" Forsythe questioned, his brows scrunching.

"We're trying to determine who, if anyone, may have been able to hear someone coming and going from the room. If anyone did," Jack explained.

Forsythe nodded in understanding. "They are on the right, second door. Only my room, on the opposite side of the hall, and Mr. Benson's are between theirs and the stairway. I heard nothing that night and to my knowledge, neither did Mr. Benson. Though, the hallway is not long. Few steps are needed to reach the stairs."

"Okay, that's helpful, thank you," Cate answered.

"You're welcome. Do you expect you may have the crime solved?"

Cate paused a moment. "No," she hedged. "Just sorting through information and trying to determine what is best to follow up on."

"I see," Forsythe answered. "Well, I shall continue to keep my ear to the ground for any further information. I must admit, the information I found on Mr. Gould that I imparted to you yesterday, Mrs. MacKenzie, seems to have direct bearing on the case."

"It is interesting. We don't want to accuse any innocent parties, though, so we need more than conjecture."

"It seems that is all the police have in the case against Miss Murray," Forsythe insisted.

"It is. However, without direct proof, the police won't take anything we say seriously," Jack explained.

Forsythe sighed. "I wish we could ferret out some information to assist. I am uncomfortable having a thief on my staff. Perhaps a search of his things?"

"I understand, though we don't know there is one. Let's hold off on doing anything rash until we can consider the information further. And if you discover any other news, please let us know. Again, thank you, Forsythe."

"You're welcome, Mrs. MacKenzie." Jack and Cate left the room, climbing upstairs to the main floor before continuing on to the servants' quarters. At this hour, the servants would be attending to their duties, so they hoped to slip in and out unseen. Using the information from Forsythe, they located the bedroom. Like Lillian's it was sparsely furnished.

"This shouldn't take long," Cate whispered. "Keep an eye on the door."

Jack nodded, taking a post at the door and peering through the crack they'd left open. Cate scanned the room before diving in. A wave of guilt passed over her as she slid open the first drawer in the dresser, but she shoved it aside, pawing through the contents. She checked each drawer with a cursory scan but found nothing. She glanced behind the dresser and under each drawer. But her search was fruitless. The wardrobe search also came up empty.

Cate glanced under the bed and felt under the mattress. Under one, she found a few notes. A quick scan of them gave her no more information than she already possessed. She stood and approached Jack. She signaled to him with a shake of her head and motioned to ask if they could retreat downstairs without being caught. He nodded, and they hurried from the quarters down to the floor containing the family's bedrooms.

They returned to their suite. Cate slogged through the door, filled with frustration. She slapped her hands against her thighs as Jack closed the door. "Well, that didn't help!" she exclaimed.

"You didn't expect to find the jewelry there, did you?"

"No, but at least some clue! Though, you're right, he'd keep nothing incriminating in his room. Perhaps the stables," Cate muttered, thinking aloud. "Do you think he could have unloaded them already?"

"I'm not sure," Jack replied. "I'm not sure how we're going to solve anything. We're reaching dead-ends at every turn."

Cate made a face and nodded. She paced the floor for a few more moments, deep in reflection. After a while, she crinkled her brow, then glanced to Jack. "What?" he inquired.

"Did you find the conversation with Forsythe strange?" Cate asked. "He seemed bound and determined to pin this on Gould."

"I suppose he's just antsy to settle this and not have a thief on his staff, as he mentioned."

"Perhaps. Although it seems he's as inflexible as Officer MacCullough."

"Why didn't you take him up on the search?"

Cate shook her head. "It seemed like a bad idea. I wanted to do it alone, without him there. I'm not sure why, but it just seemed a bad decision to involve him."

"It may not have been the best idea, you're right. If he's innocent, it could cause problems within the staff."

Cate nodded. "So, now what?"

"Up to you," Jack responded. "What's the next trick up your sleeve?"

"I haven't got one," Cate replied, showing him her empty sleeves. "If it's all the same to you, I'd like to skip dinner with the family tonight and go home."

"Sure. We'll leave a note for Rory telling him to pass along our regrets and tell the others we've gone out to dine."

"Okay," Cate agreed. Jack scribbled a note to Rory,

explaining they wouldn't attend dinner. Jack left it with Benson before returning to the suite. Cate sat on the chaise, her chin resting in her hands.

"Second thoughts, Lady Cate?" Jack asked after witnessing her glum expression.

"No," she responded. "But I have no idea what to try next."

"Don't let it get you down, Cate," Jack said, squeezing her shoulder. "Just let your mind relax. Something will come to you. I've never known you to go more than twenty-four hours without a brilliant idea."

"Brilliant, huh?"

"I have no doubt that by tomorrow, you'll have a new idea to pursue to solve this case."

"Whew, pressure's on now!" Cate joked.

"Oh, no, now you'll be in overdrive," Jack retorted. "That wasn't a challenge, Cate. It was a vote of confidence."

"I'll remember that before I accuse you of being the reason I didn't sleep all night and was up brainstorming!" Cate exclaimed with a chuckle.

"Aye, you do that. Shall we head back so you can begin your night of fretting?"

"Yes," Cate agreed with a nod. Jack pulled her to standing. They entered the bedroom and returned to the present. "At least we won't have two dinners today."

"Hey, that's my favorite part of time traveling! The double meals!"

"Wow, you have a favorite part? And here I assumed you hated everything about it."

"I told you it was growing on me," Jack answered with a wink. "Well, I'll leave you to begin your handwringing, pacing and worrying. M'lady." He gave an extravagant bow before departing from the room.

Cate chuckled as he left, though her mind immediately turned to the puzzle they'd just left behind. Jack was correct, she'd likely pore over it again and again for the rest of the day. She hoped Jack was also correct in saying that by tomorrow she'd have a new avenue to pursue. So far all they had were unsubstantiated suspicions, dead-ends and no leads to get them any closer to the culprit.

Cate spent some of her time on a long, chilly walk with Riley and Bailey. She hoped the cold winter air and mindless task of playing ball with the dogs would relax her mind into stumbling onto her next great idea. She returned to the castle with no new conclusions or objectives to pursue.

After dinner, Cate spread all her materials out on the floor of her sitting room. She added any missing information to her notes, then studied each item. She considered the case they'd built against Thomas Gould and Lucas MacKenzie forward and backward. She played devil's advocate, finding loopholes, inconsistencies in assumptions and leaps of logic.

They were missing something, she concluded. But what? Proof, her mind filled in. So far, any case they'd built had been circumstantial only. They could have built a similar case against any random stranger. Cate sighed. Unless they got a break, and soon, they'd likely never solve the case. She worried Lillian Murray would be railroaded into a prison sentence for nothing. At the very least, perhaps they could help the girl avoid that, even if they couldn't finger the guilty party and recover the jewelry.

Cate's phone chimed an incoming text alert. She opened her messaging app, reading the text from Jack: *Have you worn through the floorboards with your pacing yet?*

A chuckle escaped her as she answered: *No... no pacing, just studying.* She included a picture of her messy work area with notes and papers spread all over the floor.

Jack replied: *Ah... have you solved it yet?*

Cate responded: *No! We're missing something... and if we don't find it soon, we may never solve this!*

Within a few minutes, Jack returned the text: *No and our thief will get off scot free... pun intended ;)*

Cate shook her head at the terrible joke and wrote back: *Your jokes leave me speechless*

The response to her text was: *But you laughed, didn't you?*

Cate responded with an affirmative, admitting it elicited a chuckle from her, and Jack argued the joke couldn't possibly have been terrible if it worked.

Cate toggled off her phone after promising to get some rest. "A few more minutes won't hurt though," she murmured to herself as she stared at the papers again.

She took two clean sheets of paper. One she titled *Case Against Lucas MacKenzie* and the other she titled *Case Against Thomas Gould.* She noted every piece of evidence and every doubt for each suspect. Nothing caught her eye. Short of a miracle or additional information from Charles Forsythe tomorrow, they were stuck. With a sigh, Cate shoved the papers back into the folder, calling it a night.

When morning rolled around, Cate found herself no closer to solving anything. There were no big ideas, no new leads to try. Short of searching any area Thomas Gould frequented or finding a witness who spotted him meeting with a shady character, there seemed to be nothing else to do. Disappointed, Cate snuggled under a blanket on her chaise as the sun crested the horizon. Fog clung to the moors in heavy patches, obscuring the view. The fog also seemed to settle in Cate's mind, removing her ability to seek a solution with any clarity.

After breakfast, Cate studied the new case sheets she'd made against each suspect. She read them aloud to Riley and Bailey. "What are we missing, Riley? Do you know, Bailey? How can we figure out who committed the crime?" Neither dog offered an answer. With a frustrated sigh, she tucked the notes away and made her way to the library. As she settled at her desk, she received a text from Jack: *So, what's the big idea for today?*

Cate responded with a sigh: *Sorry to be a disappointment but I've got nothing... short of searching the entire estate or Forsythe having new information I'm fresh out!*

Jack answered within moments: *Perhaps we should up our trip? Go this morning.*

Cate considered it. Molly, ever adventurous, was using her day off to sightsee in her new country, leaving Cate alone in the castle. With no one to question Jack's appearance on his day off, she went with the plan. She responded: *Okay... unless you're busy... I hate making you work on your day off!*

Jack answered: *Not busy... not work... see you in a few*

Cate stood in the foyer waiting for Jack to arrive. The gravel driveway crunched under the weight of his car and she flung the door open to greet him. "Wow, are you psychic, Lady Cate?" Jack inquired, stepping from his car.

"No, just impatient," Cate admitted.

"You are definitely that, Lady Cate," Jack agreed.

"Let's change and go right away. I don't want to miss Forsythe."

"Or Gould," Jack added. "Meet you in thirty? Is that enough time for you?"

"I'll make it enough time. I don't want to delay this."

"Okay, see you then."

Cate hurried to her room, tossing on her dress and fixing her hair at lightning speed. She was fastening the buckle on her shoes when Jack knocked at the door. "Come in!" she shouted. "I'm almost ready," she said, glancing up at him.

"That's a pretty dress," Jack noted as he caught Riley mid-leap.

"Thank you," Cate answered. "Let's hope it's lucky in addition to pretty and we get the break we need."

"I'll admit, this one is tough. I swear, solving that murder was easier!"

Cate nodded. "Seemed like a breeze compared to this. Even with Randolph dead set on ruining the investigation!"

Cate stood, smoothing her dress. "Ready?"

"I am, but you aren't."

Cate furrowed her brow, confused. "I'm not?"

"Nope," Jack said, approaching her and sliding something off the side table.

"You're still just Cate Kensie," he said, holding up the plain gold wedding band. "And you've got to become Mrs. Jack MacKenzie."

"Oh! Yikes! I almost forgot my fake wedding ring! Sorry, I was in such a hurry, I meant to put it on as soon as I sat down, but I went straight to the shoes."

"Forgot? How could you possibly forget your wedding ring?! Don't forget it or we may have some explaining to do." He took her hand, sliding the wedding ring onto her finger. "There, that's better."

Cate smiled at him, feeling rather silly. "Now, I am ready!" she exclaimed, stepping toward the bedroom.

"Darn right," Jack responded, following her. "Come on, Mrs. MacKenzie, let's go solve a mystery."

Cate held out the timepiece, rolling her eyes at him. "Okay, Mr. MacKenzie." They activated the timepiece, slipping back to the Roaring Twenties.

"All right, Mrs. MacKenzie, let's see if we can track down any clues."

They descended to the main floor, finding Rory in the library. "Jack, Cate!" he greeted them. "We missed you at dinner last evening."

"Sorry," Jack apologized. "We weren't able to make it. We were hoping to speak with Forsythe again today. We've been following up on a few leads."

"You aren't still considering him as a suspect, are you?"

"No," Cate corrected, "he's been helping us sort through the staff member accounts and alibis. We're checking everyone's stories again to see if we've missed anything."

"Oh, I am pleased he's helpful to you. He seems to be working out well in the household." Rory consulted his timepiece; the same one Cate wore under her dress. "Hmm, at this time of the morning, he should be below stairs."

"Thanks," Jack answered as they turned to leave.

"Have you made any progress? You mentioned following leads?" Rory questioned before they could exit the room.

"We're looking into a few things," Jack hedged.

"What do you know about your groom, Thomas Gould?" Cate questioned.

"Thomas? Not much. He seems a good chap, and he's good with the horses."

"It seems he's good with liquor and cards, too," Cate confessed. "And during one of his games, he mentioned coming into some money soon. An odd admission given the theft."

Rory offered a surprised expression. "Oh! How... odd, yes. Though I can't imagine him doing something like this! For what reason?"

"His friends say he plans to open a restaurant in London. Perhaps he viewed the theft as a shortcut to funding his venture."

Rory considered it, his expression changing from shock to dismay. "How disappointing if it's true. As I mentioned, he's wonderful with the horses."

"Let's hope it's not true," Cate responded.

"Yes," Rory said, nodding his head. "Let us hope for that. Please keep me apprised, will you? And I hope you'll be able to join us for dinner. Lucas and Amelia will be departing at the end of the week, and I'm sure they'd like to spend more time with you both."

"We'll be there," Cate answered.

"Wonderful. Well, I shall let you get on with your investigation."

Cate and Jack closed the doors behind them as they exited the room. Cate shook her head as they ambled down the hall. "I swear we could catch the thief red-handed and Rory would still not believe they did it."

"Yeah, he really has an optimistic view, doesn't he? He trusts everyone to do the right and honorable thing. It's endearing in a way."

"It is. His trust is almost childlike. But it's also costly."

"No kidding. His trust has invited a thief into the household."

They descended the stairs leading to the servants' hall. They found Forsythe in the kitchen emptying a tray. "Mr. and Mrs. MacKenzie, is there something I can assist with?"

"Yes," Cate answered. "I'm sorry to interrupt, could we speak privately?"

"Of course," he said with a bow. They left the kitchen, walking down the hall to Benson's office. Forsythe closed the door behind them. "Quick thinking requesting to speak in private."

"I expect it's best to keep our conversations private. Particularly at this juncture," Cate replied.

"Yes, especially with what I've found."

"Found?" Cate asked, excitement and hope filling her voice. "What is it?"

Forsythe removed a note from his breast pocket. "This!" he exclaimed. He handed the note to Cate. "I must confess you would probably disapprove of my methods, but I believe the ends justified the means."

"What methods?" Jack inquired.

"I asked Mr. Calhoun to search Mr. Gould's things. Not very honorable, I'll admit. But, in these cases, when dealing with someone as dishonest as a thief, we must use extreme methods."

Jack raised his eyebrows at the comment as Cate unfolded the note. In what appeared to be scrawled writing, the note read:

Thomas,

Have you got the jewelry? I have a buyer ready, just say the word. We'll have that restaurant soon!

- P

Cate's pulse quickened as she read the note. Jack peered over her shoulder, also reading it. "And Mr. Calhoun found this amongst Thomas' things?" Cate queried.

"Yes, in one of his drawers."

Cate folded the note again. "Can we keep this?"

"Yes. Though at this point, I judge it's wise to go to the police!"

Cate nodded. "Mr. MacKenzie is an attorney, so I leave it to his judgement on how best to approach the police with this evidence. We want everything above board. We don't want any issues with the case because of the methods used to obtain the evidence."

Forsythe nodded. "Ah, yes, I understand. At the very least, this clears Miss Murray."

"It does, thank you," Jack replied. He took the note from Cate, stuffing it into his jacket pocket. "And we'll use it to clear her name. But as Mrs. MacKenzie mentioned, we must do it in the proper way so it may be used to create a case against the guilty party in addition to proving Miss Murray's innocence."

"This has been so helpful, Forsythe. Thank you. And we

will let Miss Murray know you and Mr. Calhoun helped to clear her name," Cate assured him.

"I didn't do it for the gratitude. It may be wise not to mention anyone's name. It may cause strife within the staff," Forsythe asserted. A knock sounded at the door. "Yes?"

"Mr. Forsythe, sorry to interrupt," a young freckle-faced maid whispered, peeking in the door. "Mr. Benson is asking for you at once."

"Thank you, Ethel," Forsythe answered. "Good day, Mr. and Mrs. MacKenzie." He nodded his head to them and turned on his heel, exiting the room.

Jack glanced to Cate, bewilderment on his face. "Oh, Forsythe!" Cate called, reaching to the floor and grasping a few folded notes. "He must have dropped this when he pulled that note out."

"Yes," Jack answered. "You can leave them on Benson's desk to return to him."

Cate didn't respond, instead her brow wrinkled as she stared at the note. "Lorne Peterson?" Cate asked, confusion filling her voice. "Who is Lorne Peterson?"

Jack shrugged. "A pen pal of Forsythe's?"

Cate shook her head. "No, this letter has already been posted and delivered. It's not an outgoing post. Why would Forsythe have Lorne Peterson's mail? Who is he?" Cate shoved the note in her dress pocket. "Let's go," she suggested.

"You're taking it?"

"Yes. Call it instinct but something is odd about this."

"You can explain it to me while we wait hours for dinner."

"Come on. We'll walk to the loch or town to pass the time."

"How about to town? Maybe hit the pub for lunch… my stomach is growling."

"Wow, is the pub there already?"

"Yes, that pub's been in business for most of the town's

history." Cate glanced to Jack, a serious expression on her face. Concern crossed Jack's face. "What is it, Cate? What's wrong?"

"Do you think they have the fish and chips?"

Jack burst into laughter. "Oh, Lady Cate," he said, stifling his laughter. "I'll bet they do, don't you worry. Should we request a car?"

"Okay, whew, good. No, we don't need to. We can walk."

"You sure?"

"Yeah," Cate assured him. "I'm good. For the fish and chips, I can walk."

They exited Benson's office, climbing to the main level and heading for the foyer. As they approached the front door, Lucas and Amelia met them.

"Well, hello, Cate and Jack!" Amelia said in greeting. She pulled Cate into an embrace, kissing her cheek. "We missed you at dinner last evening."

"We'll be there this evening," Jack assured them.

"Wonderful. We're departing the castle at the end of the week, but we'd love to spend more time with you both," Lucas added.

"Are you heading out?" Amelia asked.

"Yes. We're heading to town for the afternoon," Cate answered.

"And for lunch," Jack added. "We're dying to try the pub."

"We're also heading into town for lunch! Would you care to join us? We can share a car," Amelia said.

"Oh!" Cate exclaimed, glancing to Jack. "That would be lovely unless you were hoping for a private day."

"Not at all, Cate," Lucas chimed in. "It promises to be a lovely afternoon with you joining us."

"I'll run up for the coats," Jack said, beginning his ascent of the stairs.

"Don't forget my hat!" Cate called after him.

"No, I won't forget your hat," he assured her.

Jack returned within a few minutes. The crunch of gravel announced the car's arrival. "That sounds like the car now," Lucas added. "Shall we?"

The foursome exited the house, climbing into the car with Jack taking the front seat and the ladies and Lucas in the rear. The trip to town was quick, and they arranged for the chauffeur to pick them up in the late afternoon near the town's center. They filed into the pub and were seated in a booth near a roaring fire.

"Ah, this is lovely," Amelia said, settling into the booth next to Lucas. She perused the menu. "What looks promising?"

Cate browsed the menu finding the fish and chips were listed. She smiled to herself. "I can take one guess at what my wife will order," Jack mentioned after a glance at the menu.

"Oh?" Amelia questioned.

"Fish and chips," Jack and Cate replied together.

"Cate loves fish and chips at any pub we stop at," Jack added.

"Ah, a fish and chips connoisseur, Cate?" Amelia joked.

"Something like that," Cate admitted. In reality, she just wasn't an adventurous eater.

They placed their order with the waitress and settled in to a conversation while waiting for their meals. "So, Jack," Lucas began. "Where did you attend law school?"

Without skipping a beat, Jack rattled off, "Oxford." Cate's eyes widened at Jack's whopper of a lie.

"Ah, an Oxford man! Very good!"

"Why did you leave the work?" Amelia queried.

"I wanted something more challenging, more interesting. Land management allows me to use my legal skills but also travel."

"How interesting, what a unique blending of skills," Lucas commented.

"What about you, Lucas?" Jack inquired.

"I'm also in land, though not acquisition. I hold several different types of properties for various purposes: farms, housing, businesses. I may have to seek your expertise whenever I plan to expand my holdings."

"Are they concentrated in one area or spread out in several locations?"

"Spread out across both Scotland and England, but the majority of my holdings are in this area. The extended holiday stay here allows me to look in on things."

"A little cold to be touring properties."

"Cold, indeed," Lucas admitted, "however, not too cold to meet with tenants and discuss issues."

"Oh, you meet with them in person?"

"I do, I try to keep up with it. I believe face-to-face dealings done with a smile and a handshake make all the difference. Many of my fellow land investors have done away with all that. They only see numbers in their books, I see people. Each person has a story, triumphs and trials. It's important to be cognizant of them. Several colleagues solely review their books, toss a tenant out if they aren't meeting their due. That's quite unfair if you ask me, perhaps something happened, perhaps this is only temporary. I prefer to speak with them, determine what can be worked out. Losing a tenant is an inconvenience, but for the tenant, losing their home or livelihood can be a great deal worse."

"That's a very honorable take on land management. And a more than respectable practice," Jack noted.

"We're all here to help one another. I've been rather fortunate in my life. I'd like to share that good fortune with others."

"What a kind sentiment, Lucas," Cate commented.

Amelia smiled at her. "If you gentlemen are quite finished discussing business, perhaps a change of subject is in order. Poor Cate and I are sitting here like bumps on logs!"

"Prettiest bumps on logs I've ever seen, wouldn't you agree, Jack?" Lucas questioned.

"Quite," Jack answered.

"Well, what have you in mind, Amelia? We can't very well talk dresses with you ladies. We're out of our depths there," Lucas replied.

"I don't agree. One can still appreciate beauty whether or not one understands how it is achieved. Cate, you seem to have quite a sense of fashion. I've enjoyed many of your ensembles, both day and evening."

"Thank you," Cate responded. The clothing she wore had been stored in trunks in the castle. Previous MacKenzies placed it there for just such trips. "I inherited it." The quip, Cate figured, was true.

"Was your mother very into fashion, then?" Amelia queried.

"All those preceding me have been. They've paved the way for my choices, you could say."

Cate was spared any further clothing discussion as their food arrived. Amelia spent a few more minutes discussing recent changes in clothing styles, from hemlines to dress cuts. Conversation then turned to the delicious meals and plans for the afternoon.

"And how are the fish and chips in our little town, Cate?" Lucas inquired. "Are they quite up to your standard?"

"They are," Cate assured him. "It was an excellent choice if I do say so myself." Her comment earned a chuckle from Jack, who realized the extent of her enjoyment of the pub's fish and chips. Since Cate's arrival in Dunhaven months earlier, she'd ordered nothing but that particular dish at the pub.

The group finished their meal before emerging from the pub into the chilly winter air. Despite the nip in the air, the sun shined bright in the cloudless blue sky. "What a delightful winter day," Lucas commented. "Do you plan to do much shopping in town?" he inquired of Cate and Jack.

"No," Cate responded. "Just window shopping."

"Oh!" Amelia exclaimed. "They're skating on the pond. Shall we try?"

"I'm afraid I've never skated before," Cate admitted.

"Then today is the perfect day to change that!" Amelia replied, grabbing Cate's hand and pulling her toward the pond. Cate allowed Amelia to drag her toward the pond, issuing a helpless glance back at Jack.

"Amelia quite likes your quiet nature," Lucas commented as they approached the skate rental trolley. "If you're not careful, she'll have you racing cars next or the like."

"That's quite a leap from ice skating," Amelia chided jokingly.

Lucas insisted on treating everyone to the skate rentals and they sat down to strap the blades to their feet on a nearby bench. "Are you an experienced skater, Jack?"

"Yes," Jack responded. "Though I haven't skated in a while."

Amelia stood up, stepping onto the frozen lake. "Come on, Cate, put your feet right onto the ice and get a feel for your skates." Cate stood on wobbly legs holding tight to Amelia's hands. "Now, we'll begin by just pulling you around a bit. Don't worry, we won't let you go, will we, Jack?"

With a grin, Amelia began pulling Cate across the expanse of the icy pond with Jack's help. Lucas skated toward them. "You're doing quite well, Cate," he noted. "You've got excellent balance."

"Are you ready to try a bit of skating on your own? We

won't let you go. Just push a bit with your feet," Amelia instructed.

Cate pushed a bit too much, toppling them in a heap. Cate apologized, wide-eyed and concerned about Amelia. But Amelia laughed the incident off. "I didn't expect you to skate without taking at least one spill. I'm no worse for wear, now, come on, let's try again." Jack, who had recovered from his fall already, pulled both ladies to their feet. "Just a tiny push."

Cate gave a gentle push, tempering her movement this time, having a better feel for how the skates worked. "There you go, Cate!" Jack exclaimed. "Now, you've got it."

Cate offered a nervous grin. "I haven't toppled you a second time. Yet! But I'm far from having it down," she admitted, still clinging to both their hands.

"So, I can let go, right?" Jack joked.

"NO!" Cate shouted, tightening her grip.

Jack chuckled, looping his arm around her waist. "Don't worry, Cate. I won't let you go."

Amelia grinned at them. "You're progressing nicely, I agree."

Cate smiled at her, gaining confidence as they looped around the pond. After two loops, Cate gained enough courage to tell Amelia she could skate with Lucas.

"Are you sure? I won't leave you if you're still unsure."

Cate nodded. "I'm sure. Go have fun."

"I won't leave her," Jack chimed in.

They made their way around the pond several more times. While concentrating on her skating, Cate sneaked a few glances at Amelia and Lucas skating around the pond together. "They seem to be enjoying themselves," she mentioned to Jack.

"Yes," Jack responded. "Are you?"

Cate nodded with a smile. "I am, yes. I'd prefer not to fall again but I'm enjoying myself."

"Okay, just checking. If you get tired, let me know, I'll drag you to the bench."

"Okay. What about you? Tired of dragging me around yet?"

"No, Lady Cate, I am not."

They made several more passes around the pond before Amelia and Lucas joined them. Cate let go of Jack's hand after a few rounds, skating on her own. Jack remained watchful of her, keeping her upright when she wobbled.

"You've made a vast improvement!" Lucas noted, approaching Cate.

"Look, no hands!" Cate quipped, waving her hands in the air as she glided along on her own.

"Getting confident!" Amelia noted, applauding.

"A tad," Cate admitted. The foursome made another four passes, testing Cate's new skating skills. After the last one, they collapsed on the bench together in a heap, all smiles.

"What did you think, Cate? Did you find it fun?" Amelia asked as they removed their blades.

"I did. And thank you for teaching me," she responded.

"You're quite a good student," Lucas noted. Amelia nodded in agreement.

Lucas checked his pocket watch. "We should go back to change for dinner," he suggested.

"Goodness!" Amelia exclaimed, grabbing hold of the watch, "I didn't realize how long we'd lingered. Oh, I hope this doesn't present a problem for dinner dressing." She glanced to Cate and Jack.

"I'm sure we'll make it and anyway, it was good fun!" Cate responded.

"Come along," Lucas coaxed. "Williams is meeting us at the town's center."

They trudged up the hill to the town, navigating down the main street. The foursome piled into the car which whisked them to the castle. As they entered, a maid passed by the foyer.

"Oh, has the dressing gong rung yet?" Amelia asked the girl.

"Aye, ma'am. About thirty minutes ago."

"We'd better go straight away then," Amelia answered, glancing to the rest of them. "See you soon." She squeezed Cate's hand. They raced up the stairs, each going to their suite.

Cate blazed a trail straight to her suitcase, digging through it and pulling out two dresses. She held one up in each hand, studying them. Jack collapsed on the bed with his suit. After a few breaths, he sat up. "If you're going to stand there pondering your choice all day, I'm going to call first dibs on the bathroom!"

Cate smirked at him. "I now have a reputation to maintain!"

Jack laughed. "That you do. Nice side-stepping on the conversation. 'It runs in my family.'"

"Ha! Thank you! Although I can't touch your seamless fabrications, Oxford man."

"Hey, if you're going to fib, you may as well do it right. Besides, it's only half a fib."

"Half a fib?"

"Yes," Jack answered as he backed his way toward the bathroom. "I did go to Oxford. Two semesters."

Cate raised her eyebrows. "Really? You're full of surprises!"

"Aye," Jack agreed. "I hated it and dropped out. I may have stayed if the professors were as pretty as you." He winked at her, disappearing into the bathroom.

Cate giggled, turning her attention back to the dresses.

She selected the royal blue, silver beaded dress, tossing the burgundy back into the suitcase as Jack emerged from the bathroom.

"Have you made your choice? I moved as slow as I could."

"Yes, I made my choice. And I expect Amelia will be pleased!" Cate disappeared into the bathroom. She pulled off her day clothes, hanging the dress on a towel bar. Cate shimmied into the evening dress and took a few moments to fix her hair. Her skating excursion, while fun, left her hair a disheveled mess. She tamed it back into a low chignon. She adjusted her dress, smoothing it and adding a necklace. Satisfied, she emerged from the bathroom and sat on the bed to pull her shoes on.

"Whew, we're just going to make it!" Jack announced.

"We'll be late. This buckle can be tricky," Cate retorted, fiddling with the t-strap shoe.

"Here, let me," Jack offered, kneeling on the floor in front of her. He set her shoe on his knee, buckling the strap after his second try. "There."

"Saved the day," Cate said as he pulled her to standing. "Thank you."

"I don't want to be late. I'm hungry."

Cate pulled on her gloves as they exited the room and navigated to the sitting room. Amelia and Lucas had also just arrived. They were offering their apologies for their lateness along with those of Jack and Cate. Amelia insisted it was their fault.

"No harm done," Rory stated. "Though we should forego cocktails."

"Of course," Amelia agreed. "Shall we go straight in?"

"Yes, that might be wise," Anne agreed. They filed into the dining room, taking their seats.

"What caused you to run late, Amelia?" Anne inquired over the first course.

"We went into town earlier for lunch. Then went skating on the pond," Amelia responded.

"What fun!" Rory exclaimed. "Did you enjoy it?"

"Very much so," Amelia answered. "Cate hadn't skated before. I insisted she try. So, you see, it is rather my fault we were late."

Anne's eyebrows raised as she turned her gaze to Cate. "Did you enjoy it, Cate?" Anne questioned.

"I did," Cate admitted. "I was unsure but found it to be enjoyable."

"Well, you are more adventurous than I, Cate," Anne admitted. "I've never tried, though Amelia attempts to talk me into it every season."

"Oh, she's exceptionally adventurous, this lassie," Jack chimed in.

"Perhaps it's the American in you," Lucas suggested.

"One day, we'll make a skater of you, too," Amelia teased Anne.

The conversation continued on to winter sports, weather, travel and Amelia and Lucas' upcoming departure. Dinner sped by, with Cate enjoying the company and relaxing with her family.

Cate and Jack stayed for one post-dinner drink before retiring for the evening. Cate cited her sore muscles for her early night. She and Jack returned to their suite, changing back to their day clothes before using the timepiece to return to their time.

CHAPTER 21

"Whew! What a day!" Jack announced as they returned.

"Yeah and it's only… nine forty-eight… in the morning!" Cate announced, citing the mere forty-eight minutes that had passed in the present during the twelve hours they spent in the past.

"I'm ready for bed. And it's still morning!"

Cate nodded. "Well, perhaps you should take a nice long nap when you get home," she suggested.

"Aye, though I'd like to go over the information we received today. The note Gould received… this could be the break we've been hoping for."

"It may be a little too good of a break," Cate admitted. "We can head down to the library. We should have plenty of time to discuss it before your Sunday dinner with your grandfather."

"Why don't you join us for dinner. Pap sure won't mind. And he'll most likely be interested in our little investigation."

"Oh," Cate hedged, her brows wrinkling in thought. "I

wouldn't want to impose. It's your time with your grandfather. Plus, I've got the dogs. I hate to leave them."

"It's no imposition. Pap loves you. Pap also loves your dogs. And he's got a nice yard for them to frolic in." Cate smiled. "Besides, I won't take no for an answer."

"Oh, is that right?" Cate inquired. "I suppose I'd better just agree then!"

"You suppose right, Lady Cate! Now, we'll change and meet downstairs. We'll head down early and help him cook."

"Okay," Cate agreed. Jack left her to change. She selected an outfit, carrying it into the bathroom. She hung her dress on the towel bar, leaving it for later to put away. She fixed her hair into a suitable style for the present time before touching up her makeup.

After exiting, she made her way to the sitting room and pulled on her boots. "How about a field trip, boys? Want to go to Jack's grandfather's?" Riley agreed at the mention of Jack's name. Bailey, beginning to become excited when Riley did, leapt to his feet as well.

Cate ushered both dogs from the room. They raced ahead of her down the hall, barreling down the stairs to a waiting Jack. Cate pulled on her coat, slipping harnesses and leashes on both dogs. "I think I remember where your grandfather lives, but I'll follow you just in case."

"Nonsense," Jack said, swatting the air with his hand. "I'll drive."

"Then you'll have to bring me back, that's silly!" Cate protested. "I'm capable of driving. I even stay on the correct side of the road most times!"

"Hmm," Jack considered it, his hand on his chin. "Yes, I'd have to drive you back. That would take hours..." Cate rolled her eyes at him, chuckling. Jack continued, "May even have to stay overnight before I drive back..."

"Oh, stop," Cate said, batting at him. "Fine, fine, I'll let you drive."

They escorted the pups outside and into Jack's car. Within a matter of minutes, they were pulling up to the little cottage on the outskirts of town. Riley and Bailey reveled in the new scents as they explored every inch of the front yard before trotting to the front door.

"Well, Lady Cate!" Stanley Reid called from the doorway. "Hello!"

"Hello, Mr. Reid. I hope you don't mind my joining you for dinner!"

"Not at all, come in, come in! Add a little beauty to the meal. Better than staring at this big lug all day," Mr. Reid teased, jerking his thumb toward Jack. "Besides, can't have you eating cereal for dinner."

"Thank you for having me," Cate replied, stepping through the door. "And despite what Jack tells you, I don't always eat cereal for dinner."

"Eighty percent of the time then," Jack mentioned with a wink. "The kind with the marshmallows and the cartoon leprechaun on the box."

"And you brought the little pups. Hello, boys! When Jackie texted me you were coming, I set aside two bones for you pups."

"Aw, thank you, Mr. Reid, that's very kind of you," Cate said. "What a treat for you boys!"

Riley pranced into the living room, settling down next to the wall heater in the room. "Little laddie has made himself right at home," Jack noted. "Come on, Mr. Bailey, come over here by your buddy." Jack led him over, settling him near Riley.

"Been time traveling, eh?" Mr. Reid questioned as they headed to the kitchen. "When to?"

"Yes," Cate responded. "1925."

"Ah, the jewelry theft," Mr. Reid commented, mixing a few spices together.

"That's correct," Cate commented. "Anything I can help with?"

"Just sit yourself down, lassie," Jack answered, joining them. "We'll handle it."

"I can help, I'm not that much of a disaster in the kitchen," Cate countered.

"You'll help by sitting down and telling me what your investigation has shown so far," Mr. Reid insisted.

Cate sunk into a chair at the kitchen table. "All right, all right!"

"Who have you identified as suspects?" Stanley asked, sprinkling his mixed spices over cubed potatoes.

"A groom named Thomas Gould is our primary suspect," Jack replied, tenderizing meat.

"Or Lucas MacKenzie."

"Lucas? Rory's brother?" Stanley inquired.

"Yes, my great-grandfather."

"Though neither of us believe he did it," Jack insisted.

"Nay, I wouldn't imagine he did," Stanley agreed.

"Why do you say that, Mr. Reid?" Cate queried.

"Didn't seem the type. I met Lucas a few times. Good, decent fellow, he seemed."

"We arrived at the same conclusion after spending some time with him. Speaking of great-grandparents, I met Lachlan."

Stanley Reid stopped in his tracks, staring at Jack. "You don't say. And how was dear dad, Jackie?"

"Very friendly. We had a great conversation. Rory put all the pieces of the puzzle together pretty fast and realized we were time travelers," Jack mentioned with a roll of his eyes. "By extension, Lachlan is also aware."

Stanley shook his head, amazed by the experience Jack related. "Truly a gift we've been blessed with."

"That's what I said!" Cate exclaimed.

"Time traveling is growing on me," Jack admitted.

Mr. Reid spread the potatoes on a baking sheet, popping it into the refrigerator. "Why do you suspect Lucas?" he questioned.

"We found a note," Cate explained. "Anne MacKenzie wrote it. Oh, I should have brought it!" She planted her palm against her forehead. "In short, it spoke to an unnamed family member about how shocked Anne was that the family member could have stolen so much from her family. She mentions a theft, and she details how angry she is about it."

"Who is it addressed to?"

"No name," Cate responded. "The note mentions she cannot bear to write their name she loathes them so much."

"Odd," Stanley replied, cutting celery for a salad.

"You know, I can chop celery. I feel useless over here," Cate mentioned.

"I won't have it, lassie," Stanley repeated. Jack issued her a wry glance. "And Jackie, get the lady something to drink before her throat runs dry."

"Really, I'm fine. I can get myself a glass of water."

"Nay, Lady Cate, you're a guest!" Jack disagreed. "We can do better than a mere glass of water." He set about making her a warm cuppa.

"Okay," Mr. Reid said, returning to the previous discussion as he settled down at the table with Cate after placing the roast in the oven. "Based on Anne's note, you fingered Lucas as a suspect. But neither of you really expects he did it."

"I hope he didn't for personal reasons. But beyond that, after we investigated, I cannot imagine him or Amelia doing it. They both seem like wonderful, honest people!"

"Aye, I'd agree with that sentiment," the elder Mr. Reid commented as Jack placed a piping hot cup of tea in front of him too.

"You said you met Lucas?" Cate inquired.

"Aye," the man confirmed. "Much later than 1925, mind you, but I met him on a few occasions. He seemed a good, honest man, as you noted."

"At the castle?" Cate questioned.

"Aye, lassie. Around Christmas. They traveled here every holiday."

Cate's brow furrowed. "So... Lucas and Amelia continued to travel here many years later."

Jack sat down with his cuppa. "Which all but confirms their innocence despite Amelia's note."

Cate remained silent for a moment, considering it. "Yeah, I must agree. Given that they traveled here for years after points to their innocence. With the rhetoric in Anne's letter, I doubt they'd have been invited back if they were guilty."

"No, they'd have become estranged," Jack added.

"So that leaves your other suspect, Thomas Gould," Stanley Reid concluded.

"Aye, Pap, it does," Jack agreed. "And the evidence against him is compelling."

"Let's hear your case against him."

"He has no alibi. And we have a rather incriminating note that's been given to us suggesting he has the jewelry and intends to sell it. Those two items along with some brash statements he's made about coming into enough money to start a restaurant in London round out our full case against him."

"How did you come about this information?"

"The police accused Anne's ladies' maid of the crime. Remind Jack to fill you in on his new burgeoning legal career, by the way! When we visited her while she was in custody, she told us Rory's valet, Mr. Calhoun, was ill the night of the theft. We then questioned the staff. During that process, we found that Mr. Calhoun, who is Thomas Gould's roommate, was out of the room for part of the night. Leaving both Mr. Calhoun and Thomas without an alibi for a portion of the night."

"A fact that Mr. Gould failed to mention to Cate when she spoke with him. So, either he didn't realize his roommate was gone because he was asleep or because he wasn't in the room," Jack chimed in.

Cate nodded. "Right. After that, we focused our time and energy on Gould and Calhoun. We asked the under-butler, Forsythe, to provide any information he could. After a few inquiries, he found that most considered it a stretch that Robert Calhoun could have stolen the jewelry given his honest nature. However, Mr. Gould enjoyed gambling and drinking."

"While it's a character flaw, it's not a reason to accuse him," Mr. Reid interjected.

"No," Jack answered, "but he tends to run his mouth when he drinks and plays. And he told his gambling buddies he'd soon be coming into money to open a restaurant in London."

Cate nodded. "Which he opens mere months after leaving Dunhaven!"

"And he leaves Dunhaven only months after the theft," Jack added.

Cate's voice rose with excitement and her speech became rushed. "AND… Forsythe had Calhoun search his room and he found a note asking if he was ready to sell the jewelry."

Mr. Reid considered the information. "The evidence does point to him." Cate nodded, and they fell silent for several breaths. "Yet something is bothering you about it."

Cate nodded to confirm Stanley's suspicions. "Two

things, really. First, it seems too convenient. Second, Anne's note doesn't fit with Gould as a culprit."

"Too convenient?" Jack queried. "We've almost got him dead to rights."

Cate shook her head. "No. Forsythe said Calhoun found the note in his room. But he found it after we searched the room!"

Jack's eyebrows raised, and he glanced to Cate. "And the note wasn't there when you searched his things?"

Cate shook her head again. "Nope. And besides, would you keep such an incriminating piece of evidence in your room? The police have searched the house several times."

"Perhaps he felt untouchable. The police are focused on Lillian Murray only."

"I didn't overlook that note. It's fake."

"By whom?"

Cate considered it. "It couldn't have been anyone but Forsythe or Calhoun. Only they were involved."

"That we know of," Jack responded.

"That's where this falls apart. Why would either of them fake the note? Or ask someone else to fake it?"

"Because one of them is the guilty party," Stanley Reid deduced.

Cate scrunched her brow, considering his conclusion. "Calhoun or Forsythe? Hmm."

"Forsythe was on the original suspect list, Cate," Jack reminded her.

"Yes," Cate agreed. "And he was adamant about pinning this on Gould. When we didn't jump on the first tale about the restaurant, he gave us the note. Perhaps he wrote the note, in an effort to make the case stronger."

"It's possible," Jack agreed.

"Looks like you two have more investigating to do," Stanley suggested after checking his roast.

"Aye, looks like it, Pap," Jack agreed.

The older man plopped into his chair. "What's this about your blossoming law career, Jackie?"

Jack let out a loud laugh and shook his head. "Aye, I'm quite the legal genius. I've already gotten a man off on a murder case, and now I'm working on keeping Lillian Murray out of jail for a crime she didn't commit."

Mr. Reid wrinkled his brow, glancing between Cate and Jack. After a moment, he raised his brows. "You really are blooming as an attorney!"

"I'd expect no less from a man who graduated top of his class at Oxford," Cate joked.

Mr. Reid roared with laughter. "You do it big when you do it, don't you, Jackie?"

"Aye," Jack agreed, joining into the laughter. "I told Lady Cate, if we're going to lie, might as well make it a damn good one."

"All joking aside," Cate added, after her laughter subsided, "he may have missed his calling."

"What was that you said, Jackie? Legal genius?" Mr. Reid replied, still chuckling. "Ah, perhaps, but he didn't miss his calling. His place is right here with us and you, Lady Cate."

Cate smiled at the older man. "I couldn't agree more," she answered.

They continued their conversation as Jack and Mr. Reid prepared a few more items for the dinner then settled down for an early afternoon meal. Riley and Bailey gathered around the table, gnawing on the bones provided by Stanley Reid. Cate was not only impressed by Stanley's roast, but also by his dessert-making skills. After the meal, Mr. Reid served a delicious Cranachan, a traditional Scottish dessert. Despite it being "out of season" for the dessert, Mr. Reid insisted he make it once he learned Cate would join them for dinner.

"With cooking like this, Mr. Reid, I may come here every Sunday," Cate joked.

"Better than your cereal?" Jack questioned.

"Mmm, yes, even the marshmallow kind."

The trio continued their conversation while cleaning up after their meal, a task Cate insisted on participating in. They settled in the living room afterward, enjoying each other's company. In the late afternoon, Jack returned Cate to the castle for the evening.

"Well, I suppose we'll try our other avenue tomorrow afternoon. Follow up on Pap's idea that either Forsythe or Calhoun are the culprit," Jack promised as they drove up the drive.

Cate nodded. "Yes. This is quite the conundrum. Other than money, what reasoning is there? And how does it tie in with Anne's note?"

Jack shrugged. "I hope we can find out," he commented as he eased the car in front of the castle.

"Me too! Well, I'll see you tomorrow. Enjoy the rest of your day off."

"Thanks, Lady Cate. Enjoy your evening. And you too, Riley and Bailey." Jack gave each a pat on the head before they jumped from the car, racing to the front door. Cate ushered them into the castle, waving to Jack as he pulled away.

She climbed the stairs, the two pups racing in front of her toward their suite. Quietness filled the castle. Molly must not have returned yet. Cate entered the room, crossing to her bedroom and bathroom. Despite the early hour, she planned on changing for bed and relaxing for the rest of the evening. The extra twelve hours added to her day exhausted her. She changed and settled on her chaise. Within thirty minutes she found herself nodding off. She took the dogs for one last walk before turning in early.

CHAPTER 22

Cate slept straight through to the alarm. It buzzed at her, startling her awake. Groggy, she slapped the snooze button, rolling over for ten more minutes. The alarm screamed again, waking a dozing Cate. She groaned but dragged herself from her bed, not wanting to be late for breakfast.

She stifled a yawn as she slogged into the kitchen. "Good morning," she murmured to Mrs. Fraser and Molly.

"Good morning, Lady Cate," Mrs. Fraser answered. "Are you all right?"

"Yeah," Molly added, "you look pale."

"Aye, Molly. I noticed the same. You may be coming down with something, Lady Cate!"

"Oh, no," Cate responded, waving their concern away with her hand. "I didn't sleep well. Still waking up."

"Trouble sleeping?" Mrs. Fraser questioned. "Everything all right?"

"A little. Must be getting too much rest and not enough exercise," Cate fibbed. The real reason was her extra-long day.

"With all that walking you do with Riley and Bailey?" Molly inquired. "You get plenty of exercise!"

"I'll sleep like the dead tonight, I bet!" Cate responded. Jack and Mr. Fraser entered the kitchen as Mrs. Fraser set out the last of the breakfast.

"Well, I'd recommend you join us for a cuppa after breakfast. It'll help with your muddled mind from the lack of sleep."

"I will take you up on that," Cate agreed, happy to have a diversion to pass the time before she and Jack returned to the past this afternoon.

After finishing breakfast, Mrs. Fraser and Molly bustled about the kitchen cleaning up before making tea. Cate rose to help clear the table, but Mrs. Fraser put her firmly back in her seat, insisting she appeared too weak for physical labor.

Cate waited for her tea, stacking dishes and shoving them to the edge of the table to make it easier for the women to retrieve. "You're bound and determined to do work, aren't you, Lady Cate?" Mrs. Fraser asked.

"I'm not ill!" Cate insisted. "I'm capable of doing a little."

"We'll have it cleaned up in no time," Mrs. Fraser insisted.

It wasn't long before Cate had a piping hot cup of tea in front of her, along with one of Mrs. Fraser's famous shortbreads. "Mmm," Molly murmured, munching on one. "When are you going to teach me to bake these?"

"Soon enough. When you're ready."

"I'm more than ready," Molly assured her. "I need to learn how to make these in case I eat them all before you bake more."

Cate giggled at Molly's statement. "How was your day trip yesterday, Molly?" Cate inquired.

"Wonderful! I don't expect I'll ever get tired of this country!"

Molly discussed all aspects of her sightseeing with Cate

and Mrs. Fraser. She'd done quite a bit in one day. Not put off by the cold, she scouted several nearby sights and noted several she wanted to explore further in warmer weather. It pleased Cate to see Molly settling in so well in her new country. Molly babbled on over tea, encouraging Cate to come with her on one of her expeditions and see the countryside. Cate promised to do that once the weather improved, ceding that the dogs would love the trip.

After tea, Cate retreated to her room, using her time to work. She stared at her computer screen with glazed eyes. Only adrenaline and anticipation for her upcoming trip kept her awake. After a while, she slammed the laptop shut, opting for a walk with the dogs to fill her time before lunch.

After lunch, Cate began her preparations to return to the past. She began by sweeping her hair into a 1920s-appropriate style. She'd left the day dress she'd worn yesterday hanging in her bathroom, choosing not to put it away after her long day.

Cate pulled it from the towel bar, and it slipped from her fingers, splaying onto the bathroom floor. "Of course," Cate mumbled, bending over to retrieve it. She grasped it by the hem, pulling it upward. As she attempted to untangle it and turn it right-side up, something slid from the pocket, clattering to the floor. Cate glanced at the object, confusion crossing her face.

She set the dress aside in a heap, reaching for the envelope laying on the floor. Cate turned it over in her hands, recalling shoving it in her pocket the day before. The name on the envelope read Mr. Lorne Peterson. Cate sunk onto the edge of the tub, considering the letter. Who was Lorne Peterson, Cate wondered? Why did Forsythe have a letter addressed to Lorne Peterson? He wasn't sending the letter to Lorne Peterson, the letter had already been delivered.

With a deep inhale, Cate opened the missive, unfolding the note. Her brow furrowed as she read:

My darling Lorne,

How I cannot wait to see you! Do you have them? Are they as beautiful as I'm imagining? Oh! To have such luxuries! But one day, my darling, one day we shall!

Love, please let me try them on before you rid us of them! Could we keep just one of them? Surely selling only one piece would give us enough money to live the good life! I could wear one when you take me out on the town. How lovely I would look. Like a grand lady!

Oh, but I know we can't keep them. Sadly, we must sell them. At least once they're gone, you'll have something from your family beyond just a dull name. They owe you, love. You've been robbed of your due.

When can I see you? Please say before you sell those little beauties! I want to try it on just once, please, my love? Write when you can.

Ever yours,
Trixie
XOXOXO

Cate stared at the letter, confusion on her face. She raced into her sitting room, pulling open her folder listing all the servants in the household during 1925. She scanned the list, running her finger down the page. No listings existed for Lorne Peterson. Cate wrinkled her brow and tightened her lips together. Something wasn't adding up. Why did Forsythe have this note? What did it mean? What luxuries was the mysterious Trixie referring to?

A knock at the door interrupted Cate's musings. She

rushed to the door, greeting a prepared Jack. "Not ready?" he surmised, eyeing Cate in her normal clothes.

She shook her head. "No, but come in."

"Change in plans?" he asked, stepping into the room and bending to pet the two dogs.

"Not really," Cate answered. "But something interesting came up. As I was about to change, this note slipped out of my pocket. I'd forgotten about it after I pocketed it yesterday!"

"Ohhhh, the note Forsythe dropped?" Jack inquired, standing. "I'd forgotten about it, too."

Cate nodded. "Yes. Well, anyway, it dropped out of my pocket and I again wondered why Forsythe had it. Who is Lorne Peterson? Long story short, I read it."

"What did it say?" Jack questioned.

Cate took a deep breath. "Here you read it. I want your take without my thoughts mixed in. I don't want to influence your opinion." She handed him the note. Cate paced the floor as Jack read the note. "Well?" she queried the moment he glanced up from the missive.

"I'm confused," Jack responded. "Who are these people? And what are they talking about? And why does Forsythe have this note?"

"Same questions I had. The first thing I figured was one or both of them were servants at the house in 1925 and Forsythe, for whatever reason, confiscated the note from them. But..." Cate paused, grabbing the staff list from her folder, "there are no Lornes or Trixies on the staff in 1925."

"Perhaps Lorne is a friend of Forsythe?"

"Why give him the letter?" Cate inquired.

"Show off to his friend? Brag about his girlfriend?"

"That seems a bit of a stretch," Cate answered. "I couldn't answer the who question. So, I moved on to the next obvious question: what are they talking about? What are the luxuries?"

"Could be anything," Jack replied.

Cate paced around, biting her lower lip in thought. "Or…" she said, her mind churning in thought as her eyes grew wide, "or do they refer to something we know?"

"Like what?"

"Like the missing jewelry."

Jack stared at the note, scanning it again. "I mean it could…"

Cate sidled next to him, peering over his shoulder. "Could? It's pretty possible. Consider how she refers to these objects: beautiful, luxuries, let's sell one piece, I'll wear the other out on the town and look like a grand lady. What does a woman wear that she refers to as a beautiful luxury, that she'd wear out on the town to look like a grand lady?"

Jack shook his head as though he had no clue. "Oh, come on, think, Jack," Cate prompted.

"Luxurious clothing? A fur coat? Yeah, jewelry. It could be jewelry, sure," he agreed.

"Okay, so this note could refer to the stolen jewelry. She asks Lorne if he has it. Which means Lorne, whoever he is, is the guilty party. And it fits with Anne's note. Look here!" Cate exclaimed, pointing to a specific statement. "You'll have something from your family beyond that dull name! This implies Lorne is related to the MacKenzies somehow."

Jack remained silent, deep in thought. Cate cocked her head, biting her lower lip again. She glanced up to Jack, wide-eyed again. "What?" he questioned.

"This implies Lorne is related to the MacKenzies," she repeated. "Lorne… related to the MacKenzies… Lorne… MacKenzie. Lorne MacKenzie!"

Jack glanced around the room. "Randolph's brother?" Cate nodded. "Cate, he'd be ancient if he's still alive!"

"No, he can't be Lorne himself. That's obvious," Cate answered, pacing. "Lorne's son? No… no! Lorne's grandson! Yes, that must be it! Lorne's grandson!"

Jack knit his brows. "You're jumping to some big conclusions here, Cate," Jack warned.

Cate shrugged. "The note references taking something from his family, so he gets more than the stupid name. His name is Lorne. It can't be a coincidence that there is a Lorne MacKenzie in the family tree."

"Perhaps it's the Peterson family Trixie is referring to?" Jack questioned.

Cate shook her head, disagreeing. "It can't be a coincidence. There are far too many of those. The note refers to something luxurious… the jewelry. It refers to taking something owed to him from the family… Lorne's family. Lorne's children probably received nothing in the will. We know he had a reputation as a womanizer. Victoria confirmed that to me. It's likely they were bastard children, anyway."

"I still think it's a stretch, Cate. And even if you're correct, who is Lorne? Thomas Gould? Robert Calhoun? How can we find out?"

Cate considered it for a moment. "No," she answered. "Charles Forsythe!" She grabbed her laptop, plopping onto the chaise.

"How do you figure?"

"He's the only one I couldn't find anything out about when I researched them online! I found no information at all. Because he's using a fake name!" Cate's fingers flew over the keyboard. "Just as I suspected!"

"What?" Jack moved to peer over her shoulder.

"When I search Lorne Peterson, I find results. Death date, birth date. But when I try Charles Forsythe, nothing. I mean, I get results, but there's nothing that fits with our Charles Forsythe."

"Hmm," Jack mused aloud.

"He MUST be Lorne Peterson. He's hiding his identity because he's related to the family."

"Still," Jack replied, "it's a stretch. So, you have the name Lorne. Do you really think he and his grandfather were the only ones with that name?"

"No, but perhaps it was still too close for comfort. Or perhaps the Peterson name is known by the family. They may have kept tabs on Lorne's progeny." Jack remained unconvinced; a fact obvious from his expression. "Okay, Mr. Skeptical, what else makes sense? Who is Lorne? What does this note refer to?"

Jack sighed, pondering her queries for a moment. "I suppose you're right. This is the most likely scenario given the information we have." Cate smiled at him. "BUT," he continued, "we have limited information. This is hardly a smoking gun and we're making a lot of assumptions about who Lorne Peterson is and how he's related to the family."

"You're right," Cate answered, closing the laptop and jumping to her feet. She paced the floor. "We need more proof. And we're going to get it!"

"I hate the sound of this."

"We've got to return to 1925 and pursue this."

"How?"

"First, we prove the incriminating note is a fake. Then we need to get proof against Forsythe, a. k. a. Lorne. Perhaps search his things?"

"Ugh," Jack groaned. "Yep, I hate this plan."

"We must get proof. We can't go to the police or even Rory without it. Rory will never believe us, especially if we come with the story about this being a cousin of his."

Jack sighed. "Well, I suppose you better get changed and we better get this horrendous plan underway."

Cate nodded her head, a smile on her face. "Be right

back!" she promised. Cate raced to the bathroom, pulling on her dress. She slid her ring and shoes on, hurrying to buckle them before dashing to the bedroom and calling for Jack. "Let's go!"

"You are way too excited," Jack commented, entering the room.

"We're on to something, Jack. This is the break we've been hoping for!" She held out the timepiece, and they activated it, traveling back to 1925. "Okay, let's get going!"

"How do you plan to prove this note is fake?"

"Try to get a handwriting sample from Forsythe. Once we do that, we can compare them. If it matches, we'll move on to part two of the plan."

"Searching Forsythe's room? Ugh. I hate taking this risk, but okay, let's go!"

Cate grinned at him, hurrying from the bedroom, across the sitting room and into the hallway. Cate charged down the hall, making her way straight down to the servant's area. She sought Forsythe, finding him in Benson's office, decanting the wine to be used for dinner.

"Mr. and Mrs. MacKenzie!" he greeted them. "Have you been able to discuss the new evidence with the police?"

"Ah," Cate hesitated, glancing to Jack. "We are about to present our case to them, but we want all our ducks in a row. The police will, without doubt, want to verify any name mentioned in the note you provided us. Would you provide us with a list of all male staff members?"

Forsythe paused a moment, before nodding his head. "Yes, of course, Mrs. MacKenzie," he agreed.

"I hate to be a bother," Cate pressed, "but we'd like to gather the information now and speak with the police as soon as possible. I'm sure you understand."

"Oh, yes, of course."

"Just a handwritten note will do, thank you," Cate instructed.

Forsythe offered a brief smile, pulling a piece of paper from Benson's desk drawer and scrawling a list. "This is all of them. I hope you find it helpful and that this soon is behind us." He held the note out toward them.

Cate smiled at him, accepting the note. She glanced at it. "Yes, this will be most helpful. Thank you," Cate replied. "With any luck, we'll have this wrapped up soon!"

Cate and Jack left the man to his wine, climbing the stairs and entering the sitting room. They found the room empty. Cate pulled the note Forsythe provided yesterday and held it next to the staff list written today. Jack peered over her shoulder. "What's it look like?"

Cate squinted her eyes, peering back and forth between both notes. After a moment, she responded, "I'm no expert, but I'd say the same person wrote both notes. What do you think?"

Jack stared a moment longer. "I'd say it's a match. And that's my expert Oxford opinion talking," Jack added.

"I agree with your expert Oxford opinion. See the 'o' here and here. And 't's' are the same, crossed at an angle."

"Yeah," Jack agreed. "And the 'P' is a near identical match to the note."

"So, this note," Cate said, holding the so-called evidence up higher, "is a fake."

"A fake written by Charles Forsythe to lay the blame on someone else."

"Which puts Charles Forsythe at the top of our list."

"Yes, I'd agree."

"Now we need more evidence of his involvement, or at least his motive."

"This is the part I dread," Jack admitted.

"Well..." Cate began when the door opened across the

room, interrupting her. Amelia and Lucas entered the room. Cate folded the notes, shoving them into her pocket and pasting a smile onto her face.

"Cate!" Amelia exclaimed, rushing toward her. She pulled Cate into her arms in a tight hug. "Just the person I've been searching for."

"Oh?" Cate inquired, pulling back from her great-grandmother.

"Yes. I wanted to show you the dress I mentioned last night at cocktails. Do you have a minute now?"

"W-Well…" Cate stuttered. She glanced to Jack.

"Oh, it won't take but a moment and I do want you to see it."

"And, Jack," Lucas added. "I had a few land questions I hoped to gather your input on. This will give us the perfect opportunity. I suspect Amelia's 'moment' may last quite a bit longer than that. Women and fashion and all that!" He laughed at his joke.

Jack joined in. "Yes, I dare say we'll have enough time." He winked at Cate. "Go on, dear, enjoy your fashion while we talk business."

Cate wrinkled her nose at him but faked a laugh and told Amelia to lead the way. They left the men pouring brandies in the sitting room and sitting down to business. "Did I interrupt something?" Amelia questioned as they climbed the stairs.

"No," Cate fibbed. "We were going over our wish list for sightseeing!"

"Ah! Have you ticked all your boxes yet?"

"Not quite. There is one additional item left to be ticked."

"Well, I hope you have time to visit it. If not, we'll have to ask Rory and Anne to have you back next year for the holidays. They've both enjoyed your visit, as have Lucas and I."

"We've enjoyed it, too," Cate admitted, saddened that the

next holiday would be near the close of the year, preventing them from visiting after the new year.

They arrived at Amelia's room, entering her sitting room. "Isn't this room lovely?" Amelia commented, motioning for Cate to take a seat on the sofa near the fireplace. "We stay in this room every visit. I simply adore it. This side of the castle sees some amazing sunsets!"

"It is lovely," Cate agreed.

"How is your room? I hope you are enjoying it," Amelia shouted from the bedroom.

"We are!" Cate called in. "Contrary to your room, we have amazing sunrises."

Amelia emerged from the bedroom, carrying a dress. Cate stood, approaching her. "Sunrises? How vivacious of you to be awake to see them!"

"I'm not very good at sleeping," Cate admitted.

"Poor dear. Is it something medical?"

"No, just a racing mind, I'm afraid."

"Hmm," Amelia murmured, considering Cate's statement. "You are quite clever, Cate. I'm not surprised. If I have a daughter one day, I hope she will be as clever as you, though better at sleeping!"

The women chuckled over the joke, though the comment struck Cate square in the heart. Pride surged through her. Being the woman's great-granddaughter, she felt as though Amelia had somewhat achieved her goal.

Amelia held up the dress. "Here's the dress I was telling you about," she noted. "See the lovely detailing on the hem?"

Cate and Amelia spent the next thirty minutes discussing the dress, shoes, accessories and fashion in general. Cate enjoyed the conversation, staying much longer than she expected. It relieved her mind from the turmoil of solving the mystery.

When she and Amelia parted ways, Cate's mind returned

to the pressing business of finding evidence against Forsythe. She navigated to the foyer, approaching the sitting room. Voices carried from inside, announcing with no doubt that Jack and Lucas' conversation had not yet ended.

Cate hovered for a moment outside the doorway, determining her next steps. She checked the timepiece. If the conversation lasted much longer, they may not be able to search Lorne's room before the dressing gong rang. After a moment of debate, Cate spun on her heel and hurried up the main staircase. She wound through the halls, finding one of the back staircases leading to the servants' quarters.

Cate puffed a long breath out, steeling her nerves to climb the staircase and search Forsythe's room. "It has to be done," Cate assured herself with a whisper. Cate stared up the steep staircase for another breath. She placed one foot on the first stair, forcing her weight on it. Then she climbed to the second step. One foot after another, she forced herself up the staircase, her knees weak from tension.

She reached the top. The hallway appeared deserted. Cate stood for a moment, straining to listen for sounds. Nothing reached her ears. She tiptoed to Forsythe's door, giving it a light knock. No response greeted her. She tried again, louder this time. Again, there was no response.

Cate took a deep breath and turned the knob, pushing the door open. An empty room met her gaze. She was about to step inside when a voice halted her.

"Mrs. MacKenzie?" Forsythe called from the stairway.

Cate's stomach turned, and she jumped, startled by his presence. "Oh," she replied, her voice unsteady. "Forsythe, there you are."

Forsythe's brow furrowed as he stepped toward her. "Is there something you need? It must be very urgent for you to seek me out here."

Cate swallowed hard. "I forgot earlier," Cate fibbed. "You

dropped this note yesterday. I meant to return it and it slipped my mind with all the turmoil earlier about sorting the evidence." Cate held out the note marked Lorne Peterson toward him.

Forsythe glanced down at it. "Oh, did I? How clumsy of me." He accepted the note. "Thank you."

"You are welcome. I hated for you to have lost your personal correspondence."

"How kind of you. However, it is not mine. It was delivered in error. I'm still sorting it out, but I'm sure whoever it belongs to will be most appreciative."

Cate offered a nervous, awkward smile with a nod. "Well, I'll be on my way. Good luck finding the note's owner."

"Good day, Mrs. MacKenzie." Cate's leaden legs carried her to the stairway. She glanced back over her shoulder, finding Forsythe staring at her. She swallowed hard as she forced herself to descend the stairs at a slow, normal pace. Every inch of her body screamed for her to run, but she slowed her pace until she reached the bottom quarter of the stairs. There Cate picked up her pace, stumbling down the last few steps and spilling into the hallway below. She hastened down the hall, glancing behind her, half-expecting Forsythe to be following her. His quiet, unflappable manner disconcerted her. It should have calmed her, made her less suspicious of him, but it achieved the exact opposite.

With her thoughts distracting her, Cate almost ran into Jack as she rounded the corner.

"Oof," Cate grunted as Jack grabbed hold of her to steady her. "Oh, Jack! Sorry!"

"Cate! Where have you been?" Jack stared at her, noting something was amiss. "Are you okay?"

Cate nodded, collecting her thoughts. "Yes," she said after a breath. "I… I went to Forsythe's room."

"You what?!" Jack exclaimed. "Oh, Cate…" he trailed off, shaking his head.

"Bad idea, I realize that. Let's take a walk. I need some air."

"All right," Jack agreed, grasping Cate's elbow and leading her toward the stairs. Without a word, they traveled outside into the chilly air. Cate hugged her arms around her, squeezing her eyes shut. She gulped deep breaths of the cold air to steady her nerves.

Jack removed his jacket, placing it around Cate's shoulders. Cate opened her eyes, pulling the jacket around her tighter. "Thanks," she replied just above a whisper.

"Cate, what happened?" Jack inquired, staring intently at her.

Cate glanced to him before refocusing her gaze on the horizon. She shook her head before plowing into her story. "After Amelia and I spoke, I came to find you. You were still talking to Lucas. It didn't sound like you'd be finished anytime soon. I debated a moment but decided to try a quick search of Forsythe's room." Jack exhaled in a huff. "I know, I know. It was stupid. But I was afraid we'd run out of time before the dressing gong."

A moment of silence lasted for a breath between them before Cate continued. "I climbed up to the servants' quarters, despite my better judgment. I knocked at Forsythe's door and when no one answered, I opened it. Just before I entered, Forsythe appeared and asked if I needed anything. I didn't know what else to do, so I gave him back the note he dropped."

"What did he say?" Jack questioned.

"He claimed it wasn't his. Said he was trying to sort it out and get it to the correct person." Cate paused for a moment. "Something about him seemed disingenuous. He was almost too cool about it."

"Cate…" Jack began.

Cate held up a hand, stopping him. "Please, no lectures."

"I'm not going to lecture you, Cate," Jack responded. "I was going to say Forsythe seems to be an excellent liar. I don't trust him." Cate smiled at him. "And that I'm happy you're okay. And stop running off to investigate by yourself."

Cate chuckled at Jack's stern warning. "Don't laugh at me," Jack scolded, giving in to a laugh too. "I'm serious."

"Yes, I know," Cate admitted.

"Come on, Lady Cate, let's get out of this cold and dress for dinner."

Cate nodded to him, allowing him to lead her back inside.

Cate and Jack changed for dinner, discussing the prospect of sharing their suspicion with Rory about Forsythe. They decided to return the following morning to share their theory, agreeing this evening's dinner was not the appropriate time. They returned to the present following their dinner to wait out the rest of the day. Cate paced the floor for a good part of it, nervous about her upcoming conversation with Rory. Too many unanswered questions remained. Her mind refused to cease twirling them around her head like an amusement park carousel at full speed.

Following dinner, Cate spent an hour watching a movie before retiring. Despite her longer than typical day, Cate still experienced a fitful night. Visions of being caught by Forsythe and concoctions of the upcoming conversation with Rory danced across her mind in an endless array.

CHAPTER 23

Dawn finally brought a new day to Dunhaven Castle. A groggy Cate rose from her bed, lumbering straight past the rose gold rays painting the moors and into the shower. The steamy water helped awaken her. The pending conversation with Rory also added enough adrenaline to her system to keep her awake.

Cate ate her breakfast in the dining room, her mind whirling and her leg bouncing up and down with impatience. After breakfast, Cate took Riley and Bailey for a brief walk outside before returning to her room to change.

Jack met Cate at their prearranged time, and they traveled back to 1925, arriving in Cate's own bedroom nearly a century earlier. Jack glanced to Cate. "You ready?" he asked, throwing his arms out to the side.

Cate blew out a long breath. "I guess," she said, uncertainty creeping into her voice.

"That sounds less than ready," Jack assessed.

"There are still so many loose ends," Cate replied. "My mind hasn't stopped since we returned yesterday. So many unanswered questions are still lingering."

"Perhaps Rory can help us tie up some loose ends."

Cate nodded at Jack. "Yes, let's hope he can."

"Come on," Jack responded, grabbing Cate's hand and tugging her toward the door. "Let's get this done!"

"I never imagined I'd see the day where you were more enthusiastic than I was during one of these trips!" Cate said with a giggle.

"Me either. Now, come on, you're ruining this for me. I'm supposed to be the sour one!"

Cate chuckled as they navigated to Rory's office, finding him there going over the estate ledgers.

Jack rapped his knuckles against the door jamb. "Got a minute?" he questioned, causing Rory to glance up from his paperwork.

"Of course!" Rory answered. "Please come in! How are you?"

Cate and Jack entered the room. Cate pushed the door shut behind her. "We were hoping to discuss our investigation into the jewelry theft," Cate confessed.

"Oh," Rory muttered, as though he preferred not to. "Have you found anything? Anne is most anxious to solve the matter."

"I'm sure she is," Cate replied. "We have a suspect in mind after a thorough investigation."

Rory raised his eyebrows. "Yes, I gathered as much. My groom, I believe?" he questioned.

Cate furrowed her brow and shook her head. "No," she corrected, "not Thomas Gould."

Rory matched her expression. "Not Thomas? I understood from Forsythe the evidence against him was extremely damning."

Jack raised his eyebrows. "Forsythe told you about the evidence?"

"Yes," Rory admitted. "We discussed the matter at some

length yesterday. He inquired about the result of your discussion with the police. Have you presented the evidence to them yet?"

Cate glanced to Jack. "Uh, no." She stuttered, formulating her thoughts.

Rory answered before she spoke again. "According to Forsythe, there was no doubt. He has motive and an incriminating note stating he had the jewelry! May I ask the reason you've not shared your information with the police yet?"

"The evidence was fabricated," Cate explained.

"What?" Rory questioned, incredulous. "Fake? Why? Who? How? Oh, my apologies for the string of questions, but I'm flabbergasted!"

"I understand," Cate answered. "But Thomas Gould was framed. He isn't the thief. Yes, he has made claims that he wants to buy a restaurant and stated he'd soon have the money, but the note that provides the most incriminating evidence was forged."

"How do you know?" Rory inquired.

"We suspected the forgery and compared it to the handwriting of the person who wrote the note. It was a match," Jack explained.

"Why would anyone do that?"

"To throw us off the scent. To pin the crime on someone else and take the heat off themselves," Cate related.

Rory shook his head, confusion crossing his face. "This is all so very confusing. How appalling that someone stole our property and then lied to place the blame on an innocent man. And you say you've identified who it is by the forged note?"

Cate nodded. "Yes." Cate's heart raced as she faced the prospect of naming their suspect.

"Who is it?" Rory queried.

"Forsythe," Jack and Cate said in unison.

"What?!" Rory responded, quizzical.

Cate nodded a second time. "Yes, Forsythe. He is the one who gave us all the incriminating information. He provided us with the note that he allegedly found in Thomas Gould's possessions. A comparison of that note with this handwriting shows that they match. Forsythe wrote the note to cast suspicion onto Thomas."

Rory stood from the desk, stalking to the window and staring out. "This can't be," he claimed.

"I'm afraid it's true," Jack added.

"What made you check the handwriting?"

"We searched Thomas Gould's room for clues," Cate admitted. "The note Forsythe claimed Mr. Calhoun found was not there. Forsythe had the room searched after we searched it. Since we did not find it, we suspected it was a fake. We tested our theory by requesting a list of the male staff from Forsythe yesterday. The handwriting matches."

Rory gave a slight shake of his head. "Coincidence, perhaps."

"I don't believe so," Cate answered.

"But it must be!" Rory exclaimed, turning his head toward them before returning his gaze out the window.

Cate glanced to Jack, confused by Rory's reaction. "There's more," Cate added. Rory failed to respond, so Cate continued. "When Forsythe gave us the evidence against Thomas, another note slipped from his pocket. I picked it up, intending to give it back to him, but he disappeared before I could. It was addressed to Lorne Peterson. I read the note. It hinted that he had stolen the jewelry and even suggested a familial connection. The evidence from that note fits with certain facts we've stumbled upon."

"Who is Lorne Peterson? What is his involvement with this?" Rory questioned, spinning to face them.

"We believe Lorne Peterson is the real name of Charles

Forsythe," Cate answered. "We also have inferred that Lorne Peterson is a distant cousin of yours, a grandson of Lorne MacKenzie, your great-uncle."

"What proof have you?" Rory demanded. "I'd like to read this note." He held his hand in front of him.

"I don't have it," Cate admitted.

"You don't have it?"

"No. I returned it to Forsythe yesterday."

"So, you don't have the note. You have no proof other than your conjecture. Is that correct?" It surprised Cate to hear heat entering Rory's usually lighthearted voice.

"Well, it's a little more than just conjecture," Cate argued.

"It's not. What concrete proof is there? You can't even produce the note that hints at the theft!"

Cate's jaw dropped but she could not find the words to respond, thrown by Rory's sudden aggressive behavior.

"Rory, we..." Jack began but was also cut off by Rory.

"No!" Rory exclaimed. "None of this proves anything. And I find the entire story difficult to fathom. I am well acquainted with Forsythe. This doesn't fit his character, not at all."

"But..." Cate tried again.

"Jack, Cate, please. I have heard enough. You are barking up the wrong tree. Please, I assure you, Forsythe is not the culprit." Cate and Jack stood in stunned silence. "Look, I'd like to solve this travesty as much as you, but I cannot support your current theory. I beg you to dismiss it from your minds."

Cate glanced to Jack, giving a slight shrug at him. "All right," she agreed with a tiny nod. "All right, Rory. We'll keep searching."

"Wonderful," Rory replied, offering a slight smile. "I very much appreciate what you are doing. Oh, please don't be put off, but I am certain your theory is incorrect. I'm only trying to spare you any embarrassment."

"We understand. And thank you. Well, I hope to have more news for you soon," Cate answered. "We'll leave you to your work."

"Will I see you at dinner?" Rory questioned.

"No," Cate responded before Jack could. "We won't be able to stay for dinner."

Rory nodded, taking a seat as his desk. "We'll miss you, but hopefully tomorrow."

"Yes, tomorrow," Cate agreed with a smile.

She spun on her heel, leaving the office with Jack following her. They pulled the door shut behind them. Jack thrust his arms out, shrugging, shooting Cate a "now what?" expression. Cate pointed down the hall, signaling that they take a walk outside. Jack nodded in agreement and the two proceeded to the front door in silence.

Cate led Jack toward the loch, only speaking once they were a safe distance away from the castle. "Sorry," she apologized. "I didn't want to say anything in there since we don't seem to have a friend among us!" Cate waved her arms in the air with frustration.

Jack smirked at the statement. "I don't blame you," he replied. They walked on in silence, reaching the loch. The pair stared out over the water before speaking.

"His reaction was odd, right?" Cate began.

"Yes, I agree. The moment we mentioned Forsythe in relation to the crime, his entire mood changed. He became defensive and argumentative."

"Yes, he became combative! I found it very odd," Cate exclaimed in agreement.

"He does paint a rosy picture of the world," Jack commented.

"This was more than that. His reaction just before we

mentioned Forsythe's name was that of someone who views the world through a rosy lens. But his reaction after we mentioned Forsythe's name seemed to be more than that."

"Perhaps he feels a certain friendship with him. They must work closely together, and Forsythe fills the role of valet when needed."

Cate considered Jack's explanation for a moment. "Still…"

"Still, it seems an over-the-top reaction," Jack finished for her.

"Yes. Although…" Cate continued, pausing as her brain processed the idea.

"Yeah?" Jack asked when the silence persisted a beat too long.

"It's not that outrageous a reaction if someone is accusing your family member of being a thief!" Cate exclaimed, wide-eyed.

"What?" Jack questioned.

"Charles Forsythe," Cate explained, "otherwise known as Lorne Peterson, Rory's cousin."

Jack wrinkled his brow, his expression showing complete confusion. "Rory…" he paused, piecing together the puzzle on his end, "is aware of who Charles Forsythe is? Assuming he IS Lorne Peterson, grandson of Lorne MacKenzie, which is still a big IF, Cate."

"It makes sense, right? Rory realizes who he is, which is why he gives him the job here. It's why he's protective of him when we accused him of theft. It's why Anne wrote the note! Well aware that he is family, she pens an angry missive after he leaves and they both realize what has happened."

"Those are some huge leaps, Lady Cate," Jack disagreed. "If Rory and Anne are aware of who Forsythe is, why hire him? Why not help him some other way?"

"What way? It may not be uncommon to offer a struggling family member a position. There must be lots of families with poorer relations. Fast forward to our time and consider me. I was unaware of my family and the estate, and I lived a normal life as a working gal!"

"All right, so Rory hires him, thinking he's doing his family a favor. I can buy that. But if Anne's note refers to the theft, and they realized Forsythe was the culprit, why not turn him in?"

"Scandal. Familial obligation."

"Bah, Cate, I don't buy that one, no way. A servant robs you and you don't turn him in because it might cause scandal that he's a distant relative?"

"The MacKenzies locked a girl in their tower room because she was a bastard child, so yes, I'd believe it!"

"In the 1800s, Cate! Not 1925! Surely we're beyond the point of hiding family secrets."

Cate shook her head. "No. I'm not even sure we've reached that point in the twenty-first century! Certainly not in 1925. Plus, with this type of mentality running in the family, it's plausible."

Jack mulled over Cate's explanation, rubbing his hand on his chin. "Okay, it's a credible theory," he concluded. "Now what?"

"We stay the course, Charles Forsythe, who we assume is Lorne Peterson, is still our primary suspect. We have to find more proof. But perhaps we're at a point where we can mention this to MacCullough."

"I'm not sure he'll listen. And we may anger Rory, although…" Jack's voice broke off as a loud sound cracked through the air. Instinctively, they both ducked, searching around for the source of the noise. "CATE, GET DOWN!" Jack shouted at her, tackling her to the ground. Another crack rang out, followed by a sickening smack as a speeding object struck a nearby tree.

CHAPTER 24

Jack glanced around, his head swinging behind them, eyes darting all over. Cate followed his gaze, spotting nothing. He sighed after a moment, returning his gaze to Cate. "Are you all right? Are you hurt?"

Cate remained silent for a breath, still collecting herself. She nodded. "Yes, yes, I'm all right," she choked out. Fear still coursed through her as her mind caught up with the events of the past few moments. Realization dawned on her and she fought to steady her nerves and her trembling limbs.

Jack rolled off her. Cate remained motionless for another moment. "Are you sure you're all right, Cate?"

"Yes," Cate answered, forcing herself to sitting. "Just a little shocked. I've never been shot at before."

"Neither have I," Jack admitted. He crawled toward the tree, pulling himself to standing. His fingers dug at the bark. Cate gained her feet, her knees wobbly but able to support her weight. She joined him, peering at the object of his attention. A bullet was lodged in the tree. Cate's heart skipped a beat as she stared at the object. It provided physical evidence that they had not imagined the experience. She swallowed hard, taking a step back, a hand on her head.

"Cate?" Jack questioned.

"I'm fine," she replied. "Just thanking my lucky stars."

"Yes, we were lucky."

Cate shook her head, trying to shake the memory loose. "My God, we could have been killed!"

"I know," Jack admitted. "But we weren't. Let's focus on that." He put his arm around her shoulders, pulling her closer to him. "Okay?"

Cate took a deep breath, nodding. "Okay," she answered when she found her voice again.

A moment of silence passed between them before Jack spoke again. "I'm revising my previous statement. I think we need to talk to MacCullough. Even though we're fine, someone tried to kill us or at least scare the hell out of us. To hell with Rory's feelings."

"Not someone," Cate reminded him. "Lorne Peterson."

Jack nodded. "Perhaps we should take a car to town and talk to MacCullough."

Cate raised her eyebrows. "Perhaps we should walk. I have no interest in requesting a car from the man who just tried to kill us."

"Good point, we'll walk it. Let's grab our coats and go."

After retrieving their coats and outerwear, Cate and Jack made their way into town. Despite the cold, Cate found the fresh air calming. She drank in deep breaths. Each step further from the castle also calmed her frayed nerves.

They reached the police station, climbing the handful of steps to enter. Jack requested to speak with Officer MacCullough and they were asked to wait a moment. Cate tapped her toes on the floor as they waited. Jack placed his hand on her arm, giving it a squeeze.

After a moment, they were escorted to Officer MacCullough's desk. "Now what?" the gruff man grunted as they approached. "I've done nothing to that girl, there's no reason to come hollering at me."

"We have information to help you," Jack answered. "And an incident to report."

"Incident? Something else missing?"

"No," Cate replied. "Someone tried to kill us."

Officer MacCullough let out a long belly-laugh. Cate crossed her arms, glaring at him. "Someone tried to kill you, Mrs. MacKenzie? Oh, I can't imagine why."

"This is no joking matter, sir," Jack admonished the laughing man.

The man stood, wiping his eyes with a handkerchief as he stifled his laughter. "No, of course not, Mr. MacKenzie. Though I daresay your wife's imagination has run wild. I'm sure it's all a simple misunderstanding. Ladies can be stirred up so easily. As an officer-of-the-law, I've seen it time and time again."

Frustration showed on Jack's face. "This is no figment of my wife's imagination, Officer MacCullough. I was with her when someone shot at us. Twice! One bullet is lodged in a nearby tree as proof!"

Officer MacCullough's expression changed in an instant, sobering as he realized his mistake. "Shot at you?" he repeated, confusion entering his voice.

"Yes! Shot at us! Someone shot at us not an hour ago!" Jack exclaimed.

"Why would someone shoot at you?" the rather dense detective questioned.

"Because we're getting too close to the truth," Cate responded.

Officer MacCullough's thick eyebrows rumpled. He stared at the floor, deep in thought. "We have uncovered several key pieces of information."

"Let's hear them. Have a seat," Officer MacCullough responded, motioning to two chairs he dragged from another desk.

"First," Jack said after Cate signaled him to relay the information. "We were given an incriminating note suggesting Thomas Gould was the thief."

"Ah, so Gould's our man, then!" MacCullough exclaimed. "I suspected him, of course."

Jack shook his head. "No, no, no. Gould's innocent."

"But..."

"The note was a fake," Jack interrupted.

"Fake? By whose estimation?"

"Mine and my wife's," Jack responded. "We compared the handwriting in it with the handwriting from another note. They were a match. The note was forged to point the finger at Thomas Gould and shift any suspicion from the real criminal."

"Who is?"

"Charles Forsythe," Cate answered. "Who may be better known as Lorne Peterson."

"Forsythe? The under-butler? So, he is in cahoots with Lorne Peterson!"

"No!" Jack answered with an adamant shake of his head. "Charles Forsythe is Lorne Peterson!"

The officer rubbed his chin as he disseminated the information. "All right, Mr. MacKenzie, we'll take it from here. Thank you." The man stood, pulling his jacket closed over his bulging stomach.

"But you haven't heard half of the information we discovered!" Jack argued.

Officer MacCullough plopped into his seat with a huff. "Oh, all right. Continue," he said, waving his hand in the air, motioning for Jack to proceed. He placed his folded hands on top of his stomach, leaning back in his chair.

Jack gave Cate a disgusted glance before he continued. "When we received the forged note, which came from Charles Forsythe, he dropped another letter. Addressed to Lorne Peterson. After doing some research, we are convinced Charles Forsythe is an alias."

"And, uh, why would Mr. Forsythe need an alias?"

"No," Cate interjected. "Lorne Peterson needs the alias. We're not sure why," Cate fibbed, not wanting the truth shared just yet. "But plenty of criminals use aliases."

"Anything else?" MacCullough asked, ignoring Cate's statements.

"Mrs. MacKenzie returned the dropped note yesterday to Mr. Forsythe. And today, someone took two shots at us."

"Where were you when the shots were fired? Outside? You mentioned a tree?"

"Outside," Cate answered. "Near the loch."

"Uh-huh," the officer mumbled. "Well, I appreciate the information and we'll make a full report. There's no need for either of you to stay beyond this. I'm sure you're both tired."

Officer MacCullough's nonchalance stunned Cate. She stared at Jack, her jaw hanging open in shock. "Appreciate the information? We were almost killed!" Jack exclaimed.

"Well, Mr. MacKenzie, that remains to be determined," the officer answered. Jack was speechless. "Dinnae misunderstand. I'm not accusing you of lying. I've no doubt shots were fired. But this is rural Scotland, laddie. They could have been shooting at an animal, a bird. Hunting is great sport here."

Jack sighed. "This wasn't..." he began.

Officer MacCullough waved his hand in the air to stop him. "I've already promised we'll look into it, but I wouldn't lose sleep. I'm sure no harm was intended."

Jack opened his mouth to respond, but Cate stood, stopping him. "Thank you, Officer MacCullough. We won't take up any more of your time."

Officer MacCullough stood, smiling at Cate. "No problem, Mrs. MacKenzie. And as I said, I thank you for the information you provided. We will follow up on it."

Jack stood next to her, a dubious expression on his face. He extended a hand toward the officer. "Yes, thank you," he muttered.

"Good day, Mr. and Mrs. MacKenzie," Officer MacCullough said, dismissing them.

Cate and Jack left the police station, beginning their walk back to the castle. "Well, that was a bust," Cate sighed as they trudged toward the castle.

"Is he dense or just an ass?" Jack complained in frustration.

"Both," Cate responded. "He has no intention of continuing the investigation or following up on any information we provided him. He's also very, very dim-witted. That's half the reason he won't follow up. He couldn't follow the logic we presented at all."

Jack huffed. "Now what?"

"We're on our own. We need more information."

Jack stopped dead. "More information? Cate, are you sure we should pursue this? I mean, absolutely certain? This is becoming a dangerous game and we have no support from the police… or Rory for that matter!"

"Which is reason we must keep going! Unless we plan to return to our time and leave this alone and never return, which I do NOT want to do, we're stuck."

"Going back to our time and forgetting about it may be our best bet, Cate."

Cate remained silent for a moment, her lower lip in a frustrated pout. She thrust her arms out before speaking.

"Then what was the point! We've solved nothing! If we do that, we've just wasted our time."

"Well, you did learn to skate, and you met your great-grandparents. It wasn't a total waste. And there's no shame in giving up, given the latest developments. Even Rory would understand."

"I'm not giving up!" Cate exclaimed. They stood in silence for a few more moments. "Even Rory would understand," Cate murmured after a moment, snapping her fingers. "That's it!"

"That's what?" Jack inquired.

"With the latest developments, surely Rory will do something now that someone's tried to kill us!"

"He doesn't believe us about Forsythe, what makes you think he will now that we're accusing him of trying to kill us?"

"This makes things more serious," Cate countered. "Covering for the theft of your own property by a family member is one thing. Covering for them when they try to kill someone is quite another."

"Eh, covering for murder runs in the family, Cate. Grandpappy Randolph did it."

"For an orphaned child. Not an opportunist who's stolen valuable property."

"Still, I'm not sure he'll believe it's Forsythe."

Cate frowned. "You're right. He'll insist we're incorrect and Forsythe couldn't have done it. He'll want to believe the best of his family."

"Assuming he realizes Forsythe is his family. So we're on our own. Are you sure I can't convince you we've done enough?"

"We have done nothing but make an enemy!" Cate countered. "The jewelry is still missing, and we've brought no one to justice!"

"But how can we convince Rory or Officer MacCullough?" Jack inquired.

"We're going to need solid evidence. Like finding the jewelry in Forsythe's possession."

"I was afraid you'd say that."

Cate checked her timepiece with a frown. "Well, there's no sense trying today. It's too risky to try now. Too much likelihood of being caught. Shoot!"

"Fine by me. Tomorrow's a new day. Perhaps we can figure out a better plan. We've done enough for today. I need to decompress."

"You and me both," Cate agreed. "As much as I'd love to solve this today, I'd really love to go home. Somewhere safe."

Jack nodded at her with a tight-lipped smile. "Let's go, Lady Cate."

They returned to the castle, avoiding contact with anyone and returning to the bedroom. Within moments, they had returned to the safety of their own time. Jack breathed a long and loud sigh of relief. "Still some time before lunch," he stated. "I can't believe we've accused someone of theft, been shot at, spoken with the police and it's still before lunch."

"Yep," Cate agreed. "Such is the life of a time traveler."

"Call me crazy, but I liked my life before I was a time traveler."

"I could have done without the being shot at," Cate admitted. "But perhaps he was just trying to scare us off and not hurt us."

"I'm not sure what his intentions were. It was still too close a call for me. I'll be spending the rest of the day trying to forget about it."

"I'll spend the rest of the day trying to come up with a plan to solve this... and soon!"

"Happy scheming," Jack answered. "I'm going to change and breathe the fresh air while I assess a few repairs outside."

"Anything major?" Cate asked.

"No, nothing major. Just a few minor jobs to bid out before spring."

"Okay," Cate answered. "Got to have the place in tiptop shape for the next party Mrs. Campbell springs on us. She's got her heart set on 'bigger and better' for the next event."

"Ugh," Jack groaned. "What does that mean?"

Cate shrugged. "With her it could mean anything from a larger event to a fancier event. She keeps rambling on about having the 'upper crust of society' here like the 'old days.'"

"Old days?" Jack questioned. "I prefer not to recall any old days in this castle."

Cate chuckled at his subtle joke. "Tell that to Mrs. Campbell."

"I just might, Lady Cate! I just might," Jack answered. "Now, I leave you to your day. M'lady!" Jack gave an extravagant bow before leaving the room.

Despite the earlier scare, Jack's over-the-top mannerisms elicited a giggle from her. After he disappeared through her sitting room doors, Cate changed and took the dogs for a walk. She hoped to keep her mind from dwelling on the incident earlier. Jack's assessment was correct. This was becoming dangerous. They had little choice in becoming more aggressive in their investigation before it cost them their lives.

As her eyes gazed over the loch's still waters, she shivered, reminded of the two close calls with death, both at this location. Odd that her favorite spot on the estate in her time was the source of such terrifying experiences in the past.

Cate's mind turned to the matter of the missing jewelry and Charles Forsythe, a.k.a. Lorne Peterson. To end this, they had to gain more proof against him. They needed solid evidence for both Rory and Officer MacCullough. There was no choice but to perform a search of Lorne's room with the hope of finding anything incriminating.

Cate shivered again at the thought, though she convinced herself it was only the cold causing her to shudder. She returned to the castle, spending the afternoon searching for any information she could find on Lorne Peterson. The little she found offered no help for their predicament.

She turned her attention to a mystery novel but found it unable to hold her attention. She paced the floorboards of her sitting room for a solid hour before dinner. Afterward, Cate invited Molly to watch a movie, hoping the distraction would pass the time faster and relax her.

Despite her distracted thoughts, Molly's gregarious nature diverted Cate's troubled mind to lighter topics. Cate hated for the night to end, worried that she'd toss and turn.

As Cate lay in bed, she wondered if she was becoming psychic. Even the extra hours added to her day from time traveling failed to tire her enough to sleep. She laid awake until the clock read after midnight. Finally, as she stared at the moonlit moors, Cate drifted off to sleep.

CHAPTER 25

Cate awoke with a start. Both dogs barked at the foot of her bed. "Riley? Bailey? What is it?" she questioned, following their gaze. They stared at the ajar bedroom door. Cate climbed from the bed, her bare feet touching the cold floorboards beyond the area rug as she tiptoed to the door. As if on cue, both dogs ceased their protestations and raced, tails between their legs, to hide under the bed. Cate followed them with her eyes before turning her attention to the sitting room. "Guess I'm on my own," she murmured as she peered into the darkness in the next room.

Cate saw nothing. She returned for her robe, wrapped it around her, slipped into her slippers and padded to the sitting room door. She cracked it open, squinting into the darkened hall beyond. Movement at the end of the hall caught her attention. "Molly?" she called, receiving no response.

Cate stepped into the hallway, following the motion. "Molly? Is everything okay?" She again received no response. Cate proceeded down the hall, closing the gap between herself and the unknown figure. Before she reached the figure, it fled. Without considering her actions, Cate followed, racing down the halls behind the running individual.

Cate caught up with the unidentified figure as it entered the library. Cate flipped the light switch, but no lights lit. She pulled the flashlight from the desk drawer, pointing it at the figure hovering on the opposite side of the room. "Who…" her voice trailed off as she recognized the person. Her brows knit in confusion as she tried to make sense of it. In front of her, illuminated by the piercing flashlight's beam, stood Charles Forsythe. "Forsythe?" she questioned.

She swallowed hard as she recognized the object clutched in his hands. A stubby-nosed gun pointed at her. The muzzle flashed, evidencing a shot fired. Cate dropped the flashlight, shrieked and ducked, hoping to dodge the bullet.

She held her breath for a moment, eyes squeezed shut. After a breath, she opened her eyes to slits, peeking at the room. The figure across the room had vanished, and she lay alone on the library floor. She glanced around the room, searching for Forsythe, but he was nowhere to be found. Cate pushed up to kneeling, checking her body. No blood, no bullet holes, no pain registered. What happened, she wondered? Had she imagined the whole thing? Was this the product of her overtired mind?

She sighed, grasping the corner of the desk to pull herself to standing. A rogue wind rustled her hair as she stood. She searched the room for the source. After retrieving the flashlight from where it clattered to the floor moments ago, she trained the beam in the direction of the breeze. She gasped, stifling a yelp as she noticed the bookcase missing, replaced again by a gaping hole.

She blinked her eyes several times. Convinced her eyes weren't playing tricks on her, she took a step toward the black hole. Cate quickly decided against proceeding any further, retreating a few steps back and toggling off the flashlight. She spun and hurried to the door. Before she could exit the room, an unearthly groan commanded her attention. She whirled around to face the void, straining to hear any sounds. "Catherine!" a voice called.

Cate swallowed hard. She attempted to back from the room, but the doors slammed behind her before she could exit. She turned, pulling on them as she spun the doorknob desperately in an attempt to flee. The doors did not budge. She pounded against them, calling for help. No one came. The doors remained shut fast. "CATHERINE!" the voice boomed again.

Cate spun to face the sound again. Tears streamed down her cheeks as terror rose from the pit of her stomach. "What do you want?" she croaked.

Thunder boomed overhead, lightening lit the room. The brief flash revealed a figure standing in the open space that once held the bookcase. Cate covered her mouth with her hand, stifling a scream. "Who are you?" she demanded, pulling herself up to standing.

As thunder clapped again, its sound reverberating through the castle's stone walls, the figure approached her. As he strode closer and closer, Cate inched toward the closed doors, pressing against them. Her eyes darted around the room, searching for an escape. She found none. She tried pounding against the doors again, but no one came to help.

The figure loomed over her; the unidentifiable features shadowed by the dim moonlight. An icy hand grasped her shoulder. She turned to face the figure. Lightning tore through the sky, lighting the room for a brief second. As the man's features became more apparent, the room faded away to black. Cate experienced the sensation of falling.

* * *

Cate shot up to sitting, drenched in sweat. She'd snapped her eyes open in terror, then realized she was in her bedroom. She caught her breath, glancing around the room. The two dogs slept in their beds, Riley snoring softly.

Cate blinked a few times, checking the clock. It read quarter after two in the morning. She'd managed a few hours' sleep before the nightmare woke her. Cate collapsed back onto the pillows behind her. They had to solve this crime before it cost her her sanity.

* * *

Cate dragged herself from bed the following morning. She'd slept little, tossing and turning both before and after her nightmare. Her muddled mind found no additional solutions during that time. She slogged through her morning routine, breakfast and a walk with the dogs.

Afterward, she met Jack as she began ascending the steps. "Lady Cate, good morning. Have a minute for some estate business?"

"Sure," Cate replied, recognizing the ruse Jack used to requests her presence to discuss time traveling. "Let's step into the sitting room."

"No library?" Jack groused. "I like those armchairs."

"Sorry," Cate answered, stifling a yawn. "I'd rather avoid the library." They ushered Riley and Bailey into the sitting room before them and Cate pulled the doors closed.

"Avoiding the library again?" Jack asked, approaching the loveseat and plopping onto it. Cate nodded as she sank onto the loveseat across from Jack. "Another nightmare?"

"Another nightmare," Cate admitted, slouching in her seat.

"Same thing?"

"Sort of. This one started with spotting a figure at the end of the hall outside my bedroom. When I followed it, it went to the library. It turned into Forsythe holding a gun and he shot at me. When I ducked, he disappeared. I stood up to leave, and the bookshelf was missing again. A shadowy man stood in there. He came at me and I tried to run, but the doors were stuck shut. I couldn't get out. He grabbed me and I almost saw his face in the lightning, but I woke up. I'm assuming it was Forsythe again."

"We need a plan. This is having a terrible effect on you."

"I agree. A plan that solves this mystery. I'd like to sleep again soon!"

"So, what plans did you concoct while you weren't sleeping last night?" Jack questioned.

Cate shrugged. "None. We need proof to end this. Proof that I expect we'll find only in Forsythe's room. Unless you have another idea?"

"Nope," Jack answered with a sigh. "I'm afraid you're correct. I hate it, but I don't see a way around it."

"So, that's our plan," Cate concluded. "Shall we dress and head back there? Try to settle this?"

"Sure!" Jack agreed. Cate pushed up to standing and crossed the room to the doors. "You going to make it through? I've never seen you with such little energy."

Cate offered him a half-smile. "I'm going to make it. Don't worry, my adrenaline will kick in as soon as I'm close to solving the mystery!"

"There's the spirit, Lady Cate. Meet you in thirty in your sitting room?"

"Deal," Cate agreed, calling the dogs to follow her to her bedroom.

With the promise of time travel on the horizon, Cate dug deep to muster the energy to tackle her hair and clothes, making each appropriate for 1925. She finished with a few minutes to spare and paced the floor of her sitting room as she waited for Jack.

Within a few moments, a knock sounded at the door. Jack entered after Cate pulled the door open. "I was thinking…" she blurted as he entered the room.

"Of course you were," Jack interrupted. "There's the Cate Kensie I know!"

Cate chuckled, smiling at him. "Anyway, even if we can get that note back that I had to give to Forsythe, that's a win. We can show it to Rory. If we can win him to our side, we might stand a chance!"

Jack nodded. "I hope he didn't destroy it after you returned it to him."

"Me too," Cate said with a shake of her head. "Only one way to find out."

She strode to her bedroom with Jack in tow. They activated the watch, slipping backward in time to 1925. After a quick change of clothes into new outfits, Cate and Jack left the suite, intent on determining the whereabouts of Forsythe.

They made it a few steps down the hall when Amelia rounded the corner. "Oh, Cate! How fortunate. I was just coming to find you. I feared missing you, that you'd left for the day!"

"No, we were about to…" Cate began.

"I hope they are plans that can be broken!" Amelia exclaimed. "You don't mind, do you, Jack? Cate and I have ladies' business!"

"Oh, well…" Jack started.

"Besides, Rory has been searching for you all day. It seems urgent. You will probably find him in his office."

"Oh," Jack said, his brow furrowing, "I suppose I should seek him out." Jack shot a questioning glance to Cate.

"And that leaves you," Amelia said, wrapping her arm

around Cate's, "on your own and in need of entertainment. Search no further, Cate! I shall provide it!"

Amelia dragged a helpless Cate away as Jack headed off to find Rory. When they were alone, Amelia said, "I hope you aren't too sore at me for breaking your plans. But we are leaving Friday morning and I missed you at dinner last night! I hoped to make the most of what remains of our visit."

"Not at all," Cate assured her. Despite her desire to dive right into finding evidence against Forsythe, she, too, longed to spend more time with Amelia, her great-grandmother. The familial connection alone soothed her beyond words. "We will be leaving soon, too. It saddens me to think of it."

"But then we shall begin counting the days until we meet again here next holiday, if not sooner! We must have you and Jack out at the country estate. You'd enjoy it so!"

"It sounds very charming," Cate agreed wistfully, realizing she would never see the estate.

"I do hope Jack can carve time from his schedule. Though you are most welcome to visit on your own if Jack finds himself too busy and you find yourself alone! Women are traveling alone more and more these days!"

"Thank you. We'll certainly need to plan for it," Cate fibbed. "Now, what is this pressing ladies' business?"

"Why clothing, of course!" Amelia declared, pushing through the door to her suite. "Anne, I found her!" she announced to the woman in the room.

"Wonderful. Hello, Cate," Anne greeted her. She rose and strode to the bell pull against the wall, pulling it. "I'll ring for tea now. Amelia hoped to find you before we requested tea. She has grand plans to discuss all things fashion. And she insists she has an evening dress that makes her look gauche but would be lovely on you."

"Oh, I do, let me fetch it," Amelia stated, rushing from the room and returning in moments with a rose-colored dress in her hands. "Here it is!" She waved it in the air.

"Oh, it's beautiful!" Cate exclaimed, admiring the color and the detailed beading on the bodice.

Amelia held it out, staring at it. "It's simply ghastly on me, Cate." She held it against her. "Look, how sallow it makes me. You have handsome porcelain skin and sweet, rosy cheeks. It will look marvelous on you, I'd bet." Anne joined them as Amelia held it up to Cate. "Do you agree, Anne?"

"Hmm, yes, quite. It fits her complexion well," Anne agreed.

"Try it on? Oh, please!" Amelia requested, shoving the dress toward Cate and closing Cate's hands around it.

"Well..." Cate answered, unsure.

"There's plenty of time before tea arrives!" Amelia responded, pushing Cate toward the bedroom. "Use my room!"

Cate disappeared into the bedroom. The sounds of light conversation carried from the other room as Cate tossed the dress onto the bed and removed her clothes. She pulled the dress on, struggling to fasten it.

"How's it coming, Cate?" Amelia called in. "Do you need help?"

"I'm just fastening it!" Cate called in response. "Or trying to!"

Amelia appeared in the doorway. "Here, let me," she said, spinning Cate around and finishing the fastening in the back. "Oh, it's gorgeous on you. Very becoming! The dress requires few alterations, if any. It's nearly a perfect fit! Anne, come and see Cate in the dress!" Amelia positioned Cate in front of the mirror. "What do you think?"

Cate admired the dress in the mirror, agreeing it fit her well and was a becoming color. Anne agreed with Amelia's assessment. "Say you'll take it!" Amelia exclaimed.

"Oh, I couldn't!" Cate answered.

"Oh, please. It's such a waste for me to keep it. I'll never wear it! Take it, Cate!"

Cate grinned at her through the mirror's reflection. "I will," she answered, turning to pull Amelia into an embrace.

"Wonderful!" Amelia exclaimed. "Now, let me unfasten you so you can change. Tea has arrived! We will discuss how you shall accessorize your new dress!"

Cate nodded in agreement, and, left alone, changed back to her day dress and returned to the sitting room to join the others for tea. They spent over an hour discussing Cate's new dress, upcoming fashions, Paris fashions and other topics of the sort. Cate's nerves relaxed as she talked and laughed over shorter hemlines, sporty clothes, shopping at Selfridge's and the advancement of the modern woman. The sense of kinship played a large role in her comfort.

After tea, Anne excused herself to finish correspondence. Amelia invited Cate to take a walk. Since she planned to search Forsythe's room before lunch, Cate declined, also using the excuse of correspondence. With a hug, Amelia left her in the hallway.

Cate sneaked downstairs when she figured the coast was clear of Amelia and crept toward Rory's office. She listened at the door as voices carried from behind it. She considered knocking and requesting Jack's presence, but decided against it.

A noise down the hall sent her scurrying into the library. She hid behind the door, leaving it open a crack to peer out. Forsythe passed with two footmen trailing behind him.

"... items must be moved before lunch. It will take all three of us. I hope we finish the task in time..." His voice trailed off as they disappeared down the hall.

Cate raised her eyebrows. Forsythe would be engaged for the rest of the morning. It was a perfect time to check his room. Should she disturb Rory and Jack's meeting? Cate debated for a few moments. Yes, she decided. It was a terrible idea to go alone. Although Forsythe should be busy, so it should be safe. And how would she explain her need for Jack's presence to Rory? She couldn't explain their plan. Rory's reaction yesterday suggested he'd be less than hospitable if she explained.

"You're wasting time!" she whispered to herself.

After a moment, she harrumphed, pushing through the doors and hurrying down the hall and upstairs alone. She climbed to the servants' floor, sprinting down the empty hall to Forsythe's room. She turned the knob, pushing the door open and hurrying inside. She closed the door behind her, leaning against it with closed eyes, and let out of a sigh of relief.

Part one of her plan was complete. She made it to Forsythe's room. Now on to part two: searching it. She opened her eyes, scanning the room. While racing toward the wardrobe, she winced as she crossed a creaky floorboard, fearing she'd be given away.

Cate flung open the doors, scanning the contents of the cupboard. She pawed through the few articles of clothing inside, squeezing each article to determine if anything was concealed in the pockets or lining. She came up empty.

Cate stood on her tiptoes, sweeping her hand across the top shelf. The few items on top provided no additional information. A drawer at the bottom of the wardrobe provided her last search area in the cabinet. Cate yanked it open but found nothing but clothing items. Cate sighed, pushing the drawer shut and easing the wardrobe doors closed. She peered behind it, finding nothing. The wardrobe stood too close to the wall to have hidden anything.

Cate spun and crossed to the bed. On her hands and knees, she peered underneath. Nothing but dust bunnies greeted her. Cate frowned, sitting back on her heels and shoving her hands under the mattress. She swept them around, reaching as far as she could, but found nothing.

A chest of drawers stood against the far wall. It was the final place to search. Cate climbed to her feet, crossing the room. She cursed her careless footfalls, crossing the creaky floorboard again. Cate began with the bottom drawers, coming up empty. The middle drawers provided no information either. She pulled open the top drawers, shoving items from side to side in a desperate search for anything. Near the back of the drawer, Cate found several letters tied together. She read the address line, finding the top missive made out to Lorne Peterson. A slight smile crossed Cate's face. Proof, she reflected, flipping to the next letter in the stack. It, too, was addressed to Lorne Peterson.

Cate returned her gaze to the drawer, hoping to find more when the door popped open. Startled, Cate whipped her head to stare wide-eyed at the doorway. She swallowed hard, shock causing her jaw to hang open as she identified the figure as Charles Forsythe. Her eyes grew wider as she recognized the object clutched in his hands. A stout-nosed gun pointed at her.

CHAPTER 26

"Something I can help with, Mrs. MacKenzie?" he growled at her.

Cate swallowed hard, realizing she was trapped. "I…" she began, attempting to talk her way out of the situation. Nothing came to her, her mind remained blank.

"You what? You happen to be holding my personal property. Though I don't believe you care. You clearly can't take a hint. I attempted to scare you and your husband off yesterday. I see that did not work."

"Scare us?!" Cate exclaimed, finding her voice. "You mean kill us!"

"I wouldn't have shed too many tears had the bullet struck you," Forsythe admitted.

"Well, it didn't, Mr. Forsythe! Or should I say Mr. Peterson?"

"Yes," the man answered. "You've figured it out. I assumed you would when I dropped the note. I am Lorne Peterson."

"Lorne Peterson, grandson of Lorne MacKenzie. Am I correct?"

"What difference does it make?" Lorne snapped, raising the gun.

"I... I'd like to know. If you plan to murder me, I'd like to know why. Why you did this."

He scowled at her. "All right, Mrs. MacKenzie. You are correct. I am Lorne MacKenzie's grandson. My mother insisted on naming me after him. For all the good it does me. I've no claim to the riches of the MacKenzie clan. I pay for the sins of the mother, or rather grandmother."

"Do you mean because one of your parents was an illegitimate child of Lorne's?"

"Oh, yes, my mother was the illegitimate daughter of Lorne MacKenzie. Still, the woman worshipped her father, always insisting he'd rescue us at some point. Give us the life we'd only dreamt of. To her dying day, she professed her infatuation for him. A foolish woman. Where my mother preferred to wait and hope, I preferred to take action."

"Action? As in theft?"

"As in taking what is owed to me. What I deserve!" he shouted. Lorne raised his eyes to the ceiling, balling his free hand into a fist. "You rich people. All alike! You live a charmed life with no consideration of anyone outside yourselves, never considering how others long for only half of what you have. You can't..." His voice ceased mid-sentence and Cate heard a thump. For a splitsecond, she assumed he'd fired the gun. She braced her body for the impact. She jumped back a step when Lorne Peterson slumped to the floor, unconscious, his limbs sprawling and the gun sliding toward her.

For a moment, she remained shocked before her instincts kicked in and she grabbed for the gun. She glanced up to find Jack and Rory standing in the doorway. Jack clutched a pistol in his hand, the source of the assault on Lorne.

"Jack!" Cate exclaimed.

"Cate! Thank God," he rushed into the room and pulled her into a hug. Rory stepped over the sprawled form of Lorne, relieving Cate of the weapon she held.

"Thank heavens you're all right, Cate," Rory stated, after Jack pulled back. "I'm so very sorry I didn't listen yesterday."

"It's all right," Cate answered.

"No, no, it isn't," Rory insisted, pacing the room. "I forced you into this position by not wanting to believe what you told me."

"I found the letters addressed to Lorne Peterson," Cate said, holding them out. "Charles Forsythe is an alias."

"Yes, I know," Rory admitted, not even glancing at the notes. "I've known all along what his real name is. He's a distant cousin. The grandson of…"

"Of Lorne MacKenzie, your great-uncle," Cate finished.

Rory halted, staring at Cate. "Yes, you are correct! My, you are clever to figure that out, aren't you?" Rory answered, astonishment filling his voice.

Cate shrugged. "Once I found the letter with that name, it clicked. I never met Lorne, but we spent a great deal of time with your grandfather Randolph and we discussed his reputation. It wasn't a leap to consider there may be children and grandchildren from some of Lorne's liaisons."

"Yes," Rory responded. "When I met Lorne, he was down on his luck. I considered it a favor to employ him. And being family, I did not want to believe he would steal from us. I assumed he was grateful for the opportunity!"

Cate gave Rory a soft smile. "I'm sorry," she whispered. "But I don't think Lorne is the gentleman you assume him to be."

"I'd damn well say he's not," Jack chimed in. "He nearly killed Cate. He would have if you hadn't kept him talking! Good thinking, Lady Cate."

"Lady Cate?" Rory questioned. "So, you are the MacKenzie, not Jack! How interesting!" He paused a breath. "Though now I feel worse. My refusal to face facts nearly cost my progeny her life."

Cate laid her hand on his arm. "I'm fine," she assured him. "But there's still the matter of the missing jewelry. I'm sorry to say I haven't found it anywhere."

As Cate finished her statement, Lorne, still on the floor, moaned in pain. He stretched his limbs before his eyes fluttered open. He groaned again, grabbing at the back of his head.

"Easy there, friend," Jack warned him, hauling him up to sit on the bed. "No sudden movements."

Lorne continued to ruffle his hair, rubbing his head. "You could have killed me, FRIEND," he answered, emphasizing the last word.

"And you nearly killed both me and my wife!" Jack exclaimed. "Now the jig is up. We know who you are and what you've done. Where is the jewelry?"

"I have no idea what you're referring to."

"Please, Lorne," Rory begged, "I won't press charges, but the jewelry means more than money to me. They are heirlooms from my grandmother."

Lorne did not respond. Cate paced the floor, a nagging notion plaguing her mind. As she stalked across the floorboards, the familiar creak sounded throughout the room. Cate stopped in her tracks. She glanced down at the creaky board, rubbing over it with her toes. Her forehead wrinkled, and she bent to inspect the board closer.

"What is it, Cate?" Jack inquired, noticing Cate's intense gaze. As he questioned her, Lorne attempted to race from the room. Jack grabbed him and, with Rory's help, wrestled him back to the bed. "Where do you think you're going?" Jack asked without expecting an answer.

Cate continued her examination of the creaky floorboard.

Using a fingernail, she traced the edge of the board. She detected subtle movement as she outlined the board. Cate tried to push on the board, but it didn't budge. She attempted to grasp it and pull it upwards but could not. "Do you have a pocketknife, either of you?" Cate queried.

"I do," Jack answered, removing it from his jacket pocket. He slid it to Cate, still holding tight to Lorne. Cate caught it as it rattled across the floor, pulling it open and using the blade's edge to pry up the floorboard.

"Aha!" she exclaimed as it moved upward. "This creaky floorboard is hiding a compartment." Cate pulled the board out, setting it aside. Cate glanced into the dark hole, gasping.

"What is it, Cate?" Jack questioned.

Cate reached inside, withdrawing an object. She pulled it up, letting it dangle from her fingers. Both Rory and Jack gasped at the sight. A ruby necklace hung from Cate's fingers, its fine jewels catching the light at every angle. It remained as dazzling now as it had when Victoria MacKenzie wore it first at her Halloween ball.

"The ruby necklace!" Rory exclaimed, rushing to Cate and removing it from her hand.

"And the sapphire necklace," Cate added, retrieving the deep blue necklace from the hole.

"Oh!" Rory cried out. "Both of them! Still here. Thank heavens. I'd have felt sick if we weren't able to retrieve them. My grandmother loved these pieces." Rory clutched the two necklaces to his chest. "Anne will be so pleased."

"I'm glad we found them," Cate replied, standing and dusting her knees off.

"How?" Rory questioned, his brow furrowing as he considered the discovery. "How did you know where to look?"

"I've hit that squeaky floorboard every time I've walked

around in this room. Something about it bothered me. Just a hunch," Cate added with a shrug.

"Thank heavens for your hunch, Cate."

"And now, Mr. Peterson," Jack growled, pulling the man to his feet. "Time for you to head to your new home: a prison cell."

"No, please," Rory said, blocking Jack from moving Lorne further.

"What? We've found the jewelry in his possession. You can't still believe he's innocent."

"No, I don't," Rory assured them. "But I meant what I said. I will not press charges. He is family. I'd prefer this matter to be kept quiet. As long as you'll leave as soon as possible, Lorne. I expect no further trouble from you. I shall pay you a severance."

"You must be joking!" Jack exclaimed, shock entering his voice. "The man's a thief and a potential murderer!"

"I realize that. I do..." Rory hesitated, glancing to Cate. "But... I'd prefer to avoid the scandal."

Cate offered Rory a tight-lipped smile, placing her hand on his shoulder. "We understand." Jack opened his mouth to offer a retort to the contrary, but Cate gave him a small shake of the head to discourage him. "We must create a story that explains this to Officer MacCullough."

Rory pondered a moment. "Couldn't we just let it go unsolved?" he suggested.

"My fear is that he'll attempt to railroad poor Lillian if it remains unsolved," Cate responded.

"Ah, you may be correct. What can we do? Perhaps request the case be closed?"

"He's a stubborn man. I'm not sure that will do it," Jack answered.

"Jack's right," Cate noted, pacing the floor as she

pondered the options. "We need another solution. A way to close the case but not blame anyone."

Jack knit his brows. "How are we going to do that? How can we explain missing jewelry that no longer needs found?"

"We have to admit we found it."

"How do we say we found it without incriminating Mr. Congeniality over here?" Jack queried.

"We obviously can't say we found it here," Cate admitted.

"Perhaps we should call Officer MacCullough and be vague about the details. Let it all come out in the wash, as they say," Rory suggested.

"That's it!" Cate exclaimed.

"Do you really expect being vague will do the trick?" Jack questioned.

"No," Cate corrected. "No, not the part about being vague. The part about the wash. We'll say they must have been picked up with some other random garment and sent to the laundry. They were misplaced by mistake and no one realized until the garment was repaired or washed."

"Ohhhhh," Jack answered, realization dawning on him. "In the confusion after the party, someone grabbed clothing to launder, not realizing they also grabbed the jewelry with it and the jewelry turned up later when that clothing was being dealt with."

Cate nodded. "Yes, that's right. It's a sellable story, especially to the less-than-quick Officer MacCullough. He'll likely be glad to close the case and find it a sufficient explanation."

"All right. I agree. The secret remains between the four of us and Anne. I insist we tell Anne. I cannot keep this from her."

"Agreed," Cate answered. "And he will quietly leave and never speak a word of this to anyone."

All eyes turned to Lorne. He wrestled himself from Jack's

grasp without a word. "Well?" Jack asked, squeezing his shoulder. "We can make a lot of trouble for you if you don't agree. It's a more than fair deal."

The man grimaced but acquiesced. "Fine. I shall leave, but I will need time to prepare."

"I shall pay you for two months work, but you shall leave posthaste. I care not what excuse you give to the other servants."

"Fine," Lorne groused.

Jack unhanded the man, and they left him to commence packing his things. Cate returned the letters to the top of the bureau before exiting, Jack's wary eye making sure there was no more trouble as she did so. Rory placed the jewelry in his pocket, so it remained unseen by anyone until the ordeal was over.

He led them to Anne's suite of rooms, entering after knocking to find Anne at her desk. "Yes, darling?" she inquired before glancing up from her letters. "Oh! Cate and Jack, hello!" She stood from the desk.

"Wonderful news, Anne," Rory began. "Clever Cate has found the jewelry!"

A shocked expression painted over Anne's face. Rory revealed the two necklaces. "However, did you find them? Where were they?"

"I'm afraid that's a rather sordid tale, dear. Please, sit down."

Anne stared at him for a moment before taking a seat on her chaise. Rory explained the affair to Anne. Anne's face was aghast as he explained the familial connection of their under-butler. She whitened further when he admitted Lorne was the responsible party and the circumstances of Lorne's relationship to him. He finished by detailing the deal made between them and the story they would supply to Officer MacCullough to close the case.

When he finished, Anne leapt from her seat. "Rory!" she shouted. "How could you be so foolish? The man is a thief! He should be punished!"

"Please, Anne, try to understand. I don't want the scandal it would bring. His connection would be revealed! We couldn't hide it."

"Hogwash!" Anne exclaimed. Her reaction surprised Cate, who had never seen this level of emotion displayed by Anne.

"Anne, please!" Rory begged, preferring to be finished with the matter. "I prefer not to discuss it further! The decision has been made. I expect you to abide by it. Now, if you will excuse me, I have many details to take care of, including informing Officer MacCullough. But first I will return these beauties to the safe."

Rory departed, leaving Jack, Cate and a fuming Anne. Anne paced the length of the room. "How could he decide this? That man should be in jail!"

"If it's any consolation," Cate noted, "he'll be leaving the estate soon."

Anne collapsed onto the chaise. "It should be, but it isn't. How could he do this? To his own family?"

"It's because Lorne's family that Rory is doing it," Cate explained.

"No," Anne disagreed. "not Rory, Lorne! He lived among us, performed a job given to him by Rory to help and then stabs his own family in the back."

"I'm sorry," Cate said, easing onto the chaise next to Anne and taking her hands.

"Oh, how unbecoming this all is," Anne answered, glancing between Cate and Jack. "But I am so angry!"

"It will pass once the shock is worn off," Cate assured her.

Anne shook her head. "I want to believe that, however, I'm not sure. I'm shaking with anger at this moment. How can I look anyone in the eye and lie to them about this incident!"

An idea formed in Cate's head. She took a chance in mentioning it to Anne. "Perhaps it would be helpful to get your thoughts out. In a letter. You don't have to send it, but perhaps you should write your anger and disappointment down as though you're speaking to Lorne. It may help ease your emotions."

Anne sat in silence, clutching Cate's hands for a few breaths. "Perhaps it is a wise idea, Cate," Anne agreed. "I shall consider it. Well, I prefer not to dwell on it further right now. Oh! We are late for lunch. Will you give me a moment to compose myself?" She disappeared into her bedroom.

"Clever, Lady Cate, clever."

Cate winked at Jack. "She needs to write a letter so I can find it in our time and investigate!"

Anne reappeared, and they navigated to the dining room for lunch. They spent the afternoon discussing the case with Officer MacCullough. Cate found the man's grunts impossible to read but, at last, he agreed to close the case without assigning blame to any party.

Cate's story of finding the jewelry amidst a laundry pile made for most of the dinner conversation. Though the group shared many laughs over the investigation and its outcome, sadness crept over Cate as she realized this was the last evening she would spend with her great-grandparents.

Over cocktails before dinner, Cate and Jack announced they would depart the next morning. Dinner was a bittersweet affair for Cate, who prepared herself to say goodbye to people she'd likely never see again. There would be plans made to keep in touch, invitations extended, and Cate would make promises she couldn't keep.

But Cate could put those conversations off until tomorrow morning. She was determined to enjoy her last dinner with her family. She even wore the dress Amelia gifted her. She planned to keep the dress, putting it in her collection in case she ever returned to this time.

Cate and Jack turned in soon after dinner, feigning the excuse of packing prior to leaving. This wasn't a complete lie, Cate and Jack did pack, readying their suitcases to return with them tomorrow morning.

They returned to their time. A feeling of satisfaction settled over Cate, coupled with melancholy. "You going to be okay, Lady Cate?" Jack asked before leaving her to change.

She nodded without speaking at first. "Yeah. I'm glad it's over in a way."

"But you'll miss everyone."

"I will. Especially Amelia. But she's leaving on Friday anyway, so she wouldn't be there to visit."

"Perhaps you'll get a nice Christmas present and we'll visit again before the year is out."

Cate smiled at Jack. "Wow! YOU suggesting time travel? Are you sick?"

Jack chuckled. "I just may be, but you can hold me to this promise. I know how much your family means to you, Lady Cate."

"Careful," Cate warned. "I have a good memory. I won't forget this!"

"I don't expect you will!" Jack said, backing out of the room. "M'lady!" He bowed with his usual gusto.

CHAPTER 27

Cate rose from bed with a heavy heart. Despite solving the mystery, today she would say goodbye to the family she'd spent the past few weeks getting to know. She hated this part. It had been hard when she said goodbye to Randolph and Victoria. This farewell would be no easier. She'd grown fond of all the 1925 MacKenzies. She felt especially drawn to Amelia, her great-grandmother. Perhaps she imagined it because of the connection between them, but Cate experienced it all the same. Today would be hard.

Jack met Cate after breakfast in her sitting room for one last trip to 1925. After arriving, Cate and Jack made their way to the sitting room where Anne and Amelia sipped tea. "Good morning!" Cate said, trying to sound upbeat as they entered the room.

"Jack! Cate! All packed?" Amelia inquired.

"We are," Jack responded.

"Too bad you couldn't stay one more evening," Amelia lamented.

"Duty calls," Jack fibbed. "But we've had a lovely time."

"And we can't thank you enough for the gracious welcome," Cate added as Rory and Lucas entered the room.

"Saying our goodbyes?" Rory questioned.

"We are," Jack replied. "And thanking everyone for their hospitality."

"No thanks needed. We should thank you! Your sharp detective skills proved invaluable to us," Rory professed.

"Not necessary! I was happy to help!" Cate answered.

"All the same, thanks are extended," Anne agreed. "Also, thank you for your suggestion yesterday. I took you up on it and it helped ever so much."

Cate nodded, not responding to the comment but understanding.

Silence filled the air for a few breaths. Amelia spoke first, "Well, I suppose you two are eager to be on your way."

"I wouldn't say eager," Cate lamented. "We will miss all of you and this beautiful castle! But we need to get a start on our journey."

"Yes," Jack added. "We have a lot of ground to cover today."

"Well, let's not treat it with such finality. It will not be long before we are together again," Amelia responded.

"Yes," Anne agreed. "The holidays will be upon us before we realize it. And Amelia tells me she plans to invite you to the country home this summer. That will be lovely. Rory and I also plan to travel there."

Cate pasted a smile on her face, choking back her sadness as she realized this invitation would never pan out. She nodded. "That would be wonderful if we can fit it into our schedule."

"Oh, please, Jack," Amelia requested, placing her hand on Jack's arm for emphasis, "if you can't make it, let Cate come along herself. She'll need the break!"

"As long as I don't miss her too much!" Jack hedged.

Another moment of silence passed before Rory spoke. "Well," he said, sticking his hand out to Jack, "it has been a pleasure. We will never forget the help you've given us on your first visit. All the best to you."

Jack accepted it, giving Rory's hand a solid shake. "Thank you. It's been a wonderful visit."

Cate embraced Anne and then Amelia, lingering a tad longer with Amelia. Cate held back the tears forming in her eyes as she pulled back.

"Oh," Anne said after final goodbyes were said, "the car isn't 'round yet. Did you call for it, Rory?"

"No need. Cate and I would like to enjoy one last walk and have arranged for a car to meet us in town."

"How adventurous of you. Are you sure?" Anne inquired.

"Yes," Cate assured her.

"We've had our luggage sent into town earlier, so it will be an easy journey," Jack noted.

"Well, I suppose we'll retrieve our coats and be on our way. Thank you again," Cate said.

The group disbanded with Jack and Cate climbing the stairs and returning to the bedroom suite. Without a word, they returned with their luggage to their time from 1925 one last time.

"You okay?" Jack questioned when they returned.

Cate nodded with a tight-lipped smile. "Yeah," she said after a moment. "Yeah, I'll be okay."

"How about a post-mystery meeting? I have a few items to discuss with you for spring planning."

"Estate business… the perfect thing to get my mind off of leaving my great-grandmother in 1925!" Cate quipped.

"Roof repairs are enough to take away any of your 'missing-my-family blues," Jack retorted. Cate giggled. "See you in the library in twenty minutes, give or take?"

"How about the sitting room?"

"No, thanks, I don't think so. Library," Jack insisted. "I need those comfy armchairs."

Cate rolled her eyes at him. "Okay, okay, library it is." They parted ways and Cate changed into normal clothes, setting aside her dress. She chose not to put it away just yet, deciding she'd deal with it later.

Cate ushered Riley and Bailey to the library, finding Jack already lounging in one of the generous armchairs near the fireplace. They spent almost two hours going over the projects needed once the weather broke in the spring. After the discussion, Cate slouched back in her chair, too.

"These chairs are comfy," she admitted. "I need to overcome my fear of this room."

"Perhaps with this latest mystery solved your nightmares will subside," Jack suggested.

"I hope so!"

"By the way, you owe me twenty pounds!"

"So I do!" Cate exclaimed. "Perhaps we can go double or nothing on our next adventure."

"Okay. Just don't go finding any more adventures soon, Lady Cate," Jack quipped.

Cate grinned at him as Riley let out a earsplitting yip. Cate groaned, assuming they'd experience another bout of hysteria over the leaky bookshelf. Instead, she spotted Riley staring at the fireplace. Cate furrowed her brow, then relief coursed through her. Riley's toy moose lay on the stone in front of the hearth.

Cate chuckled. "Oh no!" she exclaimed. "Did Moose run too close to the fire?" Cate made her way over to rescue the stuffed toy. Riley, too nervous to approach the heat of the roaring fire, stared at his beloved toy from a distance.

Cate leaned forward to retrieve the moose, steadying herself on one of the large stones framing the large fireplace.

As she bent over, she stumbled, catching herself before she toppled.

"Cate?!" Jack shouted, rushing toward her.

"Whoa!" Cate exclaimed. "This stone seems to be loose. When I put my weight on it, it shifted."

"Perhaps that's the source of the leak," Jack surmised, staring at it.

Cate's brow crinkled, staring at the stone. She placed her hand on the stone again. She pushed, leaning her weight against it. A loud crack sounded, reverberating throughout the room. Cate's eyes widened, and she backed up a step, almost bumping into Jack.

The stone stuck in the pushed-in position. A creaking noise followed, and a gust of air rushed past them. The scent of must filled their nostrils. Riley and Bailey barked, backing several steps away. Cate's jaw fell open, and she glanced to Jack. He swallowed hard.

When pressed, the stone on the fireplace's right side triggered a mechanism. The leaky bookcase, the source of Cate's nightmares and the dogs' trepidation, had swung open. A black hole stared back at them.

A shiver passed through Cate, though she couldn't say whether it was from the cool air emanating from the open bookshelf or the mild dread she experienced from the situation that matched her nightmares.

Cate swallowed hard, approaching the hole, determined to face her fears. Jack followed, peering into the hole. "This explains the leak. Looks like a passage," he noted. "I'll grab some flashlights."

"I told you!" Cate whispered, breathless.

"That you did, Lady Cate, that you did," Jack answered with a shake of his head.

Jack retrieved two flashlights from a cabinet on the opposite side of the room while Cate quieted the dogs. Jack handed her one of the flashlights and they both powered them on. Cate shined her light into the blackness. The light provided a dim outline of the cavity's features.

Cate stepped inside, shining the light around the space. Cobwebs decorated it, and the air was dank and stale. "It continues this way," Cate informed Jack, shining her light to the right where the passage continued down a set of stairs.

"Careful, Cate. We've no idea the condition of those stairs. Let me go first." Jack pushed ahead of her, creeping down the steps, testing each one as he went. Cate nodded, keeping a firm grip on the dusty handrail. She tiptoed behind him, careful with her weight on the aged stairs.

They reached a landing, and the stairs turned at a right angle. They inched down the remaining stairs, stepping onto the stone floor at the bottom. Cate and Jack shined their lights around the cavernous space. Cool, damp air surrounded them, and Cate shrugged her sweater tighter around her. Jack approached the nearby wall, focusing his beam on an object there.

Cate followed his gaze. "What is it?"

"Looks like a lamp. Kerosene by the smell of it," Jack answered. "Might help to light this and any others we find. Our flashlights aren't doing very much in a space this size."

"Good idea," Cate agreed.

"I'll run up for some matches. Will you be okay here by yourself?"

Cate nodded. "Sure," she muttered, anything but sure.

Jack squeezed her shoulder, hurrying up the stairs. Within a few moments, he returned and lit the lamp. He searched around the walls, finding a few others and lighting them. The warm light illuminated the space, revealing additional details.

The space was enormous. Cate gaped around. "What is this place?" she questioned. A large desk sat in the center of the space, piled with books and papers. Storage shelves placed around the walls held various items, some housed in crates. Trunks littered the floor and several large tables stood at various spots around the room, also covered with assorted materials. A thick layer of dust covered everything.

"I have no idea," Jack admitted. "And why isn't it shown on any plans? Not even Douglas' private plans."

"Perhaps it was added after Douglas' era?" Cate conjectured.

"Maybe," Jack replied.

Cate wandered toward the desk. She blew away some of the dust covering the materials. With two fingers, Cate lifted a few items. Jack perused the shelves. Cate picked up one of the books on the desk, a thick leather-bound volume filled with script writing. She thumbed through it, dust exploding into the air as she shuffled the pages. She flipped open the cover, staring at the text written on the first page.

"I doubt this was added after Douglas' era," she commented, still staring at the page.

"Why do you say that?" Jack asked, joining her and peering over her shoulder at the page.

"This book," Cate replied. "It says *Journal of Douglas MacKenzie*."

Cate glanced around the cavernous space, awestruck. Jack rifled through the materials on the desk. "There are several journals here. Looks like they all belong to Douglas," Jack noted after opening a few.

Cate wandered to one of the tables, studying the things scattered across it. She spun to face Jack. "I think we're standing in the private research laboratory of Douglas MacKenzie."

"I think you may be right," Jack answered.

"Oh, Jack, do you realize what this means?"

Jack stared at her. A smile spread across Cate's face and

she raised an eyebrow at him. "It looks like our next adventure just found us."

Stay up to date with all my news! Be the first to find out about new releases first, sales and get free offers! Join the Nellie H. Steele's Mystery Readers' Group on Facebook! Or sign up for my newsletter at www.anovelideapublishing.com!

* * *

If you loved solving this mystery and want to continue the adventure at Dunhaven, grab book 4, Danger at Dunhaven Castle, today!

* * *

Want to her the story from Jack's perspective? Try The Secret Keepers, Book 1 of Jack's Journal!

* * *

If you love cozies, you can also check out my newest series, Lily & Cassie by the Sea. Grab book one, *Ghosts, Lore & a House by the Shore* now!

* * *

Love immersing yourself in the past? Lenora Fletcher can communicate with the dead! Can she use her unique skill to solve a mystery? Find out in *Death of a Duchess*, Book 1 in the Duchess of Blackmoore Mysteries.

* * *

Ready for adventure? Travel the globe with Maggie Edwards in search of her kidnapped uncle and Cleopatra's Tomb. Book one, *Cleopatra's Tomb,* in the Maggie Edwards Adventure series is available now!

* * *

If you prefer adventures set in the past, try my newest pirate adventure series. Book 1, *Rise of a Pirate,* is available for purchase now!

* * *

Like supernatural suspense? Try the *Shadow Slayers* series, a fast-paced page-turner! Book one, *Shadows of the Past,* is available now!

Made in the USA
Coppell, TX
04 April 2022

76005595R00223